MW01534883

AURORA
BY
ELLENE POMERANTZ

Buzzy,

I'm glad you came
back into my life.

Always your truest,

Ellene

© 2001 by Ellene Pomerantz
All rights reserved.
No part of this book may be reproduced, stored in a
retrieval system, or transmitted by any means, electronic,
mechanical, photocopying, recording, or otherwise, without
written permission from the author.

ISBN: 0-75963-327-4

This book is printed on acid free paper.

1stBooks – rev. 11/7/01

The tenth day of July, 1983, the year *TIME MAGAZINE* named the computer, "Man of the Year". The year A.T.&T. said, "Breaking up is hard to do." The year of violence against Americans in Syria. A year of welfare at peak level and unbelievably high unemployment. The year Ling Ling, a giant panda in the Washington, D.C. Zoo gave birth to the first giant panda ever born in the U.S. The year of Reaganomics; circulating the dollar, that's how our economy works.

Meggie, had been outside painting most of the day. Each time she looked at the canvas it somehow seemed obscure, as if it were trying to reach out and tell her something. Her brush strokes weren't quite right and the pigmentation of the paints were somewhat off. It looked nothing like the colorful Chinese still life she had arranged. "I think I would prefer eating to doing this!" With that thought she packed up her supplies and proceeded toward the house to prepare dinner for her family. Entering, she noticed it was 4:30 and decided to make barbecued chicken, salad, oven potatoes and fresh steamed string beans.

Too quiet!" she thought, walking over to switch on the radio. News flash!

"Ling Ling's baby, born this morning; died!"

"Poor Ling Ling", she thought. Then realized two bad things had already occurred on this day. They seem to travel in threes. She waited anxiously for her two sons to return from camp, reflecting on the day each was born and how much she loved them. Matthew was nine, a truly beautiful child who looked just like his mother. Seth at five was equally as beautiful, with wavy brown hair and his dad's beautiful light blue eyes. The camp bus pulled up to greet a very uneasy mother at 5:10 p.m.

"How was camp today, guys?" Meggie inquired.

"I'm being moved to the Cheetahs!" Seth yelled with excitement.

"What are the Cheetahs?" Meggie was curious.

"It's the swimming group up from where Seth was," stated Matthew in a way that implied he couldn't understand her ignorance.

"Listen you guys, I never experienced camp. Therefore I do not know a whole lot about camp structure. Teach me, I've always been eager to learn," Meggie proclaimed. Her two sons approached to give her a hug.

"Sorry, we forgot, you summered in Hawaii!" Matthew laughed.

Still set at the task of providing a decent meal for her family, Meggie attacked the string beans, pulling the stems off the tips, then washing them. The two boys playing outside didn't hear the phone ringing.

"Hello," Meggie hurriedly answered. Within one minute she was on the floor with the receiver in her lap. She sat there like a stone, in shock for minutes she never knew existed. Finally rising, she hung the receiver up, just long enough to receive a dial tone. Trembling she placed her call.

"Anna, can you come over here?" Meggie's voice cracked.

"Miss Meggie, what's wrong?" asked Anna, knowing her employer, caring for her and being concerned. Meggie burst into tears,

"Please come and take care of the boys."

"I'll be right there," Anna replied hanging the phone up.

Spotting Anna on her way, Meggie hysterically ran upstairs to her room, slamming and locking the door behind her. She undressed the bed, even taking the mattress off, throwing everything on the floor. In a fit of rage, she threw herself on top of it all and screamed with tears rolling from her eyes. "He promised me! He promised me!" 'Totally out of control!', she thought.

Anna, in the kitchen, hearing her scream, ran up the stairs yelling. "Miss Meggie let me help you!" She banged at the door to the bedroom. Meggie wouldn't answer. Discovering the door was locked Anna went downstairs and phoned Meggie's ma. A short while later, Ma stood at the door of Meggie's room, jiggling the door knob, "Meggie, let me in!"

"Go away, leave me alone!" Meggie shrieked.

"What the hell is going on?" Ma yelled.

"He has an annuity for seeking out truth! Thus, deceiving me!" Meggie screamed, cried, and trembled all at the same time.

"What is that supposed to mean?" Ma asked.

"His helicopter was shot down outside of San Salvador. The State Department doesn't know whether he's dead or alive!" Meggie shrieked hysterically. Her mother stood there wondering what she should do. She understood Meggie better over the recent years coupled with full knowledge of her history.

"Meg, let me in. I want to hold you," Ma said concerned.

"Ma please, if you wish to help me, go away. I need solitude. When I'm ready I'll be out!" Meggie yelled. Then, she thought to herself, he has a way of controlling my temper! I can't live without him! She lay back closing her eyes and thought how she deceived him in the past.

Hearing Ma start down the stairs, she felt relieved. Needing to be by herself, to cry by herself, to think. "It is amazing the places the mind will carry you at a time like this."

1950

The year 1950, Harry S. Truman was in the White House. Our country was engaged in the Korean War, thanks to the Soviet attack on South Korea and we no longer had relations with the Peoples Republic of China. Meggie Loren Hiken was born to the proud parents, Lillian and Morris Hiken, on the twenty-first day of May, 1950. She was their first-born. Morris, holding her for the first time, thought she was the most beautiful creature he had ever seen. Looking at this tiny person with big blue eyes and light blonde hair, he pledged his loyalty to her. Dr. Marcus entered the room;

"We have a problem," Dr. Marcus said. The two new parents looked at him expectantly with fear in their eyes.

"Your daughter has a slight heart murmur. Similar to yours Morris," Dr. Marcus explained.

"No!" Morris screamed, and Meggie started to cry. He put his daughter on his shoulder, rubbing her back. "What can be done?"

"Nothing right now, she needs to be watched. There's a 75 percent chance that she will outgrow it, if we're lucky," Dr. Marcus took the baby from Morris to examine.

Lillian and Morris brought their daughter home from the hospital with very heavy hearts, promising each other that Meggie would never know. They wanted a normal and happy life for her.

On February 2, 1951, a tremendous blizzard hit the state of Maryland. Meggie was not yet nine months old, Morris brought home a large sled, insisting on taking Meggie for a ride. Ignoring cries from an overprotective mother because it was far too late for a nine-month old to be out, Morris and Meggie hit the snow at midnight.

In 1954 Dwight David Eisenhower was our president, a republican, war general. On July 28th, Morris and Lil were blessed with the birth of Benjamin Jay Hiken. He was born eight weeks prematurely. Weighing in at four pounds, he had to remain in the hospital in an incubator, for a while. It was three months before Dr. Marcus would permit a bris.

When Ben finally came home from the hospital, Meggie was excited. That same day Dr. Marcus came to the house to check the baby and to speak with Lillian and Morris. He walked over to sit by Morris. "Please try to understand," he glanced at Morris and then Lillian. "Since Ben is a preemie, he may be a little slower then other babies."

"What the hell do you mean?" Morris yelled, looking Dr. Marcus in the eye. The good doctor was used to Morris' forthrightness.

"Please don't make the mistake of comparing your children," Dr. Marcus instructed.

"My son will never be slow!" he screamed. Morris was frightened, and being of the masculine gender he was even a little ashamed. He needed a son to carry on the family name and he was the only one left to do that. His brother's wife could not have any more children. Her tubes needed to be removed, due to complications, after giving birth to their only daughter, Lori. That was six years ago. Morris thought to himself, 'Four sisters and an inept brother.' In fear of the realities that might lie ahead of him, he cried to God, "I have one perfect child- why create one less perfect than the other? Damn you Lord!"

Meggie and Ben grew up together, loving each other. Meggie, as the oldest, always protected her little brother. She was uncomfortable with the comparisons her parents made between them. When Meggie turned 13 she saw all too clearly her family structure.

"Daddy," Meggie sat on Morris' lap, one evening. "I love you. Please get off Ben's case. See him for the special little guy that he is, not for what he is not."

Morris hugged his daughter. "I love you too, Munchie," he smiled. "Ben needs discipline, your mother doesn't understand that and there are things you don't understand."

"Is that why you and Mommy argue so much?" Meggie questioned.

"Partially," Morris sighed.

Meggie then knew it was a waste of time attempting to discuss this matter with her dad. She also realized how much more Ma loved Ben than her. Meggie felt for Ben, all of the grief Dad had given him over the years. The heartfelt warmth Ben received from Ma, he deserved, even though she could not remember what it felt like to receive love and warmth from a mother.

I

It's the end of August, 1966. The year of the Hippie Movement, Haight-Ashbury. The year of drugs: Marijuana, L.S.D., P.C.P., and let's not forget cocaine. The year of the Sexual Revolution: mothers no longer told their daughters not to have sex before marriage. The daughters were now being told to take precautions: Birth Control.

A sixteen-year-old Meggie lay back in her seat on the 6:00 p.m. American Airlines flight from Honolulu in route to Baltimore's Friendship airport, home. Every summer she visited Hawaii to be with Lori. Meggie had been taking this trip since she was eight years old, when their Zadie passed away. Their grandfather had left a large amount of money and some real estate to his two sons along with trust funds for Lori, Meggie and Ben. That's when Uncle Bob, Aunt Helen and Lori moved to Hawaii to start a new life.

Lori and Meggie grew up together, first cousins and best friends. Over two thousand miles could never separate them. This was to be Lori's first year of college and Meggie's last year of high school. She sat in thought of the conversation she had with Lori a year ago.

"I want to go to the University of Hawaii. I love these islands and I don't want to leave them!" Lori stretched her arms out wide. Meggie was heartbroken.

"Lori, you know they have a lousy art department," Meggie's bottom lip protruded, accentuating her frown.

"Meg, I know we always planned on going to school together. That's why you are the first to know. They have a great English Department. You know that's my concern. We will always be close, miles and oceans could never separate us," Lori leaned to embrace her.

Meggie sat in thought. I'll go back to Hawaii next summer and Lori will be here over Christmas, just four months. I miss her already!

Meggie closed her eyes and tried to rest. As usual, thoughts kept creeping into her head. Uncle Bob had done quite well for himself. She smiled, such good people. She loved them almost as much as her own family. In 1960, Robert Hiken moved to the new state of Hawaii and started one small car leasing company. Now he had businesses all over the islands; Maui, Hawaii, Kuai and Oahu. He had become a prominent member of the community and he was on the Board of Directors of a very exclusive country club. To Meggie, her uncle seemed to have made a wise decision when he chose to uproot his family and start over. Plus those islands are so beautiful, she couldn't blame Lori for not wanting to leave them. Lori made the right choice for herself.

Meggie arrived at Honolulu's airport in late June, 1966. Lori was waiting for her as usual. The two girls ran excitedly to each other.

"Meg, let's hurry, we have an appointment in one hour," Lori took her cousins hand, leading her toward the baggage claim. This was quite an unusual change in events. Whenever they saw each other the first priority was to catch up on everything.

"What's wrong?" Meggie curious.

"Not that big of a deal. I'm pregnant. We're going to have an abortion now. I wanted you with me. I didn't want to do this by myself, so I waited a couple of more weeks," Lori hugged her.

"You fool!" Meggie screamed. The girls retrieved the luggage and quickly exited the airport.

Meggie knew she had grown up over this past summer, physically as well as emotionally. She decided to no longer be a social recluse and she no longer was going to shelter herself or be evasive. The realization hit her that if a totally decadent individual chose to point a finger at her and say, "There goes the smart kid!", it was their problem not hers. She decided she was going to get more involved in school, not just her work. There were parties in her future now, her prime objective being to enjoy herself. "You are only young once," she laughed at the cliché.

The plane landed at Friendship Airport at 11:00 a.m. on the last Thursday in August. An exhausted Meggie greeted her Ma and gave Ben a big hug and kiss, along with all of the presents she had carried on with her. Once in the car, Ma started, "Peter's been calling, I told him when you'd be home. He'll call later. How are Uncle Bob, Aunt Helen, and Lori? Did you see her school? Did you mind your manners? Did you enjoy yourself?" Ma stated, driving down the Baltimore-Washington Parkway. Meggie thought to herself, so far nothing has changed. Always so many questions without waiting for a reply.

"Everything and everyone is fine. I had a wonderful time!" Meggie tired, sank back in her seat to cuddle Ben.

As they entered the house the phone was ringing. Meggie and Ben trudged upstairs with her suitcases.

"It's Peter!" Ma yelled.

"Hi! I heard you've been calling. Couldn't wait till I got back?" Meggie laughed.

"Funny Meg, very funny," Peter said, then paused. "There's a party tomorrow night at Lisa's. Everyone will be dated, I was hoping you would do me a favor and come with me?" Peter and Meggie were very good friends and had been for the past three years. This was a standard routine whenever either one needed a date.

"My pleasure, what time?" Meggie nonchalantly responded. Peter almost peed in his pants. She always gave him a hard time before going. Sometimes he even had to bribe her. Certain functions were okay, but never to a party with the so called 'in clique' from school. Meggie always tried to keep her distance, her low profile. Since growing up over the summer, she arrived at the realization she could no longer afford to worry about what other people thought of her, only what she thought of herself; therefore, she was going to this party and not let life pass her by any longer.

"Pick you up at eight," a surprised Peter stated.

"Bye," Meggie said, hanging up the receiver.

Being tired and jet-lagged, she sank into her bed. A few minutes later she stood to remove her clothes, watching herself the entire time in the mirror. Meggie laughed thinking how she must have shocked Peter, and tomorrow night he would be far more surprised. She crawled into bed nude, falling asleep with a smile on her face.

Screaming awoke Meggie. She thought to herself, 'I came home to exactly what I left two months ago. Dad was on Ben again and Ma would not loosen those apron strings.'

"Hi Munchie," Daddy smiled, entering her room.

"Hi Daddy," Meggie said, sleepily, dad bent to kiss her forehead.

"You look good, kid," Daddy eyed her. "Sleep, we'll talk later."

Meggie lay in thought. He's always been so good to me, so tolerant of me, and so lousy to Ben. She found her entire family relationship too perplexing to comprehend. She loved and adored Daddy so much, but at the same time she resented and mistrusted him somewhat for what he was doing to Ben. Such obscure feelings for a 16-year-old to deal with. It frightened her, so she decided to put it out of her mind and fall back to sleep.

The doorbell rang at eight o'clock Friday evening, Ma answered, "Peter, how are you?"

"Hi Mrs. Hiken, I'm fine," he responded and noticed that Meggie's dad was not home. He recalled the conversation he had with Meggie last spring. She told him her dad quite often didn't come home until late at night. He always said it was business. He's a banker, vice president of one of the largest banks in the state. She told Peter she knew he wasn't being honest, and usually managed to put the entire affair out of her mind. Peter's thoughts were interrupted by Ben punching him.

"Quit it Ben!" Peter yelled, grabbing his wrists. As he glanced up, he saw Meggie walking down the stairs. He did a double take, not believing his eyes. She always wore button up baggy blouses ten sizes too big, with pants or skirts to match (her Low Profile).

Meggie stood 5'6" tall, weighing 115 pounds. Her long wavy blonde hair flowed gently over her golden tan shoulders. She wore a white eyelet, off the shoulder sundress, with an elasticized waist. The dress, being of a light weight cotton, was somewhat sheer, thus revealing the outline of her firm round breasts.

"Meggie!" Ma said in complete astonishment, not accustomed to seeing her daughter in such attire.

"Don't you love it! Lori and I went shopping. I bought a complete new wardrobe. Daddy knows," Meggie smiled. For some reason she loved the element of shock, when she had control of it.

"You look great!" Ben looked his big sister over.

"You're my most devout fan," Meggie bent to kiss her brother. Turning to Peter, she smiled, "No comment?"

"I'm having a mental block, a complete loss for words," Peter still stared at her.

"A red letter day," Meggie smiled. At the same time, she noticed Ma's mouth was still wide open. She laughed inside, loving this.

Peter led Meggie out of the house toward his little VW. Starting the motor, he gazed admiringly at her,

"I'm going to have to watch you tonight," he paused, "Is this your coming out?"

"Coming out of what?" a puzzled Meggie asked.

"Coming out of hibernation! As long as I've known you, you have never looked like this." He laughed, finding it difficult to keep his eyes off her.

"Peter, all good things come with time," she blushed.

He wondered if he still knew this gorgeous creature sitting beside him. So unlike the Meggie of two months ago. They started talking about school and the past good times. He now knew she was the same sweet, innocent Meggie, especially after arriving at the party and finding her still so shy toward this crowd.

"Peter, will you play for us?" Lisa asked. Peter was a whiz on the piano, which was one of the reasons he and Meggie were such good friends. "I need a partner," Peter stated, then approached Meggie.

"Meg, let's play," he took her hand.

"Not here!" responded a surprised Meggie, pulling back.

"Come on," Peter led her toward the piano. "We'll start the same way we always do, when it's just us. Tchaikovsky, some Beatles, 'Splish Splash' and early rock and roll, the Beach Boys and ending with 'Boogie Woogie Bugle Boy'." They started to play and after two minutes, they switched to pop songs and all eyes turned to them. When it came time for "Boogie Woogie Bugle Boy" everyone was gathered around the piano shouting out songs for them to play. There was a by-stander at the far end of the piano who could not take his eyes off this blonde beauty. When they decided it was enough, Peter and Meggie stood knocking their backsides against each other to the rhythm of boogie woogie. When they had finished, Peter put his arms around her, lifting her slightly off the ground, spinning her around.

"You were fantastic!" Peter yelled, laughing.

"We've always played well together," Meggie blushed.

"Peter, I always knew you were talented, but, who is this?" said the by-stander with gestures from the far end of the piano prior to approaching.

"Meggie Hiken, meet Dennis Fine," Peter said, as he walked away.

"Meggie, the name is familiar. I can't quite place the rest of you though!" Dennis looked her over and liked what he saw.

"Where do you go to school?" Dennis gazed into those beautiful aquamarine eyes. Meggie, for one of the few times in her life, couldn't find the words. She knew who Dennis was, everyone did, and about his reputation. He played forward for their high school basketball team and he was captain of their tennis team. 'The school hunk!'.

"Dennis, I've seen you around," Meggie stated dismissingly as she walked away.

Dennis thought to himself, "She put me down. No female has done that in years." First shock, then intrigue. He sought out Peter,

"Where did she come from?"

"We're good friends, have been for years. I'm sure you've met her before," Peter smiled. Dennis eyed him,

"If I'd met anyone who looked like that before, I would remember! Since you're just friends, you won't care if I ask her out."

"Dennis, Meggie's terrific. It's up to her if she risks going out with you." Peter stated feeling concern. He had known Dennis since nursery school. His concern was with the neophyte of dating, Meggie.

After that remark, Dennis put two plates of food together and maneuvered Meggie away from all of the people gathered around her to the vacant patio outside.

"I thought you could use some air," Dennis said, leading her toward a table with chairs.

"That's very clever of you, Dennis," Meggie smiled as she sat down, taking the plate from him.

"It's really bugging me that I can't place you. Peter says you go to school with us," Dennis leaned back in his chair, looking at her.

"I'm even going to graduate with you!" Meggie laughed.

"Then how come I don't know you?" Dennis was perplexed. He leaned forward to look her straight in the eye.

Meeting his eye she smiled, "In deference to your limited scope of things, you should be more aware of other people and not so self-oriented." Meggie stated, very coolly staring into his beautiful deep blue eyes. 'WOW, those eyes,' she thought. She also could not believe what was coming from her mouth, not meaning to be quite so arrogant. It must be his holier-than-thou attitude that made her impulsive. She laughed inside.

Dennis felt the cut. 'Two in one night!' He wondered if he could deal with this one.

"Are you trying to impress me with your vocabulary?" he gazed into those eyes, falling in love with them. Meggie burst into laughter,

"It's not applicable!"

"You are weird, do you know that?" Dennis puzzled.

Meggie rested her elbow on the table, placed her chin in her hand, very wide-eyed and with a big smile,

"Aren't you aware all creative people are?"

Dennis moved so his face was within five inches of hers.

"No, but I plan on finding out," he kissed her. Meggie was shocked and drew back. Dennis laughed sitting back in his chair.

"Meggie, are you out here?" Peter yelled, walking from the house.

"Over here," Meggie replied, happy for the rescue.

"I told everyone you'd sing for them," Peter approached.

"No I won't!" She stated firmly and looked aggravatingly at him. Peter bent to whisper in her ear,

"If you are going to come out, you are going to do it in style," Peter laughed with Meggie joining him. She inquired,

"Do I really need this as part of my reconstruction program?"

"Yes! No, one outside your family and I, has ever heard that beautiful voice. Now, come on." Peter took her hand and pulled her up from the chair. Dennis followed, unaware of what was happening.

"Will you play with me?" Meggie asked.

"A little," he smiled. Sitting on the piano bench Meggie whispered in his ear, "I'm going to get you for this." They both laughed. Peter knew she would. He didn't know how, though. They played with her singing, then Peter left her on her own for a while. She started playing something she had never played before and no one else had ever heard. She smiled at Peter. He stared at her with an expression of "NO" in his eyes. He was quite aggravated! Meggie was all smiles since she had rearranged his lyrics and score a little. It was fantastic, Peter very surprised! He sat beside her on the piano bench, anxiously placing his hands on the keyboard,

"Which chords?"

"Third and fifth," Meggie smiled. "I believe you liked it."

"Are you kidding! It's terrific!" Peter said before kissing her cheek. All eyes were on them, especially Dennis'.

"I made a few revisions to most of your songs," Meggie whispered.

"I want to hear them! Why didn't you tell me?" Peter said.

"You didn't ask, I told you I would," she laughed. He hugged her,

"I knew that mind of yours would work them out."

"Can we go? I'm exhausted," Meggie smiled at Peter. He laughed,

"Whatever you say, the master of word and chord." They thanked Lisa, walked out the front door and turned when they heard someone yelling.

"What are you doing tomorrow?" Dennis approached. She smiled,

"I thought Peter would play some tennis with me."

"Not me, I'm no competition for you! After three years I'm not about to be a sucker any longer," Peter turned to Dennis.

"Every year after she comes home from Hawaii, she insists upon seeing how bad she can slaughter me."

"Tennis is my game," Dennis smiled.

"She's pretty good, and after being with Lori and Uncle Bob for two months, I don't even want to try," Peter responded.

"I'll play," Dennis said. He sensed from his brief encounter with Meggie that she must be pretty quick with things. This might be the way to beat her at something.

"You're on! The high school tomorrow, 9:00 a.m.," Meggie said.

"Don't you sleep?" Dennis surprised.

"I do my sleeping at night," Meggie smiled. "Besides, it's going to be over one hundred tomorrow." She turned to walk to the car.

Dennis watched as Meggie and Peter drove away.

"Listen Meg, be careful with that one," Peter said, pulling into her driveway.

"Thanks, I really do think I can handle him. I appreciate your concern though," she leaned to place a kiss on his cheek. Peter thought to himself, 'I bet she can,' and laughed as he watched her walk in her front door.

That night Meggie lay in bed trying to fall asleep, while thoughts of Dennis kept creeping into her head. She lay there for quite a while with the vision of the 6'1", dark-haired, hunk. He has deep blue-eyes and a build like an Adonis, she thought, smiling to herself.

They met at the high school on the following hot and sunny Saturday morning, precisely at 9:00. Dennis won the first set 6-4. She couldn't believe it, even though it took her time to warm up. With a vengeance she won the second set 6-2, then Meggie won the third set 6-4. She was somewhat apprehensive of what this might do to his fragile male ego, but on the other side of the coin she had her own self-image to deal with. (Typical of a female in the late 1960's).

"Where did you learn to play like that?" Dennis said, panting.

"Honolulu! That's where I play the most. I've been taking lessons since I was eight. You're pretty good yourself," she smiled as they walked off the courts, soaking wet with perspiration. "I need a drink."

"Here!" Dennis yelled, throwing her one of the sprinklers the school was using to water the grounds, soaking her.

"Hey!" Meggie screamed, lunging toward him with the sprinkler in her hand. They laughed hysterically, struggling to see who could get the other the wettest. After a while they gave up and rolled away on the grass. They lay there out of breath.

"At least we're not hot anymore," Dennis laughed. Meggie rose to her feet,

"No! Just soaked!"

"How about a pizza and a swim?" Dennis smiled, still stretched out on the ground.

"Sounds wonderful!" she grinned.

Half an hour later, Meggie, clothed in a lavender Maui Waui tee-shirt with a bathing suit under it, hopped into Dennis' Corvette. He turned to her,

"You should consider going out for the tennis team this year."

"I am, it's part of my reconstruction program," she smiled.

"Your what?" Dennis didn't understand. She ignored him. He took a good look at her while he was driving. Definitely noticing her long wavy blonde hair, her perfectly sculptured legs and that lavender material in between. He started to laugh uncontrollably.

"What's so funny?" Meggie bewildered .

"Somehow, you just don't make it in a reefer tee-shirt," Dennis still laughed. She glanced down at the front of her shirt and laughed with him.

"I was a little curious about that myself."

They sat in the snack bar eating pizza, having another race to see who could eat the most.

"Who won?" Peter asked as he walked over to the table, pulled out a chair and helped himself to a slice of pizza.

"It doesn't really matter, does it?" Meggie kissed his cheek.

"She won, she beat me! Why didn't you tell me what a wild woman she is on the court?" Dennis aggravated.

"I tried," Peter smiled. He looked at Meggie and burst out laughing, pointing a finger at her tee-shirt.

"Not you too!" she yelled, rising and heading toward the pool.

"I believe you like her," Peter glanced at Dennis.

"You know, I really do!" Dennis leaned back in his chair, watching her head to the water. "She's, she's so different, even somewhat of a mystery. I can't explain it, she's so damn unusual."

"She is different!" Replied Peter, with a slight laugh.

Approaching the pool, they saw Meggie removing her tee-shirt to expose a beautifully sculptured body to match those legs. Clothed in a skimpy, turquoise, crocheted bikini against her deep tanned skin, she immediately dove into the water, not noticing the two guys with their eyes bulging out of their heads.

Taking Meggie home that afternoon, Dennis made a detour down a dead-end street. He turned the car motor off, leaned over and kissed her. Meggie sat perfectly still, like a stoic, even though she felt something stir inside of her, a feeling she had never experienced before. It frightened and delighted her at the same time.

"There's a party tonight, how about it?" Dennis asked.

"Your friends sure have a lot of parties," Meggie said, not knowing where to look, steering clear of his eyes.

"It's Maxines' 17th, will you go or not?" Dennis inquired. There was silence, then he said, "I'd like you to go with me."

"Since you put it that way, I can hardly resist," Meggie smiled.

That evening Dennis arrived at Meggie's house at 7:45 p.m. He was greeted by her Mom, Dad and Ben, who looked him over carefully. Amenities were exchanged before Meggie walked into the den a few moments later. Dennis stood in awe staring at her, Mom was still in a state of shock and her dad seemed quite pleased. Meggie wore a hot pink, shoestring strap sundress, belted in silver around the waist. He bid her parents goodnight. She approved of his manners. In his car Dennis smiled,

"You look sensational!" She blushed.

During the party, dancing a slow dance and holding her, Dennis whispered, "I'm glad there's no piano here."

"Why?" Meggie questioned, tilting her head back.

"Because I don't want to share you with anyone tonight," he smiled. The party broke up around midnight and Dennis headed straight for the dead-end street he found earlier that day.

"Is this your parking spot, Dennis?" an arrogant Meggie uttered.

"No, it's ours!" Dennis stated. Meggie felt a chill go up her spine. She liked the sound of it, but she really didn't want to hear any of his infamous lines.

"Nice line, Dennis, do they really bite at that one?" she said, smugly.

"It's not a line! Honestly, I just found this road today with you. It's a new road," Dennis leaned over to kiss her. She wouldn't separate her teeth to allow his tongue to pass through. He had been visualizing this scene all night. He even felt himself become hard a few times when he held her during slow dances. Now he couldn't understand what was happening. "What's with you?" a distraught Dennis questioned.

"I know this is 1966, the sexual revolution and all that crap! We just met!" Meggie stated irately, never wanting anyone to take advantage of her. He looked at her and thought to himself, she looks so cute when angered. Then he got a little hot himself. He could have almost any girl in school; most would even spread their legs for him on a first date. Now he was with Miss Chastity of 1966, after spending an entire day and night with her. He leaned over, pressing his lips against hers so hard that he was able to force his tongue into her mouth. Meggie struggled, but to no avail. She felt this strange sensation come over her as his tongue searched every space of her mouth. Dennis pulled away almost as abruptly as he physically came to attack her mouth.

"That wasn't so bad, huh, Meg?" a self-righteous Dennis gloated. She was hot!

"You really think you are something special, don't you? You egotistical shit!" Meggie screamed, looking him straight in the eye. She felt her Irish starting to come to a head. "You are determined, but you have less sense than a nickel!" Meggie still screamed. "You may have no values, but I do! Who the hell do you think you are, and what the hell do you think you are doing? Raping my mouth like that! I gave no consent, it's my mouth! Never, never do that again without it, especially in a car!"

'That's it, it's the car,' Dennis thought. 'On second thought, she would never be this angry if it were just that. Boy, is she weird!' He started the car's motor and headed toward Meggie's house. Two blocks before arriving there,

"How about going to the deli to meet the gang?" He asked, not looking at her. Part of him wanted to take her home, the other part didn't want to be apart from her. It was too early for him to head home, and he couldn't go to the deli by himself. The guys would tease the shit out of him.

"Okay," Meggie responded, the only thing the pit in her throat would allow her to say. She wanted to be with him, even to kiss him, but she refused to be taken for granted, especially in a car! She felt such mixed emotions over the whole experience. Never, ever was she going to allow Dennis or any other guy to think of her as a piece of ass or a pair of tits. Never would she be placed in the position Lori was this past summer.

Little did she know how Dennis felt about her. Arriving at the deli Meggie spotted Peter and headed straight for him, leaving Dennis with his friends.

"A problem?" Bob questioned Dennis.

"I don't know," Dennis sighed. "She's getting more mysterious by the minute." He paused, "The problem is, I have never felt this way about anyone before."

"Do you know what they call that?" Bob laughed, "By George, the boy's been bitten! It's called love."

"Look at her, she's magnificent!" Dennis said to his friend. Bob was still laughing. Dennis was not the type of guy to fall like this for any girl. He had never seen him so taken.

Later, Dennis drove Meggie home with barely a word spoken between them. He walked her to the door of her house as all middle class American boys have been brought up to do. He said good night as she unlocked the front door, then headed to his car. That night she cried herself to sleep, feeling he would never ask her out again.

Sunday morning at 11:30 a.m. the phone rang. Meggie let someone else answer it. She was still crying from Ma's lecture. She felt it was a great day for tears since it was raining outside, along with the effects of the preceding night.

"Meg, it's for you," Ben yelled. She took the phone.

"Hi! Everyone's going bowling," Dennis said in a very calm voice, as if nothing had happened the night before. Meggie didn't respond, there was silence.

"Meggie I'd like you to go with me. I'll be there in an hour," Dennis stated.

"Sure," she replied, still with a pit in her throat, before she hung up the receiver. She was in a state of disbelief and thought, 'How could he be so calm after last night?' She was bewildered and excited all at the same time.

An hour later Meggie spotted Dennis' car coming down the street.

"Ma, Dad, going bowling. See you later," Meggie yelled, leaving the house because she didn't want Ma to see her with no bra again. That morning Ma had given her a lecture on the fact 'her tits were going to hang when she got older if she didn't wear a bra now.' Ma always had the knack of hitting when she was low.

Ma ran to the living room window to see Meggie sliding into Dennis' car. Ma was aggravated,

"No bra again! That's why she ran out of here."

"Lil stop worrying, her head's on pretty straight," Dad stated.

"Then why did she cry herself to sleep?" Lil asked.

"She told me what happened. She would have told you if you would have asked instead of lecturing," Morris stated, and repeated the story to Lil.

"She reacted in the way she was brought up to. I'm proud of her," Dad said, giving himself a pat on the back. "The boy would have brought her straight home if he hadn't planned on seeing her again. I told her so. I also told her he would call again soon."

"Meggie has changed over the summer, she seems so different," Ma was solemn.

"She's not that different. Meggie is fine, almost perfect," Morris smiled, thinking she was perfection. "What you are referring to is her dress. The only difference is now she is dressing like all of the other kids her age, instead of wearing those prudish clothes. She decided to wear her hair down instead of hiding it on top of her head. Face it, Lil, Meggie is a truly beautiful girl. I think you find that hard to deal with, maybe even somewhat of a challenge to you. Why, I cannot quite figure out. But, I have no intention of concerning myself about it, that is your problem. Meggie is finally enjoying herself and I cannot begin to tell you how happy I am for her."

Dennis watched Meggie as she jumped into his car with her breasts bouncing a little. He smiled when she turned to him,

"It's a great day for ducks!" She burst into laughter; she did enjoy her humor. Dennis liked her wit and laughed along with her, even harder after taking a good look at her. She wore a light-blue Kona Gold tee-shirt in which her breasts were quite pronounced, even to the point of her nipples sticking straight out. She was clothed in a pair of tightly, fitted jeans, one could see the exact shape of her body.

"You are really into reefer tee-shirts," Dennis smiled.

"I think they're cute," Meggie stated.

17

"Besides, every island has their own thing; Maui Waui, Kona Gold, Kauai Electric," she handed him a j.

"Which one is this?" Dennis took it from her.

"It goes with my tee-shirt, Kona Gold," Meggie laughed. Dennis became solemn, he glanced over at her.

"Meggie, I'm sorry."

"I know, me too," she said, biting her bottom lip and looking at him with those eyes that he adored. He had never known anyone to have aquamarine eyes before.

Dennis pulled the car off to the side of the road and turned the engine off. He leaned over and kissed her. Then a kiss putting his tongue in her mouth. He drew back to look at her, then he kissed her the same way again with his chest against hers, feeling her erect nipples through his tee-shirt and hers. Sitting back in his seat, Dennis was breathing very hard, noticing he had also managed to take her breath away. He started laughing a little. Meggie became hysterical,

"You're a pretty decent kisser."

"Why? Who am I being compared to?" Dennis smiled.

"No one, this is not my area of expertise," she smiled. The inner stimulus he aroused in her she could not explain, nor did she want to deal with it, choosing to put it out of her mind.

The following day they went on a Labor Day picnic with Dennis' friends. Then school started and he wanted to drive her there.

"Tuesdays and Thursdays I get out at 12:30 to go to the Maryland Institute of Art. I need my 'car," Meggie explained.

"How did you work that one out?" Dennis surprised. She smiled,

"Determination, along with Mr. Wells, my art teacher."

"Is that what you meant by creative?" Dennis asked, a little shocked, and feeling he better get used to it.

"Certainly!" Meggie laughed. She loved surprising people. Dennis had initially thought it was her musical ability.

"Is this your schedule?" He pulled a piece of paper from her purse.

"You want to see it?" Meggie eagerly watched him unfold the paper.

"Jesus! Calculus, Honors English!" Dennis said in shock. "Gym, we have it at the same time," he still stared at the paper. "Studies, some are the same as mine. Drama II. What do you know, we have it together."

"You are looking at a very bright person here," Meggie smiled, never having admitted this to an outsider before.

"I had that feeling from the first moment I met you," Dennis said, knowing she certainly was different. Then he kissed her. There was something about her that intrigued him. He felt he may be falling for her, if only he knew what that meant!

Tuesday morning, Meggie pulled her green MG into the school parking lot, put it in park, lifted the emergency brake and locked her up. She laughed to herself, thinking her car was a she! As she walked toward the front doors of the school, whom should she see?

"Took you long enough, I've been waiting," Dennis eyed her.

"Sorry, I dropped Ben off this morning," she smiled, shrugging her shoulders. Dennis took her books, rested his arm on her shoulder and led her into the building.

"Hold up," Meggie walked to the office with Dennis following.

"Good morning, Mrs. Ramsud," Meggie smiled to the secretary and handed her a slip of paper. "I think this will clarify things."

"What was that all about?" Dennis asked.

"I registered at the Institute last Friday. They needed the papers," she threw her head back a little.

Meggie left Dennis at her locker and headed toward her homeroom. To her surprise, she was not unnoticed. Almost everyone said hello to her, seeing this long haired blonde coming down the hall. Even the so called 'in clique' tried very hard to make her one of them. Dennis stood waiting for her outside on the two mornings a week he didn't bring her to school. He waited for her by her locker at lunch and at the end of the school day.

One morning, as Meggie walked into calculus class and took her seat beside Peter,

"Hi Meg, rumor has it you and Dennis are an item. I was a bit surprised after the talk we had last Saturday night at the deli. Just be happy, Dennis' girl." He placed a kiss on her cheek.

'So this is what it's come down to, I've been pegged as Dennis' girl.' Meggie thought, first anger, because she was her own person, then delighted because she was crazy about him. These yoyos, I am me, my own person. A large grin came to her face.

During the month of September, Meggie and Dennis had become closer than either of them had ever envisioned. Dennis disliked the fact Meggie drove to downtown Baltimore by herself two afternoons a week to attend classes at Maryland Institute of Art. She loved going there, driving down Mt. Royal Avenue and focusing on the vintage nineteenth century building. She loved the entire environment, from the statuesque surroundings to the free spirited members of society she grew to love. After a period of time Meggie realized she, too, was a nonconformist. At times she felt as if she were leading a double life: the little high school girl on one hand and on the other hand, the non conforming art student. Meggie began reading books by Jack Kerouac, Allen Ginsberg, Herman Hesse and other beat authors. She was having a good time, she was learning, she was growing and that was important to her. Meggie thought of herself as a little socialite delinquent and laughed. She then thought of Dennis, wondering, what is love? Was she honestly in love with him? Did Dennis know whether he really loved her? Could you love without ever having intercourse? She cried because she didn't know why she was having these thoughts. Meggie had so many unanswered questions, and felt it almost impossible to deal with them.

1966, the era of the Hippie Revolution, the time L.B.J. was in the White House and almost three years after J.F.K. had been assassinated. Nobody but the young thought they understood, and they didn't even do that too well. Their reaction to all of the misguidedness they had to endure was in a rebelliousness toward society. The effect Kennedy's assassination had on the entire country was the loss of optimism. The vast amount of drugs streaming into society and the worst possible thing ever, the Vietnam War. A war of addiction, a war where the U.S. did not belong and a war of no conclusion. These were her thoughts and she questioned why, why are we victims! She couldn't answer these questions, just as no other young person could. They searched in every possible way for the answers. They knew they didn't want this war or the drugs, nor did they want the growing violence in society. Nor did they want to be betrayed, feeling they were. Meggie remembered awakening one morning to her clock radio announcing an assassination in Saudi Arabia, a fire in downtown Baltimore and a man dying of a gunshot wound in Westminster, Maryland. She thought to herself, 'Lethal News'.

During this time, Dennis was finding Meggie more and more challenging as well as intriguing. Even though Meggie only allowed him to just kiss her, they had almost the perfect relationship. The mere feeling of his chest against hers stirred emotions Meggie found too difficult to understand or to explain. She knew they were adolescent hormones, but she could not stop or control them. Just as all teenagers have sexual needs and desires, so did they. Especially with the intense feelings they had for one another.

This was 1966, the era of the sexual revolution, when mothers stopped telling their daughters they shouldn't let a guy touch them before marriage. Meggie had never allowed anyone to touch her. Now she was an anarchist or a revolutionary; she didn't know what the hell she was. All she knew for certain was that she wanted to be herself. She was continuously searching, trying to find a reason for her existence. She loved going on protest marches with the kids from the Institute and, at the same time she resented herself for being so two-faced. She loved the free spirited life that Maryland Institute of Art placed before her. She felt in her present environment she was alone, solo, but she knew she needed other people. She felt so confused, with nowhere to turn for the answers or guidance. Though, knowing she was no different from anyone else with a mind and, for the first time, she realized she was like many other people. The mind is an important thing to have, she thought to herself solemnly.

One night, in the beginning of October, Meggie brought Dennis along on one of the marches against the Vietnam War in downtown Baltimore. Meggie thought it was a magnificent event, a whole new experience! Half the people were arrested. A riot squad came at them with clubs. They had never seen anything like this before. Fleeing to Dennis' car, she was trembling and clinging to him.

"Dennis, I'm sorry, it's never been like this before." He kissed her before they both sat in the car.

"I am responsible for bringing you into this bizarre..." Meggie said, without being able to finish. Dennis pressed his lips against hers, kissing her more passionately than she ever thought possible. He moved his hands from her shoulders to her waist, then up the sides of her body. She loved the way he touched her. Until she felt his hand on her breast, panic came over her. She thought if she were such a free soul she wouldn't care, but the fact was she did!

"What do you think you are doing?" Meggie yelled.

"Nothing you don't want me to," Dennis said, smugly.

"Bullshit, Dennis! It's just like you to take advantage! You have an annuity for life, it must be nice!" Meggie screamed, with Dennis taking her home in silence.

Out with Meggie the following Saturday night, Dennis ran into a former girlfriend. He made arrangements to meet her later that night. At the time, he felt no guilt. He had already gone well over a month without it. Feeling he needed someone to get off on instead of by himself, alone in his bed. After taking Pam home that night, Dennis was feeling miserable, he had thought this would be the answer. He felt guilt, something he had never experienced before. Hoping Meggie would never learn of this, and he planned on never seeing Pam again.

Dennis picked Meggie up Sunday morning after she cried herself to sleep the night before, thinking, 'No one, no way, is ever going to control me. I won't allow him to push me into something I am not ready for! I am me! Accept me for me!' Dennis was extraordinarily condescending, considerate and affectionate toward her. She knew where his anguish was coming from, and made the decision the night before not to lay any guilt trips on him. That was her decision and she was determined to stick to it, because a big part of her understood. She may not have agreed with him, but she did understand.

23

Monday morning Peter sat down beside Meggie in Calculus.

"You okay?" She asked, knowing he had been seeing Pam for the past couple of weeks.

"You know?" Peter was shocked. Meggie became very-bright eyed with an expression of, I'm far from stupid, on her face. He knew that look and laughed.

"Meg, I was only seeing her for the same reason Dennis did."

The conversation was dropped until after class as they walked to English, which they also shared.

"Well, what are you planning to do?" Peter inquired with curiosity.

"Nothing," Meggie smiled.

"Nothing!" Peter couldn't believe it. She simply smiled.

"There's a fishbowl on my desk with 25 different term paper topics. You are to go up one row at a time and draw one, signing the paper beside it. No changes," Mrs. Schotzky uttered to her class.

Meggie sat and turned to Peter, "Which one did you get?"

"One you should have! Art and Expressionism!" Peter in disbelief. Meggie burst into laughter.

"I drew one that should have been yours!" She was still laughing with tears rolling from her eyes. She wished she could control those tear ducts. "Do you remember those classic novels written for children?" Peter shrugged his shoulders.

"Horatio Algiers is my topic!" She paused, "I remember when I was seven my Dad gave me one of his books. Right now I can't even remember the name of it. Now, that is strange."

"Especially for you," Peter smiled.

"Anyway, I remember what he said to me. 'Reading is an adventure, an experience,'" she repeated. "And, he was so right! Tomorrow why don't you meet me at the Institute at three-thirty, after my class, and we'll go to the Baltimore Museum of Art. If they don't have what you need, this weekend we can go over to D.C., to the National Gallery."

"What a friend!" Peter said, knowing she knew her art.

Friday afternoon of the same week, three very strange-looking young people walked into the school cafeteria. They were all clothed in tee-shirts and paint spotted jeans. From the group, a very attractive girl with very long, straight, dark hair yelled, "Hey Meg!" She eyed Meggie, who was in the middle of eating her lunch, with Peter on one side and Dennis on the other. Hearing her name and recognizing the voice, Meggie rose from her seat, swiftly heading toward these people, with Peter following.

"Nice, you could have watched for us," Christine said, a friend from the Maryland Institute.

"Since when are you shy? Besides, you already had clearance," Meggie glanced at her watch. "You're also early." Dennis was in the background taking all of this in.

"Hi Meggie," Murry said, giving her a peck on the cheek. He was a third year painting major at the Institute, standing about 5'8" tall and adorned a dark brown scraggly beard and hair to match. Shawn then came toward her. She glanced at him and thought, 'He's too pretty for words.' He had relatively short, straight, light- blonde hair, big blue eyes and a baby doll face. He stood about 5'11" and was really built. Sculpture was his major at the Institute. Placing his arm around her shoulder,

"Hello, beauty." Meggie threw her head back a little, with a slight laugh, not noticing a very puzzled Dennis.

"Hi, Peter," Christine placed a kiss on his cheek to his surprise. They walked from the cafeteria.

"Who are they?" Dennis' friend Bob asked him.

"The hell if I know!" A bewildered Dennis stated, still sitting, not being able to finish his lunch. Through the doorway he could see Peter with his arm around Christine's waist, and this blonde guy had his arm around Meggie's shoulder, and was whispering in her ear. "This is the first time in three years I've been in a high school."

"Lucky you!" Meggie smiled. He whispered in her ear again. "You're cute, do you know that?" He placed a kiss on her cheek. Dennis took all of this in, not knowing the conversation and certainly not liking the familiarity.

They walked toward the school office where Shawn had left his guitar. After retrieving it, Mr. Parks, the principal, exited his office,

"Meggie, I would like a word with you." She was surprised, she had already spoken with him about this. What did he want? She followed Mr. Parks into his office.

"That's a motley group of people you have brought here," Mr. Parks stated. Meggie laughed a little,

"What did you expect? They go to Maryland Institute, they're artists! Give us 15 minutes to warm up, then join us in the music room, okay." She pat his arm before leaving. Mr. Parks smiled to himself, over the past two years she never ceased to amaze him.

As they entered the music room, the bell rang, signaling the end of lunch for those who had it then, and the beginning of sixth period, which was to be drama for Meggie and Dennis. As Dennis entered his class looking for Meggie, Mrs. Walsh was surprised to see him,

"I expected you to be with Meggie, Dennis."

"Where is she?" Dennis asked, very aggravated at this point.

"In the music room," Mrs. Walsh responded. Without another word Dennis gathered his books and headed out the door.

Entering the music room, he saw Peter on one piano with Christine sitting on it, Murry on the drums, Shawn tuning the guitar and Meggie on a second piano. He gave her a very peeved look which she responded to with a smile.

"Why were you keeping this a secret?" Dennis sat on the bench beside her.

"Dennis, it's obvious we don't tell each other everything. Especially you." Meggie looked him in the eye.

"I don't believe this, you know!" He said in shock. He took her hands, "I've been walking around with this guilt. It was an experience I will never forget. Do you know how lousy I feel? I thought it would help, it didn't! How did you find out?"

"I'm allergic to ignorance!" Meggie smiled.

"I never meant to hurt you. You are the one I want because I love you. I promise nothing like this will ever happen again," Dennis squeezed her hands.

"Somehow, I think you understand."

"Understanding is not necessarily accepting," said a very-bright eyed and smiling Meggie. He hugged her, whispered in her ear,

"I never want to lose you."

"Can we start now?" Murry stated, more than asked, witnessing enough of this.

"The subject is now closed forever." Meggie placed her hands on the keyboard.

"Who are these people?" Dennis whispered again.

"I'll tell you later," she laughed a little. Dennis moved across the room so he could watch her. The four played, Meggie did most of the singing. Mr. Parks came in and sat beside Dennis, followed by Mr. Carlton, the music instructor, and Mr. Corona the, vice-principal. Hearing the sounds that were coming from this room, Mr. Corona and Mr. Parks exchanged glances. Mr. Corona went to the office to switch on the master intercom without forewarning the musicians they were playing to an audience. The song was over and Mr. Carlton smiled,

"Why haven't we heard that voice before!" Meggie blushed and Peter came to her rescue.

"It was her low profile," he smiled.

They started to play again, not wanting any more interruptions, with Meggie and Peter narrating the songs. Word traveled throughout the school that it was Meggie and Peter they were hearing. The classrooms were relatively quiet with everyone enjoying the music.

"This next song Peter wrote," Meggie said proudly.

"Bull! Once they hear the words, they will know it came mostly from your brain, not mine," Peter glanced at her. Then to the adults in the room, "The score is basically mine. She changed the words and rearranged a few chords of it, just as she does everything else I do."

"That's not so!" Meggie stated emphatically.

"No? What about my English paper last year? You made me rewrite the entire thing. Remember what you told me? You don't know an adverb from an adjective from your ass!" Peter expressed himself very loudly before laughing.

"Well, you don't!" Meggie smiled.

"Pick up the top of your piano bench. There's a new song; it's dedicated to our illustrious lady of word and chord," Peter smiled.

"A Song for Meggie!" she read.

"I started it in late August. I just finished it and I know you will revise it. However, I'd like you to try it now," Peter instructed. Meggie sang the song with tears filling her eyes. To think anyone, especially Peter who was such a special friend, would have written a song for her.

"I love it! Don't you change one thing about it," she crossed the room to embrace Peter, with tears in her eyes.

The musicians played on and when they had finished, Dennis swiftly walked across the room.

"Meggie, I love you!" He blurted out, not being able to control himself, with full knowledge everyone in the room would hear. She bit her bottom lip and laughed a little,

"I love you, too. Just because it's my style to remain a virgin doesn't mean my feelings for you aren't intense."

Mr. Parks walked over and switched the intercom off. It made no difference at this point. The end of the day bell was ringing, and everyone had already heard. He and Mr. Carlton approached Meggie and Dennis.

"There's something you should know," Mr. Parks stated. Peter watched because he had an uneasy feeling.

"The entire school has heard your music this afternoon, including your last comments," Mr. Parks looked at Meggie, thinking one day she would learn to control her tongue.

"How?" Meggie screamed in anger.

"We turned the intercom on, thinking we would give everyone a treat on a Friday afternoon. It's not often we have such fine musicians here," Mr. Parks smiled. Meggie clenched her fists trying to control that Irish temper of hers. She could not, she yelled,

"You should have asked us! If that was above your grain you should have told us! What ever happened to freedom of choice?"

"Meggie, calm down, I know that temper of yours," Mr. Parks sternly stated.

"Oh! So you've heard it, too!" Dennis smiled.

"Is there a back way out of here?" Meggie glanced at Mr. Parks, then at Mr. Carlton.

"Since when have you ever been one to run and hide?" Dennis asked.

"I'm real good at it, ask Peter," Meggie said, Peter smiled.

"I want the two of you to go to your lockers. Then, I would like a word with you in my office," Mr. Parks stated.

"Let's go," Dennis placed his arm around Meggie's waist, leading her from the room. Meggie looked at him questioningly.

"It's alright," Dennis said softly. They started down the hall, she clung to his hand on her waist. Meggie was uncharacteristically quiet.

"I know what you are thinking," Dennis smiled to her.

"Do you?" Meggie felt it inconceivable anyone could know that.

"You're afraid of what this might do to my reputation," he said, still leading her down the hall.

"How did you know that?" Meggie surprised.

"Because my concern is with you," he embraced her. A girl approached them.

"I like your style, Meg."

"Some jock you are," a guy passing shouted to Dennis.

"You must be horny, I have a few numbers for you," a member of the football team stated to Dennis. Making their way to their lockers, they deposited and retrieved what they needed very swiftly.

"I need my unfinished painting from the art room," she said.

"Alright," Dennis pulled her in that direction. There was another comment that came their way. Meggie looked at Dennis,

"I think we'll forget it."

"I really do need that painting," she said.

"We are going to get it," Dennis smiled, leading her in the direction of the art room.

Walking down the main hall in the direction of Mr. Parks' office, they were still the subject of ridicule. As they approached, Mr. Parks was waiting by the door.

"Meggie, Dennis please come in," Mr. Parks led the way to the small office in the rear and closed the door behind them. Meggie, still standing, stared at her principal.

"That wasn't real nice."

"Sit down, Meggie," he said, seating himself behind his desk.   "You too," Mr. Parks motioned to Dennis. He watched the two senior students as he leaned back in his chair.

"I must admit, I am surprised," Mr. Parks smiled. Then he looked at Meggie. "Do you have any more surprises for me this year?" Mr. Parks asked, Meggie tilted her head and laughed.

"What do you mean?" Dennis said, not understanding.

"He doesn't know?" Mr. Parks smiled, watching her as she shook her head no.

"Know what!" Dennis asked, not liking to be kept in the dark. Meggie grabbed his hand.

"I'll tell you later. It has to do with the comment Peter made about my low profile." The office intercom went on, announcing Mr. Parks' wife was on the phone.

"Mrs. Parks wants to know if you can come to dinner Thursday night. She can't wait to see the new you," Mr. Parks smiled.

"Sure, thank her for me," Meggie smiled. Mr. Parks went back to the phone.

"Meggie says she'll be there. How about another guest? I would like you to meet Dennis Fine." He smiled, looking at Dennis to see him reluctantly nod his head yes. He then placed the receiver back on the phone.

"When you two walked into the office together on the first day of school I was a bit shocked and a lot concerned," Mr. Parks placed his elbows on his desk, leaning forward. "I have to admit I was fearful you were going to have a bad influence on Meggie. To my surprise, Dennis, you have made a complete turnabout. Well, almost."

Meggie leaned her elbows on Mr. Park's desk, cupping her chin between her hands,

"Can we go now?"

"Whenever you wish. I thought it might be less uncomfortable for you if the school emptied out first," Mr. Parks smiled.

"Thank you," Dennis rose, gathering his books and Meggie's. She stood, picked up her canvas, put it under her right arm, and placed her metal tool kit filled with paints in her hand under it.

Watching them leave his office, Mr. Parks inquired, "You never told me how you like it at Maryland Institute."

She turned to face him and smiled broadly,

"That should be obvious. I absolutely love it!"

Mr. Parks again leaned back in his chair, watching them make their way from the building and thought, 'Such an unlikely pair.' He shook his head in amazement.

Meggie and Dennis exited the school through the front doors when Dennis stopped, drew her toward him.

"You are the only person I have ever cared about more than myself," then he kissed her.

"You two alright?" Peter neared them.

"We'll be alright!" Dennis answered.

"Now where?" Peter asked, looking at Meggie then over to Murry and Shawn. Meggie understood what he was saying, especially after seeing Christine hanging on him. She smiled,

"To my house, Dennis has never had one of my steak subs."

"We're going to the deli," Dennis instructed .

"What, are you nuts?" Meggie yelled.

"If I'm doomed to hear the comments, I want to get them over with," Dennis led her toward his car. They watched Christine climb into Peter's V.W. and Dennis gave Murry and Shawn directions.

Sitting in his Corvette before starting the motor,

"Beauty, are you ready to explain?" Dennis smiled. Meggie started to laugh so hard her side hurt.

"You got me on that one," she was still laughing with tears rolling down her cheeks from her uncontrollable tear ducts.

"Well! I'm listening," Dennis stated.

"I need to control myself first," Meggie said, taking a deep breath. "On Tuesday, remember Peter was to meet me at the old B & O Station Building at the Institute? He chose not to wait in the parking lot as I had instructed him to do. Instead, he showed up in my painting class on the second floor as I was washing out my brushes. On the way down the hall, we heard music and of course, Peter had to make a detour. Shawn and Murry were playing and there just happened to be a piano in the background, of which Peter made good use and naturally, I started to sing. Christine was also there, the girl with the long dark hair, she's in my painting class and is completely taken with Peter's talent. To say the least, we never made it to the museum. Christine's going with him tomorrow," Meggie explained as Dennis drove.

"What about now?" Dennis said, keeping his eyes from the road.

"Use your own mind! She's in college; no parents, only a roommate. Besides, she's not one for principles," Meggie stated.

"That covers one topic, what about the other?" Dennis glanced over to her. She laughed,

"You won't let me get away with anything, will you?"

"Never!" He smiled.

"This one's a longie, I think it better wait till later," Meggie said, as they pulled into the deli's parking lot. They got out of the car and Dennis put his arms around her.

"Not too much later," he said, before kissing her. He drew his head back a little, looked at her, then kissed her again before heading into the deli.

That evening, in the rec room of Meggie's home, Dennis smiled,

"I'm still waiting."

Meggie gazed down, then rose and walked to the piano.

"Remember the song Peter wrote for me?" She sat, placing her hands on the keyboard.

"Sure, it's about a caterpillar that turns into a beautiful butterfly," Dennis responded. Meggie rose, walked toward him, and sat herself in the far corner of the sofa, with her legs bent under her.

"That's true, but if you read deeper, it's about growing up. About a young girl who hid her identity for fear of being chastised by her peers," Meggie said, solemnly.

"That was you?" Dennis moved closer to her and placed his right arm around her shoulder.

"Precisely!" Meggie smiled at him. "That's the reason you don't remember meeting me before. I spent so much time hiding behind a facade that I didn't have time to take an interest in other people." She paused, looked down, then at him. "Dennis, I skipped a grade and, in the past, I had to endure a great deal of criticism from the kids I went to school with. That's when I decided to hide, per se, becoming somewhat of a loner." Meggie had a slight tear in her eye.

"Does this have anything to do with your chumminess with Mr. Parks?" Dennis asked.

"I'm his prodigal student!" She smiled, before Dennis kissed her. They sat on the sofa kissing for a while until Meggie jumped to her feet, shocking Dennis.

"That gives me a wonderful idea!" she eagerly stated. "For Halloween you'll go as a caterpillar and me, a butterfly. As long as you are not adverse to wearing a leotard."

"I'm not adverse to wearing a leotard. I happen to have a great body, whether you want it or not," Dennis stood and placed his arms around her.

II

On the Eve of Allhallows, Dennis stood at the foot of the stairs of Meggie's house, waiting for her to finish dressing. He wore a black leotard that covered his entire body, neck to ankle. Meggie had painted caterpillar feet all over the front of it. She painted a pair of his old tennis shoes black, and found him a wonderful mask with black antennae at a costume store not too far from the Institute. He stood in awe upon seeing her walk down the stairs. She wore a turquoise leotard with tights that sculptured every curve of her body. She wore no bra, thus revealing her firm, round breasts and the erection of her nipples. Glittered wings were attached to her back, a great colorful mask covered half her face, and red glittered antennae adorned her head.

"You look fantastic!" Dennis blurted out, not being able to take his eyes off her.

"So do you! I'm glad everything worked," she smiled, walking around Dennis to check him out.

They said good-bye to her parents and Ben. After seating themselves in his car, Dennis turned to her.

"After seeing me, my parents want to see you. They want to meet the mind that put all of this together."

"That's right! I've never been to your house," Meggie said.

"The house is terrific, the family situation leaves something to be desired," Dennis said, pulling out of her driveway.

"You've never mentioned this before," she said.

"It's not something I enjoy talking about," he stopped at a red light and turned to her. "The one thing I remember about my dad as I was growing up, was his absence." Dennis paused, "I never talk about it. This, I guess you

35

could say, is a rare occasion." Meggie leaned over to kiss his cheek.

"You're not alone, my dad stays out a lot of nights, too."

"But anyone can see how much he loves you." He glanced at her.

"That's true, we have a very special relationship." Meggie paused, "Enough depression!" With Dennis pulling into his driveway.

"You live here!" Meggie surprised. She glanced around at this large, ranch-style house situated on at least an acre of land that had been lavishly landscaped.

"You don't exactly live on poverty row." He smiled leading her into the house.

"Mom, Dad, I'd like you to meet Meggie Hiken," Dennis said, as they walked into the den.

"Meggie, it's nice to meet you. We've heard so much about you." Mrs. Fine approached them. Meggie gave Dennis a look that pierced.

"All good," He laughed, placing his arm around her shoulder.

"You seem to be one talented young lady," Mr. Fine said from his seat on the sofa, referring to the costumes. There was something about him that struck a nerve with Meggie, initial dislike. Knowing it had nothing to do with what Dennis had said earlier, she formed her own opinion about people. It hit her. He seemed somewhat shady, a little like a fat Al Capone, she thought, smiling, unaware of the conversation going on around her.

"We're out of here!" Said Dennis, interrupting her thought and wondering what was going on inside her head.

"It was good to meet you," Meggie glanced at his mom and then over to the sofa where his dad still sat. After exiting the house, and again sitting in the car, Dennis turned to her.

"I'd love to know what you were thinking in there."

"Oh!" She smiled, taking three joints from her purse and handing them to Dennis. "Here, I know you, Mr. Generosity." She lit another one and passed it to him.

"I don't know how you manage to think of everything. I love you," Dennis kissed her. He started the car motor and headed toward the schools' annual Halloween Dance.

That night they parked in the car on that same dead-end street they were used to.

"A bucket seat car was not made for this," Meggie said. Dennis laughed, lying her across him while he sat in the passenger seat. Then he put his arms around her, kissing her lips.

"Let's go to my house," Meggie suggested very wide-eyed.

"I like my privacy," he kissed her so passionately again, putting his tongue in her mouth, feeling her body quiver a little.

"Do you know how you turn me on?" Dennis gazed into her eyes, then down the front of her low-cut leotard, sneaking a peek at some of her breast. He placed his hand on her hip on top of that leotard clinging to her body, and kissed her again the same way. Still kissing her, ever so passionately, he slowly moved his hand from her hip to her waist, proceeding up the side of her body feeling the side of her breast. She didn't move, keeping her arms around his neck, not wanting to remove her lips from his, as Dennis cupped her right breast and moaned. She felt a strange sensation come over her and she drew back a little. He was now massaging both of her breasts over the leotard, watching her body move in a rhythmic motion. Then he pulled her leotard from her shoulders and down her front, to her waist, exposing her breasts.

"You are so beautiful, your breasts match your beauty," Dennis said, kissing her as he touched the bare skin of her breasts.

"Virgin breasts," Meggie mumbled, kissing him.

"Virgin breasts?" Dennis repeated, laughing a little, still kissing her. He had never heard it phrased like that before.

"That's right, never touched by anyone, except myself," Meggie said, with a tilt of her head.

"You mean, you feel yourself up!" Dennis said, surprised.

"I wouldn't exactly call it that," Meggie said, becoming a little solemn, looking him in the eyes that she found breathtaking. "Sometimes, when I go to sleep at night, I feel so damn lonely. I was aware from a very young age I was different. Not your normal person and unable to decide whether I liked it or not. I imagine when I come to terms with that, finding out who I am, and being capable of accepting me, I hopefully won't feel so alone. So at night, as I lie alone in my bed, sometimes I'll place one of my hands over a breast. Falling asleep holding it, helps a little."

"I never would have thought you, of all people, felt that way," Dennis drew her toward him, hugging her so tight, feeling her bare chest against his. "I feel alone a lot too. I've never admitted that to anyone before."

"I think most of us have at least a bit of a void we can't quite place. Personally, I think a lot of the blame lies with our parents," Meggie still hugged him, liking the feeling of his chest against hers. After a few minutes, she drew back. "I don't believe my mother has hugged me since I was four years old."

"I will, I love you. That is probably because you are different, but wonderfully so," Dennis squeezed her so tight. "I have never been so totally honest with anyone in my life. It feels so good to be able to trust," Dennis whispered in her ear. "You promote that. Mr. Parks was right. You do bring out the best in me. Thank you, my love, for this feeling." He placed a kiss on her lips that she would never forget. They sat kissing and touching for a long time.

38

Dennis sucked her erect nipples, licking all of one breast with his hand on the other. She threw her head back in sheer ecstasy.

"Let's make love. I want you, I love you," Dennis said, hugging her.

"Isn't this part of making love?" Meggie leaned back a little to see him. Dennis was hopeful,

"Yes, but you know what I mean. I want all of you."

"It can't be, I'm not ready for it. Besides, I made a commitment to myself over the summer. When and if I go to bed with someone for the first time, it will never be in a car, and he will not take me home afterwards, depositing me. I want an overnight thing, preferably a couple of days when I am totally in love and ready," Meggie stated her feelings.

"You are something else," Dennis smiled, squeezing her again.

"Peter told me I should let you hump me. He said it is inconceivable for me to expect you to always take cold showers and jerk off," she whispered in his ear.

"Peter!" Dennis laughed. "You discussed this with Peter?"

"Why not? He's my best friend." Meggie looked at him very-wide eyed. He started to laugh, drawing her toward him again.

"I do love you, you are my best friend. Remind me to thank Peter," he smiled, then proceeded to make love to her face, neck and breasts, later placing his half clothed body on top of hers. After a while, they both sat in the passenger seat holding each other. Dennis glanced at her,

"You know, since I found you, I haven't been as lonely."

"What brought this on again?" Meggie curious.

"I was just thinking, you make me feel like I can say anything that's on my mind. I have never felt so loved and cared about before. Maybe that's why I'm willing to wait for you. This has already been far longer than I had ever dreamed," Dennis stated.

"Trying for a guilt trip, Dennis!" Meggie tried to pull away.

"No way! Believe it or not, I understand your feelings." He smiled, holding her. "When did you talk to Peter?"

"Tonight," she smiled. "I can hear Peter now. You sure didn't waste any time, Meg." She laughed with Dennis joining her when a light flashed into the car.

"Oh shit!" Dennis yelled, looking up, seeing a cop at the window on the driver's side of the car. He speedily moved to that seat and Meggie quickly pulled her leotard up over her shoulders.

"I'd like to see some identification," the policeman stated, still shining the light at their faces. Dennis handed him their drivers' licenses.

"Are you aware of the gravity of what you are doing, young lady?" He glanced at Meggie.

"In a totally disenfranchised society, I can assure you I am more aware than you!" Meggie said, looking him straight in the eye. Dennis turned white and the cop dropped his flashlight right in Dennis' lap. Dennis jumped as it landed on his penis.

"Sorry," the officer said, retrieving his flashlight. He was at a loss for words, standing there for a moment. "It's 2:35 in the morning, go home." He turned around and headed for his car.

Dennis rolled his car window up, Meggie burst out laughing. Since laughter is contagious, so did he. They sat there for a few minutes, hysterical and trying to catch their breaths. Dennis started the motor of the car, noticing the cop was still watching them.

"What possessed you to say that?" Dennis glanced over at her.

"I don't like being put through an inquisition," she smiled.

"You have no fear, do you?" Dennis said, driving.

"Of what? Him! What was he going to do to a couple of teenagers making out? Lock us up?" Meggie started to laugh again.

"I never looked at it that way. I'm sorry it happened." Dennis looked at her, then at her breasts, loving them.

"Don't worry about it. I take full responsibility for my actions." She took a brush from her pocketbook and ran it through her hair.

"You didn't even flinch when he first caught us," he smiled.

"Modesty has never been one of my virtues," Meggie laughed, as they pulled into her driveway.

"It has been one hell of a night!" Dennis leaned over to kiss her.

"I thought it was wonderful." Meggie kissed him back.

"You're the one who is wonderful." He sighed, kissing her again. Leaving the car, walking to the front door, Dennis stopped, threw his arms around her, and kissed her again.

"The more I know you, the more I love you," Dennis said in her ear. She kissed him.

"I love you too. See you tomorrow," Meggie walked into the house.

"Be here at twelve," he smiled. Before closing the door, Meggie smiled,

"Some privacy Dennis." He returned her smile with a slight laugh.

"Meggie, wait!" Dennis whispered loudly, walking toward her. "Let me in for a minute"

"Are you nuts? It's so late my parents will have coronaries," she stated.

"With everything that happened tonight, I forgot something," he smiled at her. Now, she was curious.

"Okay, just for a minute," Meggie opened the door wider letting him in, leading him toward the living room because it was the room farthest from her parents'. Meggie turned, staring at him, waiting.

"I'm not good at this sort of thing. I've never done anything like it before. I even rehearsed today," Dennis said, nervously .

"Out with it, Dennis!" Meggie gave him one of her looks, watching him remove something from his pocket.

"I want you to wear this," he placed his school ring on a chain he had bought that day, around her neck.

"I don't need this to tell the world how I feel about you. I know," she eyed him questioningly.

"I do, but not for the same reason. To ward off all of those guys that seem to be chasing you all of the time, especially Shawn and the others from Maryland Institute." He smiled, hugging her.

"Damn it! You don't trust me!" Meggie pulled back.

"I trust you more than anyone I've ever known. It's them I don't trust. Please wear it for me," Dennis kissed her.

"You really could have thought of a more romantic way to do this. You are about as poetic as Daffy Duck," Meggie smiled.

"I know, but I love you," Dennis laughed a little as he kissed her.

The following morning, Meggie joined her family for breakfast. She felt good about herself, no recriminations about the degree of sex she had with Dennis the previous night. She actually felt jubilant until Ma started.

"Meg, you got in a bit too late last night. Don't let it happen again," Ma ordered, with her back to Meggie, because she was frying eggs on the stove. Not waiting for a reply. "Where were you at all hours of the morning?" She then turned to look at her.

"Honestly, we were talking and lost track of time. It's amazing, we feel so much the same about so many things." Meggie replied, before taking a swig of her orange juice and thinking, 'It's a partial truth.' Ma brought the eggs to the table, serving them. When she got to Meggie, Ma yelled,

"What is that thing around your neck?" Meggie jumped from fright, then looked down.

"It's Dennis' ring. I guess you could say that I'm ringed, or I'm chained. I don't know what you call it," Meggie smiled. She couldn't help but notice Ma was irate, but she didn't understand why.

"You're too young for this and you're to give it back!" Ma yelled.

"Don't count on it!" Meggie said, resting her fork back on the table. "One of the things Dennis and I have in common is his relationship with his father is comparable to mine with you!" Meggie yelled, rising from her seat, heading out of the kitchen.

"And what is that supposed to mean?" Ma screamed after her.

"You figure it out!" Meggie yelled back, thinking, 'Damn it! Where's Daddy? She's always the hardest on me when he's not home.'

On Thanksgiving, Dennis brought Meggie to his parents' home for dessert. She had been invited for dinner, but declined. Something about his dad made her uncomfortable and she did not want to spend too much time with him. She thought it was a combination of her own natural instincts, along with what Dennis had told her over the past month. He had confided everything to her about his discontentment, his disillusionment and his mistrust of his father. When they entered the house, his mom rose from the table.

"Meggie, I'm so glad you could come," Mrs. Fine smiled, taking the coats from Dennis.

"Thanks for asking me," Meggie smiled. Dennis took her hand, leading her into the dining room.

"I want you to meet Victor," he said excitedly, not being able to wait to show her off. There sat Dennis' fat dad and his older brother, Victor, who was a junior at Penn State.

"Victor, this is Meggie," Dennis smiled and placed a hand on Meggie's shoulder.

Meggie noticed the two men did not rise as Dennis pulled out a chair for her. His mom sliced a piece of cake and handed it to Dennis to give to her. She now knew Dennis got his manners from his mom, certainly not his dad!

"Where are you going to school next year?" Victor asked, looking at her, hardly being able to keep his eyes off her.

"American University," she answered tasting the cake. "This is delicious!"

"Thank you." Mrs. Fine smiled, pleasantly.

"Mom, believe me, she knows her food," Dennis laughed, glancing at Meggie. "You look so fresh and sweet tonight."

"Straight from concentrate!" Meggie said with a slight laugh.

"Is that why you applied to American?" Mr. Fine interrupted.

"Of course. But first I have to bring my cume up to a three point O," Dennis stated.

"If you don't, you'll go to the University of Maryland. It's a lot cheaper anyway," Mr. Fine stated, putting a forkful of cake in his mouth.

"Dennis' grades have already risen a lot this year," Mrs. Fine stated.

"I don't understand this. American doesn't cost any more than Penn State," Meggie in shock. Mr. Fine turned noticeably red.

"To someone in your circumstances, money may not be an object," Mr. Fine said.

"What is that supposed to mean?" Meggie became aggravated.

"I know your dad and I went to school with your Uncle Bob," he said, not being able to take his eyes off her. He definitely could see what Dennis saw in this beautiful, bright young lady.

"Then, I think you are extremely lucky," she smiled.

"I tried to buy that piece of property in Howard County from your grandfather a few years back," said Mr. Fine. She laughed,

"He wouldn't sell it to you! I know that! His entire life, he always believed in the power of the land. Besides, he always knew that's my favorite piece and one day it will be mine. It's been promised to me since I was six years old."

"Tell me, how many millions are your father and uncle worth now?" Mr. Fine stared at her.

"I don't see where that's anyone's business!" Meggie bluntly stated, with Mrs. Fine giving her husband an evil eye.

"Let's play pool," Dennis took her hand, pulling her from the chair.

Entering the rec room in the rear of the house, Dennis put his arms around her,

"I'm sorry."

"For what? Your mom is really a nice person. You're a lot like her," Meggie said, before kissing him, noticing Victor approaching.

"I thought we were playing pool," Victor questioned.

"Good idea," Meggie smiled, starting to rack the balls.

"You actually play this game?" Victor in amazement .

"Dennis taught me a couple of weeks ago." Meggie assured him.

"Pool's not interesting unless you play for money. Let's make it a quarter a ball," Victor stated confidently.

"You don't want to do that!" Dennis warned.

"You're on," Meggie smiled.

"Ladies first" Victor motioned to her. She picked up her cue and proceeded to shoot, clearing the entire table, with Victor staring at his brother. Dennis smiled,

"I tried to warn you. She picks up things pretty fast."

The phone rang, Dennis went to answer it. Meggie headed for the juke box, Victor followed her.

"You're kind of strange," Victor looked in those eyes of hers.

"Dennis told me I was weird the first time we met. I guess your opinion fits in the same category," Meggie moved away from him to choose the songs she wanted to hear.

"You have magnificent eyes," Victor stated, putting his hands on her shoulders, turning her to face him. She removed his hands, turning back to the juke box without a comment.

"How about lunch tomorrow?" Victor asked, grabbing her arm.

"Are you asking me out?" she said, with furrowed eyebrows.

"Of course." Victor smiled.

"I believe you could use some lessons in manners. You are rude. Take your hands off me," Meggie turned her attention back to the juke box. Dennis walked back into the room. She extended her arm for him to come to her.

"Rochelle and Bob are stopping over," Dennis announced.

"Wonderful," she smiled, raising her face to kiss him. Victor decided he didn't belong and left.

"Isn't he great?" Dennis asked, referring to Victor.

"Just terrific," she lied, knowing how much Dennis loved him and she basically knew Victor felt the same way about Dennis.

The following Tuesday, Meggie pulled her car into the school parking lot. She spotted four police cars with a crowd around them. Removing her body from her little MG, saying, "See you later." (which she always did), she noticed Dennis coming toward her.

"What happened?" Meggie asked.

"They busted three guys for selling pot, one of whom I used to buy from. I'm glad I have a new connection." He kissed her.

"Me too," she laughed. Thank God for her Hawaiian connection, Lori.

They made their way into the school, going to their lockers and trying to overcome what was happening outside. The homeroom bell rang, they kissed till later, and went into their respective homerooms. Over the intercom Mr. Parks' voice was heard:

"As your grade is called you will go to your lockers. The police will be around to inspect for drugs, alcohol and anything else that does not belong. First, all twelfth graders proceed to your lockers."

Dennis started to panic because he knew Meggie had two joints in her locker for him. He managed to calm himself down a little, walking toward the lockers. Luckily, his was only 12 away from hers. He made it there so fast that he had to wait for her.

"What are we going to do?" Dennis asked, seeing her approach. She opened her locker door swiftly.

"Here!" Meggie handed him a j.

"What do you want me to do with this?," an excited Dennis stared at her.

"Eat it!" Meggie directed, stuffing the other one in her mouth and chewing. Dennis did as she instructed, watching her.

"I won't be able to get high before lunch today," he sighed.

"Dennis, you will be high all day!" Meggie laughed, not being able to control it. Tuesdays and Thursdays were his easiest days-after lunch, all studies. "Once this stuff gets into your digestive system it lasts for hours."

"How do you know so much?" Dennis smiled at her, seeing her shrug her shoulders.

"Dennis!" his homeroom teacher yelled. Seeing the police coming, Dennis moved back to his own locker.

Meggie stood by her open locker, talking to people on both sides when she saw the policeman approaching.

"You're next" he said. Then he looked at her.

"Not you again!" the officer stated. Meggie found him difficult to place, then she recognized him.

"Halloween!" she laughed. He didn't find it the least bit amusing.

"I would like you to come with me," he grabbed her by the elbow, leading her away.

Dennis witnessed what was happening and knew she should not be incriminated because there was nothing there. They had eaten it! He headed straight for Mr. Parks'.

"Can I see you for a moment?" Dennis interrupted Mr. Parks and another police officer.

"Dennis, what is it?" Mr. Parks said ending his conversation abruptly, due to his new-found respect for this young man.

"A few weeks ago, Meggie and I were parked. You know what I'm trying to say. Anyway, a policeman came shining his light in the car window. That same cop has just taken her into that room," Dennis pointed.

"Find Peter, meet me in my office," Mr. Parks walked toward the room where Dennis had pointed out.

"Officer Reynolds, I have an idea. I think you'll like it." Mr. Parks quickly glanced at a very frightened Meggie. His heart ached for her, she seemed so scared.

"Mr. Parks, how did you know?" Meggie said.

"Dennis, now shh...." Mr. Parks said to her, then laid out his plan to the police officer.

Meggie didn't like what she was hearing. She tried to object but Mr. Parks did not allow her to get a word in. She decided to whisper in his ear,

"That animated adenoid made a pass at me!" Mr. Parks had a hard time controlling his laughter.

"Go to my office, now!" he stated sternly. She left without another word, relieved to be out of there. Mr. Parks continued his conversation with the officer with a smile on his face, thinking of how Meggie used the English vocabulary.

Peter, Meggie and Dennis were sitting in the outer office as Mr. Parks entered.

"My office," he pointed to it. On entering his office, they saw only two chairs in front of the desk.

"Peter, you sit. The last time I sat there I had to go to dinner at his house," Dennis said. Mr. Parks sat himself behind his desk.

"We are going to put on an anti-drug campaign in this school. You three are going to be the ones to do it. We need a large anti-drug poster for the hallway. Officer Reynolds will be waiting at the State Police Headquarters to give you information and pamphlets. I'm giving you the rest of the day off school to do this," Mr. Parks said.

"Great!" said Meggie, aggravated.

"We'll do it" Peter stated, elbowing her in the side.

"Now can we go?" Meggie asked, looking at her principal.

"It seems you're always asking me that question, lately. Yes." He smiled.

They quickly left the school. First Meggie went to her car to get a painting, because she had to be at the Institute that afternoon. Dennis was already in his car waiting, with the engine running, when she climbed in with Peter, storing her things in the rear.

"How did we get into this?" Peter asked, feeling somewhat cramped with Meggie next to him in the same bucket seat.

"Ask principal's pet," Dennis laughed.

"Sorry! I don't feel I'm to blame for this one!" she raised her voice. He stopped the car at a red light and leaned over to kiss her.

"You are too cute for words, I bet that's exactly what that cop thought," Dennis said, pulling into the police station.

"Of all people who should be doing this!" Peter said sarcastically.

"We are, accept it!" Meggie laughed at the irony of the whole situation.

"I can't believe you find this humorous," Peter stared at her.

"Sorry, I plan to make the best of this and everything else," Meggie still laughed.

"We're also real high!" Dennis informed him.

Christmas vacation, the senior class planned a class skiing trip. They all gathered at the high school early on Wednesday morning, anticipating a four-hour drive to the mountains of upstate New York. Mrs. Walsh, the drama teacher, and Mr. Paul, the English teacher, were to be the two chaperones on the trip. They drove down Interstate 695, then onto Interstate 95.

"It's snowing!" Meggie smiled at Dennis behind the wheel of his Corvette. "Isn't it wonderful!"

"All skiers love when it snows," Dennis grinned.

Excitement came over Meggie as she glanced at Dennis beside her, then to the little twinkles of white out of the window. They crossed the Mason-Dixon line into Delaware, shortly thereafter into Pennsylvania. Next came New Jersey, followed by New York, where Dennis drove increasingly faster. They were heading for Hunter Mountain, smack in the middle of the Catskills. Spotting the resort, Meggie pulled the car to an abrupt stop, right in front of Bob.

"What took you so long? You passed us on the road doing at least a hundred," Bob yelled to them. Dennis smiled, looking at Meggie,

"We had to make a pit stop at McDonald's."

She quickly threw a snowball, smashing it into his face. He threw one at her, creating a snowball battle between the two of them until Meggie was on the ground throwing her head back.

"You blitzed me!" she yelled. He neared her laughing.

"I finally found one thing I can beat you at," he kissed her. He started to get up, pulling her with him.

"Not just yet." She bit her bottom lip. He couldn't resist and kissed her again.

"Damn, I love you," Meggie said. He kissed her again hearing those words, helping her up, leading her into this chalet of primitive people, she thought. Where else could the entire class have rented a place including meals, for the next three days.

After registering, Meggie walked up the stairs to the room she was to share with Rochelle. Glancing around this quaint room, she recalled seeing the sign, Hidden Green Resort. She laughed to herself. The room had a gray, pink and white color scheme. It was average in size. On the far wall was a lovely stone fireplace in between two, small bay windows. There was a Victorian dresser and chaise on the wall to her right. Rochelle was lying on one of the two Victorian double beds which had a small night table between them. To her left was a small bath in total pink.

"I need to talk to you. We've gotten pretty close since your coming out," Rochelle slightly smiled. Meggie stood at the foot of Rochelle's bed.

"I've been trying to figure out how to say this. There's only one way," Rochelle said, first looking at Meggie, then down. "I'm going to stay with Bob this weekend." Meggie shocked, naively questioned,

"Then where's Dennis going to sleep?"

"That's up to you," Rochelle stated, removing her tee-shirt, exposing a very thin body with small round breasts. "Bob and I have been sleeping together for almost a year now," Rochelle threw her head back with her long, brown hair falling to her shoulders. "I knew a long time ago that the only way to keep Bob was to sleep with him."

A few minutes later, the two girls entered the lobby. Seeing them, Dennis hoped Rochelle had told Meggie. He had tried. But, for one reason or another, he was unable to get it out. Watching Meggie head straight for Peter, he knew Rochelle had. A few moments later, Meggie stood dangling some keys in front of Dennis' face.

"A snow mobile! But, I drive," she laughed.

"Only for half," Dennis took her in his arms, kissing her.

They were having such a good time with her driving like a demon, until Dennis made her give it up, so he could do the same. Peter, the class historian ran out taking pictures.

At dinner that night, Bob asked Dennis.

"How come you let her drive? You've never allowed anyone to drive your car before. She drove like a wild woman, passing us all."

Dennis looked to his right at Meggie. She made a face and they both became hysterical,

"A cop stopped me for speeding. Meggie told me to trade places with her, so I did. She unzipped her ski jacket and unbuttoned her blouse midway, revealing just enough," Dennis smiled. "She got out of the car, handing him her driver's license. After looking at it he asked her a few questions, none of which I could hear, and tried to see down her blouse at the same time. She didn't get a ticket! When I went to take over the wheel, she told me, 'I got you out of this, I drive!'"

"It works every time," Meggie smiled.

"Since when?" Peter gave her a peculiar look.

"Since last summer. Lori and I went to a party on the other side of Oahu. She wanted to stay, I didn't. I took her car and headed back. I was doing 90 around some big hills that they refer to as mountains, in a 25 mile-per- hour zone with the top down, wearing only my bikini because I wanted more sun. As luck would have it, I got stopped by a cop. He couldn't keep his eyes off my chest," Meggie shrugged.

"I can't blame him," Dennis said, kissing her.

"I didn't get a ticket! And, that's how to do it!" She broadly smiled.

"It's time to play." Peter took her hand, leading her toward the piano. He played, with her singing, for a while. When they had finished, a girl in their class named Adrian, began flirting with Peter.

"Word travels fast as to your technique in bed," Meggie smiled to Peter. This time she shocked him. His eyes opened so wide, his face turned blank and white. He couldn't think of a comeback for her.

Everyone sat in front of the fire telling ghost stories. The chaperones carefully watched over them as they watched each other. Meggie thought something was definitely going on between them. Mrs. Walsh had recently been divorced.

"Tell the one about the ghost in the amusement park," Meggie gazed at Dennis. He came to the part where he jerked because of 'eerie things', seeing he still scared her.

"You will never get used to this!" He laughed, hugging her.

"Never," she smiled throwing her head back.

They lay there for a while listening to the ghost stories being told. Dennis noticed Mrs. Walsh leave and go up the stairs. A few minutes later, he saw Mr. Paul follow. It was obvious they were attempting to be discreet.

"The coast is clear," he looked at Meggie.

"Is it?" Meggie said, biting her bottom lip again, not aware of what it did to him. She didn't know whether she was quite ready for this next phase of her life. She knew she loved Dennis, but did not know whether she could go through with this. Meggie still felt she was a hypocrite, being so free-spirited at the Institute and then so prim and proper at other times. She was, in reality, searching for herself, knowing the only way to find herself was to experience new things. But, did this next phase have to happen just now? Meggie gazed up at Dennis' face, his strong masculine face, his beautiful dark hair, his deep blue eyes with long dark eyelashes. She thought, 'He is magnificent, and so sexy looking.' She smiled, still watching him.

"Meg, let's go upstairs," Dennis said, coming to kiss her.

"Now?" Was all she could manage to get out. That pit was in her throat again. It hadn't been there since that night he raped her mouth.

"Come on, Meg," Dennis pushed her up, taking her hand and leading the way. He stopped at the maid's linen room retrieving a sheet first.

Once in her room Dennis turned, locking the door, then he gave Meggie a kiss on her forehead.

"Scared? Don't be, there's no rush. I love you, you know that," Dennis gently hugged her, kissing her again. He pulled a joint from his pocket, lit it and handed it to her, "This will help you to relax." Meggie knew it would, taking it from him, watching the sway of his body as he went to light the fire. Her eyes stayed fixed on him as she sat on the chaise smoking the j, feeling her voice had definitely left her. Dennis unfolded the sheet, laying it on the floor in front of the glowing fire. Next, he moved toward the door, switching off the lights. He looked over to Meggie sitting like a statue, puffing away. He smiled, yet she looked so absolutely radiant in the light from the glowing embers. Their eyes met. Meggie knew now she did lose her voice. Dennis approached her without a word being spoken. It was a tense moment for him, too; he had dreamed about this for so long. It was finally going to happen, he had planned every detail, right down to the sheet.

Dennis came to her, putting his arms around her, kissing her. Lying next to her on the chaise, he held her. They would stay like that until Meggie felt more at ease. They passed the j back and forth, holding each other, then kissing. Dennis wasn't just kissing her lips any longer but her ear, then her neck. She felt herself becoming a little wet between her legs. Meggie could also feel the beginning of an erection against her side. She felt something wet at the base of her neck, it was his tongue. He kissed the same spot, working his way down. When he unbuttoned her blouse, Meggie felt panic. Sensing this, he stopped, leaving her full breasts exposed. He didn't touch, not yet. Instead, he went for her mouth, kissing her more passionately than ever before, researching every space in it. He kissed her ears and neck again, removing his own shirt, working his way back to where he had left. Meggie felt such pleasure, it frightened and delighted her at the same time. She felt him caress her right breast, kissing it, then sucking it gently. She threw her head back, jerking the lower half of her body. Dennis smiled to himself.

"You are so sensual," Dennis whispered, breaking the silence.

She smiled at him as he caressed her left breast, removing her blouse from her shoulders. Kissing and caressing her entire torso, he knew it was a must to take it slowly and to be extremely gentle with her; and he was. He unsnapped her pants, kissing and licking her belly button, sliding her pants off her. He stood, removing his own pants. The entire time their eyes did not leave the other's body. Watching her lie on the chaise, clothed in nothing but a pair of skimpy bikini underpants, he thought that he was finally going to have her. He's waited so long, but not yet. He knew he really wanted to make love to her first, wanting her to want it as much as he did.

Meggie looked up at his broad shoulders, his muscular, curly- haired chest and somewhat narrow hips. She saw fantastically firm muscular arms and legs and an erection through his jockey shorts. She quickly looked away into his deep blue eyes. Thinking how much she loved him, if she was going to lose her virginity, it was with the perfect person and setting. Dennis knelt on the floor beside her, kissing her, pulling his chest up over hers. Feeling her erected nipples against his chest, he slid her underpants off, then his own. He lifted Meggie up and placed her on the sheet in front of the fire. Their eyes met again. 'He kissed her as if she were the last woman on earth,' Meggie thought. Sucking her nipples, he slid his hand into the dark, thick hair between her legs. Feeling for her clitoris, he found out how wet she had already become. Smiling, he slid his body over hers.

"The first time it's going to hurt a little," Dennis whispered in her ear, before kissing her.

He was having a tough time placing his penis and controlling his orgasm, because she was a virgin. Their bodies were moving rhythmically together; finally, it was all the way in, producing ecstasy for Dennis. He rolled off her, thinking, 'The best orgasm ever!' He pulled Meggie to lay on his chest, hugged and kissed her.

"I love you so much, Meg," he said, kissing her again.

Meggie lay there in semi-shock with Dennis holding her for a while. Rising, he headed to the bathroom to get a wet washcloth. Washing the small amount of blood off of her thighs, he kissed her inner thigh,

"You are so magnificent," Dennis looked at her blank face, picking her up, placing her on the bed. Meggie couldn't take her eyes off him. She was still unable to speak. 'So this is it,' she thought. 'It was nice except for the blood, the pain and no orgasm.' She had read enough to know that's how it usually is the first time. Watching Dennis pick up the sheet with the small splattered spot of blood, she wondered if she would ever experience the ecstasy that he had felt. Dennis approached, lying beside her, touching her body all over and kissing every inch. She knew she would soon find out. They made love over and over again that night.

The following morning Dennis jumped from the bed, "Oh Shit!" He yelled, pulling some condems from his pants pocket and thinking, 'I was too anxious.'

"It doesn't matter," Meggie smiled, looking at his anguished face.

"Come here, my love," she still smiled, holding her arms out to him. Dennis came to her, their naked bodies touching again. He couldn't believe how excited he got, so quickly, with her.

"I started taking the pill," she whispered in his ear.

"When? You never said anything!" Dennis gazed into her eyes.

"The beginning of November. I went to see Dr. Marcus. He's always been wonderful to me. I knew only a benevolent deity could have prevented this!" Meggie laughed.

"You are terrific!" Dennis screamed, relieved, kissing her and making love to all of her again.

Meggie rose from the bed, stretching. He loved when she did that clothed, but nude was better. Watching her brush her hair while she was completely naked, Dennis thought he was so lucky. He laughed to himself with the thought she is even a wild woman in bed.

"I love you," Meggie said from across the room, walking toward the bathroom. She turned the shower on, allowing the water to run down her face over her body, and took the soap from the dish.

"Let me do that," Dennis walked into the shower, taking the soap from her. He washed her entire body, then his own. She left the shower, retrieving a towel. Seeing Dennis emerge from it, she bit her bottom lip. "Come here," he smiled, holding his arms out to her. She dropped the towel going to hug him, and they made love again on the bathroom floor.

Emerging from their room with Dennis' arm around her shoulder, smiling at each other, both were completely content. They walked down the stairs clinging to each other and into the dining room where a buffet was set up for breakfast. Meggie headed straight for the food.

"Good morning," Meggie smiled at Peter next to her who was making a plate for himself.

"Is it?" Peter asked, with a questioning look. She started to laugh a little. "How was it?" Peter's eyes were fixed on her.

"Wonderful! I'll tell you about it later," Meggie smiled, pulling her entire torso up, throwing her head back, feeling totally free.

"Only you!" Peter laughed.

"How was Adrian?" Meggie made a plate for herself.

"I'd rather not say," Peter answered, as they walked to the table. Meggie thought, his response said it all.

Meggie sat with Dennis on one side of her and Peter on the other. Looking at both of them, she started to giggle.

"What's so funny?" Dennis curious.

"You," she smiled, kissing him, thinking how fortunate she was to have Dennis and such a good friend as Peter.

"I have never seen so much food on one plate in my life! I can't believe you can eat all of that," Bob, sitting across from Meggie, said in total disbelief.

"Watch her!" Peter laughed.

"It doesn't seem like that much to me," Meggie glanced at her overcrowded plate.

"Damn, you're cute," Dennis kissed her cheek, thinking to himself, and so sexy.

After breakfast, Meggie smiled at Dennis and Peter.

"I think it's time we hit the slopes. Charge!" She yelled, on her way out of the door. They followed her to the ski bin, seeing her unlock her skis.

"How decent are you?" Meggie glanced at Dennis.

"Fair to Middling. I don't ski the blacks, if that's what you're asking," Dennis put his face very close to hers so their noses touched.

"Then you can stay with Peter," Meggie laughed, making her way toward the advanced slopes.

"Don't tell me; you do this too!" Dennis yelled after her.

"Okay, I won't!" Meggie yelled back to him

At noon, Dennis approached the base of the advanced slope, glanced up, and saw Meggie and Bob flying down. Before he knew it, they came to an abrupt halt directly in front of him.

"Why didn't you tell me what a wild woman she is?" Bob uttered.

"She attacks everything with such determination," Dennis laughed, seeing her red nose, with tears running down her cheeks. She wore a lime green ski jacket with matching pants that enhanced her long wavy blonde hair.

"Why are you crying?" Dennis asked, concerned.

"I'm not, my eyes are just tearing. They do it a lot, and this cold air brings it on the most. I guess they're pretty sensitive," said Meggie.

"I can't recall ever seeing an outfit quite that color before," Dennis laughed.

"Don't make fun, Dennis, it suits me," she smiled.

"Race you back for lunch," Meggie yelled, already on her way. Dennis smiled ear-to-ear. He loved her so.

That afternoon as Meggie was in the shower, there was a knock at the door. Dennis answered, hoping it wasn't Mrs. Walsh or Mr. Paul.

"I'm glad it's you guys," Dennis relieved, let Bob, Rochelle, Peter and Carol into the room.

"Meg, where's your can?" Dennis yelled to her in the bathroom.

"In the top drawer of the dresser," Meggie walked from the bathroom with a towel wrapped around her body and another around the wet hair on top of her head. She said hello to everyone as she headed toward the closet for a robe, giving Peter a very special glance, at which he started to laugh.

"We're running low," Dennis said, taking some pot from the can to roll a joint.

"There's enough, Lori will be here next week," Meggie said, walking over to him and taking the j.

"You've saved me a lot of bread on pot this year," Dennis smiled.

"But, cost you a lot on food!" she laughed, walking to the bathroom. Peter followed her, closing the door behind him. They sat on the bathroom floor passing the j, talking and laughing.

"I have a feeling Meggie has changed her style," Bob looked at Dennis, who only smiled. He somehow wasn't crazy about the fact that in the bathroom right now Meggie was undoubtedly telling Peter everything about last night. He felt he better accept the fact they confided everything to each other.

"Hey, Meg, what are you doing in there?" Dennis yelled.

"We're making out!" She laughed. 'Damn,' Dennis thought, 'She has an answer for everything.' Meggie and Peter walked from the bathroom and she jumped on top of Dennis,

"I think it's time for dinner."

"There's always that one thing on your mind," Dennis smiled.

"Better make it two, after last night," she whispered in his ear, before kissing him.

After dinner that evening, the entire class was on the floor by the fire telling ghost stories again. Meggie lay there with Dennis' arm around her, her mind drifting in thought, recalling her conversation with Peter that afternoon. She thought how interested he was hearing about her night, and how he smiled when she told him he didn't seem to be doing too bad himself. He laughed, saying they had come a long way since last year. He recalled he had a real tough time getting a date then. Meggie said, "And look at you now! They all want to go to bed with you." She smiled, Peter felt it was because of her and Christine. "No way," she told him, "I've heard the rumors about you."

"Where are you?" Dennis asked, seeing her stare into space.

"Just thinking," Meggie said, then noticed Peter and Carol walk up the stairs. Dennis followed her eyes, seeing the same.

"A clear case of fixation!" Meggie smiled to him. He hugged her.

"Let's go up," Dennis helped her up.

Entering his room, Peter put an arm around Carol, drawing her toward him, then kissing her. They walked toward the fireplace. He lit the wood as Carol sat on the floor watching him. Peter looked at her smiling, rolling the newspaper, as he lit the match;

"I want you to make love to me," Carol timidly stated, as Peter dropped the lit match on the floor. He managed to finally get the fire lit and turned to her.

"You seem surprised" she stated. Peter thought, 'The understatement of the year.'

"I am! The few times that we've gone out, you've never let me even touch you." Peter looked at this attractive girl with short light-brown hair, hazel eyes and small frame. She stood about 5'2".

"I know," Carol embarrassed, lowered her head. Peter came toward her, took her in his arms.

"I'd love to make love to you," he kissed her.

"You shocked me more because that's what was on my mind. My dilemma was how to approach you," Peter smiled. He then made love to all of her, cherishing her. Afterwards, they lay still unclothed on the floor in front of the fire.

"Why didn't you tell me you were a virgin?" Peter held her.

"Why, did it make a difference?" Carol lifted her head up to look at him. He squeezed her tighter.

"It was better," Peter kissed her.

"This was a first for me too, I've never been with a virgin before." Peter rose, helping her up and leading her toward the bed, hugging and kissing her. Laying her across the bed, he began to make love to her again, when his roommate walked in.

"Stay here," Peter told her. He went to his roommate, leading him out. When he returned, he climbed back in bed and held her.

"I want you to spend the rest of the weekend with me," he gazed into her eyes. He recalled what Meggie had told him, how rotten it would feel to go to bed with someone for the first time, then to be left alone.

"You are one special kind of guy, Peter Gould," Carol hugged him tightly..

The following Wednesday morning, the last one in December, Meggie pulled her car into the lot at Friendship Airport. She excitedly walked toward the American Airlines arrivals and carried an extra coat. She waited eagerly as the plane disembarked, then she saw her.

"Lor!" Meggie yelled, waving her arm. The girls ran toward each other, embracing on impact, then headed toward baggage pickup.

"So, tell me about your weekend" Lori said, not knowing if she could wait any longer to hear. Meggie lit up, then looked at Lori, shocked.

"What the hell did you do to your arm?" a concerned Meggie asked, seeing a new five inch, raw scar where stitches had recently been removed on her left arm.

"Oh that! It's a long story," Lori smiled, noticing her baggage come in. The girls retrieved Lori's luggage, climbed into the MG and exited the parking lot in the direction of the Baltimore Washington Parkway.

"Well, brown eyes," Meggie looked at her with half a smile.

"Somehow, I have always loved when you call·me that. But, if someone else should, I become uncontrollably hostile," Lori bent to kiss Meggie's cheek. "We always have a blast together, even my abortion was a little fun. If I told anyone about it they would have thought me nuts, having a cousin who looked over this so-called doctor's shoulder the entire time to make sure he knew what he was doing. You made him so fucking nervous. The funniest part was when he tried to make you stay outside of his tiny cubicle and you told him, 'No way, you walking disconsolate!'" Lori laughed and Meggie joined her.

"You haven't exactly induced concern right now, but I want to know what you did to your arm," Meggie said, half laughing.

"Do you remember, and I know you do, a couple of weeks ago they escalated the war in Viet Nam? Our ignorant government made a big deal out of it!" Lori said.

"Of course." Meggie was surprised. Lori wasn't one to get involved in anything about this damned war. Living in Hawaii, she felt so far removed from it. Meggie thought that it had probably even caught up to them there, the fruitlessness of it all.

"We protested on campus. Don't look so surprised!" Lori glanced at her cousin.

"Sorry, but I can't help it," Meggie approached Interstate 695.

"It was definitely a unique experience. The MP's from the Naval Base were called in to contain us. People were hurt, others jailed and, like me, many fled for safety. I was about to get hit over the head by a club when someone rescued me by pushing me to the side of the road, landing in some bushes. When I looked up, I found my American History grad assistant next to me. I asked him if he had saved me and of course he had. He witnessed what was coming down and pushed. I felt something burning on my left arm. We looked at it together and saw so much blood I was ready to pass out from the sight. I got cut on a branch when I landed in the bush. Kevin examined it, and escorted me to the hospital because he felt I needed stitches. Did I, it took 25! I've seen him nearly every night since. He's gorgeous," Lori stared into space.

"And?" Meggie smiled.

"No! I didn't go to bed with him, if that 's what you're asking. I considered staying in Honolulu for New Year's, but I knew if I did, I definitely would. I didn't think it wise, since he may be my grad assistant next semester. So, I took the chickens way out, retreating here," Lori smiled.

"A wise decision indeed. Unlike you, I may add," Meggie stated.

"Your turn, last weekend," Lori smiled with great anticipation.

"It was glorious, marvelous, fantastic. Mere words could not do it justice!" Meggie told her all there was to tell.

"Damn, you're lucky," Lori said, as they exited the Baltimore Beltway.

"Luck, maybe. I also learned from your mistakes," Meggie laughed.

"I'm glad one of us has," Lori laughed with her. Meggie proceeded to tell her about Dennis' brother Victor.

"When do I get to meet him and your Dennis?" Lori eager.

"Tonight," Meggie smiled. "Are you ready for this?" Meggie pulled the car into her driveway.

"I'm never ready for your mother," Lori bluntly stated.

At eight that evening the doorbell rang. Meggie recalled what a difficult time she had persuading Victor to meet Lori. She doesn't know why she even bothered. He's such an egotistical sexist, she thought. Ma let Dennis and Victor into the house and led them to the den where the two girls were engaged in conversation.

"Lor, this is Dennis," Meggie said, rising and going over to hug him. The look of shock on VIctor's face was obvious to everyone when Lori stood. She was about 5'5" tall, had long, wavy, dark brown hair and beautiful, big, saucer-shaped brown eyes. There was a definite resemblance between the two girls. Meggie laughed to herself recalling she had told Victor she and Lori could wear the same clothes. She loved seeing Victor like this, having him so surprised. So did Lori. They loved shocking people, seeing Victor's face absolutely enthralled! The girls smiled, aware of the conquest.

"You're Dennis," Lori greeted him, then glanced at Victor, who stood still, speechless. "And, you're big brother."

"What was it, a secret she looked so much like you?" Victor asked.

"I don't think we look alike, our coloring is entirely different!" Meggie stated emphatically. "I know she's beautiful on the outside, but wait until you know what's on the inside. She's even more beautiful."

"You are one prejudiced cousin. If I ever need a publicity agent, I sure know where to go," Lori blushed.

Meggie and Dennis left them alone, so they could get to know each other. Lori and Victor talked for a long while about their colleges, ideals, goals and themselves.

"Has your cousin told you how much she dislikes me?" Victor curious.

"Meggie, never! She loves everyone," Lori smiled.

"What do you think?" Victor looking at her, finding it difficult to take his eyes from her.

"That's a strange question, but since you asked, I think you're pushy, stubborn and you bug me a little; I like that in a person." Lori smiled again. Their eyes met, Victor put an arm around her shoulder, drawing her toward him. Kissing her passionately, he managed to take her breath away.

Their new relationship was overwhelming. Lori found it difficult to believe this was happening to her. She felt as if she were living in a fairy tale. A few weeks later Lori reluctantly left, returning to Hawaii. Victor didn't want her to go, he promised to visit when the semester was over in May.

III

It was the year 1967. The year the Hippie Movement flowered! They were the fruit of the middle class and they were telling middle America they didn't like what fate had dealt them: the Vietnam war, parental misguidance and capitalism. In fact, they were the most politically active generation this country had ever seen. They were escapists from normal society, Meggie was not sure she didn't want to be one of them. They were opposed to the everyday values that they were raised with; commercialism, mechanism and bureaucracy; the car culture, the work ethic and the quick buck! Meggie did believe in money, loving her creature comforts, and noted she didn't fit in here either. Where did she fit!

Nineteen sixty-seven, the year of racial disorders, the year of the six day war in the Mideast, the year Dr. Martin Luther King Jr., along with 100,000 others, marched the streets of New York City and assembled in front of the U.N. to protest against the Vietnam War. On December 5, 1967, 1,000 people demonstrated in an attempt to close down a New York induction center as part of "Stop the Draft Week", Dr. Benjamin Spock and the poet Allen Ginsberg were among the 264 people arrested.

Meggie had arranged to take English at the Maryland Institute of Art, receiving credit toward college. She was desperately searching for herself, looking behind every corner, so to speak. Dennis was not happy about this, feeling she would be spending more time with those social misfits. Her dad blatantly put it the same way. Dennis tried to pick an argument with her over it.

"Do you know what you are doing?" Dennis questioned her.

"Don't I always?" Meggie feeling an inquisition coming on.

"You're beginning to drive a wedge between us," he bluntly stated.

"Not unless you wish to put it there. You see, I love you," Meggie said, throwing her arms around him.

"You have a way of doing that," he held her close.

"Doing what?" She smiled.

"Making everything seem terrific," Dennis kissed her.

"Isn't it?" She slightly grinned.

"It is when I'm with you. But the mere thought of you being with those weird people so much is unnerving," he stated. Meggie laughed,

"In reality, they are no different from you and me, my love." She kissed him again, knowing the subject would be dropped for now.

In late March, Christine invited Meggie to a party at her apartment. Meggie knew convincing Dennis to go would be quite a difficult task.

"What's wrong with the kids from the Institute? Are you above them Dennis?" An angered Meggie stared at him.

"Don't get so hostile with me! I know you, remember! I'm not, there's nothing wrong with them, just...." Dennis said, with Meggie breaking in, not allowing him to finish.

"You are so narrow-minded! You're probably Republican! They're so tunnel-visioned! I'll go alone and you can stay home with your closed mind, since you don't like my friends," she yelled.

"Come off it!" A distraught Dennis raised his voice. "It's not your damn friends, it's their influence on you that gets to me. I hate all of those marches, their obscurely ridiculous outlooks and their cynical attitudes. If you really insist upon going, I'll go, okay!" She leaned over, kissing him, noting she got her way again. She wondered what would have happened if he hadn't given in. But, he always did, so she put that thought out of her mind.

Christine lived in a vintage nineteenth century building called the Beethoven Apartments, located approximately one mile from Maryland Institute. She had a roommate named Alex. Meggie thought her to be a homely looking creature, but very idealistic. Alex was a great deal of fun and into various causes. It was she who initially turned Meggie on to protesting against the war.

Meggie and Dennis walked into Christine's apartment, not being able to believe their eyes. Doing a double take, Meggie glanced around at all of the people, none of whom resembled their high school crowd. There was no furniture, the living room was adorned with only large pillows to sit on, the windows were covered with cloth from India (fabric just hanging, no attempt to make it appear like curtains). Meggie thought it to be so intriguing as she looked at Dennis' disgruntled face.

"Hi Meg, I'm glad you could make it. Well, hello, Dennis," Christine greeted them, putting her shoulder against Dennis' chest as Meggie gave her a "beware" look.

"Hi Chris," Meggie smiled.

"I got the hint," Christine said, withdrawing from Dennis and hating being called Chris, as Meggie knew.

"I'll show you around," Christine led the way to her bedroom. It happened to be decorated the same as the rest of the apartment- a large mattress on the floor, and Indian cloth on the windows. Meggie noticed all the floors in the apartment were hardwood, and each room had been painted a different color. The living room was painted white, the dining room pink and Christine's bedroom, black. Meggie couldn't imagine how anyone would want to cover up such floors. Then it struck her why! Each room had a different meaning, just as every color does. She smiled to herself, pleased she was adept enough to pick up on this. We read into everything, she thought.

"This is where you two can come later, if you get my drift," Christine smiled at Dennis, and gave Meggie an elbow in the ribs.

"Meggie, when did you get here?" Alex came to greet her, giving Meggie a kiss on the cheek. As homely as Alex looked on the outside she was equally as compassionate and sensitive on the inside.

"Alex, this is Dennis," Meggie hugged him, and Christine went to greet her other guests.

"Here, guys, have a great time! See ya later," Alex handed Meggie two little white squares of paper.

"What did she give you, let me see?" Dennis said, excited.

"LSD, I think we..." Meggie wasn't able to finish her thought as Dennis pulled the acid from her hands.

"Damn! I've always wanted to try this stuff," he smiled.

"This isn't pot! You don't know what you're fooling with here! This is dangerous shit!" Meggie raised her voice.

"One time can't hurt us. Come on!" Dennis insisted.

"Dennis!" Meggie yelled seeing him chew one square of the paper.

"Meg, you are either with me or not," he stated, putting the other square into her mouth. Meggie was now frightened. It had been her idea to come to this party with Dennis protesting the entire way. Now she was taking some chemical she had only read about, learning that one time can harm you. She didn't like this one bit, but she chewed the paper anyway.

Meggie talked to a lot of her friends from Maryland Institute and was having a wonderful time. Then she noticed, in the corner of the living room, a person sitting on the floor. It was Dennis!

"What are you doing?" Meggie approached him.

"Come here, look, what do you see?" Dennis said, as Meggie stooped to sit beside him. She could feel the acid take effect and looked at what he was pointing to.

"It looks like a butterfly creeping along the ground with so many colors on its wings. It's beautiful!" Meggie smiled.

"That's exactly what I saw," Dennis threw his arms around her. In reality what they were watching was a roach!

Dennis and Meggie stayed in the corner watching this bug, tripping their brains out, watching the people, seeing glorious colors all around them and laughing hysterically. Dennis carried her into Christines' bedroom, locking the door behind them. Meggie stared at him. She hadn't seen him so self assured in months, not caring about anyone else's opinion, going after exactly what he wanted. Dennis saw the look on her face, questioning it.

"Didn't Christine tell us if we wanted to, to just..." Dennis was not able to finish his thought, seeing Meggie remove her dress, revealing her full breasts and a pair of bikini underpants. Soon they were off as well. He was at a loss for words! She lay back on the bed, motioning for him to come to her. They made love over and over again that night, until they passed out. As for Christine, she really didn't care, staying in the living room with a friend of hers.

At sunrise, Meggie woke Dennis.

"Look, isn't it beautiful!" She said, pointing to the horizon.

"Yes, but not as beautiful as you," Dennis kissed her.

"Oh Dennis Fine, look outside and stop that." She moved away from him. He gazed through the window, feeling something strange inside, then at Meggie, nuzzling his nose into her chest. They were interrupted by the sound of the phone ringing. It was 6:OO a.m. and Meggie decided she should answer it, instead of waking everyone else.

"Is that you, Meggie? I've been so worried! Why didn't you call? Your father and I have been up half the night! When will you be home?" Ma yelled.

"Ma, I'm sorry. I told you I would be sleeping here last night. Daddy said it was alright. I'll be home later," Meggie said, before hanging up the phone.

The typical conversation with Ma, forty questions without giving her space to answer one, Meggie thought.

"I guess I'd better take you home," Dennis said.

"Not yet, it's too early," Meggie bit her bottom lip. He kissed her and gently caressed her bare breast, feeling her body quiver.

Back in January, the United States Department of Defense had announced 5,008 United States soldiers, our men, had been killed fighting in Vietnam in 1966. Then they had the unmitigated audacity to escalate this war another time in April. Meggie was involved in an all-night sit-in on the steps of the Federal Building in Baltimore. Her friends dropped her off at the high school the following morning. Seeing her get out of this beat up 1960 Chevy, in desperate need of a paint job, and noting there were at least a half dozen kids inside, mostly guys, Dennis became angry.

"Where have you been?" He demanded, approaching her.

"Don't you read the paper?" Meggie threw the morning edition of the *BALTIMORE SUN* to him. The headlines read, "Peaceful All-Night Sit-In".

"You were there?" Dennis asked.

"Of course, I asked you to come," Meggie said nonchalantly, walking into school.

"Who was that motley group of people?" Dennis grabbed her arm to get more attention than he was receiving.

"What is this, the Dennis Fine Inquisition?" Meggie yelled, becoming hostile. Dennis released her arm, he didn't want to be on her bad side. He was aware he'd get nowhere that way.

"I think I have a right to know," he sighed. She stopped. Turning to see him standing there, her heart sank.

"Look, I'm sorry. I've been up all night and I am totally exhausted. I'm not in the mood for your jealous games, Dennis. But I would like to share my experience with you," Meggie said, then she kissed him.

"I don't know why I let you get to me," Dennis smirked.

"Because you love me!" she laughed. "We sang songs all night. It was devastatingly beautiful. I met scores of interesting people who went to either the Institute, Hopkins or Peabody. It was one of the most exciting, mind-opening experiences of my life. There was absolutely no violence, it was totally peaceful," Meggie smiled, spinning her body around. She was so up from the entire experience, she didn't recall ever feeling like this before.

"What is the problem now?" She watched him stare into space.

"There's no problem," Dennis said, solemnly.

"I think there is," she tried to look in his eyes, but he wouldn't let her. The homeroom bell rang, he kissed her cheek and he was off.

After school that day, Peter stopped by Meggie's house at her request. She led him into the rec room in the basement.

"What is it?" Peter curious, seeing her squinched in the corner of the sofa with her legs tucked under her. She motioned for Peter to sit.

"Has Dennis said anything to you?" Meggie questioned.

"Lady you are perplexing," Peter said. Meggie gave him an evil eye, taking Peter back to their past.

"No! Damn it, Peter, I'm worried about Dennis. He's becoming real messed up," said Meggie, aggravated.

"He seems a little peculiar, but Dennis was always peculiar to me," Peter said, glancing over to the piano, thinking it's been a long time since they played, then realizing this was not the time.

"He's not right. He has a definite problem and he won't confide in me. I keep racking my brain, trying to come up with what it may be, but I can't and it bothers me. He also seems so insecure and so doubting of me lately it's frustrating. One would think after everything we've been through this year, he'd have more confidence in me," Meggie became a little teary-eyed.

"Maybe you are reading into this," Peter placed his arm around her to comfort her.

"I don't do that! You know it, besides there's something else," Meggie said, looking away, then toward him again. "He has this thing for drugs now. I'm not talking pot. We're talking LSD, alcohol, almost anything he can get his hands on. We argue about it all the time because I don't like what's happening to his head. I know it's all changed him, but I know there's something else. I'm worried and I don't understand. You know me, Peter, when I can't grasp something I become totally unhinged!" She cried as Peter held her.

"Jes! I wasn't aware Dennis was so into the drug scene. You've got to get through to him, and you're right, I do know you. Your determination will inevitably make the breakthrough," Peter said, trying to give her the confidence she desperately needed.

"What would I do without you?" Meggie hugged him.

"You'd work it out," Peter smiled, sitting back against the sofa, thinking how much she had changed. He still loved her, his best friend, and felt it would be like that forever.

The evening of May 21st was their senior prom. Dennis arrived to pick Meggie up and was kept waiting at the foot of the stairs. It was like her to do that, to keep him in suspense, he thought. A few moments later, he did a double take, not believing his eyes. There she stood at the top of the stairs, more beautiful than ever, he thought, feeling his heart pounding. She wore a shoulderless, white crocheted gown, with slits up the sides three inches above her knees.

It revealed all the curves of her body, especially her breasts, because she was not wearing a bra again. Meggie descended the stairs, looking at him and biting her bottom lip.

"You look unbelievable!" Dennis put his arms around her, right in front of her parents. Ma was exasperated at this blatant display of affection, thinking the boy had a great deal of nerve. Daddy, on the other hand, would rather things be done in front of him instead of behind his back. Dennis led her from the house to his car, even opening the door for the now liberated Meggie, which, under normal circumstances, she insisted doing for herself. Once in the car, he leaned over to kiss her.

"Happy Birthday," he smiled, handing her a small package.

"I can't believe you know!" Meggie said, surprised.

"You told me last October. Open it." Dennis watched her fiddle with the ribbon, tearing it off along with the paper off. Opening the case.

"It's beautiful!" Meggie was surprised, not expecting anything like this and not being able to take her eyes off a gold pinkie ring with three small diamonds and her initials engraved on it.

"Read the inscription," Dennis took the ring from the box and showed her.

"Dennis," she smiled.

"There's not a whole lot of room for anything else," he placed his right arm around her shoulder, holding the ring in his left hand. He took her left hand and placed it on her pinkie.

"The three diamonds signify that in three years we will be married," Dennis stated, before kissing her.

"It takes four years to finish college," said Meggie, being very surprised. She hadn't expected this in a million years.

"I know you, you'll do it in three! I intend to keep up with you. Besides, I would marry you right now, if you would, but you won't. It's the one thing you happen to be logical about. So, three years it is. I have an incentive!" Dennis took her in his arms and kissed her again.

"Dennis, I don't know if I can accept this. There's really only one thing I want for my birthday," Meggie pulled back to look in his eyes.

"I'm straight. I intend to stay that way, unless you have some pot," Dennis smiled at her.

"Don't I always," she laughed.

"I know I haven't been myself. I've given you a lot of grief because of the drugs. I'm sorry, Meggie. I promise it's all over with," Dennis said, hugging her again.

"I sure hope so, Dennis. I love you so much, you had me going there. As long as you promise, I'll accept the ring." Meggie kissed him.

"Damn, I love you!" Dennis held her, kissing her again.

"We're going to have a wonderful time tonight!" Meggie smiled, throwing her arms in the air. Dennis laughed.

Two weeks later, shortly before graduation, in Meggie's den.

"Cut the crap, Dennis! What is this need you always seem to have lately to escape!" Meggie yelled, as he tried to get her to chew a tiny square of white paper she didn't want. She never intended to take that stuff again. She liked her mind the way it was; at least she knew what she had.

That was better than not knowing what she might be getting.

Dennis noticed her parents were out. He found it a perfect opportunity, until this confrontation with her. Then he realized, he couldn't avoid it any longer.

"It's hard for me to talk about," Dennis said, sullenly.

"I think you better try!" Meggie hostilely.

"I know." Dennis looked at her, knowing if he could talk to anyone, it was Meggie. He had confided so many things in her already. He never felt closer to anyone in his life.

"My parents are getting divorced, but that's not all of it," Dennis took a deep breath continuing. "There's a good chance my father will be indicted by the grand jury next week for mail fraud and embezzlement." Somehow finding it to be a relief to get it off his chest.

"How long have you been keeping this inside?" Meggie asked.

"I've known for almost four months," Dennis, sullen.

"I can't believe you didn't tell me, that you didn't trust me enough to confide in me! You chose to walk around with this monkey on your back! I want the whole story!" Meggie said, hurt and angry.

"My father has had a few affairs over the years. Most of them have been pretty indiscreet. One of his liaisons went to the Securities and Exchange Commission, telling them everything she knew, which was quite a bit. She was my dad's twenty-five year old secretary. Isn't it nice, he'd been having an affair with her for three years? Anyway, she supposedly wanted him to leave my mom and us for her. He wouldn't do it. So this was her revenge," Dennis paused, upset.

"Hell hath no fury like a woman scorned," Meggie stated, noting the cliché'.

"I don't know it all. They intentionally try to be so fucking close-mouthed with me! They don't realize not knowing and anticipation are far worse than the truth, no matter how bad that may be." Dennis started to cry. Meggie embraced him, trying to comfort him, not wanting him to hurt.

"Next week, it may make the papers," he said, still crying. Meggie held him for a while.

"Dennis, I want you to throw that crap away," she pulled back a little to look at him. "There are these decisive moments in our lives when we must stop, look and take control."

Dennis walked to the trash can in the kitchen.

"Not there, in the sink," Meggie stated. Dennis put it down the garbage disposal, running the water and turning it on. Meggie turned it off when it was done.

"I'm so scared," Dennis turned to her.

"I know, me too," she hugged him. "You're not going to be alone anymore. I'm here. You forgot what weekend this is," she whispered in his ear, not wanting him to hurt because his parents made mistakes. She loved him so.

"Your parents are away," Dennis squeezed her tighter, not knowing how he deserved her, feeling she was his lifeline. God, he loved her.

Meggie left for Honolulu three weeks later. Lying back on the early morning flight out of Friendship Airport, she recalled her conversation with Victor, still with uneasy feelings. She had very mixed emotions about this trip, feeling Dennis needed her when things were so down for him. He was insistent she go. Two weeks prior, the article about his father appeared in the paper. Mr. Fine was indicted and her heart broke for Dennis when she saw it. She wanted him to come with her, even offering to pay his way. He said he couldn't do that. Principles, she thought, ex-drug addict. It brought a slight smile to her face. He still seemed strange, even though he wasn't using any longer, so she decided to let Victor in on the secret. Meggie still didn't like him, especially when he tried to put the move on her again.

"Come off it, Victor! I want to talk to you about Dennis," Meggie stated. "What about Lori?"

"I can't get there to see her now. As Dennis told me, like cousin, like cousin," Victor laughed.

"I fail to see the humor in this. In fact, I feel this is an exercise in futility," Meggie aggravated, started to walk away.

"Okay, what is it?" Victor, keeping his distance. She stopped and turned around,

"You're not that naive, you know exactly what it is. I'm worried about Dennis. I can't leave for Hawaii with a clear conscience if he's going to be so... you know what I'm saying," Meggie clenched her fists, looking at a bewildered VIctor's face. "So fucked up!" She yelled.

Victor finally realized she really did care deeply about his brother.

"You can go, I'll watch over little brother," Victor said, with a smile. Meggie gave him an evil eye and he started to laugh.

"Really, I didn't mean it like that," Victor tried to make peace with her. "You don't have to worry, he'll be alright. We Fine's are a pretty strong group," Victor took a letter from his pocket.

"Give this to Lori for me, please."

"You told me I was strange but you are stranger," Meggie said, taking it from him. "There's something else. I don't know whether you're aware of it. Dennis has gotten himself involved in drugs. He's been clean now for about three weeks. I want you to have full knowledge of what you are dealing with. I betrayed a trust by telling you this," Meggie said, becoming somewhat teary-eyed.

"I'll handle it. Dennis knows I don't believe in drugs, except for a little bit of pot. Don't worry." Victor looked at her, thinking that with someone like this on his side, how could he get himself so messed up.

"Promise!" Meggie demanded.

"Yes, I promise," Victor smiled, placing a kiss on her forehead.

Meggie was still uneasy about leaving, voicing her opinion to Lori long distance, and running up the largest phone bill Daddy ever had.

"He has to live his own life, you can't do that for him. He has to grow on his own. You can't be there for him every minute! You also need your own space; besides, I need to see you. I know you hurt, but do come for us and for yourself," Lori said Transpacifically.

"I'm coming, I need to see you too? Besides, I can't wait to see your new little beach front house. It must be wild living there. I can't believe Uncle Bob ever agreed to this. You must have done some heavy talking!" Meggie laughed.

"I did! See you soon, cous!" Lori laughed, hanging up the phone.

She smiled to herself, lying back in her first-class seat. Lori always did that to her. The conversation with her dad, before she left, came into Meggie's mind.

"Daddy, do you know what is happening with Dennis' father?" Meggie inquired, before it hit the papers.

"Come sit on my lap. Very shortly we won't be able to do this," Morris Hiken looking at his daughter, loving her. Meggie walked toward him, and sat on his lap.

"I think pretty soon is now. Daddy, I love you, but don't you think I'm a little too big for this?" Meggie laughed, putting her arms around him, feeling cramped.

"Humor me," he laughed.

"That's what I'm doing," she kissed his cheek.

"How about answering my question? I am well aware you are informed of almost everything that transpires in our community, as well as the Greater Baltimore Metropolitan area."

"I've known for quite a few months now," Morris said.

"Why didn't you tell me?" Meggie with her eyebrows raised.

"It wasn't for me to say. Other people have never been my concern, you're aware of that. Besides, we won't know how serious it is until the grand jury brings in the verdict," Morris stated.

"It's obviously serious, with or without the verdict. Dennis feels for certain he's going to be held over for trial. This is definitely not helping his already weak relationship with his father. I'm really worried about him. When I'm away, do you think you could talk to him. I don't want him to feel so alone." Meggie looked at her dad.

"If that's what you want, it would be my pleasure," Morris placed a kiss on her forehead.

"Thank you. I love you so much!" Meggie kissed his entire face as he laughed.

It had always been Meggie's style to think on planes. Every time she boarded one, she wished she had brought a book along. She thought of how much she had grown, this past year. Most of her ideals and values had changed. She even thought she was making a contribution to society. It was a good feeling. She thought about her reconstruction program and smiled. Then, thinking about Dennis again, deciding to put him out of her mind. She was good at that, filing unpleasant thoughts away into some dark closet. She fell asleep.

Seeing Lori again was like a breath of fresh air. She stood waving to Meggie, wearing a hot pink mini-dress.

"You look fantastic" Meggie said, with a slight smile.

"I wish I could say the same for you," Lori laughed.

"What do you expect after twelve hours of traveling," Meggie stated. Lori knew it was more than just that.

"How's Dennis?" Lori asked on the way to the baggage terminal.

"The same, I left him in VIctor's hands," Meggie, sullen.

"Good hands, how is Victor?" Lori asked, as Meggie handed her the letter from him.

"I certainly hope you're right. VIctor's the same. He doesn't seem too affected by what's coming down. I have a real difficult time believing you like him. He is a strange one," Meggie, in disbelief.

"Not that strange," Lori smiled.

Over the course of the following ten days, the two girls had a wonderful time together, as they always did. Now even more, because of Lori's one bedroom beach front house. Meggie loved it, being able to go to the beach anytime she wanted, to worship the sun whenever she felt like it, and, best of all, without parental supervision. She thought, 'This is heaven!' Late one afternoon Meggie received a phone call from her dad.

"Are you enjoying yourself?"

"Naturally!" Meggie laughed.

"I have someone here who is very anxious to talk to you," Dad said, handing him the receiver and leaving the room.

"Hi."

"Dennis!" Meggie yelled. "I miss you so much," her eyes swelling with tears.

"You have one fantastic father, do you know that?" Dennis asked.

"I know, but I don't think he made this call for us to discuss him," she smiled.

"I miss you, too," Dennis became solemn.

"Don't do that!" Meggie yelled.

"I won't, how's your tan?" Dennis tried to keep a stiff upper lip.

"My tan is making it. Lori's new house is fantastic! I only wish you were here to see it," Meggie stated.

"God, I love you," Dennis said, becoming somewhat depressed.

"Keep that thought. I'll be home before you know it," Meggie responded.

"Dennis, I love you too," Meggie said, feeling him start to retreat.

"I'm going to say good-bye now," Dennis said, reluctantly.

"No!" she yelled. She knew she had to talk to him for a while to find out how he was doing. He would evade a direct question.

"It must cost a fortune, long distance," Dennis said.

"Believe me, he can afford it," Meggie laughed. They talked for another half an hour. Meggie gave him Lori's phone number, telling him to call collect, she would reimburse her. Neither of the girls knew the value of the dollar. Meggie ended her conversation with Dennis, telling him to take care of himself and that she loved him. She told him to tell her dad she would call him later.

Lori walked into the room and saw her cousin wearing an ear-to-ear smile. "Dennis?"

"Via my Dad," Meggie answered, still smiling.

"Your dad is terrific, as far as your mother goes," Lori laughed.

"Believe me, I know! I keep wondering whether it's a stage I'm going through, or if she really is as strange as I think she is," Meggie still smiled.

Lori and Meggie had a wonderful month together, playing tennis every day, swimming and, of course, enjoying the sun. It was now mid-July. Meggie awoke from a horrible nightmare in the middle of the night. Her vision faded as to what it was about, leaving her with an extremely uneasy feeling and she was unable to fall back to sleep. The phone rang. It was 6:30 a.m. when Meggie looked at the clock. Who would call at this time of the morning, she thought to herself.

"I'll get it, I'm up," Meggie saw Lori stir in her sleep.

"Meg, it's Ma." Meggie didn't like the tone in her voice, "What's wrong!"

"It's a hard thing to hear and I think even harder to say," Ma said.

"Ma!" Meggie yelled, frightened, shaking her hands, becoming so frustrated with her mother.

"Obviously, there's no easy way to say this. Dennis was in a car accident last night," Ma said uneasily.

"How bad was he hurt?" Meggie asked, hardly being able to get the words out, due to the pit in her throat.

"Meg, he's dead," Ma said. Meggie's stomach sank, her legs gave way and she fell to the floor.

"Meggie, are you there?" Ma yelled into the phone. Meggie couldn't speak, she just sat on the floor, motionless, with the phone on her lap.

"What is it?" Lori asked, rising from her bed seeing her cousin. "Aunt Lil, is that you?" Lori took the phone from the lap of the stone on the floor. Aunt Lil told Lori what had happened. "Oh my God!" Lori yelled with tears running down her cheeks.

"Aunt Lil, I'm going to make plane reservations. I'll call you back to let you know exactly what time we'll be in on Saturday," Lori said, before hanging up the phone.

Lori stared at her cousin on the floor. She ached for her. Helping Meggie to stand, Lori aided her to the bedroom and Meggie fell on the bed.

"It's a bad dream, right Lor?" Meggie looked at her cousin.

"I wish I could say it was," Lori stated.

Meggie screamed uncontrollably. Her words were incoherent and Lori held her for dear life. After a while, Lori managed to calm her down a little, placing her on the bed.

"Lie here for a bit, I'll be right back," Lori told her, wanting to make the plane reservations to Friendship. She got them on a flight that evening. After a transfer, it would arrive there at 10:00 a.m. the following day.

Lori returned, carrying toast and a glass of orange juice. "Meg, I made the reservations, we leave at six. You have to eat this."

Meggie didn't cry all day, nor verbalize how she felt, nor did she eat. She simply moved around like a robot, with a very sullen face, until she boarded the plane. From that time till landing, she cried uncontrollably. There was nothing Lori could do to comfort her. She tried. Meggie sat there crying and thinking, first blaming herself, feeling guilty. She knew Dennis was having problems, she never should have left him. She also knew he must have been tripping again. She cried harder. Next, she blamed his messed-up parents and lastly, she blamed Victor. He really did a wonderful job trying to help Dennis! That putz!

Lying back in her seat, with her eyes closed, tears still running from them, she thought about parents in general, their totally deranged generation. She thought how they tried to inflict certain morals on us, when they adhered to an entirely different set. They tried to pretend they were perfect examples, role models, so to speak, when in reality they were so imperfect. Yet they expected perfection from their children. All the kids Meggie had come into contact with lately were totally confused. She understood it, the head trips their parents had laid on them. They were laden with insecurity, extreme uncertainty and feelings of betrayal. She knew Dennis felt betrayed, she cried for him, for his pain. Meggie cried for his misguidance, the lying, the cheating and the violence.

Today's youth were going to turn out to be better parents and far better individuals. They were going to improve society, instead of destroying it. She didn't know how this was going to come about, but she was certain it would. It had to! Things could not go on like this!

Still with her eyes closed and tears running from them, Meggie sat thinking about Dennis, dear Dennis. About how they met eleven months ago, in late August. About the first protest marches. About the first time they made love. He was so gentle, so concerned, so perfect! She knew she was lucky to have had that. She cried harder, aching for him. She thought about Halloween, the ski weekend and New Year's Eve. About her birthday this past May when she turned seventeen. Looking at the gold pinkie ring on her finger, she recalled he told her it was a pre-engagement ring. Remembering his kisses, the way he touched her, his facial expressions, seeing his face so vividly in front of her, Meggie cried harder. Damn you, Dennis! Then, she thought about the drugs. Poor Dennis.

Morris Hiken stood anxiously at the American Airlines arrival gate waiting for his daughter and niece to disembark. Being very nervous and concerned for Meggie, he wondered how she was handling this. He knew in life, death is the single most difficult thing we are forced to deal with. He became sullen thinking Meggie was just too young to have to endure this right now. He then became angry. His thoughts were interrupted.

"Hi, Uncle Morris," Lori kissed him on the cheek.

"Hi, girls, Meggie?" Dad questioningly looked at her. He saw her red eyes and went to hold her, trying to take this pain away from her. Meggie cried even more, clinging to her dad.

"Why! Daddy, why!" Meggie screamed, holding him with all of her might. He couldn't answer, he didn't have one. It made no sense to him. He couldn't ever recall ever being this scared. They drove from the airport, in silence the entire way home, except for the sound of Meggie's crying.

After arriving home Meggie drove her car straight to Dennis' house, not even going to see Ma first. Victor opened the door,

"Meggie," Victor said, surprised, with swollen red eyes. He extended his arm to hug her. She pushed right by him.

"What the hell happened?" She yelled, with tears still rolling from her eyes. Victor saw how overwrought she was, and thought even like this she was beautiful. He took her by the hand, leading her to the sofa in the den. Sitting down, he held both of her hands between his.

"Last Thursday, Dennis had a tremendous argument with Dad. You see, Dad was found guilty on five counts of mail fraud and three counts of embezzlement. The trial took a little over three weeks. Dennis and I were in court every day. It was a nightmare, they totally tore him apart. It was a hellish thing to live through," Victor paused, took a deep breath, then continued.

"Our system sucks! Do you know that?" Victor glanced at her blank face. "That bitch he had for a secretary really put the screws to him. The verdict came down Wednesday evening. The jury was only out for four hours, can you imagine? They already had him convicted before they went into chambers. It was the pits!" Victor releasing Meggie's hands to wipe the perspiration from his face.

"Why the argument?" Meggie looked at him.

"Dad got a five year sentence. If he's lucky, he'll be out in two. The I.R.S. is on his back for taxes on the money he supposedly embezzled. We have to sell the house to pay them, plus we have the attorney bills. There is no money!" Victor said. Meggie found it difficult to understand how people could live so high above their means.

"That must have been a shock to Dennis. I know he never worried about money before in his life," Meggie said, sullenly.

"That's an understatement! Dad told Dennis he couldn't go to American this fall. He better look into the state schools and to plan on living at home. He may even have to work at the same time. Dennis freaked!" Tears ran from Victor's eyes.

"I have only one more year of school left. I'll get a job there. Consequently, I'm not that affected, or should I say, not as affected as Dennis would have been. Dennis really went off on a tangent as to how he was going to school with you. He called Dad a bastard, telling him he wasn't going to allow him to separate the two of you because of his selfish stupidity. He would find a way to go. He called Dad a few other choice names, telling him he hated him before he stormed out of the house. As I was running after him, I heard him peel from the driveway. I thought maybe he and I together could work something out. But he was gone in a flash!" Victor still in tears.

"Meggie, he loved you so much."

"I know, and I still love him. Tell me about the accident," a tearful Meggie said.

"I want you to know something first," Victor paused before continuing. "Dennis had been straight the entire time, even during the trial. His talk with your Dad helped, it left him with hope. He thought a lot of your father." Meggie nodded, in acknowledgment.

"The accident occurred at about ten Thursday night. We're not sure exactly what happened. The police report stated Dennis' car went over the median on the Jones Falls Expressway, striking a car coming the other way. It was between Cold Spring Lane and Northern Parkway and he was coming from downtown. Dennis was killed instantly. The people in the other car were hurt, a man and a woman, but they'll be alright," Victor glanced down. Meggie stood, taking this all in, pacing a little.

"Drugs?" She stared Victor in the eye.

"Uh huh. The autopsy revealed a large quantity of acid in his bloodstream. He was literally tripping his ass off!

They also found a nice amount of cocaine. I can't imagine mixing the two," Victor glanced at her, questioningly.

They sat talking about Dennis for awhile, crying and trying to comfort each other. They were disturbed by a voice,

"Thanks, Meg," Lori said, walking toward Victor.

"I'm sorry, Lor, I forgot about you," Meggie replied, seeing Lori.

"Where are your parents?" Meggie asked, with very red eyes.

"They have each retreated to separate rooms and haven't come out since," Victor stated.

Meggie said good-bye, leaving Lori to be alone with Victor. He needed her now. She'd see his parents tomorrow at the funeral, Dennis' funeral! She didn't know whether she could go through with it. But she knew she had to say good-bye, and it was going to tear her heart out.

Sunday morning, Meggie arrived at the funeral home early. She thought the coffin would be open then, just for family. Once the services started, it would be closed, that was Jewish tradition. She had to see him one last time! Seeing the coffin made it real to her. She walked to it, looking in, feeling her heart sink again; he did look at peace. She stood there for a long time staring at him, with tears rolling from her eyes.

"Meggie, come in the back room with us," Victor placing an arm around her shoulder, starting to lead her.

"One minute," Meggie slipped an envelope out of her pocket, placing it in the coffin. A last farewell, she thought.

The course of the next hour became a complete blur to Meggie. She couldn't remember a thing that happened. All she was aware of was seeing the coffin placed in the ground. She kept hoping this was a nightmare, and someone would soon wake her. She saw the concern on the face of Lori, Peter, Bob and Rochelle. Afterwards, everyone returned to the Fine house, a house of shivah. Every time Meggie thought of that she got chills up her spine. Washing her hands on the front porch, walking in the house, seeing all of the mirrors covered, a large lit, candle in the living room, Meggie knew this was not the kind of nightmare she would awake from. It was real! Looking around again, she felt such tradition, not understanding much of it. She only knew when you returned from a cemetery, you had to wash your hands and the mirrors were covered because you shouldn't look at yourself when you are in mourning. The candle was a yhartzite candle, in remembrance of the dead. She had only been given the rules of the tradition, never the reasons behind them. None of it made any sense to her. Just as Dennis's death made no sense to her.

Adele Fine saw Meggie enter and walked toward her, taking her hand.

"You belong at the table with us," Mrs. Fine with tears in her eyes, led Meggie toward the large dining table where the family was seated.

Meggie burst into uncontrollable tears again, looking at Dennis' family, not seeing him there. Mrs. Fine glanced at Meggie's neck, which still had a simple gold chain around it. Dennis's school ring, her son's ring! She took Meggie's hand again, leading her upstairs into Dennis' room. Standing in the doorway, Meggie remembered the first time she ever saw it, on Thanksgiving weekend. His parents were out and Victor opened a closed door to find a topless Meggie on the bed with Dennis. She recalled Dennis having words with Victor that night and found herself having even less respect for Dennis' older brother.

Adele Fine walked into the room, a room she had not been able to stay away from since her son's death.

"Meggie, come sit down," Mrs. Fine motioning to Dennis' bed. Taking a seat beside Meggie, Mrs. Fine placed her arm around Meggie's waist.

"I know how much Dennis loved you; if there exists a true love I believe you and Dennis had it. Cherish those memories, they are quite rare. Dennis told me one day he planned to marry you. I helped him pick out the ring," Mrs. Fine said, with tears running from her eyes, eyeing the pinkie ring on Meggie's finger.

Hearing a voice from the living room call her name, Adele Fine left the room. Meggie lay back on the bed, Dennis' bed, a bed he would never lie in again, happy for the solitude and a chance to think. Remembering the first time they made love in this bed and every time after that. Somehow, being in his room and on his bed, she felt closer to him. She fell into sleep.

During the month that followed Dennis' death, Meggie could not explain the void in her heart. It felt as if a piece of it had been literally cut away, hurting more than any pain she had ever known. It was a feeling she had never had before in her life, a feeling that a void would be there forever. A day didn't go by she didn't think of Dennis, missing him desperately. At night she cried herself to sleep, only to awaken from nightmares. She became very withdrawn, refusing to see her friends and not going anywhere. Karl Marx became a prominent figure in Meggie's life at this point. She desired to escape, to lose herself. She read THE COMMUNIST MANIFESTO, POVERTY OF PHILOSOPHY and all three books of DAS KAPITAL .

All of this only provoked more questions in Meggie's mind, a mind that was already in an extremely confused state. She was reaching for a meaning to her existence but only making it more difficult.

Overreaction was typical of Meggie at this time in her life, especially toward Ma and even at times, toward her dad. She preferred to think of it as reacting strongly. Ma nudged all of the time, always trying to encourage her to go out. Meggie felt like Ma was always on her case!

"Meggie, all you do lately is read, eat, sleep and cry. There's more to life than that," Ma yelled at her one day. Meggie never bothered to answer, always trying to ignore her. Until one night, she overheard a conversation between her parents.

"Morris, you have to do something. She's built a wall between us and I can't get through," Lil unhappily looked at her husband.

"I know, she used to be so alive and full of spirit. There must be some way of bringing her out of this. She needs to be with people," Morris said to his wife.

This is when Meggie blew up. 'Bullshit other guys, there's only one person I want to be with and now he is dead! You two hypocrites! You are so shallow! You have no idea what hell I'm going through! You don't understand me, and, what's worse, you don't even want to try!" Meggie screamed, running out of the house, slamming the door behind her.

She drove her car heading for sanctuary at Christine and Alex's. At least there she would feel no pressure.

"Meg, it's time you started pulling yourself together," Alex said to her, after having this listless creature around for three days.

"You too, Alex," Meggie stared at her in disbelief.

"You're not aware of how I feel, or for that matter, what is going on in my head or how miserable I am all of the time," Meggie screamed, bursting into tears. Moving closer to Meggie, putting an arm around her, Alex began to cry with her.

"I do know how you feel. I've been there," Alex said, with tears rolling down her cheeks.

"What!" Meggie surprised.

"Why the hell do you think I'm so committed to protesting this war? Why do you think I'm so totally involved? Two years ago my brother, Bill, and his friend, Joe, were drafted to fight in this crazy farce they call a war. Bill was killed three months after arriving in Nam, and Joe, my future husband, was killed six months later." Alex stated with tears, seeing a very surprised Meggie. Then she continued,

"Yes, he was my first and only love. I know I don't look like the type of person anyone would be interested in, but Joe did love me. I know that with all of my heart. He wrote me letters about the conditions there, the massive amount of drugs, the merciless killings of entire villages, mostly of women and children. He hated it, being brought up as a good Christian, believing in God, not understanding murder. He used to write about all of the guys that became hooked on heroin, understanding their need to escape, swearing he never would. Before he died, I knew he did as well, from his last letter. He seemed to have nothing to look forward to anymore, I was too far away. His lack of concern and his depression grew intense. It must have been an ungodly hell to go through. Meggie, we have to keep fighting. If not, there will be nothing left to fight for. Yes, my heart went with him, but I knew I couldn't afford to sit around and sulk. And you can't either! There are too many changes that need to be made. This stupid war for one. You and I are survivors and we were put here to make a difference. Meggie, it's time to come back to the land of the living, to make a contribution, like God had intended you to."

Meggie just sat, not being able to take her eyes off Alex. She took in everything she had said, feeling hurt for her, coupled with the void in her own heart. Would that empty space and pain ever go away? Could she go on in the face of adversity? She mustered up the courage and decided she was going to try.

"Okay, Alex, I guess my spirit hasn't been entirely broken," Meggie reflected on her horse, Nozzle, before embracing her friend. The girls held each other and cried together for a while.

IV

College started for Meggie on a day in late August. She knew she was really trying to make an effort, although she realized her head was still not all there. But she was fighting to survive this lousy hand fate had dealt her. Even though her spirit was still low, she challenged herself every day. Steely determination, she thought, with a fragile smile. She still thought of Dennis every day, missing him, craving him, and cursing him all at the same time. Meggie was perseverant. She told herself over and over again, she would survive!

She walked into her dorm at American University, one hot and humid late August day.

"I'm Meggie Hiken," she informed the slender girl behind the front desk.

"You're in room 225," an average-looking, brown-haired girl stated, checking her book, then handed Meggie the key. Though Meggie approved of the number, she did not know why.

"Hi! I'm Dottie!" a five-foot-ten girl stated, slapping Meggie's back, almost knocking her over. "I'm in the room right across from ya. I'll help ya with ya thins'. Com'on, kid, I'll show ya the way," Dottie picked up some of Meggie's luggage. She had the strongest Texas accent Meggie had ever heard, 'Oh my God, how did I deserve this!' Meggie thought, clenching her fists again.

"I'm from Houston, ya know, in Texas," Dottie said, looked at a bewildered Meggie, who thought she never would have guessed.

Meggie followed Dottie, and thought they must grow them big there. Aside from Dottie's height, she must have weighed at least 145 pounds, and was extremely broad-shouldered. She had short brown hair and Meggie noticed her face revealed lines of character.

"My dad's a stock broker in Houston, just imagine!" Dottie walked briskly with Meggie still following.

"One would think livin' in Texas, he would be in oil," Dottie laughed, on her way up the stairs. "The elevator's too crowded today, one flight won't kill us."   •

Meggie agreed. 'Anything is better than to be stuck waiting with this chatterbox,' she thought.

"Listen, kid, I'm in my second year here. Ya need anythin', tell Dottie. I'll take care of ya! Where ya from?" Dottie turned to see her.

"Baltimore, the outskirts, or suburbs, as they prefer," Meggie out of breath, dragging all of her things up the stairs.

"What's yer major?" Dottie asked, still climbing the stairs in front of her.

"Painting, art," Meggie was barely able to speak, being almost breathless at this point.

"That's swell!" Dottie yelled, swinging around with suitcases in hand, almost knocking Meggie back down the stairs. "Sorry, Dearie, sometimes I don't know my own strength. I'm an art major too!" Meggie thought, 'Great! Just what I need now!

"Go on, I'm fine. I'm even getting used to your accent," Meggie smiled.

"That's good, kid, because we're goin' to be seein' a lot of each other," Dottie turned to give Meggie a big Texas grin.

"Provided you don't call me kid anymore," Meggie stated.

"Here we are," Dottie said, showing Meggie into her room. "Settle in, see ya later." She placed Meggie's' things down and turned to her. "Can I call ya Meg?" Dottie asked, with a pert look on her face. Meggie couldn't get over how cute she looked just then, not understanding how anyone so big could look so cute. She smiled, they would be good friends, knowing she could not resist her.

"Sure, anything but kid," Meggie said, still grinned.

"Good deal, as in new deal, if ya get my drift," Dottie gave Meggie another slap on the back. Meggie lost her balance a little and wondered how she could get Dottie to stop doing that!

Catching her breath after Dottie left, Meggie went into a trance about Dennis, until her thoughts were interrupted,

"Hi! I'm Melinda, my friends call me Mouse. I'm your roommate," a five-foot-one person uttered. Meggie glanced up, spotting this very short and skinny girl. 'No wonder they call her Mouse,' she thought, and disliked herself for it.

"You like that nickname?" Meggie asked, not meaning for such cruelty to come from her mouth.

"It shows some sort of endearment, don't you think?" Mouse stared at her. "I normally don't talk too much but I'm excited today, along with being nervous, so nervous," Mouse sat down, focusing on this truly beautiful girl standing in front of her. "When I walked in here today, I decided I was going to be outgoing. I'm not like that at all. I wanted to be friends with my roommate. But when I finally opened my eyes and I saw you, you're gorgeous!" Meggie now knew why she was called Mouse.

"What's to stop us from being close, we're roommates, right? We're going to share a lot. Besides, you're honest, which is more than I can say for ninety percent of this dizzy world we live in. I like that in a person, it's also my prime criteria for friendship. You're really terrific," Meggie said, going to embrace her. At first Mouse drew back, then, seeing Meggie really meant it, she returned the hug.

That evening Meggie, Mouse, Dottie and Hillary (Dottie's roommate) went out for pizza. The four girls truly enjoyed themselves. It happened to be the first time since Dennis' death that Meggie actually laughed. Dottie noticed Meggie became very quiet all of a sudden, not understanding that Meggie was feeling guilty for enjoying herself. After Mouse left the dorm the following morning, Dottie entered Meggie's room.

"Ya may think me forward, but that's how they breed us in Texas." Very cynically, Meggie thought, 'Is that all they breed there?' She didn't like herself for that thought either.

"I know somethin's wrong, one doesn't need a sixth sense to feel it," Dottie uttered in her strong Texas accent.

Meggie realized then that Dottie was an extremely bright person. She was developing respect for her and even felt Dottie seemed to genuinely care.

"This is a hard story to tell, it's even harder to live," Meggie told her the generalities.

"I'm sorry for ya, uh, Meg," Dottie said.

"You still want to call me kid?" Meggie questioned in disbelief.

"Sort of, ya need to grow a little," Dottie smiled.

"I can't quite grasp your meaning," Meggie said, perplexed.

"I'm talkin in spirit and conscience," Dottie glanced at her.

"Okay, kid! Show me the way!" Meggie stated, with a degree of vengeance in her voice. Dottie smiled,

"Sarcasm doesn't become ya, I'm tryin to be ya friend."

"Sorry," Meggie said, very flustered, finding her Texas accent was indeed growing on her. "I don't mean to be anti-social, it's really not my style. There are so many things going on in my head, so many thoughts," her eyes swelled with tears.

"Ya're goin' to find out what a real, down-home-style, girlfriend is. In a way, ya need me almost as much as I need ya. I knew from the first time I met ya, ya're special." Dottie noticed the look on Meggie's face. "Sorry, don't mean to embarrass ya. But for Christ sakes, ya are!" Dottie sat at the foot of Meggie's bed while Meggie lay on it.

"I could use a good friend right now, thank you. You've grown on me," Meggie smirked. Dottie leaned over her, looked in her eyes,

"Damn, you have pretty eyes. We all need someone to talk to. I'd like to feel free to tell ya almost anythin," a more sedate Dottie.

Dottie laid down on Mouse's bed and Meggie poured her heart out to her, leaving nothing out.

"Ya've had a pretty rough time of it, Meg," Dottie said, not pausing before she said Meg, and not even wanting to say "kid." It was difficult to believe Meggie had been through so much, to mess up her feelings, so early in life.

"I'm goin to help ya get in touch," Dottie smiled at her.

"If anyone can, I believe it's you," Meggie smiled, loving that accent now.

The two girls looked at each other, both knowing fate had dealt them this. There was a reason they were placed in each other's lives. Meggie started to cry with Dottie joining her, partially for what was left behind them and partially for what lay ahead of them.

"I knew I'd pique your interest," Meggie smiled to her new friend.

"Is that what ya call it?" Dottie, with a slight laugh.

"I gave up humiliation for Lent," she smiled pertly. Dottie laughed harder.

It was the first day of September when Meggie, Mouse and Dottie were having dinner again at the pizza house close to their dorm. Meggie thought she was on a starch diet. She smiled, still enjoying her own wit. She noticed a guy approaching their table.

"Meggie, Mouse, this is a friend of mine, Michael," Dottie introduced him.

At first Meggie thought it was her paranoia. It wasn't until she looked up again that she saw Michael was still staring at her. He could not take his eyes off her. She wore bleached-out, paint-spotted jeans with an old reefer tee-shirt. He was still staring at her!

"Hi," Meggie smiled, before getting back to her food.

"I haven't seen you around before," Michael said.

"What are you, American's answer to the CIA?" Meggie stated, still in her not-all-there state of mind.

"No, the name is Michael Groster," he extended his hand, which Meggie took. 'I was wrong,' she thought, 'Its answer to Emily Post!'

"Meg, Michael's a good friend of mine, S.D.S. We worked together last year. This year he's in charge," Dottie gave her a weary look.

"Meggie Hiken. You're right, I am new here," she said. Michael gave Dottie a look as if to say, what gives with her?

"Can I sit down?" Michael smiled at Dottie. She nodded, he sat next to her, across from Meggie, so he could still keep an eye on her.

"You guys coming to the rally tomorrow?" Michael asked.

"We wouldn't miss it," Dottie smiled, now glancing at Meggie, thinking this is what she may need. Meggie returned Dottie's smile, almost reading her mind, agreeing with her.

"I don't think I can make it," Mouse timidly stated. Her two new friends could hardly believe their ears.

"What are you saying?" Meggie asked, in shock.

"I'm not into that sort of thing," Mouse stared down at her pizza, feeling uneasy.

"That's why we're in this stupid war, because of people like you!" Meggie yelled, losing her patience.

"Meggie, she's obviously naive," Dottie hoped for a reaction from Mouse.

"Who are you calling naive?" Mouse uttered, with more emotion than either girl had ever heard from her before.

"Dottie just felt, maybe you didn't understand, and maybe you haven't been apprised of the entire situation, coming from a farm as you do," Meggie looked at her roommate. Everyone noticed that Meggie was speaking down to her.

At the same time, Michael sat back, taking it all in, enjoying himself. 'I adore an honest fight of words,' he thought, watching the blonde with a decent brain across from him. The two girls were very persistent with Mouse. They finally swayed her by doing a number on her head. On the walk back to the dorm, Mouse finally relented,

"What time is the rally?"

"Tomorrow at five" Dottie smiled, enjoying their conquest.

"See you then," Mouse walked into her room.

"And good night all!" Meggie smiled to Dottie, before moving toward her room.

"Why, ya tired?" Dottie asked, surprised.

"No, how can you ask that? I just planned on sleeping before tomorrow," Meggie yawned with a slight laugh. Dottie smiled, walking the other way.

"Meggie, she's so pushy. How can you deal with that?" Mouse stated, as Meggie walked in.

"She's not that bad. Her heart's in the right place. Let's get some sleep. Night, Mouse," Meggie said, turning out the light.

The following evening an eager Meggie and Dottie, but a not-so-eager Mouse, sat together at the rally. Michael spoke, Meggie took it all in, doubting herself for not giving him credit before. Alex would like this, she thought, making a mental note to write her later. Her thought was interrupted when Michael introduced the former president of S.D.S. at American. Michael went on to explain Steven Roth was now in graduate school at George Washington University. When he spoke, Meggie became mesmerized by his use of words, his ideals and his beliefs. 'What a hunk,' she thought, then forcing the thoughts from her head. How could she think of anyone but Dennis? But Steven Roth seemed to have such an incredible head. Sitting, watching him, she observed he had great features that she could see, but she wished she could get by that beard.

Immediately following the rally, Michael approached the three girls, inviting them to join the regulars for carry out and beer in the S.D.S. trailer. Mouse declined. This had already been plenty for her. Meggie was about to do the same when Dottie blurted out, "Meggie and I will be there!"

Michael seemed pleased; Dottie had been a positive force in the past and he definitely wanted Meggie to come. From his initial encounter with her, he sensed she was not one to sit around. She could be an asset.

"Steven will be there, he's doing me a favor," Michael walked away. Dottie gave Meggie a nudge in the rib cage,

"I saw yer face when the chief got up to speak."

"You're eluding me at the present," Meggie indifferently.

"Come off it! Steven Roth!" Dottie with an ear-to-ear grin.

"You're definitely inhabiting another world," Meggie stated. 'I better watch what I think around her,' she thought.

"Remember, I told you I have ESP with some chosen few," Dottie smiled.

Everyone sat around a large table in the S.D.S. office exchanging ideas and eating. Their main objective right now was how to get more involvement from the student body. So much bullshit and garbage was coming down. Meggie thought, 'A duck had more sense.'

"We should get hold of a mimeograph machine, so we can verbalize what we are doing here. People in general are ill-informed, let's inform them!" Michael stated. Meggie thought, 'Great idea, the only decent one I've heard all day.'

"Freedom demands participation?" She stated, acknowledging agreement with Michael. All heads turned toward her. No one had noticed this blonde before. Steven Roth took a good look as well.

"Well, maybe they'll contain this war," Peggy uttered. Meggie rose from her chair. She had enough!

"This trailer has been a veritable cesspool today, and now the liberal from fantasyland is heard from!" Meggie stated, before leaving the trailer for some fresh air.

Everyone sat in shock, except for Steven Roth. Totally intrigued, he followed her outside.

"That was really uncalled for," Steven approached Meggie.

"Sorry, I become frustrated at times; listening to an airhead doesn't help. She wouldn't know a fact if it begged her all night long," Meggie said, clenching her fists. Steven walked so he faced her, placing his hand on her shoulder.

"I'm not going to argue with you, Peggy isn't all that bright. But she means well, and she's a hard worker. We need more like her around here," Steven stared at her, being captivated by how truly beautiful he found her to be. Meggie looked up at him, meeting his eyes. 'Those eyes,' he thought, 'They're beautiful.'

"Do you know what Einstein once said?" She didn't wait for an answer. "He said he didn't know how they were going to fight World War Three, but he did know how they were going to fight World War Four, with sticks and stones."

Steven couldn't get over her mind, and didn't know how to answer something like that. He had never come across anyone like this before, such a rare combination of brainpower and beauty.

"That's what frightens me the most. You do happen to be right. I should be more compassionate toward other people's feelings," Meggie said, solemnly.

Steven was totally amazed and placed his arm on her shoulder.

"Let's go in and eat before it's gone," he smiled, leading her in.

Once inside he couldn't keep his eyes off her, watching her eat, seeing how much she enjoyed it. Every time Meggie glanced up, she caught his eye on her. She smiled each time, biting her bottom lip.

Later that evening, after Meggie and Dottie left, Steven turned to Michael with a great deal of curiosity,

"Who is she?"

"Who?" Michael questioned.

"The pretty blonde with a mouth," Steven smiled.

"Oh! Meggie," Michael laughed.

"Where did you find her? She's a spellbinder, she's absolutely beautiful," Steven said.

"She's a real question mark! Full of surprises! Somehow I have the feeling you'll find out the hard way, won't you?" Michael smirked.

Back at the dorm,

"He liked ya, Meg, he kept starin at ya." Dottie poked her in the ribs again.

"Your imagination is working again; besides who cares?" Meggie, nonchalantly.

"Ya do, say what ya want, I know ya do," Dottie smiled.

"Goodnight, Dottie," Meggie walked into her room.

Meggie usually worked in the S.D.S. office on Wednesday afternoons. On this particular Wednesday, near the end of September, she walked into the broken-down trailer they used for an office. Smiling, she glanced around at three table-type desks, a beat-up old sofa, one typewriter and a tiny, dirty lavatory.

"Meg, do you know how to work a mimeograph machine?" Michael asked, before she had time to remove her sweater. 'There's always more work than people to do it,' she thought.

"You got one! I never have before but I'm sure it's not too difficult," Meggie walked toward the machine.

Michael gave her some basic instructions and before long, she was printing the flyers he wanted. Dottie approached to pick up some flyers to distribute.

"Look who's in the back watchin ya," she whispered to Meggie.

She glanced back to see Steven watching her. She smiled and he did the same before he went back to his work.

"Meg, when you're finished, just leave them. Dottie and I will be back for them later," Michael instructed, putting on his coat.

"Oh thanks, cutie," he said, throwing her a kiss. Meggie smiled, shaking her head.

While running the flyers off, she had time to think. She wondered if they really had a shot at changing this world they lived in. Her arm was getting really tired as she inked the machine for its final run. Looking up, she saw Steven standing next to her.

"You almost done, it's getting late?"

"Almost," she smiled at him, then was shocked. The machine sprayed black ink all over his face. Meggie burst out laughing. Steven started to laugh with her, putting a couple of his fingers into the ink, flicking them toward Meggie's face. They laughed hysterically and uncontrollably, both falling back on the sofa to catch their breath.

"You hungry?" Steven smiled.

"Starving, what time is it?" Meggie asked.

"Seven-fifteen," he told her.

"Michael and Dottie never came back," she stated. Steven broadly grinned,

"They went to dinner and left you here to work."

"You're probably right," Meggie said, before she burst into laughter again, looking at his ink-laden face.

"You should see yourself if you think I look funny," Steven laughed, watching her.

They both squeezed into the tiny cubicle of a bathroom to look in the mirror. They stood there laughing, not being able to stop, looking at each other. Steven finally controlled himself a little and went to search for a towel. He finally came up with a rag, wet it and started washing Meggie's face. He couldn't get over how naturally beautiful she was without makeup. He thought that unusual, since most of the girls he knew used some. Meggie didn't need any, he noticed, as he looked into those large aquamarine eyes. He knew then he wanted to know her better.

"Let's get some dinner. I know the perfect place for starving, ink laden people," Steven smiled. Meggie laughed again,

"Okay, I pay my own way."

"You liberated woman, you. Only if I can take you another time," Steven said.

"Maybe," she smiled. "But, right now, feed me!"

On the way out of the door, Steven turned to her,

"You're Jewish, right?"

"So!" she was curious.

"Then you must like Chinese food," he smiled.

"It's one of my passions," she laughed.

Steven took her to a very small Chinese restaurant. When she spotted the red neon lights, she was out of the car fast, heading straight for the restaurant.

"Wait!" Steven yelled. Meggie couldn't believe her ears. 'Is he joking, as famished as I am,' she thought. Steven took her hand, leading her into the liquor store next door.

"Red or white?" He turned toward her, wondering which wine she preferred.

"Red as far as colors go. As for wine it's white," Meggie glanced around, taking it all in. She had never been in a liquor store before.

"Great! How about a Riesling?" Steven asked. She nodded yes, not knowing what he was talking about.

The Chinese restaurant appeared small from the outside but it was smaller from the inside, having only six tables. There were people already seated at two of them. They sat themselves at a table in the far left corner. A Chinese lady approached, carrying a corkscrew and wine glasses.

"Ello Steven," she smiled.

"Mai Wong, this is Meggie," Steven said. "I told her how delicious your food is."

"It true, you like," Mai Wong smiled, then left for the kitchen.

He poured the wine as Meggie gave him a questioning look,

"Don't we order?" All she could think about was her stomach.

"We get what they have. Don't worry, you like," Steven laughed, seeing the surprise on her face.

While they waited for the food to come,

"Let's see, what do you like?" Steven smiled.

"I like daisies in the summer, glowing embers in fireplaces, I like the leaves when they turn colors," she smiled into space.

"A true romantic," he said. Meggie laughed,

"In all honesty: food, painting and my independence." She gazed up at Steven, thinking, 'He is really cute,' and wondering what he would look like without that beard.

"What's your criteria for happiness?" She asked, taking a sip of wine. He watched her rose-colored lips touch the glass. 'Such sensual lips,' he thought.

"Sunsets on wintry beaches, relating over a fine bottle of wine," Steven mused, as Meggie broke in,

"And you call me a romantic!"

"I like my freedom, books and sex," he said with a grin, watching Meggie blush, finding her refreshing. She thought him fascinating while she listened to stories of his college days.

Driving back to her dorm in Steven's '63 Cutlass, she smiled,

"That was a wonderful meal. I think, maybe the best since I've been here."

Steven thought, not just a great meal, but fantastic company, not recalling when he had enjoyed himself so much. They had spent over two and one half hours in the restaurant, enjoying every minute of it. He sensed Meggie did as well. At times they laughed to the point of tears, at other times they were quite serious and at still other times, they didn't say a word but looking into each other's eyes. He thought it an enjoyable and an unusually enlightening evening. Steven stopped the car in front of Meggie's dorm, turning the motor off.

"I'm delighted you enjoyed the food," he placed his right arm around the back of her seat.

"Are you kidding? It was..." Meggie was unable to finish as Steven leaned over, kissing her.

Meggie ran from the car quickly, without even a word, heading into her dorm. Steven sat there in total shock! He didn't understand, not knowing what he did. He was definitely puzzled.

Meggie ran through the lobby of her dorm, up a flight of stairs, crying the whole way to her room.

"What's wrong?" Mouse asked, concerned.

"Mouse, not now!" Meggie yelled, flopping herself on her bed, burying her face in her pillow, crying.

How dare she enjoy herself? How could she possibly show interest in someone else? How could she? Meggie thought, and cried. She grabbed the ring she still wore on a chain around her neck, crying even harder. 'Dennis, I still love you, and at the same time I hate you for doing this to me,' she thought, still crying to herself. How can I enjoy myself? That question kept going over and over again through her mind. She cried herself to sleep, still fully dressed.

Meggie avoided Steven at all times, which was not too difficult, since he didn't go to school on her campus any longer. What she did was not go to the S.D.S. office too much, and never on a Wednesday afternoon. Above all, she never joined Michael when he invited her to have dinner with the group.

It was nearing the end of October and a sit-in had been arranged. Meggie felt she had no choice if she wanted to be involved, if she wanted to make a contribution, if she wanted to do something for herself and her country. On her walk to the S.D.S. office, anticipating seeing Steven again, Meggie thought about her conversation with Dottie after her dinner with him.

"I can't believe ya are so upset," Dottie gave her a strange look.

"I know! It's far beyond your comprehension," Meggie arrogantly.

"Meggie!" Dottie yelled, grabbing and shaking her, trying to make her sensible. "This may have happened even if Dennis was alive!"

"Get lost!" Meggie yelled irately.

"No! Accept it, he's attracted to ya. The time has come for ya to admit ya feel the same way," Dottie said, sternly.

"You have absolutely no idea what the hell you are talking about," Meggie cried, tears running from her eyes.

"No! Read me, feel my vibes, I feel yers," Dottie left for class.

'Personal feelings had to be put aside,' she thought, walking into the S.D.S. office. She was confronted again with more than she could possibly deal with. Michael, the organizer approached her.

"Meg, I'm glad you're here. Can you run this off for me?" He handed her a stencil.

"What am I, the mimeographer?" She smiled.

"That's it," Michael returned her smile.

Hearing her voice, Steven glanced up. Meggie caught his eye and smiled. He did the same. Later he sat staring at her, recalling his conversation with Michael,

"Remember, you told me how strange she is," Steven said.

"What are you talking about?" Michael looked up from the paper he was working on.

"Meggie," Steven smiled.

"Oh, right, Meggie, she's a real puzzle. Right!," Michael smirked.

"In your own words, she's a real question mark," Steven stated.

Steven sat in his seat, smiling as he thought of that conversation. He rose nearing Meggie.

"My roommates and I are having a Halloween party Saturday night. Can you come?" Steven looking at her, risking what kind of response he may get. She glanced down, preparing to say no.

"I told him we'd be there, Meg," Dottie said, giving Meggie a very disconcerted look.

"The only costume I have is at home," said Meggie, trying to find an excuse not to go.

"So, we'll go get it," Dottie smiled. Meggie knew when to quit, knew she was in a spot she could not get out of.

That evening on the way back to their dorm.

"I am so angry with you!" Meggie bluntly stated.

"Why?" Dottie laughed, aware of the reason.

"You know!" Meggie screamed. "Because of that stupid party I have no desire to go to!"

"Ya know as well as I do, ya need it. We'll have a great time," Dottie smiled.

"You may, I won't. Another thing, I don't appreciate people answering for me!" Meggie said, still very aggravated.

"Sorry, I feel ya should go. Besides, I'm a great believer in positive aura's and ya have one!" Said Dottie. Meggie smiled. She always did when Dottie started talking like this.

The day prior to Halloween, due to Dottie's persuasion, Meggie and she drove to Baltimore. Meggie pulled her car into the parking lot next door to the Beethoven Apartments.

"Ya live here?" Dottie said in shock.

"No. Christine and Alex do. I don't plan on spending any more time with Ma than necessary," Meggie said, getting out of the car.

The two girls walked into the building and took the elevator up to the fifth floor, as Dottie took it all in. Meggie knew the architecture would pique her interest.

"Hi!" Alex was surprised to see her when as opened the door.

"Hi, Alex, this is my friend, Dottie. How are you?" Meggie smiled.

"Hi," Alex looked at Dottie. "I'm fine, school is great and the people are fantastic," Alex led them toward the pillows in the living room.

"Hi Meg, you look good. Sorry, can't stay," Christine flew by.

"Wait!" Meggie yelled, following her into her room. After a very brief chat, Christine was gone.

"What the hell is she on?" Meggie asked Alex.

"Coke," Alex said, nonchalantly.

"How can you let her do that?" Meggie aggravated.

"I'm not her keeper, though I've tried," Alex sadly responded.

"How could you have allowed this to happen, especially after Dennis!" Meggie stated very distraught. Dottie sat, taking all of this in, fully aware she didn't know all there was to know about Dennis.

"Damn you, Meg! I really don't need a guilt trip laid on me! I've tried to control the situation but I can't. As a mother is with a child, I'm forced to sit by and allow her to make her own mistakes. I don't like it, but the alternative I don't like either, moving out. If I do , she'll have no one who really cares," Alex looked at her.

"I'm sorry, Alex, I had no right to jump on you like that. It brought back such bad memories," Meggie said, with a tear in her eye. Alex nodded, understanding. "How long has this been going on?"

"She used it occasionally last year but it's been daily since July," Alex stated, giving Meggie a look. Meggie then knew where Dennis got his coke.

Meggie checked her watch, turned to Dottie, "We've got to go, it's five o'clock. Alex, can you help her?"

"I'm here for her, that's all I can really do. Christine has an addictive personality," Alex stated.

The girls said their good-byes with Meggie and Alex hugging, promising next time wouldn't be so long before they saw each other again. Meggie drove for nearly thirty minutes from downtown, with hardly a word said between them. It was the first time since Dennis' accident that Meggie had taken the Jones Falls Expressway, not thinking clearly when she got on. Riding past the Cold Spring Lane exit, she tried seeing if she could figure out where it happened but she couldn't. Meggie finally broke the silence,

"Dot, sometimes I get this feeling the whole world is closing in on me. Do you know what I'm trying to say?"

"Honestly, no," Dottie stated. "There's one thin' for certain though, bein' with ya is never dull," Dottie smiled, trying to lighten the mood.

With that comment, they pulled into Meggie's middle-class driveway. It was 5:30 p.m.

"Ma," Meggie yelled as they entered the house. Ma was aware they were coming for dinner.

"Meggie, is that you?" Ma rushed down the stairs with Ben.

Ben hugged her. They hadn't seen her since the High Holy days in late September.

"Ma, Ben, this is Dottie," Meggie smiled.

"I'm happy to meet you," Ma said. Ben started to punch this large girl.

They followed Ma to the kitchen to help her with dinner. After a few minutes, Meggie excused herself to search for her costume.

"Dottie, tell me how she's doing" Ma said. Dottie was a little taken aback. From everything Meggie had told her, she thought her mother hated her!

"She's alright," Dottie surprised.

"Is she getting out, doing things? Is she any happier?" Ma asked, with a few tears in her eyes.

"Mrs. Hiken, that's why we're here. I'm tryin' to get her to go and to do. She's a real special person," Dottie said, feeling sorry for Meggie's mom.

"My ears are burning and I have the hiccups," Meggie walked into the kitchen. "Ma, you always told me that meant one thing-people are talking about me."

"Let's see your costume!" Dottie said, trying to change the subject.

"Later," Meggie spotted her Dad walk in.

"Munchkin!" Daddy smiled.

"Hi, Daddy," she said, flinging herself into his arms.

Dinner was excellent, as usual, even quite pleasant. Later that night, Dottie was in the other twin bed in Meggie's room.

"It's time to let go, Meg," Dottie instructed.

"Please don't start again," Meggie propped her head up on an elbow to look at Dottie.

"Ya don't want to let go, or should I say, let him rest," Dottie stated.

"You're not being fair," Meggie became depressed.

"I'm bein' more than fair. Ya're the one who's not bein' fair to Steven," Dottie watched her for some reaction.

"Enough is enough, and goodnight," Meggie said, turning out the light, knowing Dottie was right. But she couldn't help the way she felt, it hurt too much. Dottie fell to sleep quickly. Meggie was up for most of the night thinking, just thinking, feeling that her mind was always at work.

The following day the two girls drove back to D.C. That night, Dottie walked into Meggie's room to inform her Michael was waiting downstairs.

"My god! Look at ya!" Dottie, in a beautiful peasant dress, was astonished.

"Look at me! Look at you! You look beautiful!" Meggie said in awe.

"Only a rare person, built like ya, could wear what's on yer body," Dottie smiled, Meggie blushed.

She was wearing the same butterfly costume she wore last year with Dennis. It hurt when she looked at herself in the mirror, bringing back memories.

"Here, take this," Dottie said, breaking a white pill in half.

"What is it?" Meggie questioned.

"It's called a Quaalude. Just half though. Alex gave me some yesterday. It will help ya relax, take it from me, ya need some relaxin'," Dottie handed her half of the pill.

"No, I don't think so. Drugs, you know how I feel, nothing stronger than pot," Meggie stared at the white half moon in her hand.

"It's really medication. Ya know I would never do anythin' heavy," Dottie took her half of the pill, watching Meggie do the same.

Seeing Michael and Dottie walk in, Steven approached them.

"Your costumes are great! Who is this? Meggie?" Steven laughed, not recognizing her at first because her mask covered at least half of her face. When Meggie removed her coat, sprouting glittered, butterfly wings attached to a tightly-fitted turquoise leotard, Dottie thought she was going to have to pick Steven's eyes up off the floor. By the same token, Meggie barely recognized Steven.

"A pirate, wonderful idea! It goes well with your beard, about the only thing that does," Meggie laughed, walking by him toward the food.

"Always thinking about your stomach," Steven approached her.

Meggie laughed with a mouthful of food, noting she did happen to be in rare humor that night; it must be the Quaalude.

"Let's dance," Steven took her hand.

"Where'd she come from?" Roger, one of Steven's roommates, inquired.

"Luck, or maybe not" Steven smiled.

They danced together quite a bit that night. She mingled like she never had before, not being able to recall when she ever talked so much. A slow song came on and Steven held her so very close. Meggie remembered this feeling, liking it; she did like Steven. Dottie approached her at 12:30 a.m.,

"I'm leavin' with Perry." Meggie gave her a peculiar look. "Ya're not my mother. I've told ya about him before," Dottie smiled.

"Have fun! But not too much," Meggie said, with a very cynical look, thinking all of these guys are on the make!

"I'm leaving, Steven said he'd take you home. Later, cutie," Michael gave Meggie a familiar peck on the cheek.

Things seem to be pre-arranged, Meggie thought, then realized it must be her own paranoia. About an hour later, she walked into the kitchen to throw away her cup.

"Morris, you ready to go?" Steven stood looking at her.

"Morris?" Meggie laughed questioningly. He smiled,

"Sure, you know, the cat. You have as many moods as one."

"Not..." she didn't have a chance to finish; Steven kissed her. Afterwards, she had to lean against the refrigerator for support, feeling her legs could barely hold her up. "I think it's time," Meggie's voice cracked.

Steven grinned, seeing her a little shaky. He enjoyed being able to do that to her. He put his arm around her shoulders, trying to steady her.

"Come on, Morris," Steven laughed a little, leading her out.

The following day, a Sunday, Steven phoned, asking her to have dinner with him that night; she declined. Damn, he couldn't understand her, she totally baffled him. The night before, he kissed her in his car in front of her dorm. Walking her to the door, he pushed her gently against the wall, this time really kissing her. Placing his tongue in her mouth, he relished every crevice of it; she didn't run away. He asked himself, why won't she have dinner with me and why did she run away before. Morris, he thought to himself, perfect for her!

On Wednesday, when Meggie walked into the S.D.S. office, Steven wasn't there. She was surprised and disappointed at the same time. She was even a little sad, though she wouldn't admit it to herself or to Dottie. Michael put her right to work as usual, allowing Meggie to put it out of her mind.

Entering the trailer the following Tuesday, Meggie found it bustling. Everyone, including Dottie, Michael and even Steven were busy at work. Seeing Steven, she smiled to herself, such a unique individual, she could use so many different adjectives to describe him. Quickly, she became solemn again, thinking of Dennis.

"What's happening?" She walked toward Michael.

"I'm glad you're here, run this off," Michael handed her a stencil.

Meggie read it. This one was on atomic warfare. "Ban the Bomb" was printed in large block letters at the top. She walked over to the mimeograph machine, removing the cover.

"Hello, Morris," Steven neared her. "I'll help you."

"Are you sure you really want to do that. Remember the last time you tried to help me," Meggie laughed, partly because of recalling the incident, and partially because he called her Morris again.

"Come on, Morris. Let's get to work," Steven laughed, aware he got to her.

The flyers were finished, everyone else took them out to circulate, leaving Steven and Meggie alone in the trailer. Meggie's arm hurt so badly, she felt as if it were going to fall off. She fell back into a seat on the dilapidated sofa.

"Morris, you tired?" Steven asked.

"More than that," she smiled.

"I know, hungry!" he laughed. "I know just the place for tired, hungry people."

"I can't wait to hear this one," Meggie smiled at him.

"Come on Morris," he handed her jacket to her.

"Where are we going?" Meggie inquired, sitting in his car.

"I told you a place for tired, hungry people. Mexican, it's fast and great!" Steven smiled.

"No way! I respect my stomach and I don't plan on abusing it!" Meggie laughed. "Guacamole, an avocado with heartburn."

Steven was shocked as well as disappointed. He intended on letting her know it, pulling his car into a market in northwest D.C.

"Let's go, Morris," Steven said, getting out of the car.

"This isn't a restaurant!" Meggie surprised, following him.

"I know, but it's one place I can certainly please you!" He said.

Meggie laughed on the inside, he's going to be in for a real shock. She retrieved a cart, giving it to Steven and proceeded to the fish counter, ordering two and a half pounds of jumbo gulf shrimp.

"That's a lot. Who are you feeding, the District of Columbia?" Steven smiled at her.

"You jest! I know what I'm doing!" She laughed slightly, enthralled with his mind.

She proceeded around the market with Steven following, gathering what she needed to make dinner. Romaine lettuce, clove garlic, butter, fresh string beans and rice. Steven watched her in amazement, at the same time hoping she really did know what she was doing. At the check-out, Meggie had already paid for everything before he could get to his wallet.

Seeing the shock written all over his face, she smiled, "This way, if I should poison you, you wouldn't have lost anything.".

"Only my life, Morris," Steven laughed, walking out of the market with his arm around her shoulder.

Steven lived in a brownstone townhouse in Georgetown. Meggie couldn't believe she hadn't noticed this before, figuring it had to have been the "Q" on Halloween that blurred her vision. Once inside, she got to work.

"What can I do?" Steven placed his arm around her waist.

"Do the shrimp," she handed him the scissors, showing him how to remove the shell. "Take the vein out, then wash the shrimp."

"I've always eaten the black line," he said, questioningly.

"You wouldn't if you were aware of what it was," Meggie tossed her head back a little.

"Out with it, Morris, what is it?" Steven asked, sopping wet with scissors and shrimp in his hands. Watching him, Meggie couldn't help but laugh.

"You really don't know, do you," she still laughed, trying to keep the tears from flowing from her eyes. "I'm looking for a polite way to say this. It's part of a normal bodily function, going to the bathroom." Steven looked at her with surprise.

"I bet you won't eat that black line anymore," she smiled.

"Finished, anything else?" Steven glanced at her. Meggie laughed,

"Yes, go change. I can't believe you made such a mess."

A few minutes later, Steven entered the dining room to a fully set table. Meggie had already placed the food on it. She had made a Caesar salad, steamed string beans and shrimp scampi over rice.

"Ready," she yelled before seeing him.

"Okay, let's eat," Steven pulled a chair out for her.

"So formal, Mr. Roth," Meggie smiled.

"You forgot one thing," he walked to the kitchen.

Meggie looked around the table, surprised. Steven returned with a bottle of white wine they had purchased that afternoon.

"You alky!" she laughed slightly.

After devouring everything there was to eat, Steven smiled.

"Where did you learn to cook like this? It was fantastic!"

"Thank you. My ma's a super cook. Now you can help clean up," Meggie blushed. Accepting compliments was one of the things she had never done very well .

Steven carried the empty plates into the kitchen and stood in awe. "Morris, come here!"

"What?" Meggie rushed toward him.

"I have never seen anyone do so much damage in such a short period of time," Steven stared at the disaster area of a kitchen.

"Sorry, maybe all good cooks do this," she took his hand, stared into his light blue eyes with a tilt of her head. "Wasn't it worth it?"

"Maybe," Steven laughed a little. "It was a gastronomical triumph!" he gazed directly into those eyes of hers, before kissing her.

After cleaning the kitchen, which looked like a tornado had struck, they retired to the living room, sitting on the sofa in front of the fireplace. It was now giving off a great deal of heat, since Steven, with his infinite wisdom, had lit it earlier. Meggie always loved the feel of the burning embers, of their warmth. 'Such a calming effect,' she thought. The lights were dim and Steven sat beside her, resting his arm around her on the back of the sofa.

"Where are your roommates?" Meggie gazed into the fire.

"They both have classes on Tuesday and Thursday evenings," Steven leaned to kiss her.

"Morris, it was a great meal, mess and all!" He laughed, thinking about the kitchen.

"Gee thanks! Next time I believe I'll let you cook," she stated.

"I'd be delighted to, but I know that's not where my talent lies," Steven kissed her again.

On the way back to her dorm, Steven turned toward her.

"Morris, you like Peter, Paul and Mary?"

"Of course!" She smiled.

"I have two tickets for their concert Friday night, you want to go?" Steven asked, watching the road ahead.

Meggie thought for a short bit before answering.

"Why not," she mumbled. Not knowing Steven heard her.

"Cute! Some people would kill to see them!" He yelled in shock.

"Right! To be seen in public with the bearded wonder!" Meggie bluntly. She didn't mean to be so arrogant but she had this bizarre need to cover up her true feelings, not just from him, but also from herself.

"You really take such offense to my beard?" He inquired.

"No, not really. I just wonder if there's a face under it," she smiled.

Peter, Paul and Mary performed fantastically. Steven took her to this neat little delicatessen, one of the very few in D.C.. Meggie was astounded he had found it. He ordered hamburgers, French fries with gravy and egg creams. It was her first egg cream in years, she hadn't had one since her last visit to New York. Taking her back to her dorm, Steven asked her out for the next Saturday night but she told him she was busy, even though she had no plans. The following day he phoned, asking her to have dinner with him, since eating seemed to be her hobby. She turned him down again. He had difficulty figuring her out, feeling she enjoyed his company as much as he did hers.

Monday afternoon the phone rang again. Meggie refused to answer it, so Mouse did.

"It's for you." Mouse handed her the receiver.

"Tell him I'm not in," Meggie bluntly.

"It's your father!" Mouse stated with disgust.

"Hi, Daddy," Meggie said, grabbing the phone.

"Munchie, I'm in D.C. for the day. How about dinner?"

"Great Daddy!"

"Pick you up at six-thirty. By the way, who aren't you in for?" Dad asked.

"Oh, Daddy, see you later," Meggie put the receiver in place.

That evening Dad took her to a steak restaurant near school.

"How's it going?" Dad looked at her.

"Okay; Ma and Ben alright?" Meggie smiled to him, knowing he desired an honest answer, feeling his concern. She knew for months now he wanted to take her pain from her, but he couldn't, nobody could.

"You know your Ma, she'll never change, still on me all of the time," Dad glanced at the menu.

"You had another fight," Meggie said, knowing her dad's history of fooling around. Dad glanced up,

"What else is new, nothing for you to be bothered about."

"Daddy, tell me something. Did you ever love Ma?" Meggie leaned across the table toward him after they ordered.

"Certainly, years ago when we first married; then something happened. I still love Lil, but in a different way," Morris Hiken stared into space. Meggie asked, curiously,

"What happened? How can you love differently?"

"Hi, surprised to see you here," Steven said, as Meggie looked up at him.

Dad, being the gentleman he was, stood, inviting Steven to join them. Meggie noticed the shock on Steven's face at seeing her father. Morris Hiken stood six feet tall, having the same eyes as his daughter and wonderfully thick, dark blonde hair. He was an extremely young looking, forty year old man, and quite handsome. Before Steven could answer, Meggie smiled,

"Steven, this is my dad." Noticing the relief on his face.

"Mr. Hiken, pleased to meet you. I'm here with my roommates, but thanks anyway," Steven shook his hand. He turned toward Meggie.

"Morris, I'll see you Wednesday, right?" He waited for a reply before walking away.

"Right, Wednesday," Meggie watched him sit with Roger and Paul.

"Morris, why? Is he aware that's my name?" Dad interested.

"No, Daddy, he's not aware of your name. He calls me Morris, after the cat. He thinks I have as many moods as one," Meggie smiled.

"Smart guy. Is he the one you weren't in for?" Dad smiled.

"You're very perceptive!" She laughed. "You know Daddy, I really do love you. It's so good to see you."

They talked, finishing the meal, with Meggie frequently glancing over to Steven.

"Let's hear about him," Dad smiled to her.

"I can't put anything over on you, can I?" Meggie blushed.

"You know better," he smiled.

"I really don't know much about him. We've only gone out a couple of times," Meggie said.

"He seems to know you, Morris," Dad laughed, slightly.

"Oh, Daddy! He works in the S.D.S. office with me and he's in grad school at G.W. That's it. Can we go now?" Meggie asked, wanting an end to this conversation.

They left the restaurant with Dad's arm around her waist, leading her out, not noticing anything or anyone, not even the young man with the beard who was intently watching their every move.

Two days later, Wednesday afternoon, Meggie walked into the S.D.S. trailer, seeing no one but Steven.

"Hi Morris. Not too much happening today," he said.

"Where's everyone?" She glanced around, never seeing it empty before. He smiled,

"Not a soul was here when I arrived a few minutes ago."

Meggie sat on the sofa taking her boots off. Steven sat himself a few feet away, eyeing her,

"Your dad seems okay. I imagine you got your looks from him."

"He's terrific! Sometimes I think he can read my mind," she said.

"It's nice to know someone's aware of what's going on inside that pretty little head of yours," Steven laughed.

Meggie put her boots back on, somewhat offended.

"Hey, where are you going?" Steven looked at her.

"Back to the dorm. There's nothing to do here, and I'm not real good at being idle lately," Meggie put her coat on.

"Let's go someplace, the Smithsonian!" Steven hopeful.

"The Natural History and the Air and Space museums," she smiled.

"Terrific," Steven grabbed his coat, leading her out.

They had a delightful, informative and fun afternoon. Meggie felt her stomach gurgle,

"I'm starving," she waited for his normal response.

"For a change! I know just the place to take a beautiful, starving young lady," Steven smiled.

"For a change!" Meggie laughed. "Where are we going?" Thinking of her stomach and definitely not wanting Mexican food.

"To a wonderful little Greek restaurant. No complaints about shish kebob, I hope." He smiled. She simply nodded approval.

After dinner, on the way back to her dorm, Meggie smiled,

"Steven, you really do know some strange places."

"You didn't like it?"

"Great, but tasteless furnishings," she laughed.

"American people are spoiled," he smiled.

Steven stopped his car in front of her dorm.

"Thanks for a wonderful day," she started to step from the car with Steven grabbing her left arm.

"Where do you think you're going?" He kissed her.

"I guess nowhere. Anything else you want to say?" She smiled. He kissed her far more passionately than before.

"Yes, I got hold of a couple of tickets for the Bullets game on Saturday night. You want to go?" Steven asked, with apprehension.

"I love basketball," Meggie smiled, before getting out of the car.

"See you at six-thirty, Saturday," Steven yelled, watching her enter the dorm.

Meggie didn't understand her own emotions. She knew she was confused, so out of touch with her feelings but she was attempting desperately to deal with them. She had never felt like this before. She tried hard to put everything out of her mind, finding it impossible. In the past, so many things were either black or they were white, now it was different. Why was it when Steven phoned her, she inevitably turned him down, but when she was with him, and she loved being with him, he made her laugh-she would say yes. She thought about Dennis; they always went to the Bullets games together, his parents had season tickets and he adored basketball. She must have been out of her mind to even consider going with Steven! She simply couldn't do it! Meggie decided tomorrow she would phone him, informing him she made a mistake, she would be unable to go Saturday night. The end!

"Where ya been?" Dottie spotted Meggie walking down the hall.

"Where have you been!" Meggie a little hostilly.

"Where I usually am on Wednesday afternoons, the S.D.S. office," Dottie smiled. Meggie became arrogant,

"Bullshit! I was there and you weren't; in fact, no one was."

"Sorry, I know ya've been with Steven. He scooted us out of there," Dottie smiled. "Did ya have a good time?" Dottie glanced at her surprised face.

"Okay," Meggie said, walking into her room. Dottie flopped herself down on Meggie's bed,

"Well, tell me about it."

"You're so nosey, you're more dependable than the C.I.A.," Meggie smiled.

"I'd prefer to be equated with Dear Abby'," Dottie said, with the two girls laughing.

"We went to the Smithsonian and a little hole-in-the-wall Greek restaurant for dinner," Meggie said, undressing. "Your turn, tell me about your love life." Meggie sat, brushing her hair.

"Not as interesting as yours, it's nil." Dottie flipped through a *HARPERS BAZAAR* magazine.

"What about Perry?" Meggie questioned.

"I haven't seen him since Halloween," Dottie said, with Meggie giving her a strange look. "No, I didn't do anythin'!" Dottie yelled, looking at Meggie's eager eye. "Maybe I should have, maybe then he would have called. Why am I telling you this?"

"Why not? You've been playing Dr. Freud with my life, it's my turn now," Meggie smiled.

The two girls were up most of the night talking. Dottie tried to convince her not to break the date with Steven. It was totally irrelevant anyway, because Meggie never had the nerve to call him.

Saturday evening at exactly 6:30 p.m., Meggie waited outside her dorm for approximately 30 seconds before Steven drove up.

"Morris, been waiting long?" He asked, as she opened the car door, seating herself on the passengers side of the front seat.

"Only a few seconds," she shut the door.

The Bullets game was quite exciting. Meggie was pleased she had gone. 'It's been a long time,' she thought. They even won! Afterwards, sitting in Steven's car, before he started the motor,

"You know this city, where should I feed you?"

"Very funny. Suppose I told you I wasn't hungry," she stated.

"I'd call you a liar," he smiled, before kissing her.

"Little Italy, Sabatino's, my favorite," Meggie laughed, giving him directions from the Baltimore Civic Center.

They drank the house wine, with Steven having far too much. Meggie refused to allow him to drive and sat in the drivers seat asking him for the keys.

"Do you get inebriated often?" She inquired.

"You do this to me," Steven stated

"Me!" Meggie said, very bright-eyed.

"You make me drink too much!" Steven yelled.

"Oh! Go to sleep, I'll see you get home safely," she laughed a little..

"No! You don't understand, do you," he stated.

"No, I guess I don't," Meggie half laughed, looking at this blob, on the seat beside her, who could barely speak.

"You won't go out with me that often, so-oo-oo I intend to be a perfect gentleman and stay awake," Steven gave her a drunken smile.

She started to laugh so hard she had to hold her stomach while she drove. "Can you handle some conversation?"

"Would you like to talk about how much you want to make love to me?" Steven asked, with a drunken smile again. She gave him a very evil look.

"Sorry, I stepped out of bounds! What would you like to talk about?"

"You already know where my roots lie, how about yours?" Meggie glanced at him.

"Monologue time," Steven sat straight up, noticing they were on the Baltimore-Washington Parkway heading toward D.C.

"Let's be serious now" he tried to regain his composure. "I grew up in urban New York City, the home of the asphalt playground, the New York Yankees, the Statue of Liberty and egg creams. We moved to Phoenix, Arizona, when I was fourteen. My parents own an orange grove. I guess you could say they're orcharders," Steven laughed, still pretty drunk. "I also grew up with the benefit of two religions. My mom is Jewish and my dad Protestant. I'm a spoiled only child and I lived in Phoenix until I started American four years ago. No special interests, except I love music and I love to write. That's what I want to do, to write."

"You call those no special interests, what about S.D.S.?" Meggie asked, curious.

"Students for a Democratic Society. So it filled my time, I think I'm beginning to outgrow it," Steven stated.

"Bullshit!" Meggie yelled. Then glanced over at him,

"I suppose that's why you still come around."

"It's because of you I come around," Steven leaned toward her.

"Steven, I don't buy that. You were there long before ever meeting me," she said.

"Sure, Michael asked me. Somehow you have a way of making me fess up," Steven smiled to her.

"Especially when you're too high," Meggie laughed.

"It's one of my pets alright! I hate the way this country is run, the manipulation, this stupid war, the bomb, the starving people in Appalachia. The corruption, the very fabric of things! I'm simply doing what I believe in, standing by my convictions!" Steven stated, becoming more and more angry as he spoke.

The entire conversation had sobered him up a lot. Meggie stopped his car in front of her dorm,

"Do you think you're capable of driving home?"

"I'll be fine," Steven leaned to kiss her. "Morris, I have to tell you something."

"What?" Meggie asked, with aroused curiosity.

"You're something else. Do you know that? Michael and I call you a real question mark," Steven looked at her for some reaction.

"Gee thanks, I don't know when I've been paid a higher compliment," she started to step from the car. Steven leaned, grabbing her, not allowing her to move.

"Listen Morris, I believe you know how I feel. I'm pretty straight right now, so I know what I'm saying. I care," he kissed her.

"I've got to go. See you. Oh thanks," Meggie said, running out of the car into the dorm.

"Shit!" Steven yelled, thinking, 'What the hell did I do wrong now?' He drove home in thought and bewilderment.

Meggie ran up the flight of stairs leading to her room, happy to find Mouse not in yet and Dottie gone too. She took a long hot shower cleansing herself, crying the entire time. She fell into bed nude, still with tears flowing from her eyes. She kept asking herself, why did he have to say he cared? Nobody cared like Dennis! She cried even more because if that were true, he wouldn't have done what he did to himself, or to her! He'd still be alive! Maybe Dottie was right. Maybe this would have happened even if Dennis was alive. I don't know, I'm so confused, I think I need help. Meggie fell asleep with her mind still working and crying at the same time.

The following day, Sunday at noon, the phone rang.

"Meg, it's for you," Mouse yelled across to Dottie's room for her.

"Who is it?" Meggie asked, walking in.

"Steven," Mouse smiled.

"Tell him I'm not in, please," Meggie said.

"No way! You do it!" Mouse left the room with Meggie giving her a very discomforting look.

"Thanks," Meggie sarcastically. "Hello."

"Morris, I'm sorry I got so drunk last night," Steven said.

"It's alright, I'm glad you made it home safely," she stated.

"How about dinner tonight?" Steven asked. She became sullen,

"I don't think so."

"I need to talk to you, to clear up some things," he pleaded.

"No need, the only clearing up is in my own head," she sighed.

"Morris, I want to see you!" Steven yelled.

"I know, another time, okay? Bye," Meggie hung up the receiver.

Thanksgiving vacation Meggie returned home, making an appointment with Dr. Marcus.

"Meggie, how's school?" Dr. Marcus entered the examining room.

"I think I need a shrink," she said, sadly.

"What makes you say something like that?" Dr. Marcus inquired, examining her.

"I'm totally confused. I don't know where I'm headed, or where I'm coming from, seventy-five percent of the time. At other times I simply want to close the entire world out." Meggie was in tears.

"Meggie, get dressed, we'll talk in my office." Dr. Marcus stated.

A few moments later she walked into Dr. Marcus' office.

"You're one hundred percent physically. Now, what is this about a psychiatrist?" He questioned.

"Oh, Dr. Marcus! Sometimes I am so frustrated and I find myself not being able to deal with life," Meggie cried.

Dr. Marcus rose from his chair. He was a kindly gentleman of about fifty years. Placing his arm around her, he tried to comfort her as a parent would. My God! He brought her into this godforsaken world, he did care. She told him about Steven; he was already aware of Dennis. She told him of her confusion and her guilt, crying the entire time.

"Meggie, you are still growing up. This is what it's like, unfortunately. You're only seventeen years old. Don't expect life to be perfect; you are well aware it isn't. Be strong, you have to be to survive in the world today. I know you can," Dr. Marcus with his arms around her, holding her head against his chest.

"I don't know where to begin," Meggie still cried.

"You have to start with tearing down that wall you have built around yourself. The first time I noticed it, you were eleven, then, last year, it came down, only to go up higher and stronger than before, after Dennis died. You have to start enjoying your life again. God gave it to you and he meant for you to be happy. I know you loved Dennis, but he's dead. He would want you to be happy, to go on living. If someone such as Steven really cares, it's because you deserve it. Tear down that wall, let him in. I promise you won't be sorry. Remember, anything worth having is worth fighting for," Dr. Marcus moved back to sit behind his desk.

"Thank you for always being here for me," Meggie said, with tears still running from her eyes.

"You know I'm always honest with you," Dr. Marcus smiled.

"I know, I feel better just getting it out. Thanks for listening," Meggie forced a slight smile.

Dr. Marcus sank back in his chair with thoughts of Meggie. From the first time he had brought her into this world, to the beautiful child she had become. She would always be a child to him, no matter her age. It wasn't fair she had to deal with such pain. Damn, life wasn't fair!

At the same time, Steven was in Phoenix, Arizona, visiting his parents over this four-day vacation.

"What's wrong?" Steven's dad asked his son during their ritualistic stroll through the orange grove.

"It's nothing," Steven replied, glancing down.

"Not true. I know you son," Ian Roth said.

"Her name is Meggie," Steven smiled.

"So tell me, what is a Meggie?" His dad inquired.

"A Meggie." Steven laughed, partly because of how his dad phrased it, and partly because the mere thought of her did that to him.

"She's beautiful, she's talented and there is something mystifying about her. She is a truly fantastic creature, inside and out. She's a walking question mark, and yet the kind of girl you'd want to give a bunch of daisies to," Steven smiled to his dad.

"So, what's the problem?" Ian Roth asked.

"I can't figure her out! This has been the most mind-boggling experience of my life. She eludes, my rationale, my wisdom, my experience," Steven picked an orange from a tree and began to peel it. "She has a mind I would equate with my own. I've never been able to relate with anyone as I do her. Dad, I wish you could see her, she's absolutely beautiful!"

"I think you're in love, Steven!" Ian Roth said, surprised.

"Maybe. She is so exasperating and unequivocally frustrating," Steven said, staring to the ground. He went on, telling his father everything there was to tell about her.

"Steven, you're going to have tell her you want to know why she keeps running away from you. It may mean a confrontation, be prepared. You have no other choice because you care so deeply. It is obvious something is troubling her, you have to find out what it is. Remember, honesty is the single most important ingredient to any relationship," Dad embraced him.

During the course of next few weeks, Meggie and Steven saw each other occasionally, mostly in the S.D.S. trailer and dinner afterwards. She was still refusing to go out with him, until the Saturday just before the semester was to be over. Steven phoned her,

"Hello, Morris, would you like to go to an art gallery opening in Georgetown tonight?" Meggie hesitated,

"Okay."

"Pick you up at eight," Steven said, before hanging up the phone.

Meggie sat back in her bed, asking herself why she said yes. Shoot! She loved going to art galleries.

Steven happened to be quite pleased with himself, waiting to ask her and finding something he knew she would appreciate. He laughed, thinking about her, she was so unusual. Most girls demanded being asked out days ahead of time; he had to deal with their immature egos, not Meggie, only last minute invites for her. Steven decided that was her positive self-image.

Later that evening at the art gallery,

"You didn't tell me it was Chinese art." Meggie stated, not being able to take her eyes off the landscapes.

"I'm not familiar with art, Morris. I didn't ask when invited," Steven watched her so engrossed.

"It's difficult to understand a Chinese Landscape. It's as if the artist wants you to jump right into it," she gazed at another landscape.

"Isn't it marvelous!" She smiled at him. "I am so totally in love with Chinese art," Meggie took his hand, leading him across the room.

"Look at this! The strange paper and the unusual pigmentation of the paints," she stared at a painting. Steven smiled watching her.

"It must be ancient, like a priceless piece of art from another millennium!" she smiled. Her enthusiasm amazed him, drawing him closer to her.

Sitting in a dimly lit bistro in Georgetown later, Steven eyed her,

"I'm impressed, Morris. You really know your art."

"That's my thing," Meggie bit into her sandwich.

"Mine is history," he said.

"History, the accumulated events of mankind! It's never been one of my best subjects," she smiled. "I thought it was writing?"

"You need history to write. Do you know who made George Washington's false teeth?" Steven asked. Meggie laughed,

"No, I never really thought about it, either."

"Paul Revere," he grinned.

"I thought he was the one who rode his horse around warning the colonists, 'The British are coming, The British are coming'?" She laughed.

"He did that, too," Steven laughed with her.

"What color is yak's milk?" She smiled.

"I would imagine, white," Steven said.

"Wrong, pink," she laughed.

On the way back to her dorm,

"Morris, if you'll go out with me on New Years', I'll postpone my trip home." He stopped at a red light, looking at her expression.

"Don't change anything then, because I can't," Meggie stared out the car window at a street person.

"Why not?" He yelled, becoming more frustrated. "You're certainly not going to spend it alone."

"No, I'll be in Honolulu," she smiled at him.

"You're joking?" He said, surprised.

"Hardly," Meggie stated.

"How long are you going to be there?" Steven drove down Wisconsin Avenue.

"I'm leaving on the 16th for about six weeks," Meggie said.

"Six weeks!" He said in shock. Meggie started to laugh again.

"I don't believe I've told you about my family there, especially Lori." Meggie continued to explain the relationship, talking about Lori most of the time. She couldn't wait to see her again, missing her. As she spoke, Steven thought how much he still didn't know about her. Parking his car in front of her dorm, he watched her chattering away, never seeing her so wound up before. He leaned over,

"Shut up for a minute," he kissed her.

"I guess I was rambling, I do when it comes to Lori," Meggie smiled. Steven kissed her again.

Sunday, Steven phoned asking her to have dinner with him. Again, Meggie turned him down. Prior to this, he thought that he had been making some progress with her. Apparently he wasn't. He was totally perplexed. The night before they had a wonderful time, again. They laughed relentlessly, they agreed constantly; it was obvious they thought alike, in harmony.

Monday evening, the phone rang as Meggie was engrossed in a book for finals.

"Hello," she said, flipping through some pages.

"Morris, I'll be over in half an hour," Steven stated emphatically.

"No! I have work!" Meggie yelled.

"Listen, I'm leaving tomorrow, and I need to talk to you. This won't hold for a month and a half," Steven sternly stated.

"Meet you outside," Meggie said, taking a deep breath, hanging up the phone. She finished reading the chapter and headed quickly out of the dorm. Steven was waiting. She hopped in his car,

"What's up?" He didn't answer.

"Steven!" She loudly said. Still no answer, no acknowledgment.

They drove in silence until Steven pulled the car into Rock Creek Park, putting it in park and turning off the motor. He turned his body toward her, looking her right in the eyes,

"Okay, clever lady, I have had just about enough!" Steven stated harshly.

"What are you referring to?" A puzzled Meggie asked, staring down. Steven made her look at him,

"I need to know what is going on with you!"

"What?" Meggie wrinkled her nose. Steven grabbed her shoulders, shaking her a little. That really startled her.

"From the beginning! Why do you keep running away from me? From the first time I kissed you to the present, you've been refusing to see me more often! I know you enjoy being with me, we have a wonderful time together.

Damn it, Meggie, you're a paradox of ambiguity! You know exactly how I feel about you, you are driving me crazy! What the hell is your story?" Steven angrily screamed. The impact of what Steven had stated was starting to hit her. Shock was written all over her face, but she made no response.

"Well!" Steven yelled. Meggie burst into tears. He was surprised, never expecting her to fall apart like this. She obviously wasn't as strong as she pretended to be. Feeling somewhat badly, he put his arms around her.

"Oh, Steven," Meggie cried, resting her head on his shoulder.

"It's so hard to explain," tears still flowed from her eyes. "I can't talk about it, not yet." Meggie, still crying, hugged him.

He held her until her tears stopped, then he kissed her. They sat kissing for quite awhile.

"While you're away, think about this conversation. I hope when you return, you can level with me. I need to understand, Morris," Steven said, sincerely.

After driving back and stopping in front of her dorm, Steven grabbed her, kissing her again.

"Say hello to Pele' and Captain Cook for me," he smiled, before kissing her again so passionately.

"And don't forget the macadamia nuts!" He yelled, as she walked toward her dorm.

Approximately one week later, Meggie spent a day with Peter, then another one with Christine, Alex was not available. She boarded her flight to Chicago with a connection on to Honolulu. Daddy drove her to the airport,

"Daddy, what happened years ago between you and Ma," Meggie asked.

"Meggie, I really can't talk about it," Dad calmly stated, driving down Interstate 695. He was sorry he had allowed it to slip before, knowing he would inevitably be questioned about it. Once she had an idea she never let go, he smiled to himself.

"Why are you still keeping secrets from me. I'm older and wiser now, and I honestly resent it," Meggie coarsely stated. Morris Hiken laughed to himself, thinking, 'She thinks she's so old.'

"It's none of your business. It's not your place to be involved. What happens between a man and a woman is their private concern," Dad glanced toward her.

'Avoiding an issue—so typical of parents today;' Meggie thought.

On the plane there was nothing but time to think. First, she thought about her Zadie, such a marvelously strange person. She loved him so much, thinking about all of the happiness he had created. She remembered the time when they were little; he would bounce Lori on one knee and Meggie on the other, telling them how pretty they were, and how much he loved them. There were two things about Zadie that stood out in Meggie's mind: his love for his family and his prejudice.

Zadie had six children and eight grandchildren. Ben was the only grandson. He came to this country from Russia with his uncle, leaving his parents and brothers behind, in the late 1880's, at the age of eight. She remembered his broken English; he never learned the language well, even up to his death. She recollected her Bubbie with her long white hair, so long, always wearing it up with small combs. She recalled the home-canned fruits and vegetables from the farm. It brought tears to her eyes. In the early 1930's, Zadie was the first person to ever transport cattle by truck across this country, bringing them from Colorado to his farm in Pennsylvania. He built the first school there, he was even the only Jew living there. Meggie thought about all of the prejudice that existed back then. It still exists today, but not quite as bad. Zadie always believed in hard work and the fruit of the land; he lived by his beliefs, accumulating a small fortune before he died. He started from nothing. Meggie recalled him telling her, "When I was eight, I used to walk the streets selling shoe shines, so I could eat". She smiled to herself, trying to picture this. It was hard to visualize him as a young boy; she only knew him as an old man. She remembered the horse she named Nozzle he bought for her on her fifth birthday. It brought a tear to her eye. In January, 1958, Zadie died, leaving behind a legacy of memories, love and wealth.

Meggie sat back in her seat thinking of the time Zadie told her, "Toughness makes life bearable." She never really understood it, always thinking it was his bitterness, but she really wasn't sure.

In his lifetime, Zadie had worked hard to acquire three large dairy farms, supplying the states of Maryland, Pennsylvania and Delaware with the majority of their dairy products. He owned a vast amount of real estate, always acquiring, never liquidating. The farms were huge. Meggie couldn't imagine how many acres there were, knowing, when the time was right, Daddy would fill her in. He and Uncle Bob never sold them; they rented them out. She recalled the red brick rancher, which was her grandparent's home, sitting on top of a knoll, overlooking the largest section of land. They built it in the late 1930's. She remembered the long summer weeks she spent at the farm. Zadie used to drive her all over it, telling her stories. The biggest story was the one she had to tell. No one could know Zadie drove. His license had been revoked years prior due to his poor eyesight. He felt this was his land and he could do what he wanted on it. She recalled him saying, "The more land you own, the more you are your own man."

When Zadie died, the majority of his estate went to his two sons, Robert and Morris. Meggie knew he had set up trust funds for Lori, her and Ben. At the time they were eighteen, they could receive interest from the funds. When they turned twenty-one, they could have the principal. Zadie had always told her the importance of being your own person, making your own decisions; he felt money helped. Meggie thought to herself, such a wise man, before she fell to sleep.

Meggie awoke with a jolt, recalling her conversation with Christine a few days ago. She was sitting on her bed, snorting some coke, when Meggie walked in.

"It eludes me as to why you are doing this!" Meggie irately stated.

"I'm not in the mood to hear it," Christine looked down to the mirror in front of her.

"There's a question I need answered. Is this where Dennis got it?" Meggie asked.

"You, Meggie, sometimes you're like a mother hen, Dennis probably felt the same way!" Christine yelled.

"You little cunt! How the hell would you know anything!" Meggie screamed. (She couldn't believe that came from her mouth.)

"You'd be surprised!" Christine snickered. Meggie eyed her with such vehemence now. Christine rose from the bed and walked toward her. "You know, Meg, you never should have gone to Hawaii last summer and left him."

"I've been trying to deal with my guilt about that for a long time. I really don't need a guilt trip right now, even if it is coming from a totally fucked up person, who really doesn't know what the hell she is saying!" Meggie yelled, putting her coat on to leave.

"No! Then you better listen, little lady! The night Dennis died, he came here; he needed to talk to someone. But we didn't talk, we made love!" Christine smugly, standing with her right hand on her hip.

"You are a deceitful, cruel, vicious and destructive non-person!" Meggie shrieked, running from the apartment, almost knocking Alex down on her way in.

Meggie cried the entire time she drove home, changing directions, heading toward Peter's. She told him everything that had transpired between her and Christine. She cried the entire time she spoke with him, he was always a good listener and such a comfort. Her emotions were running rampant. The betrayal she felt was like a knife cutting inside her. The hurt, the pain, it was as if she was reliving Dennis' death, and she did not know whether she was tough enough to deal with this.

"I believe this was meant to happen," Peter held her, trying to comfort her. Meggie only looked at him questioningly.

"Maybe now you'll be able to start letting go. Dennis wasn't a saint! And now, maybe you can finally deal with his death," Peter brushed her hair away from her face, so he could see her.

The plane landed and it was wonderful to see Lori again. The two girls were up all night talking about their lives over the past few months. Lori had invites for herself and Meggie to many parties but Meggie refused to go. Lori had also lined up dates for her cousin but Meggie refused again. There was one time Uncle Bob had arranged a date for her and Meggie found she could not refuse. It was the night before Christmas Eve; he was the twenty-one year-old son of a business acquaintance of her uncle's.

"What's he like?" Meggie asked.

"He's a ten, but shy," Lori smiled.

Later that evening when Meggie returned home, Lori inquired,

"It seems he didn't appeal to you?"

"Shy should not necessarily mean a bore!" Meggie stated. The two girls laughed.

That was it for her. She had fulfilled her commitment; no more dates! She took to walking and thinking on the beach, knowing she needed to sort things out in her head. During one of her many nightly beach strolls, a young man approached her,

"I've seen you moping around out here lately."

"It escapes me as to where it's your concern," Meggie stated to this person, keeping pace with her.

"True! Did you ever consider talking it out with someone, an unbiased someone, an uninvolved someone, a non-judgmental someone?" He still walked with her. Meggie thought to herself, how could she bare her soul to a perfect stranger? As if he were reading her mind,

"Sometimes it's easier to talk to someone you don't know. They're more objective. Don't you think?"

For some strange reason, she rambled on about her problems to this person as they walked along the beach, for over two hours. She confided everything to this perfect stranger, she was in total shock that she had when she finally looked at him. He sported a beard and a mustache, dark brown, and long, very long dark brown hair fixed in a ponytail in the back. He stood about five-foot-nine. She felt him to be not attractive. She then smiled at him,

"Why am I telling you all of this?" He broadly grinned,

"Because you needed to get it out, and I'm a great listener."

"Who are you? And where did you come from?" Meggie curious.

"The name is Richard, and I came from the house over there." He pointed to a run-down shack. "How about something to drink?" He noticed Meggie hesitating. "Certainly you can trust me, after all, you just told me your life story. Come on," Richard moved his head, motioning for her to follow, which she did.

His house on the inside wasn't as bad as she had anticipated. It had a very small but adequate kitchen and a living room with large pillows for seating. A totally filled, floor-to-ceiling bookshelf encompassed one wall. A similar bookshelf stood against the opposite wall, filled with record albums and a stereo. He handed her a cup of tea,

"It has honey in it, only natural foods for me."

"So Richard, what do you do?" Meggie sipped her tea, sitting back on the pillows.

"I know everything about you, except your name," Richard smiled.

"Oh!" she started to laugh. "It's Meggie."

"Meggie, not bad. It fits. What's your sign?" Richard looked into her eyes, finding himself mesmerized by them.

"I don't know," she smiled.

"When were you born?" He asked in disbelief.

"May twenty-first," she said. Richard smiled,

"You're a Gemini."

"You never answered my question; what do you do?" Meggie said again. He laughed a little because his intention was avoidance. He never meant to allow anyone in.

"I'm an Aquarius and I eat all natural foods. I smoke a little pot and I do a lude occasionally."

"I certainly hope there's more." She gave him a questioning look.

They talked for over half the night, Meggie learned he had graduated from Berkeley as an English major, then decided to drop out of society. He came to Hawaii because he thought it to be the most copacetic place to do so. He wrote poetry, selling it basically to children's' magazines, and bringing in enough money for him to barely get by. Richard pointed to a bookshelf.

"That's the heavy stuff; no one has ever read it."

"That's a waste, why not share it with the rest of humanity?" Asked Meggie in hesitancy.

"Because they're not ready for it!" Richard stated.

Meggie saw him every day after that, thoroughly enjoying their conversations, feeling she was growing from them. She thought he had a great head, intellectually stimulating.

On New Year's Eve Lori started on her again.

"Come on, Meg, it's New Year's. It's going to be a fun party," Lori said, trying to persuade her to go.

"No, I'm not in the mood," Meggie flipped through a magazine.

"You're going to stay here all by yourself, making me feel guilty for going," said Lori, getting angry. Meggie smiled,

"No need for guilt. I'll probably go over Richard's."

"He's a waste! He's a beach bum!" Lori yelled.

"Hardly, he's far too intelligent to be a beach bum! How can you judge someone you don't know?" Meggie glanced at her.

That evening, Meggie took her familiar stroll along the beach, intentionally ending up at Richard's door.

"You bringing in the New Year alone?" She smiled.

"I usually do," Richard said.

"How about some company?" She asked.

"Why didn't you go to the party with Lori?" Richard asked.

"I'm not up for idle conversation. You avoided my question again," Meggie laughed.

"Sure, come on in." Richard started to laugh, seeing her still standing by the door.

They drank some wine, took a lude and at midnight, they toasted in the New Year, 1968. The year of college campus unrest, the year of runaway teenagers, the year of riots. The tragic year! The year two great men were assassinated: Dr. Martin Luther King Jr. and Senator Robert F. Kennedy. Both men had the knowledge and wisdom to bring some sort of substance to this archaic society we live in. They were shot down trying, relinquishing any remaining hope.

Meggie lay back on the pillows in Richard's living room, being fully aware of how high she was,

"You want to make love?" She laughed after saying it, this was not her style, though she felt the need to be close with someone.

"Not with you! You're too fucked up; I don't intend to add to that," Richard put another record on the stereo.

Later when he walked her home, Richard smiled,

"Meggie, you have to know how attractive you are. At another time I would be ecstatic to make love to you. Right now, it's imperative you get your head together first." He placed a kiss on her forehead. She hugged him,

"Thank you, you're a wonderful person and a good friend."

As he walked away, looking back at her, he thought to himself, 'I must be out of my mind.'

During the course of the next couple of weeks, Meggie saw a great deal of Richard. Their relationship was not one of lovers, but one of good friends, totally platonic. She convinced him to allow her to read some of his poetry, and was impressed. She thought him to be very gifted, telling him so. One night, he saw this beautiful girl lying on his pillows again, with a forlorn facial expression.

"Hey, you there! Open your eyes and see what's coming down!" Richard yelled to her. Meggie glanced up, startled by what he had said and by the tone of his voice.

"I'm sick and tired of seeing you like this. Life is for the living, if you haven't noticed. What gives you the right to waste yours? If you desire to throw yours away, why not walk out this door into the Pacific Ocean and keep going until it swallows you up for the fish to feed on! You're far from the only person on this earth who has had to deal with death. It's a part of living! It's about time you grew up and accepted life!" Richard screamed.

"Oh! You're into reading my mind lately!" Meggie yelled, with tears filling her eyes.

"I don't bother with trash novels!" Richard candidly stated. Meggie felt the cut, crying even harder.

"I know it's hard to lose someone you love, but that doesn't mean you can't care about someone else, or allow someone to care about you. Life does not stop. Every experience, no matter how bad it feels, has something positive in it. Take the positive, keep the memories, throw the other shit away," Richard said, meeting her eye.

"And another thing, take that thing off from around your neck. It's like an albatross hanging there!" he screamed.

Meggie rose, running from the house without a word to him, heading down the beach, crying hysterically. 'Albatross!' she thought to herself, crying the whole way back to Lori's. Finding her not home yet, Meggie flopped herself on the bed, crying herself to sleep, for at least the hundredth time since Dennis's death.

At 5:45 a.m. Meggie awoke with a sudden shock. She sat on her bed for a couple of minutes before moving to the dresser and took a small box from the top drawer. She glanced at Lori, sound asleep, before climbing back on her bed, placing her legs in a yoga position, sitting with a straight back. Staring at the box in her hands, tears rolled down her cheeks. After a few minutes, she removed the chain with Dennis' ring from around her neck, placing it gently in the box. Looking at the pinkie ring, she removed it, placing it there also. She cried, staring at it for awhile. Then she placed the box, now having contents, back into the top drawer of the dresser, closing it very slowly. Dressing quickly in a pair of shorts and a tee-shirt, Meggie left for the beach. The tears were still flowing from her eyes; the sun was coming up-the beginning of a new day. 'Aurora!' She thought, 'The dawn, a new beginning!' She started to run, thinking, 'The beginning of a brand new life. Mine!'

That evening Meggie went to see Richard. Not knocking, she let herself in and saw him standing by the kitchen sink. He was surprised to see her.

"Someone can wallow in their grief for so long. Then comes along a friend to bash her head in. Thanks, I deserved it." Meggie said, with a few tears and a big smile.

"Welcome back," he smiled, embracing her. Then he neared his bookshelf. "Stop thinking so much, especially on airplanes. It's obviously not healthy for you. You should read more." He handed her a book.

"*WAR AND PEACE*, " she stated, reading the cover.

"You will love it!" He smiled.

In the next two weeks, Meggie had Lori take her shopping, since she hadn't bought anything new for herself for over seven months. She started to play tennis again, she started to live! Still seeing a great deal of Richard, she would never forget what a wonderful friend he had been. She started looking toward the future for the first time in so long.

"Let's go to Europe this summer," Lori smiled. Meggie stared at her in shock. "You'll be eighteen by then; we have our own money! As females we are legally adult. We don't need anyone's permission."

"You have a devious mind," Meggie laughed.

"I know, isn't it wonderful?" Lori smiled.

"It's a great idea; let's do it!" Meggie smiled. The girls made their plans before Meggie boarded her flight home.

V

Late one Tuesday afternoon, toward the end of January, Meggie entered the S.D.S. office, throwing Michael a newspaper she had picked up in Honolulu a week prior.

"What was this all about?"

Hearing the sound of her voice, Steven glanced up. Rising, walking toward her, he did a double take. Her tan was unbelievable, he thought, her hair even blonder, obviously streaked from the sun. And that sweater—purple, perfect for her. He saw Michael unfolding the paper to the front page. Curiosity got to him. He neared where Michael was seated. Gazing at the paper and seeing a picture of Michael on the front page, he was shocked. Michael smiled,

"Me and Kennedy Airport had this disagreement, like, sitting in front of the Eastern counter for three days, protesting a ticket price hike they laid on me at the last minute." He stared at the picture.

"When did you get back?" Dottie asked, seeing Meggie sinking into the sofa.

"This morning," Meggie smiled at Steven, then turned back toward Dottie. "I'm totally exhausted, still suffering from jet lag. I thought I left this morning in plenty of time to get here for registration. Of course I got stuck in traffic on the B. W. Parkway, therefore I was quite late! Would you believe Sparks' class was closed! I was forced to seek him out, it took me over two hours to convince him to let me in," she yawned. She stood, putting on her coat.

"Morris, where are you going?" Steven watched her.

"Oh, here are your nuts," Meggie threw him a can of macadamias. He smiled, she remembered!

"First to get something to eat, because I haven't all day, then to sleep," she smiled.

"Wait! I know just the place for exhausted, empty-stomached people," Steven chuckled. Meggie laughed, stepping outside into the frigid weather,

"It's button-up weather." Steven placed his arm around her.

During the following month, Meggie and Steven saw a great deal of each other. No longer turning him down, always going with him, she loved being with him. Steven questioned her new attitude toward him, and at the same time, wondered why she hadn't said anything concerning their conversation this past December. He decided to wait until she was ready, not wanting to chance another confrontation. Everything appeared to be going along well at this point, why risk it?

Hillary, Dottie's roommate, had become engaged over the vacation. Wedding plans were set for June. Meggie informed Dottie of her planned trip to Europe this summer with Lori, and asked her to join them. Dottie's dad would not permit it. One weekend, to Steven's dismay, Meggie persuaded Dottie to go skiing with her. It felt so good to ski again, to feel the cold wind against her face, to feel the freedom as she came down the slope. Damn, she loved it.

After returning home from the ski trip, Mouse blurted out,

"I'm pregnant," as she watched Meggie study.

"What?" Surprised Meggie said, thinking she didn't understand.

"I'm pregnant," Mouse stated, again.

"How? When? Why? What are you going to do? We'll find out about an abortion!" Meggie yelled, excited.

"Aren't they illegal?" Mouse questioned.

"Sure, but when did that ever stop anyone?" Meggie responded. "So, tell me about this."

"He's in one of my drama classes, I went out with him a few times, that's all," Mouse said, with tears in her eyes.

"That's all!" Meggie yelled. The only response from Mouse was tears. "Does he know?"

"No! And I don't intend to tell him," Mouse stated emphatically.

"Why not? It's his responsibility too," Meggie angrily.

"He hasn't phoned me since December. In class he practically ignores me now," Mouse cried. Meggie put her arm around her,

"We'll take care of it. Everything will work out, you'll see."

'Oh God!' Meggie thought to herself, 'What a mess! These goddamn, irresponsible guys!' Meggie found out the names of some so called doctors who performed abortions. She told Mouse about them.

"I don't think so. I'm planning on having my baby," Mouse stated, placing Meggie into shock.

"What, are you nuts?" Meggie yelled, as Mouse walked from the room. She had never won an argument with Meggie and she knew she would never get her to understand. She didn't expect Meggie to, she could not give up a part of herself. Her mom had died a year ago and since that time she had felt so unloved. There was an unexplainable void! Her dad retreated into himself, only having time for his farm. Now she would have someone to love and someone who would love her back. She needed that.

The following Saturday morning , a short stocky man entered the lobby of their dorm.

"I'm Mr. Donlop. Where can I find my daughter Melissa?" He asked the girl behind the desk. She directed him.

"Oh, baby," he walked into the room and looked at Mouse, before hugging her. "Everything's going to be alright. Papa's here. I know I haven't been for some time, but I am now," he stated with tears in his eye, still hugging Mouse. It brought tears to Meggie's eyes.

"I'm sorry. I love you so much. You are all I have in the world," he still embraced her. He turned to Meggie who was taking all of this in.

"Thanks for being such a good friend to Melissa. I want you to come visit us," he picked up Mouse's luggage.

"Mouse!" Meggie yelled, running to hug her. "Be happy."

"Oh Meg!" Mouse cried, holding her so tight.

Meggie walked back into her room and sank into her bed, recalling the first time Mouse had walked into her life. She remembered her conversation with Ma before Christmas.

"Tell me, how's your roommate?" Ma asked, being busy for a change, not even looking at her as she spoke.

" Mouse? Oh, she's fine. You know that's exactly what she is, squeaking around and cleaning most of the time," Meggie laughed.

"I'm delighted one of you is neat," Ma stated, now looking at her. Meggie felt the intended cut.

Sitting back, smiling to herself, she thought, 'Who's going to clean this room now? I wonder if I can get a service,' she laughed.

A couple of weeks later, Dottie walked in and saw Meggie on the bed studying.

"Why don't you clean up this place?" Dottie went around the room, picking things up off the floor.

"Are you kidding? Cleaning is a disgusting job," Meggie watched her, now knowing who was going to do her cleaning.

The last Saturday in February, Meggie made Steven another wonderful meal. Afterward they curled up on the sofa in front of the fire together.

"Is there anything you can't do?" Steven asked her. She smiled,

"I'd like to know, is there anything you don't think of."

"What are you talking about?" Steven asked.

"The Valentine cards you sent me. One was postmarked, Kissimmee, Florida; the other, Valentine, Nebraska!" She smiled. Steven hugged, then kissed her.

"You haven't answered my question yet," he stated.

"There are plenty of things I can't do," Meggie said.

"Okay, Morris, name one," Steven smiled.

"I can't clean, I'm the worst at it," she said. Steven laughed.

Leaning over her, he kissed her again and again. With his hand moving up the side of her body, he started caressing her breast. Meggie jumped to the other side of the couch.

"I'm not ready for this!" She screamed.

"Why not?" Steven grabbed her arm. "We have more chemistry than DuPont!" .

"Accept it, I can't handle it!" Meggie became frustrated, clenching her fists.

"You know how I feel about you! I thought you felt the same way!" Steven yelled at her. "Damn it! I want you! You know what," Steven stood and stared at her sitting on the sofa. "You are the most exasperating person I have ever had the pleasure of meeting!" He looked her in the eye, holding it there and continued.

"You with your long blonde hair, your tight fitting sweaters, revealing your breasts and erect nipples. Your body-fitting jeans, that make me want to grab your ass. Don't you think the way you dress can entice a guy, especially me! There's a difference between looking and touching, which means frustration! I feel like you are always putting me on the back burner to sizzle for a while! You really have a way of making me angry; I'm getting pretty damn tired of it! There's a limit to my patience and to my understanding!" Steven angrily.

Meggie clenched her fist again, glanced down at her chest; then she started to cry. Steven sat beside her, placing his arm around her shoulder. Somehow, she had a way of getting to him, he smiled to himself. Sometimes she seemed so mature and at other times like a little girl.

"I can't," Meggie said, still crying. "Help the way I look in clothes," she bit her bottom lip.

"Morris, I guess you can't," Steven smiled. "You know what, I wouldn't want it any other way."

Almost a week later, on a Friday afternoon, Meggie and Steven were alone in the brownstone. Meggie was supposed to be painting by the front window. Instead, she stood gazing through it with the end of the paintbrush in her mouth.

"You look as if you're in a trance," Steven placed his hands on her waist, kissing the back of her neck. She turned around,

"Steven sit down," she walked toward the sofa, sitting in a corner of it. From the tone of her voice he knew she was serious. His curiosity was aroused, therefore doing as she instructed.

"I've been trying to figure out how to say this. There' s only one way—honestly." Meggie looked at him.

"Growing up was different for me. I've had to do it in odder ways than most." She glanced down, then toward him again.

"Back in December, you demanded answers. I do appreciate the fact you haven't pressured me. You know the old saying, truth is stranger than fiction. I am now prepared to give you your answers. I hope you're ready to hear them," Meggie rose and started to pace.

"The summer before last, I spent in Hawaii. I grew up a lot that summer, in many ways. I had never had a boyfriend, nor did I date; I was too brainy, choosing not to socialize. The stigmatism of being labeled a smart kid can really do a number on a person's head." Meggie paused, trying to get her thoughts in order. Steven thought, 'That's it, some jerk dumped her.' She began pacing again,

"Anyway, when I returned, I met Dennis and fell in love. We were totally in love. I know that for a fact! He was a wonderful person, the first and only guy I ever made love with. It happened on our class skiing trip, the Christmas before this." Having Steven's full attention,

"The entire mess started last spring. I insisted he go to a party with me at Christine and Alex's, girls I know from Maryland Institute. Alex gave us some acid but Dennis enjoyed doing it too much. We fought over it all of the time. Shortly after our prom, I found out his parents were having extremely heavy problems. They were getting divorced for one, which alone is enough to mess up a person's mind. His dad was also about to be indicted for mail fraud and embezzlement. After graduation, I left him in the hands of his older brother, Victor, and I left for Honolulu. I needed a break; I have always spent my summers in Hawaii since I was eight. Four weeks later I received a phone call from Ma. Dennis was dead!" Meggie stopped and looked at Steven's surprised face. She sat back in the corner of the sofa, bending her legs against her chest, putting her arms around them and resting her chin on top of her knees.

"He was involved a car accident. An autopsy revealed he was tripping his head off, along with a nice amount of cocaine. He went off the deep end when his dad was found guilty. His dad received five years, and everything they had was going to be lost, nothing left. Of course, Lori and I flew home immediately for the funeral, a very shadowy flight, I may add. It was the most difficult thing I have ever had to do in my whole life. I loved him so much! I had been going through hell and then I met you. You were like a life raft to a drowning me!" Meggie had tears in her eyes, Steven was still in shock.

"You always seemed to be able to make me laugh. You know, you have a way of doing that, making me feel better!" She smiled to him.

"I felt like I was in a dark tunnel and I couldn't find my way out. You helped show me the way! If it wasn't for you and the help of good friends, I may never have lived through this nightmare," tears rolled from her eyes.

"It must be unbearable to see someone you love behind bars," she whimpered.

"It must be harder to bury him," Steven put his arms around her.

"I started playing tennis again, going shopping and that's why I went skiing. It's sort of like when you fall off a bike as a kid, you get right back up and try again," Meggie said.

"Don't you see, you accomplished the impossible; you made me relax, you made me laugh," she said, still with tears in her eyes.

"Morris, in my wildest imagination I never thought of this. That must have been his ring you wore around your neck," he embraced her.

"I didn't think you noticed! I was sort of in a time warp. It's put back in the past too, I believe I finally let go. Now you know why I ran out of the car, why I couldn't see you too much, being guilty and fearful all at the same time. Why I'm not ready to go to bed with you. You are right, you deserved an explanation, probably before this. I simply wasn't ready to give it to you or to myself, before now," Meggie's tears still rolled down her cheeks.

"Shh, it's all behind you now," Steven held her tight. "I'm glad you finally told me." He stared into her watery eyes before kissing her.

That night as Steven lay in his bed thinking about what Meggie had confided in him, tears came to his eyes. He thought about all of the hurt, guilt and anger she had felt. He thought of all of the pain she had to endure and that she was far more sensitive than he had ever imagined. He realized at the same time, she would be afraid to love so deeply again. He planned on changing that, being so in love with her. She was so different from anyone he had ever known. He had even taken the ribbings from his roommates over the past few months because he couldn't get her into bed. None of this mattered any longer, because now he understood, he knew where she was coming from. 'His Meggie,' he thought, and one day that would be so. He fell asleep with a smile on his face.

The following month seemed to literally fly by. Meggie wrote telling Lori everything, along with plans for Europe. Steven and Meggie were seeing more and more of each other. The week before a sit-in was planned for late March, their relationship got a little too hot and heavy for Meggie.

"Steven, it's not time yet," she gave him a leery look. They were sitting on the sofa in his living room with her sweater off; he was trying to undo her jeans.

"Morris, it's time to live in the present, to look toward the future, and the past is where it belongs, in the past. You, of all people, should know life is too short to waste it arguing," Steven said, hugging her. "Come on, I'll take you home," he stood, handing her sweater to her. He looked at Meggie very sad-eyed, knowing he wouldn't push, part of him understanding, but not quite being able to accept.

The day prior to the sit-in, the S.D.S. office was bustling. Everyone was there helping to get it organized. They despised this damn war. Far more effort went into this protest than the ones before since they hoped to bring out more people.

"Meet you here tomorrow," Meggie said to Steven, before he left.

"I won't be here," he stated, hoping to avoid it, not wanting to get into another confrontation with her.

"Why not?" Meggie in disbelief. This was so unlike him.

"I have a paper to finish. Morris, that's not the whole truth. I have bad feelings about this one. I've learned over the years to go with my instincts, they're damn good. Stay with me tomorrow, don't go," Steven placed his hands on her shoulders, looking into her eyes... that literally lit up with fire after his statement.

"I'm going with or without you!" She yelled, turning around giving him her back. Meggie turned back to him,

"Aren't you the one who told me, when you have principles you believe in, you do something about them?"

"Morris, you're right. This is different, though." Steven hugged her, thinking, 'I better watch what I say to her in the future.'

Dottie, Michael, Meggie and at least a thousand other people sat in Market Square, protesting this pitiful war. It was pouring down rain. Meggie figured she was sure to get sick and thought, 'What an experience!' What started out as a peaceful demonstration turned into something horrifying. Policemen came storming at them bearing clubs. She wasn't prepared for them or the rain. Wearing only a sweatshirt and a pair of jeans, she started running for her life, after seeing a cop, swinging a club, coming toward her.

"Remember the First Amendment!" Meggie yelled in fear. He grabbed her arm and she didn't resist, he led her away. She saw people literally getting their heads banged in, bodies covered with blood. She witnessed one cop standing over a nineteen year-old kid, clubbing him, until he could no longer move. 'Masochists!' She thought. 'Oh my God! Steven was right, how is he so perceptive?' As she climbed into the paddy wagon, this ogre of a cop spoke to her,

"You're going to find yourself spending the night in a nice cold jail cell."

'Such bastards,' she thought, on the way to the lock-up. She remembered her first confrontation with a cop. He wanted to make her; she would never trust any of them. Never! Then, wondering where Dottie and Michael were, she prayed they weren't hurt.

A short while later, in the police station, some cop yelled,

"Meggie Hiken." She thought, 'Jes!, they took my fingerprints, my picture and my identification. What else could they want from me?'

"Over here," her voice cracked as she answered.

"Follow me," he opened the cell, letting her out. Frightened, she followed him into the sergeant's office.

"Miss Hiken, you're a juvenile, you're under eighteen. We have to call your parents to come pick you up," Sergeant Williams looked at her. Meggie stared at this huge, black sergeant, remembering what Daddy said last October, when he came to get her, Dottie and Michael.

"Next time, young lady, if there should be one, and I certainly hope not, you are coming home to live and to go to school. I mean that, Meggie!" Dad yelled.

"You kids are so damn idealistic. Haven't you realized yet you're not going to change anything?" Dad was angrier than Meggie had ever seen him.

She thought quickly, "My parents are out of town," she struggled for words. "They're out of the country, in Europe," a very scared Meggie uttered, looking at Sergeant Williams.

"What do you suppose we should do with you? Juvenile Hall?" Sergeant Williams asked, not quite believing her.

"I have an older brother in grad school at G.W.," Meggie said, still frightened, hoping Steven would pick up on this.

"What's his number?" Sergeant Williams picked the receiver up from the phone. Meggie gave it to him, hoping, praying and watching him dial. She was able to tell when someone answered on the other end, she trembled with her fists clenched again.

"I would like to speak with Steven Hiken," Sergeant Williams stated into the receiver. Meggie's stomach was doing somersaults. There was silence on the other end of the phone. After a few seconds Steven thought, 'Meggie!' He decided to play this through.

"Speaking," Steven curiously.

"This is Sergeant Arnold Williams from the sixty-third precinct. I have your sister Meggie with me. She was picked up during a protest demonstration tonight. Can you come down and take her home?"

"Leaving now, Sergeant," Steven said, before slamming down the phone, grabbing his coat and running to his car. "Damn it!" He said to himself, driving there. The entire way, he kept repeating, "I knew it! I knew it! Why didn't I stop her?" Walking into Sergeant William's office he took one look at Meggie, and his heart sank. He'd never seen her such a mess! She was still soaked from the rain, her hair was scraggly and wet. There were smudge marks from dirt on her face. He neared her, and placed his arm on her shoulder, showing brotherly concern.

"Sergeant Williams, I'm Steven Hiken."

"Sign here; then you can go," Sergeant Williams handed him a pen and pointed to a paper on his desk.

"Let's get out of here," Steven stated. He led her to his car and helped her in. She trembled the entire time. After he started the motor, Meggie spoke for the first time.

"You lied for me!"

"What should I have done? Let you rot in jail? What the hell happened, anyway?" Steven asked in a hyped-up tone. Aside from still being soaking wet and shaking, she was now crying too. He placed his coat around her, trying to warm her.

"You must be freezing, we'll discuss this later," Steven extended one arm around her, trying to warm her more, he drove home that way. After parking, he led her up the stairs of the brownstone.

"I think a hot shower would do you a great deal of good right now," Steven stated. Taking a shirt from his drawer and handing it to her, he went into the bathroom to turn the shower on. When he returned, Meggie was removing her wet sweatshirt, revealing her beautiful, firm, orange shaped breasts. Steven stood back in awe!

"Listen, I'll be downstairs when you're finished," he said, receiving a nod from Meggie before leaving the room. Hearing the bathroom door close, he returned to his room, gathering Meggie's clothes from the floor. Heading back downstairs, he threw them in the dryer in the kitchen, took a bottle of wine from the refrigerator and made a fire in the living room fireplace. He poured himself a glass of wine, sat back and thought how frightened she looked. He had never seen her so scared, recalling her eyes had turned green.

Upstairs in the shower Meggie thought luck or fate must have brought Steven into her life. She did not know what she would have done without him tonight. Maybe Daddy was right when he told her, "God places people in our lives for a reason." Thinking about her recent experience she became angry. Then she cried, being so disillusioned about life!

Steven heard the water in the shower go off. After a few minutes he saw Meggie walk down the stairs in his shirt, which came to her mid-thigh. Those legs, they're gorgeous, just like everything else about her, I've never seen them before. Meggie walked in and stood in front of him.

"Steven, thank you. I don't know what I would have done without you," she said, with Steven pulling her to sit on his lap. He looked in her eyes, noticing they were back to normal.

"Tell me what happened," he said. Meggie started to cry again, sliding from his lap to a sitting position next to him. He placed a comforter over her legs. She was still cold.

"Here," he handed her a glass of wine, not being able to take his eyes off of her. Even with red eyes she was a beauty. Meggie drank the wine, motioned for more. Steven fulfilled her request.

"We have no rights!" Meggie angrily stated. She proceeded to tell him about the whole unfortunate experience, about her disillusionment!

"Feel better now?" Steven smiled, with his arm around her.

"I feel like the world is out there, and it's just you and me," she smiled a little, he leaned to kiss her.

They continued kissing with Steven's hand on her hip, feeling her bare skin, because she had nothing to put on other than his shirt. He unbuttoned the shirt, revealing her breasts. She made no protests this time when he caressed and kissed them. She smiled at him when he looked at her. He smiled back, taking her hand, leading her up the stairs to his room. He kissed her more passionately than she'd ever been kissed, she thought, losing her balance, falling on the bed. She lay there watching him undress. He has a great body, Meggie realized for the first time. He came to her, placing his arms around her, holding her so securely, never wanting anything to ever harm her again. He kissed her, his tongue exploring every space in her mouth.

"I love you, I have for months. I believe you knew that. I love your eyes," Steven stared into them, kissing them. Then he kissed her nose.

"I love your nose, I love your lips." He kissed them, then kissed the top of her head.

"I love your hair, your ears; in fact, I love everything about you," he whispered, kissing her ear. He fondled her entire torso, sucking those beautiful breasts. He wanted every square inch of her, making love to all of her: her legs and her back. He smiled at how aroused she became when he ran his hands down her back. Meggie thought, 'He has the most extraordinary hands!' He proceeded to fondle and kiss her lower body. Then finally the hairy space in between her legs, discovering how wet she had already become.

"You are so magnificently beautiful," Steven said softly, kissing her again. Moving his hands up and down the sides of her body, feeling her rhythmic movements, then sliding himself over her, moving with her. Shortly after, they became one, two people entwined in each other. Steven thought, 'Just you and me.' That is exactly how it was as they made love two more times that night.

"Morris, I love you," Steven smiled at 6:00 a.m. after the last time. Meggie didn't respond, feigning sleep.

Later that morning Meggie awoke, finding Steven not beside her and hearing voices coming from the kitchen. She rose from the bed putting Steven's shirt back on, making her way down the stairs. Steven stood by the sink drinking a cup of coffee. Roger and Paul were sitting at the kitchen table eating cereal. She noticed their surprise as she walked into the room, heading toward the box of corn flakes and milk on the counter. She turned, giving Steven a kiss,

"Good morning." He blushed, never having seen this side of her before. She sat herself at the kitchen table, eating her corn flakes.

"Hey, Meg, were you at that riot last night?" Roger questioned.

"That's why I'm here, I was arrested," she smiled, looking toward Steven. "Do you have time to take me back before your class?"

"Only if you hurry!" Steven pulled her clothes from the dryer, throwing them to her. Finishing her cereal she ran up the stairs to dress, removing his shirt on the way up. Immediately after she closed the door to Steven's room, he walked in and took her in his arms,

"Why don't you stay here? My class is only an hour."

"I need to finish a painting," Meggie said. Steven kissed her and they fell on the bed again.

"On second thought, maybe I won't go to my class today," he kissed her again.

"You have a paper due, remember!" She laughed, standing nude in front of him. She dressed quickly and Steven took her to her dorm.

"Have I told you I love you lately?" Steven looked at her, wanting a response. Meggie leaned over to kiss his cheek and he grabbed her and really kissed her.

Driving to his class, Steven thought about the shock written all over his roommate's faces, he laughed.

Meggie walked into her dorm, peeked into Dottie's room, finding her safe and sound asleep. After taking a quick shower, she took out her paints.

"Oh shit!" She said to herself, finding it impossible to paint. She put everything away and headed out of her room toward the stairs.

"Where are you going?" Dottie sleepily yelled from behind her.

"Out!" Meggie yelled, not knowing where, nor did she feel like talking.

"Meggie!" Dottie yelled again, as her friend turned around. "Damn it! I saw them get you last night. Are you alright?"

"I'm standing right here, aren't I?" Meggie said, sarcastically. "What about Michael?"

"We managed to escape," Dottie stated. Meggie proceeded out of the dorm without another word.

At dusk that evening, Meggie ran across the street in front of her dorm, turning when she heard her name.

"Morris! Where have you been?" He yelled, stopping his car. She opened the door, sliding herself into the passenger's seat.

"I've been to London to see the queen," she laughed. It even brought a slight smile to Steven's distraught face.

"That's not funny! I've been worried!" He said, thinking, 'Anxious and angry also;' though, knowing her history, he was still more concerned. He had wanted to spend the entire day with her, phoning all day to find her not in. Damn, he was disappointed!

"It was not my intention to alarm you. I've been to the National Gallery," Meggie glanced at him, biting her bottom lip.

"For eight hours!" Steven raised his voice.

"Sure! It's a great place to think and lose yourself. I always thought art could avenge the soul, even when the soul resisted. I guess I lost track of time," Meggie smiled.

"Obviously!" Steven still irritated. "What did you think about?" He asked, not taking his eyes from her.

"You!" Meggie leaned over to kiss him. Which was partially true.

"Where should we eat?" Steven embraced her.

"You read my mind; any place but Mexican," Meggie smiled, holding onto one of his hands, not letting go.

"I know the perfect place for people who have been thinking about their lovers all day," Steven laughed, seeing her do the same.

They had a wonderful dinner, enjoying each other more than ever before, probably because of the recent closeness. During dinner, Steven found it difficult to keep his hands off her, touching and kissing her constantly. He was disappointed again because Meggie wouldn't go home with him, due to her unfinished painting. 'She's a contradiction in terms, this time being so righteous,' he thought.

Four o'clock the following morning, Meggie awoke to finish her painting. She couldn't sleep anymore, partly because she had never been a big sleeper like most teenagers. Also, she knew how unhappy Steven was the night before, because she couldn't spend the night with him. She wouldn't intentionally hurt him for anything—that wonderfully intelligent, sexy person. By 9:30 a.m. she was finished, probably because she was uninterrupted. Everyone was still asleep. She dressed, headed for the food store and arrived at Steven's by 11 a.m.

"What are you doing here?" Roger opened the front door, surprised to see her.

"Gee! It's nice to see you too! Where's Steven?" Meggie with bundles in her hands, making her way through the house to the kitchen.

"Still sleeping," Roger watched her take out the pots and pans.

"I was hoping so. You want some breakfast?" She smiled. He nodded yes, being amazed, seeing her busy at work. She brewed coffee, squeezed oranges for juice, and made eggs Benedict. Meggie handed him his and placed the rest on a tray. Taking one red rose from the bag, she started upstairs with the tray. Opening the door to Steven's room, she saw him sound asleep. She entered, placing the tray on the night table, and leaned over, kissing his tender lips.

"Time to get up bright-eyes," she smiled, watching him open his eyes. He embraced her tightly, to make sure this wasn't a dream.

"Morris! What a fantastic breakfast," Steven smiled, before kissing her all over.

"Steven, stop! I did make you breakfast," Meggie laughed.

"I thought you were it," he smiled, still half asleep.

"Come on, lazy bones, sit up," she propped the pillows behind him. Then placed the tray over his legs in front of him and they both ate from it. She never ceased to amaze him; seeing her the first thing in the morning, he thought he couldn't ask for more.

"The best breakfast I think I have ever had," Steven smiled, laying her back on the bed, kissing her. He gazed into her eyes,

"How's the kitchen?"

"Oh! I have to clean it!" Meggie very-bright eyed, tried to get up.

"Later, Morris," Steven smiled. He kissed her and rubbed the palm of his hand over her breasts. He couldn't get over how sensual she was, becoming excited so quickly. He nuzzled his head into her breasts, Meggie even liked the feel of his beard on her skin. But, she noted, his hands were the best! Especially when he ran them up and down her entire body, she quivered. Steven smiled, loving making love to her.

Afterward Meggie fell asleep in Steven's arms. He enjoyed that. He took the dirty dishes downstairs, looked at the kitchen and laughed to himself before he cleaned up the mess. A couple of hours later, he came to wake her.

"Morris, rise and shine," Steven bent over her.

"The kitchen!" Meggie jumped up.

"I took care of it," Steven hugged her.

"You did!" Meggie kissed him, throwing her arms around him.

That night they lay in bed holding one another, completely satisfied. Steven turned to face her, with both arms still around her,

"Morris, I've been reading the papers. It seems everyone arrested Thursday night at Market Square was booked, spending the night in jail before being released on bail. Why were you different?"

"I guess they liked my smile," Meggie laughed.

"That I can understand, because it lights up a room for me," he laughed with her.

"Seriously, now," Steven said, directly meeting her eye.

"Maybe because they told me I was a juvenile. I won't be eighteen for another six weeks," she looked at him, feeling him go limp. "I know what you're thinking-jail bait!"

"No! I'm not saying I'm not surprised. I am! You're far too much woman to be jail bait. You're just advanced beyond your years. In every way," Steven rolled over on top of her.

"God, I love you," he said, rubbing his hands all over her body.

Easter vacation was a week later, a four-day weekend. It was also Passover. On occasion they fell at the same time and this was one.

"I'm going home for the Seders. I'll be leaving Friday afternoon, but I'll be back Sunday evening," Meggie said, witnessing the surprise and hurt on his face. She refused to explain, being tired of it: first to Ma and now to him. No way! She needed her space and now was a perfect time for Steven to be made aware of that.

Friday evening, Meggie sat at the dining room table with the rest of her family. Ma said the blessing over the candles and Dad read the Haggadah. Amazed and bewildered, she was trying to understand why on holidays, such as this, her parents seemed so loving toward each other, when at other times they were distant. Her thoughts went well with the four questions, she imagined. Her parents relationship was strange, far beyond her grasp, she concluded. Finishing her fourth cup of wine and feeling a little tipsy, she thought about Steven but decided to put him out of her mind. Ma made a wonderful meal as usual. The doorbell rang; it was Peter. Meggie led him into the den. She sat on the sofa with her legs bent under her.

"How's school?" She smiled.

"Great! The best move I've made yet! Mardi Gras was not to be believed," Peter handed her a poster. "Next year you must come." He watched Meggie's expression when she unrolled the poster.

"I love it! Thank you," she said, kissing his cheek.

"You look good! So tell me, what's been happening since I saw you last Christmas?" Peter leaned back on the sofa. Her life always seemed so interesting to him. Watching her he couldn't help but smile, recalling all of their experiences. Meggie told him about Hawaii and Richard, about Mouse, about her relationship with Steven and the last sit-in. He listened, taking it all in curiously.

"He's important to you," Peter said, referring to Steven.

"True, I feel good when I'm with him. But, I don't think I can love anyone the way I did Dennis," Meggie said. Peter looked at her,

"Or, you won't allow yourself to."

"How can you say that?" Meggie yelled in anger.

"Meg, you can't live with that ghost forever, you know." Peter smiled, knowing he got to her and her mind would eventually start to work on it.

"Maybe not, time will only tell. I've learned time is a good healer. The void isn't there so much anymore and sometimes, weeks or even more go by without my even thinking of him," Meggie held Peter's hand, happy for his friendship. "Peter, you have to understand, I won't allow myself to hurt like that again."

"You're making progress, even if your defenses are still up. I guess we can thank Steven," Peter smiled.

"Him, time and good friends," Meggie kissed his cheek.

They were up till three in the morning, talking, playing the piano, singing and reminiscing.

Saturday afternoon, Meggie met with Rochelle. It was good to see her. It's been too long, Meggie told her.

"Bob and I aren't together anymore," Rochelle stated.

"I'm shocked, what happened?" Meggie asked.

"Some of it had to do with Dennis' death," Rochelle eyed the ground.. "If you don't want me to go on, it's okay." Rochelle looked at her now. Meggie thought, one person's death can affect so many lives; only because he affected so many when he lived.

"I need you to talk to me." Meggie said.

"I became pregnant, something must have been wrong with the diaphragm I was using. Bob wanted to keep the baby and name it after Dennis. I wasn't ready for motherhood, not just yet, and I knew it would never have worked. As immature as we were! At that point in our relationship we had been arguing for months. A baby would have made things worse. Bob was drinking too much, missing Dennis too much and using me to take out his frustrations. I had the abortion by myself because he wouldn't have any part of it. That was the end of it. It's probably better this way. It's strange, every time we looked at each other we thought of Dennis." Rochelle had tears in her eyes.

"I guess, it's like, when two people share a secret; when they're far apart it's no longer a secret," Meggie hugged her friend.

After Rochelle's visit, Bob called before coming to see her. He told his side of the story. They were both her friends; she decided not to get in the middle. This was Saturday night after the second Seder and he was still there when Peter arrived. The three old high school friends went out together on this cool, moonlit night in April.

Sunday morning Meggie rose, showered and headed toward the kitchen to find Ma. She walked to the refrigerator, opening it.

"I'm going back to school today, can I take some stuff for Steven?" Meggie asked, taking food from the refrigerator.

"You should have brought him home for the holiday," Ma looked at her. It must have been the first time her mother looked at her when she spoke.

"But, I didn't!" Meggie stated.

Ma knew better than to question her about this. Meggie always had a reason for doing the things she did, even if her mother didn't agree. Ma quietly packed up the food her daughter wanted to take.

Meggie thanked Ma, gave Ben a kiss and walked toward Dad to do the same.

"I think we should talk," Morris Hiken glanced at his daughter before walking to the den. Meggie followed him.

"Is that for Steven?" Dad eyed the bags of food.

"Sure," Meggie placed the bags on the floor.

"Come sit by me," Dad pat the sofa next to him. Meggie sat with her eyes focused on him.

"I can't believe how you have matured over the past couple of years. It seems like yesterday you were a baby," he glanced at her, aware the rest was not going to be easy to say, especially to a daughter.

"Are you aware of the ramifications the physical act of love carries with it?" He was still looking in her eyes, noticing an element of surprise. There was silence for a moment; he had never spoken to her about such things before.

"No need to worry, Daddy, I am aware," Meggie placed her arms around him, hugging him, not noticing the tears in her dad's eyes.

After she left, Morris made himself a stiff drink and sat back in his big chair in the den. He really wasn't surprised. Meggie was always independent and intelligently advanced. Now she's a young woman. He downed his drink.

Driving back to school, Meggie thought about her weekend, smiling. She enjoyed herself immensely. She parked in front of Steven's, glancing at her watch. It was 1:30 p.m., she was early. With bundles in hand and a small suitcase, Meggie, overloaded, rang the bell. Steven, clothed in nothing but a pair of jogging shorts, opened the door. 'How I love his hairy muscular chest,' she thought.

"I brought you a care package from Ma," Meggie kissed his cheek before walking by him toward the kitchen. Steven followed her, watching her unload the bags without a word.

"You look surprised to see me," she smiled, going back to what she was doing.

"Surprised and peeved!" Steven turned her to face him.

"Why?" Meggie asked, very bright-eyed.

"You could have asked me to come home with you!" Steven stated, becoming angry.

"And you could have voiced your feelings! I thought we were going to have an honest and up-front relationship. That won't be possible if you choose not to speak what's on your mind," Meggie looked at him, then turned around to continue what she was doing.

Steven thought, how did she do that? Turn it around that way! Meggie realized she wasn't being fair. She walked near him, put her arms around his neck, and gazed into those light-blue eyes.

"I wasn't ready to tackle any questions from Ma, not just yet. Sometimes, we all need our own space and I wanted to spend some time with Peter," said Meggie, with Steven now holding her.

"Who's Peter?" Steven looked into those eyes.

"A very old and dear friend. He goes to Tulane, he wants to be an archaeologist. Can you imagine, a Jewish archaeologist! I asked him if he planned on opening a kosher deli in Saudi Arabia," Meggie threw her head back laughing. 'Damn it!' he thought, 'She gets to me every time.'

"I haven't seen Peter since before Christmas. Last night, he, Bob, another friend and I went down to The Block. I witnessed my first striptease show. It was wonderful," Meggie smiled.

"It would have been a tragedy if you missed such a cultural experience," Steven smiled.

"Think about this-how could you have slept, knowing I was in the next room," she laughed.

"Morris, it's not the truth that matters, it's what the mind can conjure up!" He said, emphatically. She giggled,

"You're a writer; you're always looking for a little mystery."

Steven pulled her closer to him, kissing her, feeling her go limp again. He smiled to himself and led her up the stairs. He undressed her as he held her and gently moved his hands down her back. He loved how sensual she was and knew she was made for him. Passionately he kissed her and squeezed her tightly.

That night, during dinner from Ma's care package, Meggie glanced at Steven, "How long have you had that growth?" He looked at her questioningly.

"Oh, my beard! You have such a unique way with words. I guess about four years," he laughed. "Why? I thought you were getting used to it."

"I just wanted to know," she replied, nonchalantly.

"Out with it, Morris! Up front, remember," Steven said.

"I'd just like to know what you look like, that's all," she smiled.

"Your Ma's a great cook," Steven said, changing the subject of the conversation.

The following morning Steven slid back into bed beside her.

"Morris," he whispered in her ear. Sleepily, she turned over then jumped to a sitting position, reaching to touch his face.

"You're gorgeous!" She screamed, kissing every square inch of it.

"If I'd known you'd react like this, I would have shaved long ago," Steven laughed, drawing her toward him, stroking her bare breasts.

During the course of the next few weeks, the S.D.S. office was bustling. There was a great deal of mimeographing to do because many future sit-ins were planned. After her previous experience, Meggie chose to write articles on the war for the American University paper, instead of participating in the sit-ins. This also left more time for her to paint.

One afternoon in Steven's house, where Meggie had become a permanent fixture, partly because he always wanted her with him, and partly because she loved painting scenes in Georgetown.

"Hey, Meg, why don't you put your paints away? I'm getting tired of looking at them," Paul yelled to her. Meggie walked from the kitchen drinking a glass of water. Steven stood beside her.

"She's the only person I know who uses the floor as a closet," Steven laughed. Meggie almost choked as she swallowed, taking the three-quarters full glass of water, and dumping it over Steven's head before running. Before she could even make it up two steps, Steven caught her by the waist and they fell on the floor at the foot of the stairs. Pushing his way on top of her, the water dripped on her face,

"I imagine all creative people have at least one idiosyncrasy." They both laughed, kissed and started doing more than that on the living room floor.

"Take it upstairs, you two," Paul laughed, being genuinely happy Steven had finally found someone special after all of these years.

Early that evening, Meggie awoke to find Steven not next to her. She walked down the stairs.

"Where are my paints?" She was looking for them.

"I put them away," Steven laughed, putting his arms around her.

"I've been cleaning up after you for over a month now, I may as well continue," he smiled. She kissed and threw her arms around him.

"Hey! We've got to be out of here soon," Roger entered the room, becoming aggravated. They remembered Steven had promised Roger the use of his car for the night after they got Meggie's.

"I'm going to take a quick shower, be ready in fifteen minutes," Meggie ran up the stairs. She stopped abruptly mid-way,

"What are we celebrating that I have to get dressed to go to a fancy French restaurant?"

"Our anniversary, Morris; two months of truth and honesty," Steven laughed.

"Oh!" She smiled, running up the stairs.

Two minutes later Steven walked into the shower, watching the water run from her head to her toes. Taking the soap from her, he washed her entire body, then she, his. He hugged and kissed her, touching her all over.

"Not now, Steven! Roger's in a hurry," Meggie said.

"He can wait a couple of minutes," Steven smiled, getting his way.

Hearing the noise coming from upstairs, Roger turned to Paul,

"She's really inconsiderate; she knows I'm in a rush."

"Calm down! You always blame Meggie; it's probably Steven," Paul smiled.

Within ten minutes Steven was dressed and downstairs, seeing a very irritated Roger.

"Meggie will be down in a minute," he said, then saw her walk down the stairs in a low-cut, turquoise mini-dress.

"No matter what you may think of her, or my relationship with her, you have to admit she's beautiful," Steven smiled, watching her.

"You're prejudiced, but she is a real looker," Roger stared at her and wondered where she ever found white leather boots.

A half an hour later, Meggie and Steven sat in her car with him trying to start it. No such luck. He stood from the car and looked under the hood.

"Morris, some rejected retard stole your battery!" Steven yelled.

"Shit!" Meggie got out of the car, walking toward her dorm.

"Where are you going?" He followed her.

"To call a service station," she replied.

"Sure, who's coming out on a Saturday night?" Steven asked, keeping step with her.

"Mr. Nachio will," she smiled to him. "He's Korean. My Dad's bank gave him a minority loan. I've been dealing with him since I've been here. Really a nice man, he'll tow it, fix it, and probably sometime Monday, I'll be able to pick her up. But that doesn't do us any good right now."

"We'll take a cab!" Steven smiled.

"You are really wonderful, not allowing an experience such as this to put a damper on our celebration; instead, making it work for us," Meggie kissed him.

They went back to the brownstone in a taxi, after a perfectly marvelous meal.

"I could become used to traveling like this, having someone else do the driving so I could sit back, hugging and kissing you," Steven said, with his arms around her.

"The problem is, I don't like an audience to our conversation, our kissing, or to where your hand now is," Meggie laughed, feeling his hand on her right breast.

"I am in love with you, don't you realize that?" He kissed her.

"Steven, I know, you've told me enough. But are you aware of the amount of time we spend in bed?" She inquired.

"Remember the first time we had dinner together, I told you how much I liked sex? It's one of my passions. With you, it's making love and total perfection," Steven smiled.

"True!" She laughed, with Steven placing his hand in her dress to feel her bare breast.

"You know why that is?" Steven took her in his arms, looking into her eyes. "We're so alike, we enjoy the same things, we learn from each other. We even think alike. We have the same ideals and beliefs and we desire the same things out of life," he kissed her. "Morris, we're meant for each other. I sensed that from the first time you opened your mouth. Then I took a good look and knew you were meant for me."

The cab dropped them off in front of the brownstone. As they walked in, Paul inquired,

"Why don't you come to the party with us?"

"I'd love to go!" Meggie excitedly answered.

"I wouldn't," Steven stated.

"What's the matter? You afraid I'll find out what a Don Juan you are? Your reputation precedes you," Meggie laughed, throwing her head back with her hair dangling down. Steven drew her toward him, forcing her to look at him.

"I haven't seen, touched or done anything with any other female for months now!" Meggie gave him a strange look out of the corner of her eye.

"Paul, you tell her," Steven said to his roommate.

"I don't have to, she knows," Paul smiled. Hell everyone knew!

"Tonight, we celebrate two months of truth and honesty. I know you're telling the truth, Marathon Man," Meggie laughed, throwing her arms around him. She whispered in his ear, "Besides, things travel too fast around my campus."

"If you really want to go to this party, we'll go." Steven said.

"It would be nice to be out in public again. This hermitdom is starting to get to me. I really don't care about the women in your life prior to me," she smiled.

"We'll go," Steven laughed, looking at his roommate. Then, turning to Meggie, "Marathon Man?"

"Aren't you?" She smiled as Steven drew her close.

"In fact, I love your wit, too." Then he kissed her.

The following morning, Steven awoke to find Meggie still asleep. He decided he would serve her breakfast in bed for a change; she had done it for him so often. On his way up the stairs with the tray, she was coming down,

"Morris! You should be in bed; that's where you're having breakfast."

"Wonderful!" Meggie yelled, running back up the stairs, sitting on the bed waiting for him.

He placed the tray in front of her. Meggie looked it over carefully. Coffee, fresh squeezed orange juice, toast, scrambled eggs and bacon.

"Thank you, Marathon Man," she placed a kiss on his cheek.

While they were eating, the phone rang.

"Meg, it's for you," Paul yelled from downstairs.

"Hello," Meggie said into the receiver.

"Where have you been? I've been trying to get in touch with you for days. If I didn't hound Dottie, I wouldn't have this number now!" Ma said angrily.

"Hi, Ma." Meggie said, nonchalantly.

"Well, where are you?" Ma screamed.

"At Steven's," Meggie uttered.

"What are you doing there?" Ma was still angry as Meggie still ate.

"Eating breakfast," she smiled.

"Where were you yesterday?" Ma demanded.

"Ma, what do you want?" Meggie was becoming hostile, not appreciating this inquisition.

"I wanted to know how you are," Ma stated.

"You need to put me through a tyrannical rage to find out how I am?" Meggie asked with tears. "Ma, I'm wonderful, anything else?"

"No." Ma never knew how to answer her when she turned things around.

"Bye, then," Meggie said, before hanging up the receiver, leaning back on the bed with tears running from her eyes.

"Morris, what's the problem?" Steven put his arm around her.

"With Ma, there's always a problem," Meggie stated, solemnly. "Most girls I know have a relatively decent relationship with their mothers, not me. I never have; I happen to have one who doesn't love me and never did!" Tears flowed down her cheeks. Steven tightly squeezed her,

"I don't believe that for a minute! To know you is to love you."

"You'll see," Meggie cried on his shoulder.

"Even so, I have enough love it won't matter." He kissed her, made love to her without either of them finishing breakfast. Afterward, Steven rolled over to look at her.

"I'm going to Europe this summer with Roger and Paul. I'd love for you to come with me." Meggie laughed hysterically.

"I can hear my Dad now. Don't you think he'd give his blessing?" Meggie said sarcastically, laughing. She tried to calm herself. "Besides, Lori and I have planned a trip there this summer."

"I told you we think alike!" Steven hugged her. "Great minds do work alike, don't they, Morris?" Steven placed an arm under her and brought her to lie on his chest. She didn't respond.

VI

The semester was over a few weeks later. Steven drove back to Phoenix for a couple of weeks before leaving for Europe. His plane abroad was leaving one week before Meggie's and landing in London; hers was to land in Paris. They compared itineraries, deciding they had to find each other somewhere along the line. If by chance they didn't, they would go to the American Express office in Rome to claim mail. Before getting into his loaded-down car in front of Meggie's dorm, Steven took her in his arms.

"See you in Europe, Morris," he smiled, before kissing her. "I'm going to miss you."

"I'm going to miss you," Meggie sadly, not wanting him to leave.

"I love you, Morris." Steven looked into her eyes for some expression. He turned, climbed into his car and waved to her standing there as he drove away.

Once home with his parents, Steven and his Dad took their familiar walk among the orange trees.

"From the looks of you, son, things with Meggie must have worked out," Ian Roth slightly smiled.

"She's wonderful. She's a human jigsaw puzzle with a supercharged imagination," Steven laughed.

"How'd she get you to shave your beard?" Dad smiled.

"She told me she wanted to see my face," Steven laughed.

"Bright girl," dad said. Meggie accomplished what he had been trying to for four years; she accomplished what he thought the impossible.

"That she is! You know, no matter how worldly or sophisticated she tries to appear, there's a certain degree of vulnerability about her." Steven looked at his father before continuing,

"One problem, she won't tell me she loves me, though I know she does. Every time I say it, it only seems natural she respond. It would be nice to hear."

"It's harder for some people, though I know how you may feel. Reassurance aids security," Ian Roth placed a hand on his son's shoulder. "Not bad, only one fault."

"Wrong! She's a slob, not about herself, her appearance or her work. She's incredibly talented, her paintings are unbelievably orderly. She refuses to put anything away or clean up, and you wouldn't believe the messes she is capable of creating. She says cleaning is not the manner in which she wishes to channel her energies. Besides, it's a disgusting job," Steven laughed. His father joined him,

"I can't wait to meet her. She sounds like a real card!"

Back in Baltimore, Meggie was picking Lori up from the airport. The girls chattered incessantly about their forthcoming trip. First stop, Paris.

"I wonder if it's true French men are the best lovers?" Lori smiled; the two girls laughed.

"Have you spoken to Victor?" Lori asked her cousin.

"No," Meggie bluntly stated.

"He'll call today," Lori confidently said. Meggie loved her cousin, but hoped he wouldn't. She managed to avoid him until one night when he came to pick Lori up, and Meggie had to answer the door.

"Hi," Victor said, walking in.

"Hello," Meggie replied coolly. "Lori will be right down." Meggie started to walk away.

"Wait, don't run off." Victor looked at her. "Lori tells me you have a new boyfriend."

"So," Meggie replied, sarcastically.

"So, I can't believe you! Dennis hasn't been dead for even a year yet! You didn't even wait for his body to get cold before you let someone else in your pants," Victor screamed angrily.

"It would be fine if it were you, right?" Meggie yelled back.

"That was uncalled for!" Victor yelled, knowing he had given her reason to feel that way in the past. But not now!

"Right! And I'm King Tut! My life is none of your goddamn business!" Meggie shrieked.

"Obviously, you couldn't have felt the way about Dennis you claimed. You're nothing but a hypocrite!" Victor still yelled.

"Look who's calling who a hypocrite, the master of the trade!" Meggie screeched, with all of her vocal chords.

"What is going on in here?" Lori came busting in, turning to Victor. "Shut up!" she screamed.

Meggie ran up the stairs with Lori following.

"You okay?" Lori concerned, touching her cousins hand.

"I knew this was going to happen. I'll be fine. You know, I never liked him." Meggie said, angrily.

"I know, you've told me enough," Lori smiled.

"Go on, I'll be alright," Meggie smiled to her.

Meggie decided she wasn't going to stay around for four more days until her flight left. She phoned Peter, who was now working in Ocean City. He told her of course she could come stay for a few days. She packed her bag and told Ma and Ben. She wrote Lori a note; and of course, Daddy wasn't home when she left for the ocean.

Meggie returned from the ocean with just enough time to pack. On the way to the airport, Dad lay down some rules for the girls. He made them aware he didn't think this trip was a good idea.

"Oh, Uncle Morris, you know we can take care of ourselves," Lori smiled excitedly.

"I question that at times," Morris Hiken stated.

Meggie was sort of in a trance through all of this. She hated being lectured to, especially since she had turned eighteen. She was feeling her independence. The legal age of adulthood, she thought.

"What about you, Meggie?" Dad looked at her.

"What!" Meggie glanced up, unaware of the conversation.

"You didn't hear a word I said!" He yelled.

"Daddy, we'll be fine. Don't worry so much. Give us some credit," Meggie smiled, feeling unfair rules were made to be broken.

"You worry me, you know that?" Dad motored down Interstate 695. He cursed his father to himself for leaving her that money.

Upon arriving at Dulles Airport, outside of Washington D.C., the excitement amidst the two girls was at a fever pitch. Morris watched them board their flight, feeling his heart sink. His Munchie was no longer a baby. She had let him know last spring but this only made it far more apparent.

The plane circled Orly Airport for over an hour before landing. On disembarking, Meggie screamed, "Bonjour Paree!" and threw her arms in the air, spinning her body around.

After collecting their luggage, they looked in their *EUROPE FOR $5.00 A DAY* by Arthur Frommer, to find a decent place to stay. They found a wonderful little hotel on the left bank, in the Latin Quarter.

The following day the first stop was the Louvre. At night they walked by the Arc de Triomphe and Notre Dame. They went up the Eiffel Tower, losing their hearts to this wondrous city. Meggie thought her favorite place in Paris was going to be the Louvre. It wasn't, she loved sitting by the St. Germain, finding intellectual conversation in French, along with great food. On the way out of the city they stopped at Versailles, wondering how anyone could have lived in this massive palace. All of the gold, silver and mirrors: what a waste, too gaudy. Meggie knew Steven would agree with her. He was beginning to be a part of her, more than she ever realized or chose to admit to anyone, including herself.

They took a train out of France, eventual destination, Madrid. They stayed for a day on the northwest coast, in the beautiful ocean-front city of San Sebastian. Then heading south through the Spanish mountains, where many an American Western had been made, to the beautiful, fantastic and energetic city of Madrid. Looking through their book again, they chose a pension and hoped it would have a room.

After spending two days at the Prado, Lori stated, "I've had about enough of this museum."

"Not me! I'll never get enough of it; the Goya's, El Greco's, Velasquez," Meggie sighed.

They exited the museum, heading toward the great Royal Palace. Then to a bullfight on a Sunday afternoon, seeing thousands of people cheer at the slaughter of a defenseless creature. Meggie thought she must be strange for hating it—the blood, depressing.

One evening, their waiter from the pension took them to the Caverns of Madrid. They expected to find caves; instead, it was a bar and restaurant below ground level. People were drinking and singing. The girls joined in, enjoying themselves immensely. They learned they should go where the people go, not to Barcelona, but to Tossa del Mar, an old fishing village thirty kilometers north of Barcelona on the Costa Brava. Barcelona was too expensive and touristy, a young man informed them.

Disembarking from the train, totally amazed, they marveled at this little village. Cars were not allowed in the village and the very narrow roads were blocked off for pedestrian use only. The old Spanish-style buildings butted up right against the edge of the roads. They found satisfactory accommodations, unpacked, ate a late lunch and set out for the beach. The beach was made up of little cream-colored pebbles approximately one sixteenth of an inch in diameter. It was a different type of sand, one they had never seen before, visually beautiful. They spread their blanket and removed their shoes.

"They hurt my feet, these little pebbles," Lori stared at the strange sand.

"I know. Race you to the Mediterranean!" Meggie smiled, running toward the water.

"I have never seen anything so clear and green before. Look down Meg, see your feet. Can you believe this!" Lori said excitedly. They were completely entranced by the beauty of the Mediterranean.

A short distance away, a young man watched the two turquoise bikinis frolicking in the water.

"It can't be. It is!" He said, staring.

"It is what?" His friend asked, sitting up. Too late, he was gone. He hadn't seen her for five weeks. He ran toward the girls,

"Morris!" Startled, she turned around.

"Steven!" She screamed with excitement, running toward him. Steven lifted her off the ground, spinning her around, kissing her. Lori walked toward them,

"I'm glad to finally meet you, to know you're not a fragment of her vivid imagination."

"This has to be Lori?" Steven said, seeing Meggie shake her head yes, then he shook Lori's hand.

Back on the beach, Roger was disappointed.

"Oh, it's only Meggie."

"But, who's the brunette?" said Paul, rising.

"Hi, Meg," Paul kissed her cheek, glancing at Lori.

"Hi, this is my cousin, Lori." Meggie smiled toward her. "This doll baby here is Paul," Meggie hugged him. At the same time she saw Roger approach.

"And this is Roger."

Steven took Meggie's hand, leading her away from the group. Walking down the beach, they talked about their experiences, the different places they had been. They wanted to share everything!

"I want to show you something!" Steven said, still holding her hand. He pulled her, running up a hill.

"Look, it's an old fortress! They must have defended the village from here. Come on!" Steven excited, led her through a six-foot tunnel. She stopped in amazement. He placed his arms around her.

"You can see for miles and miles," Meggie sighed, gazing over the Mediterranean.

"It's wondrously beautiful," Steven said, neither of them being able to take their eyes from it.

"It's romantic," Meggie smiled. Steven smiled before kissing her. They stood, holding each other and watching the sea for a long time.

"Morris, stay with me tonight," Steven said.

"I was planning on it," Meggie smiled, with a tilt of the head.

"Race you to the bottom!" She yelled, running. He smiled, running after her, keeping an eye on her the entire way down. They approached the group of three they left earlier.

"Lor, would you mind if I spent some time with Steven, like the night?" Meggie said to her cousin.

"Go, I think these two will keep me company," Lori smiled, expecting it.

"I can't imagine a prettier girl to be with," Paul said. Steven led Meggie away with his arm around her.

"It figures," Roger said, not to happily.

"Ignore him," Paul glanced at Lori.

Meggie and Steven stopped by an outdoor market, buying grapes, cherries, French bread, a large hunk of Swiss cheese and a bottle of Spanish wine. They entered the room of a nice hotel they checked into, over-looking the Mediterranean.

"This romantic enough for you, Morris?" He laughed, loving when he was able to please her.

"Oh Steven! It's wonderful!" Meggie smiled, glancing around the room. There was a double bed with a large headboard, Spanish-style furnishings and a private bath (which was rare for Europe when you traveled middle class). This was the first time she had a private bath since being there. It even had a bidet. Spotting the balcony, Meggie stepped out of her wet bathing suit, opened the double doors and walked out to watch the sea. Steven grinned watching her, happy modesty wasn't one of her virtues, thankful for that. He removed his bathing trunks and stepped behind her, taking her in his arms.

"It's beautiful, isn't it?" Steven whispered in her ear.

"We're so lucky," Meggie put her arms over his, watching the sea.

"We're the luckiest!" Steven turned her around to face him, looking into her eyes. "We have love." He kissed her, again and again. Holding her in his arms again felt better than he envisioned. Leading her into the room, he lay her on the bed.

"You gorgeous thing, have you any idea how much I love you?" Steven kissed her ears, her neck, her entire body. She did the same to his, until she felt his hands all over her. She threw her head back, jerking the lower half of her body. Steven smiled at her sensuality, he felt the moist hairy spot between her legs and moved his body on top of hers. He held her for a while, not wanting to let go. Then turned to her, moving her hair from her face,

"Morris, do you realize we're a perfect fit." She smiled,

"I felt that too." They both laughed at the pun. He squeezed her.

Afterwards,

"Now for a romantic dinner." He brought all of the food to the bed, laying it out, feeding Meggie. Later, after they had finished dinner and Steven had cleaned up.

"What are you doing?" Steven laughed.

"I've never used one of these things; I'm trying to figure out how it works," Meggie said, inspecting and sitting on the bidet. Steven laughed. She always did that to him, he thought.

"I'm terrific with inanimate objects! Get up, silly lady," he still laughed, walking toward her. He started to fool with some knobs and water came spraying out all over the place. Meggie laughed so hard it brought tears to her eyes, looking at a drenched Steven. She grabbed a towel and stood to dry him.

"You and your bright ideas," he laughed.

"Why, Mr. Roth, you burst my bubble. I thought you knew everything," she smiled, with a certain sparkle in her eye. Steven picked her up and lay her on the bed again,

"Damn, you have a way of getting to me."

"Marathon Man," Meggie smiled.

Having a continental breakfast in bed the following morning, Meggie and Steven discussed their future destinations. Steven and his friends were headed to Mallorca, an island off the eastern coast of Spain. Meggie and Lori were off to Marseilles; after that, Monaco.

"You girls are certainly partial to the better things in life," Steven said, drinking coffee.

"You know how I feel. Living only once, you must live it right! Besides, you know me, my creature comforts!" Meggie smiled. Steven hugged her. They made love one last time, not knowing when they would see each other again.

"How's Roger's Mom doing?" Meggie asked as she dressed .

"The same. When she dies, I'll hate to see what will happen to him," Steven sullenly.

"Look, we know it's not easy. I'm living proof of it. He'll have to deal with it; he has no choice," Meggie stated.

"Wrong! When his dad died almost four years ago, it nearly destroyed him. I don't feel he'll be able to handle this," Steven glanced down. Meggie walked close to him. He extended his arms around her,

"You see, Morris, everyone handles death differently. You're a lot stronger, more stable, more independent than Roger. Your parents always gave you the space to be your own person, to make mistakes, to grow. It's important to know how to stand on your own two feet, to learn to take care of yourself. In Roger's case, he was sheltered far too much. That's why they wouldn't allow him to go away to school. He lived home his first two years at American," Steven released her and walked out on the balcony. She neared him from behind, embracing him, resting her cheek against his back.

"It's baffling what parents can do to a head without meaning to," Meggie said with tears, thinking of Dennis. Steven turned, looked into those eyes, touched her face before kissing her.

Later that day Steven, Roger and Paul boarded their boat for Mallorca. Meggie and Lori planned on spending one more day in Tossa, for the sun. They found the Spanish such warm, friendly people and prolonged leaving this wonderful country.

"How was your night? You like Paul?" Meggie asked.

"He's a nice guy. It's Roger who's on my mind," Lori smiled.

"Roger! You always like the strange ones," Meggie laughed.

"You know, I always like a challenge," Lori smiled.

"He can't stand me, just like Victor," Meggie stated.

"Wrong! Let's leave Victor out of this," Lori grabbed Meggie's arm as they walked down the narrow streets of Tossa. "He's jealous of you and Steven. He's never had a real relationship with anyone, outside of his mother. She over-protected him. It really messed him up."

"Now his mom has cancer, she's dying. He has a big problem and he knows it," said Lori, with a tear in her eye.

"Lor, you have to be the most compassionate and perceptive person in this world. It confounds me you were able to arrive to this conclusion from one evening," Meggie stared at her.

That night they sat in El Club, a nightclub-type place in Tossa.

"I wonder if he's been circumcised?" Lori stared into space.

"Who?" Meggie questioned. Lori smiled,

"Roger propositioned me last night. I know he's not Jewish."

"The things your mind is capable of thinking up!" Meggie laughed.

They walked back to the pension, still in good humor, laughing a lot. They were both quite giddy, due to the lack of sleep from the night before. They decided to take a shortcut through the park.

"Bonjour, jeune filles," one of three French guys approaching them said. Meggie eyed them before responding, figuring they were in their early twenties.

"Bonjour," she and Lori smiled.

Within seconds, they found themselves on the ground, trying to wrestle these three guys off of them. Meggie thought quickly, 'What did daddy say to do?' Holding that thought, Meggie drew her knee up and with all of her strength she slammed it into the crotch of one of them. He rolled over, grabbing himself in excruciating pain.

"Get out of here, you perverts!" One of two American guys yelled, running toward them. One grabbed one of the French attackers who was trying to force himself on Meggie, giving him a full right to the jaw. On impact one could hear a crack. The other American kicked the one who forced himself on top of Lori in the stomach. The three French assaulters ran, one limping, holding his crotch.

"Thank you," Meggie rose from the ground, looking toward a redhead. She extended her hand,

"My name is Meggie Hiken and this is Lori Hiken. We're truly indebted to you," Meggie said, seeing Lori still struggling to her feet.

"You sisters?" The redhead asked.

"No, cousins. You got here in the nick of time. Thank you," Lori said, brushing the grass off her.

"From the looks of things, I think you could have handled them," a brown-haired guy said, extending his arm.

"I'm Jay Marks, my redhead friend here is Barry Schwartz," he said. The girls smiled at each other. Lori glanced around,

"Can we get out of here? This place is giving me the creeps."

They walked to a cantina close by, ordered some vino and Barry lit a joint. Meggie and Lori watched in shock.

"It's cool here," Barry said.

They talked for hours, learning their saviors went to school at U.C.L.A., and had two more years before graduation. Jay was from Cleveland, Ohio and Barry's home was in Vineland, New Jersey, not too far from Atlantic City, he explained. They had eight more weeks left in Europe, intending to make every minute worthwhile. After landing in Paris, Barry bought a VW bus for them to travel in. He planned on shipping it back to the States afterward.

"I think you two could use some bodyguards," Jay stated. The girls were in shock but didn't say a word. Seeing this Barry smiled,

"Listen, it won't be like that."

"You'll share the expenses, drive across the continent. It will be fun. Friends, promise." Jay said. Meggie looked at him,

"We're not exactly located on the plains of Galilee."

"Hands off, I promise. But how about some engaging conversation?" Jay smiled, liking her mind.

"We'll think about it," Lori stated. The girls said goodnight.

Walking to their pension, they discussed the situation, finding more pros than cons.

The following day, the four students left for Switzerland, a change in plans for the girls. After riding for quite a while, Meggie decided to do something constructive.

"Who are you writing?" Lori asked.

"Michael. He stayed in D.C. for the summer to keep the S.D.S. office going," said Meggie, still writing.

"Bullshit!" Jay screamed.

"What?" Meggie surprised.

"S.D.S., marches against the war," Jay said, sitting in the front passenger seat, with the two girls behind him.

"Somebody slam-dunked your brain! I can't believe you said that. At least we're trying to do something!" Meggie said in shock.

"Right! And Venus is twenty-seven million miles away. You have as much of a chance of doing anything as you have of going to Venus," Jay stared out the window.

"It's my right to make my own choice and I resent your cynicism," Meggie spoke to the back of his head.

"Then you're naive as shit!" Jay turned around to see her.

"Your credibility is a little suspect right now, so why don't you elaborate?" Said Meggie, angrily.

"Sometimes in life there are things that should be so clear to us and then we are oblivious. You have a great deal to learn. I was in Nam!" Jay stated.

"Some luck! Words fail me!" Meggie felt the cut and was being sarcastic. "I'm sorry, Jay, but you elude definitive classification. You're quite puzzling. When were you in Vietnam?" She showed concern.

"I spent two years at U.C.L.A. and, like a fool, I decided to take a year off school. I was drafted because I no longer had a college deferment. It was far from a pleasant experience. I nearly freaked out, and all because I needed some time to think about what I wanted to do with my life. I was there for the worst two years of my life. God help me, because I will never forget the hell I went through, the nightmarish hell!" Jay paused, taking a few deep breaths.

"You S.D.S.ers can protest all you want, it won't do any good. Those bureaucrats in D.C. have a tight hold on all of the strings. We're innocent victims of society; they decide whether we stay or leave. They decide the outcome of this war. They don't care about us. Don't you know a young mind is an undisciplined one?" Jay glanced at them.

"You lost me," Lori said to him.

"It's not my thought, it's what those middle-aged, ancient war mongrels in the Pentagon are all about," Jay stated.

"Tell us about Vietnam," Meggie said, curious.

"You're blind to what is really happening over there. It's something I do not talk about," Jay sternly said.

"That's the problem, nobody wants to talk about it. Put it in the closet, close the door, and come down on all of us who have not been there! It's easier that way!" Meggie yelled, thinking about her conversation with one Vietnam war veteran last winter.

"We live in the age of the atomic bomb. One day we're here, the next we're gone! That's what Nam is like, but worse," Jay stated.

"Sardonic wit!" Meggie smiled, liking his head.

"If people aren't made aware of what has happened, how do you expect change to come about? You have to have faith in the human race!" Lori stated. Meggie smiled inside. Lori always seemed to have this natural tact for everything.

"Who's going to change things, the S.D.S.ers?" Jay asked sarcastically. Meggie leaned into the front seat so she faced Jay.

"Obviously, you think poorly of us. We just want to help. Let us! Someone has to take the first step, let it be you," she placed her right hand on his left shoulder, then touched his face, feeling some sort of closeness to him, she could not explain.

"Somehow, I have the feeling we're not talking about informational use for protest marches." Jay said. Meggie smiled,

"I write for the American University paper. I don't march anymore. Like you, I feel they're making little impact. Information is the key ingredient to awareness. Awareness will bring change."

"I have never told these stories before. If you use them, I would appreciate it if you didn't use my name," Jay said.

"We've heard rumors of horrid atrocities happening there but it's important the whole world be made aware. Sometimes when you can't back up a source, it's not believed. If you choose to remain in the background I do understand. I will accept it, until you are ready to come out of the closet and make your story more believable," she said.

"You have a lot of brain power, don't you?" Jay looked at this beautiful, blonde S.D.S. person, finding he had developed a certain degree of respect for her.

"Here it is, two years of one Vietnam war veteran's life, December, 1965 through January, 1968," Jay said, pausing to think.

"You know L.B.J. inherited the legacy of this irrational war from Kennedy. When I was shipped over to that God-forgotten land, and that is exactly what it is, I had made one good friend, he was black. Believe it or not, his name was Jim Dean. I used to tease him all of the time." Jay paused again, reflecting with a smile.

"God, how I loved that guy. He was something special. There were two other guys in our platoon we became sort of friendly with, one black, the other Catholic. I guess the minorities stuck together. One day the Viet Cong charged us at Dong Hoi, that's in North Vietnam. A grenade came at me, Jim saw it first, pulling me out of range. He saved my life! I wish, with all of my heart and soul I could have done the same for him in Quang. We were engaged in heavy battle and I didn't know where Jim was. When it was over I went looking for him. I found him; I wish I hadn't. His head was blown off! It was the most horrid sight I have ever seen. I went into shock for days afterwards." Jay stopped talking, taking a bottle of Scotch from the glove compartment of the van. He took a swig and offered it around. Barry was the only one to take him up on his offer.

"After that, I was afraid to get close to anyone over there. Too much blood, pain and misery. One-third of the men who arrived by boat with me were dead after six months. Another third were addicted to heroin. Only ten percent of us survived that atrocious place. Out of five hundred, that means fifty, and half of us left disabled. To understand it, you had to be there," Jay said, with tears, drinking some more Scotch.

"I had no idea the statistics were that high," Meggie sadly.

"Not to mention the raping of a beautiful people, land and world. They had such an extraordinary gift of hope, even when so many Vietnamese were ruthlessly killed, murdered, slaughtered." Jay took another swig of Scotch before continuing.

"I had a wonderful Vietnamese girlfriend after being there for a year. She was the only one I allowed to get close to me; I was so lonely. She was so beautiful, I can still see her face! All of the Vietnamese were beautiful people. They didn't deserve this war; they were so unaware of what was happening. How they got it, I honestly will never know, unless it was from such outside forces that could not be reckoned with. I don't want to believe the U.S. inflicted it on them. They happen to be such a kind and gentle people.

Anyway, getting back to Nan, she lived in a small village outside of An Khe. One day I had leave. I was going to see her, I found the village flattened. That was the first time in years I prayed to God. Nan was pregnant with my child. We planned on being married in a week. I had gotten leave to bring her to see the base minister. I loved her... she was so gentle and kind, so tender and loving. She may not have been from our world, or understood our language or even what Jews are; but she was so good, sweet and, yes, innocent," Jay said, crying.

Meggie leaned into the front seat, putting her arms around him. She felt for him-his pain, his agony, his loss. Jay looked at her,

"I'm not finished, far from it." His tears still ran from his eyes. She was at a loss for words, hugging him. He pulled away, taking another drink, before continuing.

"A few months later, we were out on a maneuver. My captain had reason to believe the villagers at Quang Tri were sympathetic to the Viet Cong. Quang Tri is located a few miles below the northern border of South Vietnam. He set us up for an ambush on the village, really wanting blood. We were on the outskirts of the village. It was pitch black that night-it must have been around midnight-you couldn't even see your own hand in front of your face. No moon that night! There was one lone house, about two hundred feet in front of the village. A shot was fired from the house and our captain panicked. He ordered us to open fire on it." Jay stopped again, taking another swig of Scotch, with tears running from his eyes.

"We heard a sound from the house when we stopped. A small voice was calling out, 'Mama, Mama.' It's amazing how we hold onto life! Our captain ordered Bill, the Catholic, and I to go check. Do you have any idea what an automatic weapon can do to the human body? It's disgusting! Bill picked up a little boy, who couldn't have even been three years old. He tried to stop the blood from pouring out of his body but the boy died in Bill's arms. That night we slaughtered three women and nine children under the age of eight. Two were babies!" Jay cried.

"I have spent the past year trying to forget; now you have resurrected it! You have no idea how much I hate this war or would do to see it discontinued," Jay still cried. Meggie leaned to hold him,

"It was not in your control; you had no choice but to follow orders."

"It was sheer craziness, I lost part of me over there," Jay said, looking away from her.

"The villagers opened fire on us. Bill got it in the back. He's paralyzed from the waist down. The last time I saw him was before they shipped him home. He was so different. This war had taken it all out of him. His eyes were dull, like when you get old." Jay paused, thinking.

"Our captain was killed. I would say justifiable homicide. Do you remember what Thomas Wolfe wrote?" He looked at her, both with red eyes. She didn't answer.

"You can never go home again," Jay stated, still crying. Everyone in the van got the message. He would never be the same, no matter how hard he tried to close the door on the past. Heavy hearts were in the van that night. Everyone felt badly for him and those in Vietnam.

Four weary, teary-eyed students in a van pulled into Geneva that afternoon, after being up all night listening to a sorry tale.

"Is anyone in the mood for a big city?" Lori asked.

"No!" Jay, Meggie and Barry replied, in unison.

They ate lunch at a friendly little restaurant, learning they should go to Interlaken. They drove an hour and a half northeast of Geneva.

Meggie thought Interlaken had to be one of the most beautiful places in the world: awe-inspiring. A small village around a lake, surrounded by the snow-capped Alps was breathtaking. The beautiful deep green grass, the crystal blue water and the mountain peaks soared into the light blue sky. Swiss chalet-type homes spotted the mountain's terrain, like a fairy tale land. They took a train up the Grindewald and hiked for miles to play in the snow in summer. Swimming in Lake Brienz, eating Wiener schnitzel, they thought it was heaven. That night, she sank into her bed, exhausted, under a one-foot-thick down comforter, thinking she must get one of these. She thought of Jay, with great sadness coming over her. Steven then popped into her mind. How she missed him, and wished he were there to hold her.

They drove through the Swiss Alps to Lake Como in northern Italy, another Alpine village surrounded by mountains, but ethnically, so different. They marveled at the beauty of these two countries.

After that, to Florence, the city of art! It appeared so old, so ancient- the tales it could reveal! Meggie was insistent they see Michelangelo's "David", they did that first to shut her up. They took in the Uffizi galleries, the Pitti Palace, the Baptistery, the Duomo and went up the bell tower. They went to the church of Santa Croce, marveling at its memorials to Dante, Galileo and Michelangelo. They didn't leave the Medici Chapels all day. At dusk, they saw the Piazzale Michelangelo that overlooked the entire city, and one of the most fantastic sunsets they had ever laid eyes on.

The following day, on to Rome, savoring everything their eyes beheld on the way. The first stop was the American Express Office. Meggie found a letter from Steven waiting for her.

July 7, 1968

Hi Morris!

Isn't Europe fantastic! It's like an old world! You can read about a place but it's never the same as when you come to see it, is it? From here we're going to Pisa, you know how I've always wanted to see that tower lean. Plans from there aren't real clear right now. We should be in Athens by the end of the month.

I miss you Morris. Last night in bed I really wanted you with me. I fell asleep thinking about the mole near your belly button. By the way, you know I love it! I love you!

Can't Wait!

Steven

Meggie folded the letter and held it tightly against her chest with tears flowing from her eyes.

They drove down the Dalmation Coast of Yugoslavia to Dubrovnik, staying a day, before heading across country to Bulgaria. Destination Istanbul, Turkey. Jay and Barry were told they could score some hash there.

'A city of an entirely different culture, from a different time and space,' Meggie thought. They saw the Blue

199

Mosque, took a boat ride on the Black Sea, and snook a peak at the Soviet Union.

After that enlightening experience they headed toward Athens, with an overnight stop in Kavala, a wonderful little city in Northern Greece. There, they ate souvlaki, roasted and spitted chunks of lamb served on pita bread.

The following evening, the four students arrived in Athens and checked into the Hotel Plaka. Having a quick bite to eat, they sat, watching the Acropolis. Meggie thought, 'Tomorrow!'

"Let's see this glorious city at night," Barry declared to his traveling companions. They all agreed and after their meal, they walked the streets of this wondrous ancient city.

"Another era, another age, another world," Meggie said, throwing her arms in the air. Watching her, Jay knew in the future, his new friend would somehow help him make it through. They stopped at a little taverna located near their hotel, it seemed to be a pretty happening place.

"Meg, where are you going?" Lori yelled to her cousin, seeing her head toward a group of people, sitting around a table in the rear.

Meggie placed a finger over her mouth, signaling, don't say word. She leaned behind him, whispered in his ear.

"Hello, bright eyes." He jumped up and embraced her,

"Morris!" He kissed her and led her to a small table in the corner.

Lori followed her to the table with Jay and Barry.

"Hi, guys," Lori smiled at Roger. "Meet our saviors, Barry and Jay," she placed an arm around each of them.

"Here, sit. I'm Paul and this is Roger," he moved over.

"That must be Steven," Jay whispered in Lori's ear. She nodded.

Meggie and Steven sat across from each other at a little round table, staring into one another's eyes. They held hands tightly, not wanting to ever let go. Drinking ouzo and discussing experiences, they were all smiles, happy to be together again.

"How was the tower?" Meggie smiled.

"Not to be believed. You got my letter!" Steven said happily. "What did you do?"

"Looking back, I have to laugh," she laughed a little. Steven looked at her curiously, still astounded by her natural beauty.

"Barry and Jay insisted upon going to Istanbul to score some hash. On the way we had an accident on a major highway, up a mountain in Yugoslavia. It was a one lane dirt road! We came within inches of being killed, of going off the mountain! I'm delighted I can laugh about it now. At the time it was not the least bit funny," Meggie had tears rolling from her eyes due to laughter. Pausing to compose herself, she continued.

"After that wonderful experience, we were able to obtain a twenty-four hour visa to travel through Bulgaria. It's amazing. They are both Communist countries but Yugoslavia is so filthy, poor and backwards. I guess Tito doesn't rank too high with the Russians," Meggie placed her elbows on the table, leaning closer to Steven.

"Bulgaria's capital, Sophia, is the cleanest city I have ever seen. It's as if you could eat off the streets. Plus modern architecture. It's far from being under-developed or poor. One thing though-the Bulgarians wouldn't let us out," she smiled.

"Why, Morris? What did you do?" Steven laughed.

"Nothing! They wanted our money at the border. We didn't save our receipts when we exchanged it coming into the country and they wouldn't exchange it back without them. Nor would they allow us to leave the country with Bulgarian money! At the border, Lori and I went from car to car asking people if they would exchange with us. Most of them didn't know what we were talking about, not being able to understand us," she laughed. Steven visualized these two running from car to car. He laughed, thinking about what those straight-laced Bulgarians must have thought of them.

"Consequently, we stayed the night in the most expensive hotel we could find. We had a wonderful dinner, steak and bought all kinds of snacks and anything else we could find for the ride to Istanbul. The entire excursion cost a grand total of twenty-one dollars among the four of us! Can you believe it!" Meggie laughed so hard her eyes watered again.

"The following morning, the same border guard was there. We weren't planning on seeing him, thus being able to make our escape. He allowed us through, though. I believe he became sick of us. Between us, we still have over three hundred dollars in Bulgarian money. We haven't been able to exchange it anywhere. We've been told to try in Switzerland," she smiled.

"Only you, Morris!" Steven watched her admiringly.

"The irony of the whole situation is, after finally arriving in Istanbul, we were informed how totally uncool it was to try to score anything there-no hash; it's far too dangerous. The rumors about the Turkish prisons were horrifying! On leaving the country, at the border, the Turkish police took the entire van apart, even the doors, looking for dope. I watched in amazement. It was beautiful, educational and so totally different, but I'm glad I'm out of there," Meggie smiled, Steven leaned across the table to kiss her.

On the other side of the room, Lori sat down beside Roger.

"Hi, you okay?" She asked, seeing him stare at Steven and Meggie. He didn't respond, swirling the liquid around in his glass.

"She's peculiar," Roger stated. No one noticed, being engrossed in conversation.

Meggie and Steven approached the table. She motioned to Lori, who followed them outside. When Lori returned Roger stated sarcastically,

"It doesn't take a genius to figure out where they went!"

"What's the big deal?" Lori sneered.

"Your cousin has one hobby! It surprises me, after everything he went through to get her there," Roger took a swig of his drink.

"You're disgusting!" Lori yelled.

"He's jealous and grossly exaggerating," Paul glanced at Lori.

"Why do you have such a problem accepting they love each other?" Lori said bitterly to Roger.

"Because it's a one sided-relationship. All Steven!" Roger took another swig.

"If you think that, I suggest you get your head out of the clouds," Lori proclaimed.

"Steven's been a good friend to me. I don't want to see him hurt by a bimbo who is too independent! She would state her feelings if she had any. She's one cold broad," Roger uttered, still drinking.

"You obviously never took the time to know my cousin at all. Has it ever crossed that single digit IQ of yours there could be extenuating circumstances? You have the world market on problems cornered; no one else, but Roger has any!" Lori, angry, rose from the table, leaving the taverna.

"What circumstances?" Roger followed her, grabbed her shoulders and turned her to face him.

"It' none of your business! Get your hands off of me!" Lori enraged.

"Sorry." Roger, upset, removed his hands from her shoulder.

"I never should have let you get to me," she smiled, slightly. They walked down the street, with his arm around her shoulder.

Meggie and Steven walked toward the Hotel Plaka,

"We're staying here!" Meggie said, grabbing his arm.

"I always said you girls like to live high," Steven smiled, leading her into the lobby.

"We can't register. I already have!" She gently tugged on his arm.

"Would you care to bet?" He smirked.

"What about a different hotel?" Meggie said with raised eyebrows.

"This is the nicest budget-priced hotel. Only the best for you, Morris." Steven placed his arm around her shoulder, kissing her forehead. They walked to the desk and Steven registered as Mr. and Mrs. Steven Roth. On the way to the room on the sixth floor, Meggie turned to him.

"Why did you have to register like that?" There was a not too pleasant tone in her voice.

"Don't start, Morris," Steven looked at her out of the corner of his eye, laughing on the inside.

"Oh, Steven," Meggie sighed, entering the room. She stepped out to the balcony, looking up at the Acropolis on this moonlit, Athenian night. He stood behind her, placing his hands on her shoulders, resting his chin on top of her head.

"It's breathtaking," Meggie placed her hands over his. Her exuberance always got to him. He turned her around to face him.

"Not as breathtaking as you," Steven said, before kissing her. They hugged each other tightly.

"Alone at last, just you and me," he smiled, unzipping her dress, kissing her as it fell to the terrace. Leading her into the room, laying her on the bed, he couldn't take his eyes off of her while he undressed. She lay there, extending her arms for him.

"My Venus, my love goddess," Steven smiled again, looking into those eyes before making love to her.

Afterward, they lay entwined, staring out at the Acropolis, both happy they were together again.

"I only have two more weeks left in Europe. Come with me," Steven said, putting his fingers through her hair. God he loved her hair; he loved everything about her.

"You know better. I wouldn't do that to Lori," Meggie lifted her head a little to look at him.

"Why do you have to be so righteous?" Steven smiled, moving his wonderful hands all over her body, making love to her again. A couple of hours later he awoke. No Meggie. He sat up and saw her bend down on the balcony,

"What are you doing?" She stood up with her sundress in her hands and threw it at him.

"Hey, it's soaked!" He yelled.

"You left it out there! It was baptized!" Meggie laughed as Steven chased her around the room with the wet dress.

"Steven, don't," she laughed, before falling on the floor. He spread the cold wet dress over her body. He moved on top of her, feeling the wetness against his chest, kissing her, making love to her on the floor. 'I somehow never got enough of her,' he thought. Still lying on the floor, holding each other, she turned to him.

"How come you didn't get drafted?"

"I did," Steven stated.

"You did!" Meggie surprised.

"Why, Morris? You disappointed?" He kissed her, "It was right after I graduated from American, the summer before I met you, 1967."

"How'd you evade it?" Meggie lifted her head to see him.

"With the help of my doctor," he smiled. "I took a couple of speed, amphetamines, about an hour before the medical exam. They told me I had high blood pressure; therefore, I was not admissible. I was rejected, happily so. I was never so delighted in my life, except for right now."

"I was frightened. In fact, it went far beyond that. I couldn't even envision myself as a soldier," he reflected.

Meggie nudged Steven's shoulder, when awakening.

"Come on, get up! We're going to miss it!" She scurried out of bed.

"Miss what? It's still dark," Steven opening his eyes, unaware of what the rush was all about.

"The sunrise," Meggie threw his clothes to him. "Now, get up!" She smiled, tilting her head.

"Why do I want to see the sunrise in the middle of the night?" Steven, still lying in bed. Meggie walked over and leaned so her face was only inches from his.

"Because, silly, how often are you going to get a chance to see it rise from on top of the Acropolis? It's been said to be one of the most magnificent sights this world has to offer." She moved away, brushing her hair, with him watching. He could never get over her exhilaration for living.

"Morris, what time is it?" Steven finally rose from the bed, beginning to dress. "How did you get up?"

"I guess I have one of those built-in clock radios in my head," she smiled pertly. He approached her, drawing her close, kissing her.

"Steven, not now," she said, moving away.

A few moments later they were on the way up the hill,

"How's the dress?" Steven touched it.

"Still a little damp. I think I'll live," she smiled, grabbing his hand, pulling him to walk faster.

They stood on top of the Acropolis with their arms around each other, watching the sun as it rose from the Aegean Sea. It certainly was one of the most glorious sights this world has to offer. 'Definitely worth getting up for,' Meggie thought. Turning to Steven, she placed his face between her hands.

"You sorry you didn't stay in bed, Marathon Man?"

"You jest!" Steven placed both arms around her. "You are something else, Meggie Hiken."

They spent two more days together, sightseers by day and lovers by night. Parting was harder each time, becoming more difficult.

"Call you in three weeks," Steven said, holding her. "I don't think I'll be able to make it much longer than that before seeing you." He kissed her.

"Me, too!" Meggie had tears in her eyes. Steven kissed her better than ever, she thought. She watched him board his train with Roger and Paul. They were heading northeast; their final destination, Paris.

Lori, Meggie, Jay and Barry headed north in a beat-up van to Switzerland, hoping to be able to exchange their Bulgarian money.

In mid-August, Meggie and Lori arrived home from Europe, via TWA, landing at Dulles airport. Lori planned on staying for a week before returning to Honolulu. Being home for a few days,

"I think I'll go see Peter; you're busy with Victor, anyway." Meggie was sitting on her bed after a phone call from Steven.

"But Steven will be here in a couple of days," Lori looked at her.

"I know, but what should I do until then? Listen to Victor chastise me!" Meggie said, noticing Lori's acknowledgment.

The following morning the girls embraced, said their farewells and Meggie drove three hours to Ocean City. She parked on Fourth Street, got out of the car and walked to the boardwalk. She didn't notice the heads turning as she walked by, in a pair of white shorts and green top that tied right under, revealing her nice breasts. Walking into a little restaurant located on the boardwalk between Fourth and

Fifth streets, she sat herself at the counter and spoke to the guy on the other side.

"I'll have a coke please."

"Meggie!" Peter excited, ran from behind the counter to embrace her. "How was Europe? You lucky person."

"Wonderful! Can I stay with you for a few days?" Meggie smiled.

"Of course! But first I want to hear everything," Peter said, going behind the counter, handing her a coke then leading her to a booth in the rear. They talked for almost an hour. Peter handed her a key to a little beach front house he rented with two other guys.

"I have to get back to work now," Peter saw his boss walk in.

"I plan to lie on the beach, soak in those rays. See you when you get done. Thanks, Peter," Meggie kissed his cheek.

That night when they were out to dinner, Peter inquired,

"Meg, you know you're welcome, always; but, where are you going to sleep? The last time you were here, Alan and Stan weren't in yet. Now there are no extra beds, no sofas, only floor. I need my rest!"

"I'll sleep with you," Meggie eyed him slyly.

"You trust me!" Peter was shocked, but Meggie was quite serious,

"Listen, Peter, if we should consummate the lust that exists between us, we would end up with an eternal wall of separation. I know we wouldn't want to risk that. Therefore, I trust you," she said, trying to control herself before laughing hysterically.

"You know, you really had me going there. Something else, you are so right," Peter laughed, hugging her. "I have really missed you."

Over the course of the next couple of days, Peter and Meggie enjoyed their friendship again. It was Peter's day off, they were on the beach when the phone rang. He dashed toward the house.

"Hello," said an out-of-breath Peter.

"Is Meggie Hiken there? I was given this number by her mom," a voice on the other end stated.

"She's outside, worshipping the sun. I'll get her," Peter lay the receiver down. With a second thought, he picked it back up,

"Is this by chance, Steven?"

"Yes, it is." Steven surprised. Peter broadly grinned,

"It's good to finally meet you, even if it is through Ma Bell."

"Peter?" Steven asked.

"You're on. Why don't you come down?" Peter said.

"It's not a bad thought, but I've been driving for a day and a half. I'm a bit bushed right now. Maybe tomorrow," Steven remarked, even though he wanted to see Meggie. It had been nearly a month since he last laid eyes on her.

"They run shuttles out of Friendship to the airport here. It only takes half an hour to get here. One way it's not too costly. I bet you could get a three-thirty and surprise her. I'll pick you up," he said.

"What a mind! No wonder Meggie adores you. I'll call you right back and let you know if I can get on. By the way, how would I know you?" Steven curious.

"It's a small airport, more like a landing strip. Just look for the character standing by a red VW Bug," Peter laughed.

"Thanks, Peter I mean that," Steven sincerely.

"No need," Peter said, hanging the receiver back on the phone.

Peter went back to the beach. Seeing Meggie floating in the water he thought, 'Neptune's daughter.' He laughed. At three-thirty he informed her he had to go out for awhile, but would be back in an hour.

"We'll go out for dinner," Peter smiled.

"Where are you going?" Meggie curious.

"Can't I have some space? Since you're staying here does that make you my guardian?" Peter put on a pair of shorts.

"Sorry," Meggie said, backing off. She left the room, heading back to the beach. At four-fifteen she came in, had a drink of water and disrobed for the shower.

"Where's Meggie?" Peter said to Stan, walking in with Steven.

"In the shower," Stan looked up, acknowledging Steven's presence. "Can't you hear her singing?"

Standing outside of the bathroom, Steven undressed before opening the door so slowly hoping she wouldn't hear. Very quietly, he pulled the shower curtain back a little and stepped in. She still didn't notice, being so engrossed in song.

"Hello, Morris," he whispered in her ear. Meggie started kissing him, then pulled back,

"You could have scared the life out of me!"

"You! Never!" Steven laughed before starting to make love to her. He kissed her-soaking wet body, licking all of the water off as he laid her on the bathroom floor.

"Oh, Steven," Meggie sighed.

Meggie and Steven decided they would stay at her parents' place in Rehoboth Beach, forty-five minutes up the road. There would be a lot more room there, even a bed. Steven turned to Peter,

"Have dinner with us tonight."

"Not tonight, how about tomorrow? I'd like to get to know you, but after my house guest, there's some straightening I have to do," Peter laughed.

"I understand," Steven laughed. They both knew her so well.

"Peter, you're the best friend a girl could have. I love you!" Meggie said, before kissing his cheek. Steven extended his hand.

"Thanks a lot. Tomorrow, dinner; don't forget," Steven put his arm around Meggie's shoulder, leading her toward her car. Peter smiled watching them pull away, feeling they were meant for each other. After his brief meeting with this man, he already liked him. 'Meggie's always had good taste,' he thought, 'Look who she chose for a friend.' He laughed out loud before walking into the house.

The following evening Peter told them to meet him at a small restaurant in Ocean City, called The Goldrusher. The meal was decent and they laughed most of the time. Afterward, Meggie excused herself to visit the ladies' room.

"You've known her for a long time," Steven said to Peter.

"We've been good friends for a very long time, even during her caterpillar days," Peter smiled.

"She's special. She's more of a sharer than a taker. I find that unusual today," Peter rubbed his finger around the rim of his glass. Steven looked on curiously. "I'm certain she didn't tell you about the youth center."

"What youth center?" Steven questioned.

"I don't think I would have found out if I hadn't walked in on a heated argument she was having with her dad at the time. I had never heard them yell at each other before. He owned a piece of real estate in south Baltimore, and she wanted him to donate the use of it to the city for a youth center. He told her that piece of property was far too valuable and she may as well forget the entire idea. Meggie looked him right in the eye, and said. 'I don't throw away an idea unless I know how to replace it!' She hugged him, saying, 'There are so many people with so much less than us, don't you think it's our responsibility to help?' She got what she wanted. Somehow she has a way of wrapping that man around her little finger," Peter laughed.

"Afterward I commented to her about her attitude. She told me it was steely determination and perseverance.

Imagine this coming out of the mouth of a fourteen year old? Then she informed me of her view. 'These kids can't help that they are underprivileged, or black, or who their parents are, or what they are, for that matter. They are innocent, helpless and powerless. It is up to us to do what we can-they are our responsibility!'" Peter smiled, recalling the conversation.

Steven listened intently. There were still so many things about her he didn't know. She was far more complex than he had envisioned. It seemed she always stood up for her principles, even before he came into her life. He leaned back in his chair, thinking.

"Miss me?" Meggie asked, returning to the table.

"Always," Steven kissed her.

After a few days of a lot of fun and a great deal of sun and ocean, Meggie turned to Steven one morning as they lay in bed.

"You want to come home with me?"

"Are you actually asking me, Morris, to see you in your natural habitat?" Steven smiled, hugging her.

"I want you to. It'll only be for a day or two, just to get my stuff," she said, returning his hug.

Before leaving to return to school, after spending a couple of enlightening days with Meggie's family, Steven took her car keys.

"I'll drive."

"Why? Women drivers aren't as good as men?" She said, giving him a rotten eye. He drew her toward him,

"Morris, you drive too fast! When that cop stopped us on the way back from Ocean City and you unbuttoned your blouse, I thought I was going to take gas. Then you told him I was your older brother. To top it all off, you didn't get a ticket with that immature act," Steven paused. "I'm tired of being big brother!" He smiled before kissing her.

"You don't exactly remind me of George Orwell!" Meggie laughed. "What should I have done?"

"Let me drive. Now get in!" Steven opened the car door for her.

Morris Hiken watched and heard this interchange of dialogue from the living room window and smiled. He liked this young man, his strength of character, his wisdom and the way he was able to handle Meggie. Knowing his daughter was not easy to deal with, he thought Steven was obviously as bright as she was. He sensed a great deal of love between them, a great deal of caring and understanding. Not having seen his daughter this happy in such a long time, he knew he was right. He smiled, watching Steven drive the car from the driveway.

On the drive to D.C., Meggie smiled at Steven.

"I think my parents really like you, especially my dad."

"I like them too, especially your dad," Steven laughed. "You never told me what happened to your Bulgarian money."

"We finally did exchange it in Switzerland for one-third of its original value. We took a loss. I imagine that's why they're so insistent about exchanging there," said Meggie, staring out the window.

"The best part of the past two days was when you came into my room last night and climbed into bed with me," Steven smiled to her.

"You didn't think I was going to allow you to be alone in a strange house or a strange bed! Did you?" She kissed his neck, unbuttoning his shirt and placing her hand on his left breast.

"Don't do that now, Morris!" Steven laughed, glancing at her and trying to drive at the same time.

VII

Approximately one week into the semester, Meggie lay in bed in the dorm, thinking about Mouse. She and Dottie had spent the day with her and her new little baby girl. The baby was adorable and seemed so fragile. Meggie wasn't used to being around babies. A part of her hurt for Mouse and all she was missing out on in life. Mouse had named the baby Rebecca, after the story, *REBECCA OF SUNNYBROOK FARM* . Meggie found no logic in that, finding it strange, but almost everything Mouse ever did was strange. She was undoubtedly different. Maybe that's why she was attracted to her, always finding pleasure outside of the norm. Meggie thought about what Mouse had said to her and had a difficult time accepting it,

"Now I have someone who will always love me for me. You see, I grew up a very sad and lonely little girl. This is the first time I feel whole!" Mouse smiled with a sparkle in her eye. She didn't expect Meggie or Dottie to understand, but now she could give her love freely, with no fear of rejection, and unconditionally.

The following day, Meggie reported to Michael what she had learned about the war in Vietnam over the summer.

"Haven't you grasped it yet! They don't concern themselves with us; they merely use us to fight their stupid battles!" Michael yelled.

"We're not individual human beings. They group us together as one. Don't you see? We're the new generation, we're achievers. We are, in reality, a threat to them!" Michael still angry.

Meggie could not entirely agree with him, even though she was open-minded enough to see his point of view. She continued to work in the S.D.S. office and decided to write more articles for the school paper in protest of this war. The first in a series of editorials began;

Vietnam is like sending one hundred men into the face of fire with the knowledge they will never return. Vietnam is like sending one hundred men with nothing but guns, against one hundred enemy tanks. Here is one mans' war.

She used no name. Later, after it was printed, she mailed a copy of the paper to Jay.

Sometime in mid-September, not quite a month into the semester, Roger received a phone call. His mom had died. Meggie, feeling for him, tried to put her arms around him.

"Get the hell away from me! Have you any idea how much I hate you?" Roger screamed. She walked away to gather her things.

"Where are you going?" Steven concerned..

"I think I better leave," Meggie said, on her way out the door.

"I don't want you to," Steven followed her.

"Roger needs you now, far more than you are aware of. He's made it quite clear he doesn't want me around. At a time like this, I plan on respecting his wishes," Meggie said, getting into her car. Steven hopped into the passenger seat,

"He's upset."

"Don't you think I know that!" Meggie yelled, trying to control her tears, her hurt. She knew there was more pressing business in front of Steven right now, yet she knew he sensed how she felt.

"Listen, Steven," she hugged him." Roger is a good friend of yours. Right now he is hurting and in dire need of your strength and wisdom."

"I'm worried about you, Morris," Steven concerned, looking into her eyes. He only saw them green on two other occasions. The first time was the night he gave her the ultimatum, and the second, was when she was arrested. Knowing her well enough at this point in time, he knew, seeing green eyes, she was really upset. It bothered him she wouldn't admit it or allow him in.

"No need, I'll be fine," Meggie forced a smile.

"Morris, you sure?" Steven said, getting out of the car, not knowing what to do. Roger did need him.

"Positive," she replied, before driving away.

Meggie awoke the following morning, not in the mood for classes. Deciding to skip them, she showed up at Steven's. Paul opened the door, letting her in, telling her he never realized Roger had such a diabolical side to him before. Death has a way of making people grieve in strange ways, she told him. He was sorry Roger reacted that way to her. She didn't deserve it. Roger went to stay at his mother's last night, with his step-father. They haven't been able to reach his younger brother yet. He was traveling around the Far East. Meggie embraced Paul before she started up the stairs to Steven's room.

"Steven, time to get up," she whispered in his ear, sitting on the edge of the bed by him.

"Morris, why aren't you in class?" Steven sleepily, stretching his arms a little.

"I wasn't in the mood. Besides, we have to decide what we're going to send Roger. What do you think, dairy, meat or sweets?" Meggie was very sullen. Steven laughed.

"I fail to see the humor!" She said, aggravated.

"You are funny," Steven smiled, seeing her surprised face. "Morris, Roger's not Jewish, we don't send him food."

"Why not? He still has to eat," Meggie said, in disbelief.

"Oh, my dear sweet Meggie, do you have any idea how I love you?" Steven embraced her.

"Later we'll send flowers," he whispered in her ear, before caressing her breast.

"Come on, Steven, this is not the time," she struggled to get up.

"No! I can't think of a better time," he kissed her, unbuttoning her blouse.

The funeral was held the following Sunday, Steven stood with a very teary-eyed Meggie, not realizing beforehand how hard it was going to be on her. He thought, Lord, the more I know her the more I love her. He never thought it possible to love her more than he did last year. Every day it grew stronger. After spending some time with Roger, while Meggie was extremely quiet and distant, they headed back to school.

"It brought back memories," Steven glanced at her as he drove.

"Uh-huh," Meggie mumbled, with tears running down her cheeks.

"Oh Morris," he extended his arm around her and drew her toward him. All he wanted to do was make her pain go away, though he knew that was an impossibility. Later, they drove into the city.

"Steven, take me to my dorm," Meggie remarked, still upset.

"No, I'm not letting you be alone," Steven drove in the direction of Georgetown.

"I need my space!" Meggie cried.

"You can have all the space that you want, just not alone! You'll never be alone as long as I'm around," he kissed her forehead.

Meggie couldn't understand where she came off deserving him. Her thoughts had been with Dennis all day; memories of the day he was buried and all of the pain, the void and the loss involved. She sensed Steven knew this and took comfort in knowing that. She fell asleep with his strong, warm arms around her.

217

One week later, Meggie walked into Roger's room, finding he and Steven lying on their backs with their arms folded behind their heads on the double bed.

"Hi, you two," she smiled.

"Morris, I didn't know you were coming tonight!" Steven surprised, rising to his feet to hug her.

"Steven, I'd like some time with Roger," she stated coolly. He had been aware of her many tones by this point in their relationship, and he knew this was a serious one. He left the room after kissing her.

"What do you want?" Roger said rather cruelly, not looking at her.

Meggie leaned to kick the door shut with her foot. Seeing a chair in the far corner of the room, she brought it near the bed and sat so she could face Roger.

"It doesn't take a genius to figure out you don't like me. I honestly wish I could say I didn't care, but I do. That's something I needed to get out, and I will have to learn to live with it. Just as you will have to learn to live with the loss of your mom. I'm here, because I've been where you are right now, maybe not in the exact same context, but-never-the less, I've taken this horrid journey into never-never land."

"Sure! Who are you kidding? You have both of your parents," Roger stated sarcastically.

"That's true. I lost someone very close to me. Society, as it is, can accept the death more readily of someone older, but dealing with the death of someone younger or one of your peers, is an entirely different ball game. My plan is not to take anything away from your grief. We all need it, we have to have it at a time like this. I'm sure losing a parent is quite a devastating experience, one I hope I won't have to deal with for many years. I need for you to know where I am coming from." Meggie paused. He finally raised his eyes to see her.

"A guy I loved with all of my heart and soul, a guy I considered to be my other half, a large part of me... the first boy I ever loved or who ever loved me... died the summer before I started at American. He was supposed to go here too. He was eighteen; such a waste of a young life!" Meggie started to cry. Sitting up, Roger took her hands. Instead, she put his in between hers.

"Roger, I have experienced the void you feel, the total emptiness, that is exactly what it is. Sometimes you feel like your heart is going to fall right through your body, or like someone reached in and cut out a big chunk of it. It hurts a lot, especially when you can't control the tears flowing from your eyes." Meggie leaned to hug him; Roger placed both of his arms around her. They both cried, holding each other.

"You know, somehow it manages to heal itself. Our bodies are like that, fighting for survival. I don't really understand it. It comes from good friends and time, but it does happen. You should know from when your Dad passed away." Meggie sat there holding him, with his head resting on her shoulder.

"Why are you trying to help me, feeling compassion for me?" Roger leaned back to see her.

"If you are a friend of Steven's, there is no way you could be a bad person. Only one going through a bad time. Besides, it's my nature to care," Meggie smiled slightly.

"After the way I've treated you, why?" Roger with a few tears.

"I don't believe you meant the things you said to me, but at the time you may have felt them. You may have felt me to even be a threat to you in some way. Your defenses were up and have been for so long. Let's leave the past, just there, behind us," Meggie hugged him again.

"Please hold me for a while longer. It feels good," Roger said, crying. They both cried.

"Peace of mind doesn't come easy, it takes about eight and a half hours to get." She whispered in his ear, trying to lighten up the situation a little. She even heard a slight snicker from him.

"Hey, what's going on in here?" Steven said, walking in.

"You have one fantastic lady here," Roger pulled back, looking at Meggie and then at Steven.

"I've been trying to tell you that," Steven smiled, nearing them, seeing Meggie's red eyes. Before she left the room, Meggie embraced Roger again. No words were spoken, none were necessary. Steven led her down the hall with his arm around her. She headed toward the stairs, making it down three of them.

"Hey Morris, where you going?" Steven stopped her.

"I came tonight to see Roger." Meggie looked at Steven and he drew her toward him on the stairs.

"I really feel for him," she said, before Steven kissed her.

"You know, Roger's right, you are fantastic!" He smiled.

"Come on, Steven, I have work to do," Meggie tried to pull away. Steven kissed her again, putting his tongue in her mouth.

"You can stay? Can't you?" He smiled, feeling her go limp again, loving when he got to her.

"I guess I can," she smiled.

During the course of the following month, Steven noticed Meggie had endeared herself to Roger. He was happy for that because Roger could use every friend he could find right now, and having no more tension between them was a real pleasure. Roger was even picking up after her and not complaining about her things around all of the time like he used to. Steven thought to himself, she is unusually special, she's mine. I wonder if she knows it yet?

Meggie still worked in the S.D.S. office, even though Steven wasn't around much anymore. 'Maybe he is outgrowing it,' she thought. Receiving pictures of Mouse's baby, she cried for Mouse, for all of the things she had missed out on and for her baby. She couldn't understand how happy she was. The situation totally confused Meggie: accepting the responsibility for another living soul, and the total dependency Mouse was accepting at such a young age.

Dottie was the perfect roommate: not prying, giving space, far more sedate than last year and-she cleaned. Meggie thought about how much she did love Dottie. She was a good friend, worthy of the finer things in life and she hoped she would have them. Dottie had helped her so much, more than she could ever have anticipated.

One week before Thanksgiving, a Wednesday morning at 7:OO a.m., Meggie received a phone call from Ma. Ben had been rushed to the hospital during the middle of the night. He was in intensive care; they thought it might be his kidneys. Meggie was shaking so as she dressed that Dottie wouldn't allow her drive, so she drove her to Baltimore.

Later that same day, Steven entered the S.D.S. office.

"Have you seen Meggie?" He looked at Michael.

"You know, I haven't, nor Dottie. That's unusual! Maybe she forgot," Michael said.

"That may work for some people, but not for her. She's too responsible," Steven sat down to wait, in hopes she would show up. A half an hour later, the phone rang.

"It's for you." Michael motioned to Steven.

"Steven, it's Dottie. We're in Baltimore at Johns Hopkins Hospital."

"Is Meggie alright?" Steven asked, scared.

"Yes! No! I don't know! She's not sick or hurt or anything like that. It's Ben, he needs a kidney transplant.

All hell is breaking loose around here! Her dad left in a huff and nobody will talk to me, not even Meggie. She keeps running away, crying. Now she's roaming the halls, talking to herself, cussing! I don't know what to do! You have got to get here, I don't want to leave her. I can't handle this much longer and I have a Modern Art History test this afternoon. It's frustrating not to know what to do, sensing something terrible is happening," Dottie aggravated.

"I'm leaving now, you may as well go. It'll take me about fifty minutes," Steven said, hanging up the phone. Driving down the BW Parkway he wondered what was wrong, concerned for Meggie. It didn't take Einstein to figure out it had to be more than Ben's kidney. Considering himself lucky to find a space on Broadway to park, he entered the antiquated building and learned where intensive care was. Taking the elevator up, walking down the hall on the fifth floor, he spotted Mrs. Hiken in a waiting room, standing close to a window.

"Mrs. Hiken." Steven approached and noticed she had been crying. "Where's Meggie?"

Lil Hiken looked out the window to the courtyard below without saying a word. Steven saw Meggie walking around in a circle down there. He fled for the elevators, but, not wanting to wait, he ran down five flights of stairs. Walking outside to the courtyard, he briskly approached her, grabbing and hugging her tighter than he ever had.

"Oh, Steven," Meggie cried, placing her arms around him.

"You're freezing! Let's go inside," Steven said, holding her.

"No! Take me home, please," she looked up at him with tears rolling from her eyes.

They got into his car, with Meggie still crying, her nose red and her cheeks chaffed from her tears and the cold.

"Come here, Morris," Steven placed both of his arms around her, trying to warm her.

He drove to her parents' house, with one arm around her and Meggie leaning her head on his shoulder, in silence the entire way, except for the sound of her tears. She unlocked the front door.

"What's going on?" Steven concerned.

Meggie walked to the kitchen, opened the refrigerator and handed Steven a bottle of wine to open. She never drank wine in her parents home before, except during holidays, she thought. You have to be twenty-one, the legal drinking age in the state of Maryland. Another first for her. Putting it out of her mind, then retrieving two wine glasses from the cupboard, she walked to the den. Steven followed, sensing something out of the ordinary had taken place, aside from Ben's illness. He decided to keep his mouth shut until she was ready to speak. He knew her so well. Pouring the wine into the glasses, Meggie finally broke the silence.

"Do you realize you are always asking me what's wrong?" She glanced at him.

"Not always," Steven smiled.

"Don't you get tired of rescuing me?" Meggie asked, with tears.

"From time to time I've thought about it," Steven with a slight laugh. "Morris, don't you realize by now you are a large part of my life, a very large part of it? I love you." He hugged her.

"Three times in the past year you have been my salvation. There must be something wrong with me for all of these things to happen," Meggie cried on his shoulder.

"God gives us what he thinks we should be able to handle. Whatever this is, we will deal with it together. I love you so much, I wouldn't be here if I didn't," Steven held her tightly.

Meggie sat in the corner of the couch with the glass of wine in her right hand, bending her legs under her. Steven sat beside her.

She didn't wait for him to ask again. Swirling the wine around in the glass before taking a sip, she began.

"Ma called this morning to say Ben was in the hospital with kidney problems," she paused.

"I guess about an hour after Dottie and I arrived at the hospital, Dr. Marcus came into the waiting room with a specialist. He told us very tactfully Ben needs a kidney transplant. Naturally I jumped up. Take one of mine I don't need two!"

"Just like you, Morris!" Steven smiled, kissing her.

"That's what I like about you. No matter how bad things are, you have always been there for a good laugh! Honestly, this is not a joking moment," said Meggie, sadly.

"Sorry, just trying to lighten up a bad situation," he said.

"I'm sorry, I know you are. Ben will be on dialysis. He has total kidney failure. They need to find the perfect kidney, one from a solid blood relative, having the right tissue match. Dr. Marcus told Ma since she's a woman and a little too old, hers were not feasible. So of course Dad offered his. At that point, Ma asked to be left alone with Daddy and me. The doctors and Dottie left the room immediately. Ma stood, closing the door behind them. She then came to hold my hands and told me Ben's my half brother; therefore, he couldn't use my kidney. I know I was in shock, but when I looked at Daddy, he was white. She turned to him, telling him Ben wasn't his son. Daddy dashed from the room without a word. I followed, I hurt for him and for me! Can you imagine raising a child and finding out when he's fourteen years old he's not yours? He was gone before I could reach him, I haven't been able to find him all day. Not at his office nor his answering service." Meggie paused, tears still running down her cheeks.

"I went back to see Ma; there were questions that needed answering, whether she wanted to or not. She was going to! I discovered she had an affair with a trumpet player almost three and a half years after I was born. Can you imagine, a trumpet player!" Meggie yelled.

"That is a little uncharacteristic of your ma," Steven remarked.

"Not really, didn't I tell you? She was a concert pianist before she married Daddy. He made her give it up. You know the old adage, a woman's place is in the home. I believe she resented it, having to compromise who she really was," Meggie said, solemnly.

"No! You never told me! Is that where you get your musical talent?" he joked.

"You've never heard it. Singing in the shower does not exactly depict musical ability," Meggie said, with raised eyebrows. She moved toward the living room with Steven following. She eyed the baby grand piano that was Ma's. Meggie was only permitted to touch it on special occasions. Hers was in the rec room in the basement. Meggie thought, 'Look who's subservient now! I'm going to play on this,' playing has always released a great deal of anxiety and tension. She glanced at Steven before sitting down.

"Naturally, I play classical beautifully, thanks to my mother. I really don't feel like doing that now." Meggie saw her hands in fists, realizing they hadn't been that way for such a long time.

"The songs I'm going to sing, Peter wrote. There's one song he wrote for me, I remember crying when he gave it to me. I have played and sung by myself or with Peter, I haven't done this with any sort of audience for over sixteen months now," she said, sadly. He realized, that's how long Dennis had been dead.

Meggie played and sang. Steven was in bewilderment.

"That's it!" Meggie stood, stretching, when she had enough. He neared to embrace her.

"You certainly are full of surprises," Steven kissed her. "I can't believe you kept this a secret; you never shared it with me before."

"Would you like to hear the rest of this sorry tale?" she inquired.

"No, but I know I have to. So, go on," Steven smiled, leading her toward the den.

"At the time Daddy found out about their affair, or their tete-a-tete, and put an end to it. Ma had me and she wasn't willing to risk it. She didn't know she was pregnant, finding out only a few weeks later. That's what Daddy meant when he told me at one time he loved her, then something happened and now he loved her differently. Now their estranged relationship seems so clear. The way he has always treated Ben, I have a feeling he may have been a little suspicious." Meggie cried more, thinking of her dad's pain.

"Morris, I hurt for you," Steven kissed her forehead.

"Well, don't! Hurt for everyone else in this godforsaken world who has been betrayed by their parents, misled, mistreated and misguided. You know, they have two sets of morals, one for us and one for them. Their lies, their irony, their sadism and their contradiction! They are like goddamn chameleons! I'm sure you are familiar with the old saying, don't do as I do, but do as I say? Then they wonder why their children turn out to be rebels or so totally messed up. It's a joke, a real joke. Parents are shields of artificial love!" Meggie cried harder then before.

"Oh, come on," Steven hugged her.

"Sure, your whole world isn't falling out from under you," Meggie said, still in tears.

"Thanks a lot, I thought I was part of your world." Steven leaned back to look at her.

"Steven, you are, you know exactly what I mean," she said, with Steven holding her tighter because he did understand. He sat there holding her, comforting her until she stopped crying.

"What about a kidney for Ben? But, no more tears," Steven said.

"Ma reached her old paramour, knowing just where to find him, in New York. He's flying in tonight. For many years now, he's been playing with the New York Symphony. As it turns out, he's seen Ben and has been aware he's his son. Can you beat that one?" Meggie sarcastically.

"This entire story is a lot to digest, especially for someone like you," Steven held her again, when the phone rang.

"I don't want to, but I have to get that." Meggie gazed into his light blue eyes, wondering if they were the source of his strength.

"Hello," she coolly said, picking up the receiver. "Daddy! Are you okay?" Meggie yelled, relieved to hear his voice.

"I'll be fine once the shock wears off. How are you?" Morris Hiken, on the other end of the phone.

"Where are you?" Meggie asked, concerned.

"Take this number down. I still want to know how Ben's doing and I know you'll keep me informed. In my own way, I do love him and always have. He's still my son, whether he has my genes or not," Dad said, very sullenly.

"I know, Daddy. Ben's kidney is flying in tonight. I'm concerned about you," Meggie said.

"Don't be, Baby, I'm in good hands. Are you alone?" Dad asked. She understood his meaning about the hands, pausing before she answered.

"No, Steven's with me."

"Good, let me speak with him," Dad instructed.

"Hello, sir," Steven stated. Meggie marveled at his manners, even at a time like this.

"Mere words can not express how much I appreciate your being there for Meggie. I fear for her; she's been through so much for such a young woman. This I am sure hasn't helped matters. I am sorry she has to lean on you again, but I am thankful for it," Dad said, depressed.

"Words fail me right now, not knowing the appropriate thing to say at a time like this. Except, I'm sorry," Steven sadly said.

"Thank you, Steven. My mind will find some relative peace with the knowledge you are there. Put Meggie back on the phone," Dad said.

"I love you. I'll see you in a couple of days," Dad said, before hanging up the receiver.

Later, Meggie made another wonderful meal. Steven loved how she could cook. This time it was Delmonico steaks with a Bernaise sauce, Caesar salad, potatoes and a string bean casserole. He smiled at her talents, holding her in bed, both fully clothed. Meggie looked at him with tears in her eyes again,

"Nothing is what it seems to be. Reality is only what each individual's perception is, never truth."

"Stop being so philosophical, Morris," he kissed her.

"It escapes my comprehension how she could do this! She's lied to me my entire life. How could she do a thing like that?" Meggie cried.

"Think of it this way. She's been living a lie! How difficult do you think that can be? I'm sure she had her reasons, Morris, whether you agree with them or not. I'm certain your ma did what she felt best," Steven held her tighter.

"I am sure you are aware the wall between Ma and me will be higher now," Meggie said, still with tears.

"I know." Steven pushed her hair off her face, feeling for her, knowing the loneliness she had felt, thanks to her mom, for so long now. He resented Lil Hiken for doing this to her and everything she had done over the years to make Meggie feel so unloved and unwanted. He was thankful her dad loved her the way he did.

Watching Steven as he slept, Meggie marveled at his strong features, how truly handsome he was. She thought about his strength and wisdom, his intelligence and courage. She fell to sleep with a secure feeling, thinking she didn't know what she would do without that strength of his. He had become her backbone!

Friday morning, Ben's kidney transplant was performed. The doctors said they thought it was a success, only time telling for sure. Meggie refused to meet Ma's friend and had very little to say to her. The relationship was definitely strained. Steven noticed you could cut the tension with a knife.

Sunday night, Steven wanted Meggie to return to school with him but she wouldn't leave until Ben was out of the woods, so to speak. Reluctantly, he drove back by himself, reflecting on the past few days. 'She is constantly surprising me,' he thought. He never imagined she could play the piano or sing like that. He laughed. Then, becoming a little sullen, he thought about her inner strength, her power of deduction, her will for survival. Even Ben kept his wits about him. He recalled a conversation the other day.

"We'll always be brother and sister. I was with you when you bought your first tube of Clearasil," Ben laughed. Meggie did also.

He thought, their ma must have done something right to have raised two children who turned out like this, though his respect for Lil had become nil.

The following Wednesday morning, the day before Thanksgiving, Steven walked into the Hiken house to find Meggie's ma staring out of the living room window.

"Mrs. Hiken, is anything wrong?" He realized everything was, what an idiotic question! He was hoping there were no new developments.

"I'm waiting for Meggie to return with my car so I can go to the hospital," Mrs. Hiken still with her back to him.

"Where is she?" Steven questioned.

"The same place she's been every day this week," Lil Hiken said, finally turning around to face him. "I will never understand her, the things she does, her reasons for doing them, or even the manner in which she thinks. God, I wish I could; it might have helped us make it through this, if only I were more perceptive." Tears running down her cheeks. She turned back toward the window.

"Her first stop is the hospital to see Ben. Then, the cemetery," Lil was still crying.

"The cemetery!" Steven became excited. "Will you go with me? I haven't any idea how to get there. You can get your car."

Pulling into the Oheb Shalom Memorial Park, he spotted Meggie. He parked his car, walked about a half a block, approaching her from her back, and put his arms around her.

"Come on, Morris, what are you doing here?" Steven read the gravestone:

January 18,1949 —— July 25,1967, DENNIS BARRY FINE.

"I've been depressed," Meggie whimpered.

"Oh, Morris, Dennis wouldn't want you to do this, and neither do I." Steven hugged her and led her toward the car.

"You're ruining a perfectly marvelous depression. I hope you realize that," Meggie looked at him, glassy-eyed.

Lil Hiken watched for a short time, happy Meggie had someone like Steven, even if she did sense they slept together. She may have slept with Dennis, too, for all she knew. Who was she to pass judgment on anyone, especially her own daughter, whom she had brought into this world, loved and hurt so badly? She pulled away from the cemetery in tears.

Steven and Meggie climbed into his car.

"I'm taking you away for a few days. I spoke to your dad, he thinks it's a wonderful idea. He gave me the keys to the Rehoboth house," Steven held her. Meggie leaned her head on his shoulder.

"How do I deserve you?" she cried. Steven thought to himself, 'Because you are terrific and I love you.'

"Steven did you know the word Rehoboth means, broad places. It's from early Hebrew," she forced a slight smile. It brought a smile to Steven's face, that mind of hers!.

The remainder of the semester went by relatively quickly. Meggie kept busy with her painting. The S.D.S. had an anti-war sit-in on the steps of the Justice Department and the school paper asked her to write more articles about the war. She spent every spare moment with Steven. She felt closer to him than she had ever felt to anyone, yet still not admitting it.

"Let's go to New York for Christmas and New Years," Steven suggested.

"The Guggenheim Museum!" Meggie said, very-bright eyed.

"If you wish." Steven drew her toward him, kissing her.

"Steven, have you ever seen it?" she said, excitedly.

"No, I haven't been back to my ancient stomping grounds since I left. I was fourteen, remember,." he smiled.

"It looks like a cupcake!" she yelled, throwing her arms in the air.

They spent the holiday in New York, standing in Times Square, watching the ball drop down, bringing in the New Year, 1969. The year "Tricky Dick" (Richard Nixon) took the oath to be the 37th President of the United States. The year anti-U.S. demonstrations were taking place around the world. The year the SATURDAY EVENING POST, after 148 years of publishing, stopped publication. The year South Vietnam President Thieu stated the withdrawal of U.S. troops would take years and years, because they had no ambition to take over the fighting. The year Howard University in Washington, D.C., closed after students seized eight campus buildings. The year Apollo 11 landed on the moon and the first man ever stepped on it.

> "One small step for man and one giant
> leap for mankind"

The immortal words of Astronaut Neil Armstrong on July 20,1969. He was accompanied by Air Force Colonel Edwin Aldrin and Air Force Lieutenant Colonel Michael Collins.

The year this country was informed the Vietnam war deaths exceeded those of Korea. The year of "Hair," a Broadway musical, and the movie, *2001: A SPACE ODYSSEY*. The year "Sesame Street" made its' debut on Public Television.

Shortly after New Year's, Meggie and Steven said their good-byes at Kennedy Airport in New York. He was going to Phoenix and she to Honolulu, a two week separation. Steven watched her walk down the narrow corridor toward her plane. Just before her boarding he yelled,

"Don't forget the macadamias." Meggie turned around with a slight tilt of her head.

"How about some oranges?" she yelled, prior to stepping onto her plane. Steven ran through the narrow corridor, catching her before she could board, grabbing her by the arm.

"Morris, I love you," he kissed her, not caring who was watching.

Boarding her flight, sitting in her first class seat, she took out the copy of *WAR AND PEACE* Richard had given her. Still taking his advice, she read the entire flight. No more thinking on airplanes.

Arriving in Phoenix, Steven told his Dad he wanted to take some oranges back for Meggie.

"You should have brought her this time," Ian Roth walked with his son among the orange trees.

"I wanted to but she had other plans. She went to Honolulu, to visit her cousin, Lori, for a couple of weeks." Steven bent down to tie his tennis shoe.

"She's even more incredible than I ever could have imagined." Steven told his dad the situation with Ben and Meggie's parents. "She has such extraordinary strength and character. It truly amazes me."

"Personally, I think she was mighty lucky to have you," his dad said, kicking a stone. "You're no slouch, you know."

"I'm lucky to have her. She brings out the best in me. That's because she settles for nothing less than that for herself," Steven smiled. "She's like this ferocious person so engaged to life."

"Steven, I'm delighted you're happy. But what are your plans after you get your Master's in May?" His dad looked at him.

"I haven't made any. You are aware of the fact I want to write. Whatever I choose to do, I want Meggie with me, of that I am certain." Steven paused, "Dad, I don't intend to lean on you any longer. I don't expect you to pay my way for the rest of my life. I would like to travel and write-you can't write about life unless you experience it."

"Without any incoming money, what do you plan to live on?" Ian Roth inquired.

"I have made some connections. I'll probably be able to sell some articles to magazines and newspapers while I work on my book. I'll work something out," Steven smiled, unconcerned.

"You'd make me happy if you allowed us to help you. We can't take it with us; you're all we've got," dad placed an arm around Steven's shoulder.

"Dad, without a doubt, I have the most wonderful parents in the world. Not because of the money, that is so minor. But because you ˙ have always been behind whatever I do, always believing in me, so willing to listen. It's a terrific feeling," Steven embraced his father. "I'll make a deal with you. If I should find myself in need of your assistance, I'll ask for it." His dad backed off, knowing when Steven made his mind up, he followed through.

At the same time, in Hawaii, Meggie was informing Lori about everything that had transpired with her parents. Lori had already heard bits and pieces of the story from her dad.

"So what's going to happen now?" Lori asked. The two girls were on the floor doing sit ups.

"They're getting divorced! Why not? Irreconcilable differences, too much hurt there. I'm capable of comprehending that. At least they waited for Ben to recover, I give them credit for that," Meggie said, out of breath.

"And you call me understanding," Lori stood up.

"That was a nice note you wrote Roger," Meggie glanced at her.

"Thanks, he's a nice person, part of me is afraid for him," Lori stretched.

"So true," Meggie sighed, thinking of Roger.

"Have you heard from Victor lately?" Meggie touched her toes.

"He called the other night. I really do love him, you know," Lori smiled.

"I am sure you are aware of the fact I curse the day I introduced you to him," Meggie said, bending down again.

"Meg, you don't know him like I do. One day, I promise you, you'll like him," said Lori, on the floor, doing push-ups.

"Somehow, I have difficulty visualizing that," Meggie laughed.

"Why are we doing this?" Lori asked. The two girls were dripping wet with perspiration. Meggie laughed,

"It's supposed to be good for our bodies?"

Meggie went to see Richard the following day, noticing his hair was much longer, though still tied in a ponytail in the back.

"Why do you keep your hair like that?" she questioned.

"It saves money at the barber's," Richard smiled.

"Okay, I guess I can accept that," she laughed slightly.

They sat, drinking herbal tea and talked for quite some time.

"Why do I always end up telling you everything?" Meggie gazed at this man with very strong, pronounced features. He makes me think! she thought to herself.

"I've told you before, I'm a great listener," Richard placed a record on the stereo.

"Your wonderful poetry, have you written any more?" Meggie lay back on the pillows.

"Of course," Richard walked to the bookshelves, knowing there was no way of getting around her. He threw them to her,

"Can you read it?"

Two hours later Meggie closed the notebooks and stared into space for quite some time.

"You're searching for Utopia. Haven't you realized by now it doesn't exist? No matter what our achievements bring, how hard we try, nothing will ever be perfect," she said with furrowed eyebrows.

"Some would say there's a slight edge to your voice," Richard responded, somewhat ired.

"Some would say you're being a bit paranoid," Meggie neared him.

"Moi, jamais! (me, never) You're the one who has that market cornered!" He yelled.

"You're overreacting, or reacting strongly," she stated.

"I write what I see!" Richard stated.

"Wrong! You write what you want to see, what you would like the world to see, what you would like the world to be, rearranging it to suit yourself," Meggie in a raised voice.

"I would never prostitute my talents that way!" Richard stated harshly.

"You tell me I think too much. You see too much, reading into things something that simply isn't there," Meggie said, trying to get through. There was a lull for a few seconds.

"I do understand what you're trying to say," he walked closer to her. He didn't know too many people who were as honest as she.

"Our first creative disagreement," she smiled. Richard hugged her.

The flight returning from Honolulu landed at Baltimore's Friendship Airport. Meggie closed the book and disembarked, looking for her dad.

"What are you doing here?" Meggie was puzzled.

"Thanks, that's one hell of a welcome to someone you haven't seen for over two weeks," Steven smiled at her.

"Sorry." She kissed him. "I was under the impression my dad was going to pick me up."

"I called and told him I would. Any objections, Morris?" Steven said, holding her.

"None! You're as sly as a fox," she laughed.

While waiting for the baggage, he noticed her tan, which made her look even more beautiful. She swung her head around and her hair, streaked from the sun, flew back. God, he loved it. After retrieving her two suitcases, he started for the door.

"Wait!" Meggie yelled.

"You can't possibly have more luggage," Steven said, surprised.

"No, only a case of macadamias for someone who's been on my mind," she smiled.

"I brought back a crate of oranges for the woman I love," Steven smiled, still standing, holding both suitcases.

"Wonderful! We can have fresh-squeezed orange juice in the winter!" she yelled, jumping up and down. Her zest for living never ceased to amaze him.

Later that morning, at Steven's house, Meggie squeezed the oranges, Steven kissed the back of her neck.

"Steven, stop that! Don't you want juice?" she laughed.

"I can't believe the way you attacked those oranges! Didn't you get fresh orange juice in those glorious islands of yours?" Steven smiled.

"Of course, but none from oranges grown out of love, such as these," Meggie said, barely finishing her comment before he kissed her.

"Here." She handed him a glass of juice. "It's healthy for you, lots of vitamin C."

"I can think of something healthier," Steven laughed, as they stood drinking the juice, looking at each other. He took her in his arms.

"You beautiful creature, have you any idea how I have missed you?" he kissed her, picking her up, carrying her up the stairs.

"Steven, my Adonis, you are going to get a hernia," she laughed.

237

He laid her on the bed, undressing her tanned body, checking out every bathing suit line, gazing at her beauty. He kissed her lips, her neck, her ears, then her breasts and entire torso.

"Morris, I love you, more than I think you know," Steven said, right before they became one. He honestly felt it would be like this forever. Mid-day, they slept, holding each other. They had missed one another too much.

The phone rang, a few hours later and groggily Steven answered.

"Is this Steven Roth?" a voice from the other end asked.

"Yes," Steven barely opening his eyes, with Meggie beside him stretching, his arm still around her.

"This is Sergeant Allen at the 23rd Precinct. We have a friend of yours here." Steven abruptly sat up, finished his conversation, and turned toward Meggie.

"I should be back in a couple of hours."

"Oh no! I have this strange feeling Roger has gotten himself in trouble," she looked at him.

"He has," Steven rose from the bed quickly.

"Then, I'm coming." Meggie started to dress.

Steven had no plans of arguing with her. Number one, when she made her mind up to do something, there was no talking her out of it. Number two, believe it or not, he even found it difficult to believe, she was the only one who had been able to get through to Roger over the past few months.

Driving toward downtown D.C., Steven told her,

"He was creating a disturbance in the pizza place across the street from your dorm." He sighed, "Not just a disturbance. To put it more bluntly, he took the food from everyone in there, threw it on the floor, then he started eating it off the floor like a dog." Steven expected a reaction from her. Instead, she said,

"I was afraid something dreadful was going to happen; the signs were there. We were too wrapped up in ourselves to see them." Meggie, extended her arm around Steven's shoulder.

They drove the remaining five minutes in silence. Entering the police station, Steven approached the man behind the desk.

"I'm Steven Roth. Sergeant Allen phoned me in regard to Roger Moore."

"Sergeant Allen would like to speak with you, Mr. Roth," the police officer rose from his seat.

"Can I see Roger?" Meggie tugged on Steven's arm.

"You sure?" Steven asked her.

"Of course!" she said.

"She's a good friend of Roger Moore's; she'd like to see him," Steven told the officer.

"We'll see," he stated, before walking away.

The officer returned, leading Steven into Detective Allen's office, then Meggie to a small room where she waited for Roger. Thirty minutes later, she emerged from the room, passed a waiting Steven, headed for the phones. Steven stood beside her as she placed the call.

"What are you doing?" he asked.

"I called Daddy. I think he can help Roger. Are you aware they are planning to put him in a state sanitarium?" Meggie was upset.

"What can we do about it? He's the one who got himself arrested. It's out of our hands." Steven said.

"Daddy's calling Dr. Marcus; he may be able to get him into Sheppard Pratt. It's far better than any state institution," Meggie stated.

They waited for her dad to phone back. It took twenty minutes. She answered it, smiled at Steven, and thanked her father. That night, they followed the ambulance with Roger to Sheppard Pratt Hospital in Baltimore, for their own peace of mind, needing to know he was safe and somewhat peaceful.

Meggie kept herself busy as usual for the next month and a half. She and Steven went to visit Roger many times, eating dinner in Baltimore at all of her favorite restaurants: Sabatino's, the Palmer House, the Pimlico Hotel. He never allowed her to help with the bill.

"I've said before, you like the finer things in life," Steven smiled, after picking up the dinner check.

"Give it to me! I'll take care of it," Meggie became somewhat aggravated. Steven leaned across the table in front of her.

"Haven't you got it yet? It's not a problem for me. I enjoy teasing you," he kissed her. He was aware she came from money-how much, he didn't know, nor did he care. He loved her for her.

"This isn't fair!" Meggie said. "It's not your responsibility."

He smiled, thinking it would be quite soon, hoping to get his way.

On their drive back to D.C. that evening,

"Steven, do you have any bad memories of your parents from your childhood?" Meggie, curious.

"What brought this about?" he inquired.

"Somehow, I have the feeling Roger has quite a few, coupled with everything else he has had to deal with. I have a few rotten memories myself, one in particular always creeps back," she said.

"Out with it, Morris." Steven glanced at her.

"I was in the second grade. After school, I wanted to talk to my first grade teacher. She was getting married that weekend, and I was afraid I would never see her again. I lost track of time, missing my school bus home. I walked the eight blocks home with two girls whose mothers didn't insist they take the bus. When I arrived home, Ma was a neurotic mess! I was punished and put in my room till the following morning. It was a beautiful spring day and all of the kids were outside playing. From that time on, I decided I would behave for her, but neither she nor anyone else was going to tell me what to do. Can you believe this? This was her way of showing affection for me: yelling and punishing!" Meggie leaned back with watery eyes.

"You were a bit young," Steven smiled.

"I needed my space then, just as I do now." Meggie looked at him. "How about you, any bad experiences?"

"We all have anxieties left over from childhood-it's part of living. I think I was four or five when I awakened from a nap in the afternoon and found no one home. I left the house in search of my mother. I roamed the streets of New York City all night-a very frightening experience! They found me at about three in the morning. I was punished for days. I never did it again. My mom was next door borrowing some milk when I awoke," Steven recollected.

After visiting Roger on one occasion, Meggie took Steven to meet her grandparents (her maternal grandparents). Her grandfather was from Ireland, the source of her temper. 'Such a neat old guy,' Meggie thought. Her grandmother was the daughter of a Rabbi. What a unusual pair. They entered the small two-bedroom ranch house in the suburbs of Baltimore.

"Grandpa, this is Steven," Meggie kissed the old man's cheek. Grandpa rose from his fifty-year-old chair to shake Steven's hand.

"Cookelah, come eat," Grandma called from the kitchen. Grandpa sat back in his chair and continued to watch television.

Meggie led Steven into the tiny kitchen, seeing Grandma at the stove and two places already set at the small table. She leaned to kiss the short, gray haired lady,

"Grandma, meet Steven."

"You're the first boy Meggie ever brought here. Do you love her?" Grandma looked straight at him. Shock came over him. He turned red,

"Probably more than she knows."

"Sit, eat while it's hot." Grandma motioned with her hands for them to go to the table.

The first course was chicken soup with kreplach.

"My mother makes this but not as good as you do," Steven said, seeing a smiling Grandma. What a bunch of baloney, Meggie thought. He found a way to endear himself to her. After that came little hamburger steaks, about an inch thick and extremely soft.

Grandma never sat down, staying by her stove, pretending to be doing something, but really keeping an eye on them. Noticing Steven's plate was empty, she loaded it with more food.

"Grandma, it's delicious, but I've had enough," he said in disbelief.

"You're a growing boy, you need your strength, eat," she instructed, before walking away. He ate to be polite. When they finished, Meggie took the dishes to the sink, located two steps away.

"Thanks, everything was delicious as usual," Meggie leaned to kiss her. Steven walked into the living room.

"The old lady make you eat a lot?" Grandpa still watched T.V.

"I think I'm going to bust," Steven smiled.

"That reminds me of a story," Grandpa still not taking his eyes from the television, as he told his tale.

In the kitchen, Grandma wouldn't allow Meggie help her.

"Take this to Steven," Grandma handed her a bowl.

"Taiglach! Thank you," Meggie walked from the kitchen.

"My grandmother makes the best taiglach," she took a piece before handing the rest to Steven. Walking back into the kitchen, only to find Grandma finished, the two women returned to the living room. Meggie looked at Steven and the half empty dish.

"Oh! You didn't like the taiglach!" She laughed.

"Morris, you have to get this recipe," he smiled at her.

After talking to Grandma for a while as Grandpa still watched T.V., they decided it was time to head back to school. Grandma walked them to the car as she did with all her grandchildren.

"Cookelah, did you see the paper yesterday?" asked Grandma, with her arm on Meggie's shoulder.

"What happened now?" Meggie smiled, knowing what would follow.

"Some guy got into the dorm at the University of Maryland. Do you know what he did to those girls? They got him!" Grandma stroked her granddaughters hair..

"Don't worry, I have Steven," Meggie smiled, knowing he was taking in all of this.

"He doesn't sleep with you, so you be careful," Grandma stated. Meggie thought, 'If she only knew,' laughing inside.

"I also have Dottie. She's from Texas, they breed them big there. Stop worrying!" Meggie hugged and kissed her grandmother.

After they got into the car, Grandma motioned for them to buckle up. She swung her arm around the front of her body. Then motioned to the door locks. Meggie raised her arms to make her aware they were listening.

"We're buckled and the doors are locked," she yelled, and laughed at the same time as they pulled away.

"Your grandmother is a real trip." Steven laughed, seeing Meggie undoing her seat belt so she could move closer to him.

"She's terrific! One of a kind, and a worry wart. Grandpa's a neat guy. What story did he tell you?" Meggie laughed.

"The one when your parents were first married, he drove them to Atlantic City. After arriving there..." Steven laughed, Meggie broke in.

"Daddy got out of the car, kissed the ground. Thank you Lord! I can't believe we made it here!"

"You know the story," he glanced at her.

"Of course. I know all of his stories. That happens to be his favorite," she smiled.

"I guarantee you before I even get back to the dorm, she'll phone, expecting me to return her call. She always has to make sure that I get home safely," Meggie laughed. Steven extended his arm around her,

"I think you will have to call from my place. I'm not letting you out of my sight tonight," he pulled up to a red light, kissing her.

"Your beauty came from your father, your talent from your mother and your effrontery, from your grandmother," Steven laughed.

Time seemed to be passing quickly; it was already the end of March. Meggie and Steven were lying on the floor by the fire in the living room.

"I have to get married," Paul announced, walking into the room.

"If the Catholic Church allowed me to use one of those little rubber thingies, I wouldn't be in this bind," Paul sat himself on the sofa. Meggie burst into laughter.

"It figures; only she would find some humor in this situation," Paul glanced at Steven.

"It's not funny; it's just the way you said 'little rubber thingies,'" Meggie was tearing from her laughter.

"The wedding has to be by the end of April. Steven, be my best man," Paul asked, sullenly.

"Sure," Steven smiled.

"Why didn't she use something?" Meggie asked, cynically.

"She's Catholic, too," Paul stated.

"In that case, you should have abstained!" Meggie said, very bright-eyed. Her comment brought on laughter from everyone.

Later that night, she lay in bed with Steven.

"I feel bad for them: having to begin like this, with strings attached," Meggie, with her head on his shoulder.

"Oh, Morris, don't you know by now people make their own choices, whether they mean to or not. You can't feel bad for everyone who makes a mistake or has some bad luck," he said, before kissing her. "There are two people in this world I know of who should be married and spend the rest of their lives together."

"Who?" Meggie curious.

"You and me," Steven smiled, gazing into her eyes.

"Marriage is a very complicated relationship," she looked away.

"True, but when two people love each other, it can work," Steven put his arm around her, pulling her on top of him.

"Do you know what I'm saying?" he looked into those eyes again.

"Yes, do us both a favor. Give it a rest. It's not the right time," Meggie said.

One month later, Paul and Marriane were married. It happened to be the first Catholic wedding Meggie had ever attended. She was excited, always hoping for the best; it was the romantic in her. They were able to take Roger out of the hospital for the day. Motherhood definitely agreed with Marriane-she never looked better. She was not a pretty girl, but looked quite attractive today. She stood about 5'3" tall, had light brown hair, freckles and brown eyes. The ceremony took place in a small Catholic Church and the guest list was limited. Afterward, everyone returned to Marriane's family's home for the reception. Meggie stayed close to Roger, not wanting him to be alone or afraid. She somewhat mothered him.

"Be careful what you say to me; I may be falling in love with you," Roger smiled.

"Shove it!" Meggie told him. She wasn't aware of his state of mind; anyone who paid such attention to him was dear.

Steven and Meggie drove Roger back to the hospital afterward. He rambled on incessantly! Heading back toward D.C., they were happy he was gone, feeling somewhat guilty for that thought.

"You're alone in the brownstone now. Would you like Dottie and me to move in?" Meggie smiled. Steven stretched his arm to bring her toward him.

"You, not Dottie," he looked at her out of the corner of his eye.

"Sorry, you can't have one without the other," she laughed.

Entering the brownstone, Steven glanced around before taking her in his arms. They stood like that for a while. Steven thought of all the past experiences he had shared with Roger and Paul here. It would be different now.

"I never realized how quiet it is here," he said.

Steven lit the wood in the fireplace and Meggie went to the kitchen, opened a bottle of wine, and brought it, along with two glasses, into the living room. Placing everything on the table, she stood in front of the glowing embers. Steven poured the wine, watching her. Their eyes met as Meggie unbuttoned the front of her turquoise silk shirtwaist dress. She untied the belt and the dress slipped from her shoulders, falling to the floor. Having nothing on, she walked toward Steven, who simply sat in shock. She took her glass of wine and stood in front of him, drank it, and asked for more. He poured it before he stood.

"You never cease to amaze me," he smiled, taking her nude body in his arms, kissing her. Extending his tongue in her mouth, he felt every space of it, feeling her go limp again. Meggie knew, for some reason, Steven had a certain power over her. She lay on the floor in front of the fire, waiting for him to undress, their eyes never leaving each other's. He came to her.

"My beautiful Meggie," he whispered in her ear, before making love to her. Needing her to know she was his, would be his, forever.

Still lying in front of the fire, he placed his hand on her cheek, turning her face to him.

"Morris, why can't you tell me you love me? I know you do." Steven picked his torso up to look in her eyes.

"Love doesn't stay," Meggie tried to move away. He wouldn't allow her to.

"Don't you see, either someone dies, or someone gets hurt, betrayed, or love itself dies!" She looked at him.

"It doesn't have to be like that," he said.

"No? Then why is it they say, 'When the mystery is gone, love is gone,'" Meggie, seriously.

"I agree, mystery can be quite intoxicating," he smiled.

"Oh, Morris" Steven hugged her. "Don't run away from your feelings. Don't be afraid. If you don't take chances with your feelings, you're only existing. Make room in your heart for me. I have a feeling it's already there, but you won't admit to it." Steven glanced into her watery eyes.

The following evening, after making wonderful love again, they lay in bed entwined in each other. Steven thought their bodies were definitely meant for one another. It was always better than perfect.

Meggie jumped out of bed, yelling, "Oh no!"

"What's wrong?" Steven, surprised, saw her dash out of the room without a stitch on.

"The spaghetti!" she yelled.

He followed her down the stairs and stood in the kitchen doorway, laughing, watching her clean up the spaghetti noodles that had boiled over, and run down the front of the stove to the floor.

"Come here," Steven grabbed her by the elbow, lifting her up till she faced him.

"Marry me, I love you," he looked into her eyes, seeing fear shoot into them. Putting his arms around her, he drew her toward him. Their bodies touched, her head was on his shoulder.

"Don't be scared, I know you have reason to be cautious. I wouldn't hurt you for the world," Steven said, feeling something wet on his shoulder, realizing it was her tears.

"Marriage! It seems to be a popular piece of conversation with you lately! I'm not ready for this, you know that," Meggie cried, with a trace of a crack in her voice. Steven stepped back to look into her teary green eyes.

"I'm out of here in three weeks. School is over and my lease is up. I would like to travel and write. I want you with me. I've tried talking to you about this before."

"Oh, Steven," Meggie hugged him. "I have at least another year and a half of school left."

"College is an assembly line. They turn out everyone the same. You don't know what you want, you're too fickle," he smiled, trying to lighten up the situation for her. It didn't work.

"I don't know what you want from me! I enjoy being with you. I respect you, I trust you and I make love with you," she declared.

"Morris, I want you to tell me you love me! I want a commitment!" Steven finally stated his feelings..

"I'm not ready for that! There are some things you can't control. Like me!" Meggie turned around, giving him her back. Steven placed his hands on her shoulders, turned her around to face him. He smiled,

"Juliet was only thirteen when she married Romeo."

"And they had a wonderful wedding night-they both died!" Meggie said half in anger, half in jest

"Morris, I love you! I know you're aware of that. I also know you love me!" Steven said, before kissing her. They made love on the kitchen floor with the wet noodles.

The next morning, on their way out to breakfast, Meggie thought everything from the preceding night was behind her. She ordered three pancakes, bacon, two eggs over light, whole wheat toast, and a small orange juice. No, wait! Make it a large orange juice. Steven sat across from her.

"Your appetite never ceases to amaze me!" he watched her finish everything. He took her hands in his,

"Meg, I love you, probably more than you are aware. It's not possible for us to see each other again until you can say the same to me."

"What are you saying?" Meggie said, in shock.

"You are quite aware of what I am saying. Believe me, I'm going to miss you. I'm going to miss your smiling face, I'm going to miss even a trace of your laughter, your smell, I'm going to miss making love to you, I'm going to miss your sense of humor and your wit. But I think it best like this. You see, Morris, I love you too much. I need for you to admit how much you love me to yourself." Steven watched her-she was in a state of total disbelief.

"You can't be serious," tears rolling down her cheeks.

"Oh, my dear, sweet, lovable Meggie, I am. When you feel you can finally come to me, commit yourself to me and tell me you love me, I will find a way to let you know where I can be reached. I want you to keep in mind how much I love you and I always will," Steven still held her hands, with tears in his eyes.

"But," Meggie cried.

"No buts! I want all or nothing. I'm willing to wait for it if necessary, and it appears necessary," he stood, hugging her. He whispered in her ear, "Morris, always remember how much I love you."

"If you loved me, you wouldn't leave me," she cried.

"That's not so. It's because I love you, I must go," Steven said, with tears rolling down his cheeks.

"What am I going to do without you?" Meggie cried harder.

Taking her back to the dorm, there was not a word spoken between them. He stopped the car in front. Meggie leaned toward him,

"Please think about this."

"I already have," he kissed her one last time.

Steven drove back to Georgetown with tears running from his eyes. It has to be this way, he told himself, for both of us.

That evening, after she was told by Dottie she was a fool for not marrying Steven and not going with him, Meggie climbed into her bed, talking to herself,

"I won't be pushed. He's trying to force me to do what he wants, I won't be controlled! I'm my own person!" She thought about what Dottie had said. Double digit I.Q.'s filled her mind, falling to sleep.

During the course of the following two weeks, Meggie found herself too deep in thought.

"You seem despondent," Dottie stated.

"Not despondent, just depressed," Meggie never realized before how much she had depended on Steven.

One week later was the day of Steven's graduation. Awakening that morning with tears in her eyes, Meggie dressed and left hurriedly.

That same morning, Steven awoke extremely early. He had never been an early riser, except lately, because he missed Meggie so much. All he wanted was to have her with him, he thought, for the rest of his life. He climbed out of bed, took a shower and thought about her, sometimes even having a smile on his face. He dressed, thinking this should be a milestone in his life, but it certainly didn't feel that way. It was the day he would receive his Master's degree. He cried, knowing he was going out into the world alone, not being bothered by it, not being one for fear. It was Meggie-he wanted her with him; he felt like half a person without her. At the time, he felt he was doing the right thing, giving her space to grow up in. Right now he wasn't so sure. He wanted and needed her-God how he loved her! He felt he loved her more than life itself. He stood in front of the mirror in his bedroom.

"You are strong. You made an excellent decision, not an easy one, probably the hardest one you will ever have to make. You are going to live with it." Steven looked himself in the eye in the mirror, before he finished dressing.

Later that day, after the graduation, Steven's dad approached him, taking his son in his arms.

"I'm proud of you, son! Meggie was here," he whispered in his ear. Steven stood back.

"What! Where is she?" He glanced around.

"I recognized her from your slides of Europe. She sat in one of the back rows," Ian Roth stated.

Steven looked toward the back, seeing a little green car pull out of a parking space before driving away. He wished she would have stayed; he really needed to see her.

"Steven, I think you did the right thing. It's obvious she does love you, she just needs time to realize it." Dad put an arm on his shoulder.

"You know, I hurt sometimes. I sure hope she realizes it soon," Steven embraced his father.

Driving through downtown D.C., heading toward her dorm, Meggie cried the entire way. She didn't know why she even went; it hurt more than she would allow herself to admit. She simply wanted to lay her eyes on him one last time! Then, going into a trance about Steven, she found herself in front of her dorm, not remembering how she got there.

A few days later, just a few hours before his flight to Paris (after that, a connection to the Middle East- destination: Tel Aviv), a young man stopped and parked his car a half a block from a dorm on the American University campus. Waiting for a while, he saw a pretty blonde walk from the building and cross the street. He marveled at her grace, her beauty. He heard someone from a group of people yell to her.

"Meggie, over here!" He saw her raise her right arm to signal she had heard. He sat watching for a few minutes, her freedom for living. Pulling out of the parking space with tears, he headed toward Dulles Airport. He had to see her one last time before leaving the country, still wishing she were going with him.

Meggie had made no plans for the summer, not bothering to look ahead. Dottie was going back to Houston. Peter chose to stay in New Orleans, working in the French Quarter. He told her to join him but she wasn't in the mood for joviality. She couldn't handle spending three months with Chris and Alex, so she flew to Honolulu, deciding to take a few courses in liberal arts at the University of Hawaii. She knew she couldn't stay at home with Ma, though she loved Ben. She simply couldn't do it! She refused to stay in D.C. by herself: no Steven, no Dottie and no Michael. Realizing this, she decided, by May, she would graduate also! Choosing not to be there without her friends or Steven.

VIII

Arriving in Honolulu, Meggie handed Lori a letter.

"I'm not going to read it yet. Tell me what happened," Lori, curious. Meggie told her the complete and honest truth about Steven and the situation.

"You fool! Don't you realize most girls would give their eyeteeth to be in your shoes! To have someone like Steven love them, as he does you! To even want to marry them," Lori in disbelief.

"I am not most girls! I am me! Everyone I love must accept this, even Steven," Meggie said, irately.

"Pardon me, Miss Martyr!" Lori said, sarcastically.

"Standing by one's principles, doesn't make one a martyr! I'm simply conveying where I am coming from and what I believe in," Meggie said, not knowing where her own head was. Tears poured from her eyes.

"Look Lor, I love you, you know that. I'm simply not ready; that's all there is to it. I don't like being pushed! So many things have happened over the past couple of years. I need some space to sort out everything," Meggie cried. Lori put her arm around her cousin,

"I think Steven's giving you that space."

Later, Lori read her letter.

"Great! VIctor's coming!" Lori was excited.

"That's great? I think I'll leave." Meggie said in disgust.

"Daddy offered him a job, he'll be here in August. Come on, Meg, give him a chance," Lori pleaded.

Meggie chose to keep busy, finding that to be her best therapy. She registered to take three courses at the University of Hawaii. She played tennis, swam and she still saw a great deal of Richard. One day, she sat in his living room.

254

"I still tell you everything, don't I?" she curled herself up on some pillows.

"Meggie Hiken, you are something else!" Richard smiled.

"What is that supposed to mean?" Meggie raised her eyebrows.

"Most girls these days have a prime objective of getting married. They really don't care to whom, as long as they do. They go to college to receive their MRS.," Richard came to sit by her.

"I'll tell you like I told Lori. I'm not most girls, I'm me!" Meggie stated emphatically.

"I know, and I thank God for that, for giving you a mind of your own. That's very important," Richard hugged her. "But Steven does love you and I think you love him."

"I'm not capable of loving anyone," Meggie said.

"No!" Richard tried to look her in the eyes.

"No!" she yelled.

A week later was the Fourth of July. Lori wanted Meggie to go with her to the dance at the country club.

"Can Richard go?" Meggie asked, laying on the bed.

"He doesn't fit in there," Lori stated.

"Then, good-bye. I'll see you later," Meggie picked up a magazine.

"I don't know what you see in him," Lori said.

"I like his continuity. He impresses me, he's a straight thinker; he's got his priorities in line," Meggie smiled.

"I know you like the guys at the club," Lori not understanding her.

"Sure, to play tennis with. Otherwise, they are mere abstracts of their parents." Meggie flipped the pages of the magazine.

"If you are interested in becoming an armadillo junkie, I know where I can find you work!" Lori said, aggravated and left in a huff.

"That was good, Lor!" Meggie yelled after her. Lori returned,

"I'm sorry. It's just sometimes I have difficulty understanding you."

"I know-I'm not your normal person. I'm sorry to cause you such grief," Meggie, looking at her cousin.

"Don't be sorry. You're very special, and I love you," Lori embraced her before going out for the evening.

Richard stopped by an hour later and invited Meggie to see the fireworks. She jumped at the chance, loving them since she was a kid.

The following morning Meggie awoke with her normal stretch.

"You called me Steven last night," Richard glanced at her beside him.

"I'm sorry," she replied.

"No need. You're beautiful, do you know that? Especially in the morning." Richard rose from the bed, getting dressed. Afterward, he came to sit by her. She hadn't moved.

"What happened last night will not happen again. We're good friends, that's just what it was: two friends needing each other, closeness and contact. You love Steven. I know for certain now," he gazed into those eyes of hers.

Meggie simply stared at him, not saying a word. On his way out of the room, he paused at the doorway thinking, 'She's magnificent in so many ways-it would be easy to fall in love with her.' He already loved her as a friend and that's how it would stay. She's in love with Steven. He told himself before he walked away, this was just an expression of their friendship.

They were both thankful their friendship was able to continue as usual. They felt it was due to the respect they had for one another and wanting the very best for each other.

Mid-August, Victor arrived and had another confrontation with Meggie. She made reservations to return home the following day. Before she left, Victor approached her.

"I'd like you to try to understand. Dennis was the glue of the Fine family, and without him, we fell apart." Victor took her elbow and led her toward the beach.

"You were apart before that!" Meggie said, in disbelief.

"I came to that realization last night, thanks to Lori. At the same time, I discovered I have been blaming you for his death. I was wrong about so many things, especially about the way I have treated you. I believe that you did love Dennis. After my conversation with Lori, I am now aware of what hell you have had to go through. Can you ever find a way to forgive me?" Victor placed his hands on her shoulders, trying to express how sincere he was.

"Death is a very difficult thing to deal with. We all deal with it in our own way," Meggie glanced up at him, before he hugged her.

"Be good to Lori. She deserves the best," tears were in her eyes.

"I'm aware of that! She's one special person and I love her with all of my heart." Victor led her back toward the house. "Are you still going home today?"

"I think it best. I'm glad we had this talk. It will help in the future," Meggie smiled slightly.

"I don't resent you anymore. I've always liked you. I think you know that," Victor said, turning her face to look at him.

"I know. Let's leave the past behind us," Meggie said.

On her flight home, she read a couple of more chapters of *WAR AND PEACE* . Leaning back in her seat, she thought it had been a constructive summer: she earned nine more credits, felt far closer to Richard, and reached some sort of peace with Victor. After arriving home, she spent some time with Alex and Christine. Arriving at the conclusion Alex was spacier then ever and Christine more addicted, she wasn't able to take too much of either of them. She thought her tolerance level was low because she lost patience so easily. Rochelle had a new boyfriend, and Bob was spending his summer in Europe. Peter was having a great time in New Orleans, not returning home at all that summer. Ma and Ben were doing well. Ma was seeing a great deal of her old paramour, Albert. Meggie hated his name; she thought she even hated him.

The realization hit her that her parent's divorce would be final by the end of December. Trying to put it out of her mind, she went to visit Roger. He appeared to be doing much better; they planned on releasing him in a few weeks. Steven would be pleased, she thought, missing him; putting him out of her mind as well. She moved back to D.C. and registered for the up-coming semester. Her work continued in the S.D.S. office and she continued to write for the school paper. Writing her latest article on nuclear war, it was apparent she was unhappy.

> Sometimes the truth is hard to tell. It's also hard to hear. In 1962, our country faced the Cuban Missile Crisis, President Kennedy gave the Russians an ultimatum, forcing them to turn their boats around. We know the score. We know about nuclear bombs, about fallout; we've known for over 24 years. Atomic war would be like two suns exploding directly over you!

Sitting back and reading her article later, Meggie noted it was definitely depressing. It went with her state of mind.

Late in September, Roger was released from the hospital. Meggie met with him a few times. Each time, she felt he was getting worse, believing they released him too soon. He avoided her questions as to whether he was taking his medication. One weekend in mid-October, Meggie was dressing when she sensed something behind her, she turned around.

"Roger! How did you get up here?"

He smiled before dropping his pants, chasing her around the entire second floor of the dorm. She fled back to her room, trying to close the door as Roger pushed on the other side. It's amazing the strength one could muster up at a time like this, but it wasn't enough. He was able to force his entry, pushing her on the bed.

"I know you want it as bad as I do. Besides, women are to be used, then thrown away like a Handi-Wipe," Roger stated, with a twinkle in his eye, before reaching for her blouse.

Panic came over Meggie. She froze for a moment in disbelief, then struggled to get away. She couldn't, he was too strong. Out of the corner of her eye she saw Dottie moving quietly into the room. Before Roger knew what hit him he was in a hammer hold. He pushed Dottie back and she lost her balance, releasing her grip, and he was able to run from the room.

"What are you doing?" Dottie asked, seeing Meggie scanning through her phone directory.

"Calling his brother, Ted. Steven's not around to help him. Someone has to, and it's not going to be me!" Meggie upset.

After laying the receiver back down, Meggie finally heard the police sirens. The dorm mother heard what was happening and phoned them. 'They would have been too late, for a change,' Meggie thought. She approached Dottie.

"Thank you! Thank you! Thank you!" she kissed every inch of Dottie's face.

"Get lost!" Dottie laughed.

Ted arrived, and had no choice but to have his brother give himself up to the police and return to the hospital. He looked for Meggie,

"Are you Meggie?" Ted asked in disbelief, thinking, 'If so, I should have remembered her.'

"Yes," she said.

"I have to apologize for my brother; I'm sorry he frightened you." He stared at her.

"I didn't have much else to do today," she smiled.

He stepped back. Her mere presence aroused his emotions; he knew he was already hard. He wanted to be with her at some time, to know her and that body of hers. He said good-bye, thinking he would find a way.

Ted phoned Meggie in the beginning of November, inviting her to a party at his house. Even though Dottie was engaged to some person in Texas, Meggie talked her into going with her. They had a wonderful time, both girls deciding to sketch these colorful people. Meggie was intrigued, never knowing anyone quite like them before. Ted and his house mate, Tim, both wore clothing from India; acquired during their travels, they told her. A whole new experience, she thought, taking it all in, loving it. She and Dottie smoked some pot with them and took the lude Ted generously gave them. The only thing that brought Meggie down was Dottie, during the drive back to school. Being high, she was in the mood to talk.

"I lost my virginity last summer with Mark," Dottie blurted out.

"So, you're going to marry him," Meggie said, surprised.

"True, but I didn't like it. I wanted to talk to ya before this, but I didn't have the nerve. I was raised in an environment in which one doesn't speak of such matters," Dottie started to cry.

"I presently live in a very open environment, so don't be embarrassed," Meggie smiled.

"His parents were out for the night and we had dinner in their home. We had some wine and smoked some pot and before I knew it, we were in bed. Not that I objected. I love him; I was just a little scared. Before I knew it he was in me, then ejaculating on the sheets," Dottie said with tears.

"Why not in you?" Meggie asked.

"I've never used birth control before; there was no reason for it. I thought it would be better after that first time but it wasn't. The same thing happened three more times that night before he made it all of the way in me. When he took me home at two in the morning, I crawled into my bed alone. I felt no satisfaction, only a big emptiness inside. I wanted to die. I made excuses after that as to why we couldn't be together. I'm glad school started when it did. I know he loves me and I love him. Why do I feel like this?" Dottie burst into tears.

"Why didn't he use a rubber?" Meggie drove down Route 29.

"I asked that same question. He told me he receives no satisfaction that way," Dottie mumbled.

"This weekend I'll take you to see Dr. Marcus. You'll go on the pill. I promise, you will enjoy it," Meggie thought, 'What a selfish bastard.'

Thanksgiving crept up on her without Meggie knowing what to do with herself for the holiday. Dottie was flying back to Houston with high expectations. Ma phoned and invited her to spend the holiday with Ben, Albert and her. Meggie quickly declined, thinking, 'Albert, yuck.' She cried herself to sleep that night, wishing Steven were there. She missed him, his touch, his wisdom and wondered where he was, hoping he was well. They could have spent the holiday in Phoenix-he had such a stable family. Three days later, the phone rang.

"Hi, Munchie."

"Daddy!" Meggie, excited.

"I'd like you to spend Thanksgiving with me. Can you?" Dad asked.

"I would love it! Do you really want me? I don't want to cramp your style," she laughed.

"Are you kidding? You are the light of my life. We belong together on a holiday," he said.

"I'll be in on Wednesday night, okay?" Meggie smiled.

Meggie was excited. She hadn't seen her dad's new apartment in the newly constructed Charles Center. She hadn't even seen her Dad for a couple of months. Being single now, Morris Hiken had an entirely different lifestyle, and Meggie felt awkward about intruding.

One day, at the beginning of December, Meggie went to see Ted again. Dottie wanted some ludes to take back to Texas with her over Christmas vacation. The girls had learned Ted and Tim were drug dealers: acid, coke, ludes and pot. Meggie chose not to pass judgment-she enjoyed being around them too much. They were a good time-that's how she looked at it, a momentary thing. That's what intrigued her about them because she wasn't into drugs herself, except for an occasional lude or a smoke here and there. Her pot consumption had even slowed down since Dennis' death. In fact, she was afraid of drugs. She decided they were simply colorful people who made her laugh. Pulling into the driveway of the mansion they were renting, she sensed something out of place before noticing there were no cars around. She thought that unusual-there were always a lot of people around, creating a great deal of excitement. Meggie rang the doorbell. She glanced around but the place seemed barren. After a few seconds, Ted answered.

"What's going on, or what isn't going on?" Meggie questioned, still scanning the place. She followed him into the massive living area.

"Tim was busted," he frankly stated.

"What?" Meggie, surprised, never having known anyone who had been busted for dealing before.

"Paula you've met her," Ted said. She nodded, recalling one of Tim's girlfriends.

"Her husband set him up! Tim was selling him some acid when the cops arrived. They found him with a couple of pounds of pot in the car, along with the acid transaction. They have him on possession with intent to sell L.S.D. and marijuana," Ted paced back and forth.

"Jesus! What are you going to do?" Meggie in shock.

"Our attorney's with him now. Undoubtedly, we'll get him out on bail. How much, I don't know yet. We have to keep it cool for a while," he said, then kissed her. "I want you." Noticing the shock on her face. "Come off it! You can't possibly be that naive."

Meggie knew sex was his favorite hobby. On one occasion when she was there, he was in bed with two girls; on another, it was he, Tim and Paula. In fact, he was usually in bed with someone. She recalled him telling her, no strings, no hang-ups, no involvements. I love them all.

"No, Ted, I'm far from naive. I believed we were friends," Meggie stated, very-wide eyed.

"We are, but friends can enjoy each other," he said softly, touching her cheek.

Meggie remembered that one night with Richard, thinking it entirely different.

"It's not my style," she said, nervously, looking away. He smiled,

"I won't push. I do want to make you feel wonderful. I know I can."

She felt he wouldn't push; it was not his style. He liked his women to want it as much as he did. Believe it or not, she thought him somewhat of a gentleman. Retrieving the ludes for Dottie and wishing he and Tim luck, she left. She was sorry she hadn't asked about Roger, but she had no intention of going back. In fact, she thought she may never return there again.

A few days prior to the end of the semester, on a rainy Thursday afternoon, Meggie's phone rang.

"Hello, Meg?" a voice on the other end questioned. Meggie thought it sounded familiar.

"Jay!" she yelled. She hadn't seen him nor heard his voice since they said their good-byes in Paris well over a year ago. However, they did write to one another.

"Alright, bright lady, if you want another article for your school paper, you'll meet me," Jay drearily stated.

"You don't sound quite right," Meggie said, concerned.

"I'm not!" Jay answered, angrily.

"What the hell happened?" Meggie was curious and worried.

"Just meet me!" he yelled.

"Calm down! How do you expect me to fly to California on the spur of the moment?" Meggie held the receiver, feeling the sweat from the palm of her hand.

"We can do what ever we want to do, if we want it bad enough. Besides, I need you in Chicago," Jay said, sounding very shaky.

"Give me your number. I'll call you back if I can manage to get on a flight," she said, before placing the receiver down, feeling something was drastically wrong.

Meggie boarded a 7:35 p.m. flight leaving from Washington Airport to O'Hare Airport in Chicago. Landing at 8:45 p.m.. Chicago time, she disembarked and there was a frazzled-looking Jay waiting for her. She gave him an extremely curious look.

"You hungry?" he asked.

"My curiosity is piqued! But I didn't have any dinner nor did they include it on this flight," Meggie said, with Jay taking her carry-on garment bag from her. He led her toward the car he had rented and drove her to a coffee shop not too far from the airport. She ordered a club sandwich and a coke. He ordered the same, plus French fries, onion rings and soup. Meggie stared at him in bewilderment.

"I haven't eaten all day and I'm now beginning to feel it," Jay said, when the waitress left.

"You look terrible! Are you going to tell me what's going on?" Meggie looked at him, wanting some answers.

Jay pulled an envelope from his shirt pocket and handed it to her. She read the name written on the front,

"Gumboat?"

"A year before I left for Nam, I quit smoking. On the boat over I chewed gum continuously. I must have chewed at least a case of the stuff. Consequently, they nicknamed me Gumboat," Jay explained.

"It seems you picked your old habit back up," Meggie watched him puff away on a cigarette like a dragon.

Jay's soup arrived and Meggie took the letter from the envelope. It was dated December 7th, two days prior.

Gumboat,

> *I decided to check out. I can't handle the images my mind keeps feeding to me any longer. It's like a horror movie that plays continuously. You're the only one who can understand. Please explain it to my folks.*

Bill

"Did he do what I think he did?" Meggie looked up at Jay.

Jay took his right hand, stuck his pointer finger out, raised it to his temple and said, "Pop!"

"Oh my God!" Meggie said in semi shock, never visualizing before anyone shooting themselves in the head. Her elbows were on the table; holding her forehead with her left hand.

"Why you? You told me you weren't friendly with anyone but Jim Dean," she questioned.

"He's the one who had the kid die in his arms, then got it in the back, remember?" Jay glanced at her, feeling badly for dumping this on her. "You don't see, do you? He wasn't feeling sorry for himself; he simply couldn't live with what we did over there any longer," Jay started to cry. Meggie reached for his hand.

"Some people are stronger then others, more stable. Maybe sitting around in a wheelchair gave him too much time to think," she tried to console him.

"He worked! He was a mechanical engineer. True, he couldn't hold down a job for too long, having at least a dozen since being released from the hospital and the army. What you really mean, is some people are better at pushing bad experiences out of their minds than others," Jay stated, with Meggie relating to it.

"I received a phone call very early this morning from the Chicago Police Department, informing me what he had done and that he had left a letter for me-with no address. They asked me to fly out immediately, there were a lot of loose ends. After arriving here, I checked into a motel room before meeting with them and getting the letter. I returned to the room to read it. I didn't know what was in it but I felt Bill deserved that last bit of privacy. That's when I called you. You were the first person that popped into my head, I haven't shared this wonderful experience with too many people. After hanging up with you, I had to phone the police and inform them of the contents of the letter. I have to meet them at Bill's apartment tomorrow morning at nine-thirty," Jay said, paying the check and driving them to the motel where he was staying. He unlocked the door to his room.

"I'll go register," Meggie started toward the office.

"No!" Jay yelled, grabbing and hugging her. "We traveled through Europe together for nearly seven weeks. We practically lived together and I never once made any advances toward you. Honestly, at this moment, that is the farthest thing from my mind. I called you for selfish reasons. I don't want to be alone. I thought knowing what you already know, you would understand," Jay cried, Meggie hugged him.

"It's alright, I'll stay with you," she rubbed the back of his head. "Are we going to stay out here all night, or can we go in?"

Entering the room, she smiled. It had two double beds. She knew him, it was not like him to take advantage of anyone.

"First things first. I'm tired and in dire need of a shower," Meggie said with a slight laugh. Jay moved toward the small bathroom,

"It's all yours, my salubrious friend."

Meggie took her time in the shower. She walked back into the room wearing an extra-large, red, Hawaiian Magic tee-shirt which came to her mid-calf.

"Is that how you sleep?" Jay asked, with a slight smile, lying in bed under the covers, watching her.

"Either like this or in the raw," she smiled, being thankful she was able to make him forget a little, even if it was for a short period of time. She leaned to kiss him on the forehead.

"Goodnight, my boon companion," she climbed into her bed, turned the lights out. A few minutes later, she heard crying. She climbed from her bed and into Jay's.

"Shh," Meggie put her arms around him, feeling for him, the pain he was suffering. That is how they slept all night.

The following morning, Meggie awoke abruptly to the sound of the shower. She groggily gathered her thoughts and realized it was Jay. She rose and dressed in a royal blue shirtwaist dress, happy she thought ahead, this was not going to be a pleasure-seeking expedition. She had brought conservative attire with her. They left the motel room and walked one block to the nearest coffee shop.

After they ordered breakfast, Meggie asked Jay,

"Why do the police want to meet you at Bill's apartment?"

"Bill wants me to explain to his parents. I can't do that if I don't know how to reach them. His last name is Jones! Have you any idea how many Jones's there are in the Chicago phone directory?" Jay said as their breakfast arrived.

They pulled up to Bill's apartment and stood from the car.

"Alright, guy, take a deep breath," Jay said. Meggie knew he was talking to himself.

Bill's apartment was located on the first floor of a three story-dwelling. Meggie glanced around. It wasn't nearly as bad as she had imagined; it was far from being in the slums. They walked to the front porch where there was a man waiting.

"Mr. Marks, I'm glad you could come," the man stated, extending his hand. Jay shook it,

"Detective Daniels, this is Meggie, a friend of mine."

After exchanging amenities, all three walked into a small, one bedroom apartment. Meggie got the chills at first.

"I think we should start in the bedroom. That's where most people keep their personal belongings," Detective Daniels led the way. Jay started going through the dresser, directing Meggie to the night tables. Detective Daniels took the closet.

"What exactly am I looking for?" Meggie inquired, with the drawer from the night table on her lap.

"Anything that could give us even a hint of a clue as to where to reach his parents. It could be on a piece of scrap paper or an old match book. Sometimes people hide stuff in their underwear. You'd be surprised where things turn up, usually in the strangest places," Detective Daniels looked right into her eyes. He thought, 'What a beauty.' Meggie turned away, starting her search. 'How did some guy like this get her,' he wondered. 'It takes all kinds,' he thought, continuing his search through the closet.

Meggie finished with the night tables and walked from the room. The two men tore the bedroom apart, coming up empty.

"Detective Daniels," Meggie called from the living room. He walked in, to find her sitting behind an old roll-top desk.

"It's locked; can you get it open?" she asked. He was stunned for a moment looking at her again and motioned for her to rise.

"Let me see," he sat down, reaching into his pocket and pulling out a Swiss army knife. Within thirty seconds he had it open.

"There," Detective Daniels rose from the chair.

"The wonders of modern criminology!" Meggie laughed slightly, sitting down again. Detective Daniels stood staring at her.

About five minutes after Meggie started her search through the desk, "Look at this." She glanced up and saw Detective Daniels' eyes fixed on her. She wondered how long he had been doing that!.

"Look at what?" Jay walked into the room. Meggie handed him a photograph. He stared at it for a moment before stooping to be on her eye level. "This is me."

"I didn't need a higher mental power to tell me that! Which one is Bill?" Meggie eyed the photo. Jay pointed to Bill, then stood back up.

Detective Daniels was now in the kitchen, going through the drawers and cabinets. Meggie continued her search through the desk with Jay standing beside her, still staring at the photo.

"This was my platoon," he said, sullenly. "Only six of us came back, Bill was one. That makes it five, now." Tears rolled from his eyes.

"Jay, do us a favor and stop wasting time," she prescribed.

"It can be beneficial to have a friend like you," Jay moved toward a large chest in the living room.

Detective Daniels left the kitchen, announcing there was nothing there.

"I think I have something," Meggie smiled a little. Both men approached. "It seems to be an old scratch pad with a number on it." Detective Daniels took it from her.

He placed a call to trace the number. Hanging the receiver up, all eyes were on him.

"I didn't want to check it myself; I felt his parents should be informed in person. It's his parents' alright," he glanced at his notes.

"They are Elizabeth and William Jones; 12292 Iowa Place is the address. I think they should know as soon as possible; it's already been long enough," Detective Daniels said, putting his coat on.

"I'll follow you," Jay led Meggie through the door. Standing on the porch in the wind, Detective Daniels gave Jay directions.

"I'll meet you in the car," Meggie stated, before running to it.

A few minutes later, Jay sat in the driver's seat.

"It's only fifteen minutes away," he said, then started to laugh a little. Meggie didn't say a word, simply looking at him, concerned.

"He's enthralled with you! He overheard our conversation and discovered we're friends," Jay smiled.

"I'm delighted you are finding this so humorous! Please keep your eyes on the road because I value my life and yours!" Meggie was becoming upset.

"Meg, it's flattering! Especially when he wanted to know if I would mind if he called you. I told him, sure, no problem, but she lives in D.C. You should have seen the look on his face!" Jay was still laughing. Meggie started to laugh with him.

"You know, I thought I saw him staring at me," she smiled. "How old do you think he is, about twenty-eight. He's sort of cute," she wondered. Jay laughed harder,

"Cute! I'm no beauty, but next to this guy I look great!"

"True!" she laughed again.

Jay stopped the car in front of Bill's parents' house. He saw Detective Daniels getting out of the car parked in front of him.

"Oh shit!" Jay said, before opening the car door. Jay put his arm around Meggie's shoulder and she around his waist, Detective Daniels led the way, then rang the doorbell.

"Mrs. Jones, my name is Arthur Daniels, I'm a detective with the Chicago Police Department," he flashed his badge. Mrs. Jones stood staring at him.

"This concerns your son," he stated, as Mrs. Jones motioned for them to come in.

"Please sit down," Detective Daniels said, seeing her husband seated in an extremely old chair. Meggie thought, 'Older men apparently like broken-in things.'

"Bill Jones is your son. Would you rather I call him William?" the detective asked, looking at Bill's mother.

Meggie was amazed by his tact, something she never had. He also seemed to have a wonderful sense for other people's feelings.

"We call him Bill," Mrs. Jones said, frightened.

"Can you find him in this picture?" Detective Daniels handed them the photo of the platoon.

They both pointed to the same person Jay had; he matched the photos and I.D. from the crime lab.

"Your son was found two days ago in his apartment, dead," Detective Daniels reached to touch their hands.

Mr. and Mrs. Jones held each other, crying, for a while.

"How?" Mr. Jones asked, the tears still flowed from her eyes.

"Suicide, he obviously had a lot to deal with. He took a gun to his head," Detective Daniels had a few tears in his eye. He didn't want to hurt them if only that were possible. Meggie marveled at his strength; she hadn't had that thought since Steven.

"Mr. and Mrs. Jones, my name is Jay Marks. Bill wrote me, he wanted me to explain some things to you. We were in Nam together." He stopped, glanced at Meggie.

"Go on, you're doing fine," she smiled a little.

Deciding Jay should have some space, Meggie walked outside with Detective Daniels. Jay explained the entire, hideous, sordid story to Bill's parents, and cried with them.

On the front porch, standing and shaking from the Chicago cold and wind, Meggie now knew how it got its name: the Windy City.

"You're from Washington, D.C.," Detective Daniels said.

"No, I'm from Baltimore. I go to school in D.C.," she smiled.

"When will you graduate?" He asked.

"Hopefully, this spring," Meggie said, shaking from the cold, staring out at the street. He moved toward her.

"You're cold," He put his arms around her, to warm her.

"I'm not used to this. I do ski, but when I stand still, it gets to me," she welcomed the warmth of his arms.

Jay walked from the house with very watery eyes. Meggie moved toward him,

"You okay?"

"I don't know," Jay said, sullenly.

Meggie grabbed Jay's arm, holding on to him as they walked to the car. Detective Daniels followed, not taking his eyes off her. Jay opened the car door with Meggie sliding in. He started to walk around to the driver's side when Detective Daniels motioned to him. Jay was with him for over five minutes while Meggie sat in the car shaking and freezing. Jay finally got in.

"Cute! It took you long enough; I'm freezing," she exclaimed.

"I'm not the one in this group who is so damn attractive," Jay, with red eyes, smiled at her.

"And what is that supposed to mean?" Meggie, a little aggravated.

"Oh, Meg," Jay placed his arm around her, trying to warm her. He also needed some compassion right now. Tears rolled from his eyes. "Our good detective friend obviously has the hots for you." They both laughed a little. He pulled from the space with his arm around a still shaking Meggie.

"What happened back there?" she asked, trying to warm her hands.

"I told my story, they thanked me and I left. They'll call as soon as they know when the funeral will be," Jay became upset again. He pulled the car to a stop in front of a liquor store, Meggie looked at her watch. It was one-fifteen.

"What are you doing?" she asked.

"I want to get drunk, do you mind?" he stated, infatically.

"No, but I want to eat," she said.

273

"There's a grocery store next door," Jay got out of the car, heading toward the liquor store.

Meggie went to the grocery store and purchased what she wanted. Jay was waiting, when she returned to the car.

"Did you get your food?" he inquired.

"Of course! You know me, I never ignore my stomach," she smiled.

Arriving back at the motel, Meggie took out what she had bought, displaying them for Jay to see.

"Nuts, chips, pretzels, cheese, crackers and two ready-made turkey sandwiches. How'd I do?" she asked.

"You did terrific," Jay embraced her. "You have a way of putting a smile on my face." He still had some tears but was smiling a little.

"Now, let's get drunk," he took the ice bucket and left for the ice machine.

When Jay returned, they ate and they drank.

"What is this?" Meggie questioned, making a raunchy sound.

"It's Scotch," Jay laughed.

"It tastes terrible," she made a face.

"You'll develop a taste for it," he said.

They drank and ate some more, Meggie's two drinks to his seven. When three-quarters of the bottle of Scotch was gone, Meggie laid back on the bed,

"I'm too high," she sighed.

"That's fine by me," Jay lay on top of her before he kissed her.

"Sorry, Meg," Jay moved to the other bed, starting to cry again. Meggie came to him, placing her arms around him.

"It's okay, I understand," she held him as he cried. They fell to sleep holding each other, late that afternoon. The phone rang, awakening them at eight in the evening.

Jay answered it. Placing the receiver back down, he looked at an open-eyed Meggie.

"The funeral is planned for Sunday morning."

There was silence. She had nothing to say. Jay came to her, hugging her,

"You are one special lady, and I am taking you to the finest restaurant Chicago has to offer."

"That's not necessary," Meggie said, half-asleep.

"This is a first! You, turning down food!" Jay lay next to her.

"You saved me once, remember?" she whispered in his ear.

Sunday morning, Jay and Meggie stood by Bill's graveside for his funeral. Only a few other people were there: his parents, his brother and sister-in-law, an aunt and uncle, a cousin and Detective Daniels. Afterward, Bill's parents invited everyone to come back to their home. Jay went to speak with Mrs. Jones.

"We're flying out today. Meggie's plane leaves in an hour and a half and mine shortly after that. I wish we could have met under different circumstances," Jay said, with Bill's mom embracing him.

"I'm thankful my son had a friend like you in this world," Mrs. Jones cried, not letting go of Jay.

At the same time, Detective Daniels approached Meggie,

"You leaving today?"

"Shortly," she gazed at the ground. Funerals depressed her-too much history.

"Hey! You're upset," Detective Daniels took out his handkerchief to wipe her tears, thinking, 'What a beautiful girl.'

"Death does that to people, you know," Meggie looked at him.

"If I'm ever in D.C. or Baltimore may I call you?" he asked.

"Certainly," she smiled, with red eyes.

"You should do that more often." Detective Daniels smiled at her.

"Do what?" she asked, with furrowed eyebrows.

"Smile. You're so beautiful when you do," he still smiled, with Meggie starting to blush. Then she was saved.

"You ready? Detective Daniels, thanks for your help," Jay extended his hand. The detective took it.

"It's my job" he said, still watching Meggie.

"Hardly. There's a lot of human spirit there. I am happy to have met you," Meggie touched his hand.

They said their good-byes and Detective Daniels watched them as they walked away.

Jay's plane was due to leave an hour after Meggie's. He dropped her off to get her boarding pass, telling her he would meet her at the gate after he returned the rented car to Hertz. He showed up twenty minutes before boarding.

"It took you long enough!" Meggie said as Jay entered the waiting area.

"You know how it is with these rental companies," Jay sat beside her, extending his arm around the back of her seat.

"You were a real life saver-a virtual well of moral support. I'll never forget this," he looked at her.

"That's what friends are for. You deserve the best; you are an incredibly good person, one of a kind," she kissed his cheek. Jay leaned back in the seat, stretching his legs in front of him.

"Do you know what's going to get me home?" he smiled.

"Yes! A plane," Meggie laughed.

"No! Detective Daniel's' crush on you!" Jay said, they laughed. A few moments later, Jay became solemn again.

"A problem?" Meggie took his hand.

"Not anymore, I don't think. I was just struck by the thought I buried a piece of the past back there. I was wondering if I should feel a little guilty for feeling freer and better," he said. Meggie put both of her arms around him.

"You should never feel guilty about anything, especially things that are out of your control. You're too fine a person. Promise me, no more guilt for anything from here on." She gazed into his brown eyes.

"You know, you have beautiful eyes," Jay said, looking into them.

"They are one of my better attributes, but don't change the subject," Meggie smiled. He hugged her, hearing the call for her to board her flight.

"You have to go," Jay said.

"Not until I get an answer," Meggie whispered in his ear.

"I don't know whether I can promise, but I can try," he hugged her.

"That's all a person can ask from a friend. I love you," Meggie said, with tears running down her cheeks. Hearing the call for final boarding.

"I think you'll be fine," she headed toward the gate.

"Thanks to you," Jay said. Meggie turned around, gave him a big smile and waved her arm in the air.

"I love you, too," he yelled to her.

Her plane took off, Meggie leaned back in her seat, thinking how easy it was for her to express her feelings to her friends. She decided to put it out of her mind, getting out pen and paper. She knew it wouldn't be published until the beginning of the following semester, the end of January. Right now it was fresh on her mind and she wanted to get it on paper. Deciding to write the article,

> Vietnam, the killer of minds, of souls, of spirit, of people.

Vietnam, the making of trumpery from the masses. Last year I wrote an editorial on one man's war; this is a follow-up.

Meggie walked into their room, and saw Dottie reading on her stomach, propped up on her elbows on the bed.

"How was Chicago?" Dottie asked.

"Windy," Meggie removed her coat and threw all of her things on her bed.

"You know that's not what I meant." Dottie arrogantly.

"Read this, then you'll know," Meggie threw her the article she had just written.

Meggie disrobed for the shower, when she returned, Dottie looked at her with tears in her eyes.

"Was it as bad as this?"

"Worse!" Meggie stated, climbing into bed with nothing but a towel around her.

Over Christmas vacation and semester break, Meggie decided not to go to Hawaii. Instead, she would stay at school and earn six more credits during the mini-mester, so she could graduate in May. She went home for only a day to see Ben, feeling she couldn't stay, she didn't belong there any longer with Ma and Albert. One night in the dorm, alone in her bed, she felt totally alone, not having anyone or a place in this world where she belonged. She felt far more alone than she had ever felt, with the knowledge, she had been spending a great deal of time by herself lately. She cried herself to sleep, feeling completely empty and abandoned. Where's Steven?

Peter came in from New Orleans for a few days for New Year's; she thanked God for that. Meggie spent those few days at his parents' home with him. His folks couldn't get over the change in her, mostly her sarcastic attitude.

"I'm considering taking a summer job with an archaeologist in Chichen Itza, Mexico," Peter informed her.

"I thought you were considering geology instead?" Meggie questioned.

"A person can change his mind; freedom of choice. I believe I'll be happy in archeology," Peter smiled.

"In simpler terms, you want to be a grave digger!" Meggie said, sarcastically. Peter laughed, always loving her comments.

Meggie was well aware she was going through a bad time. She tried desperately to find a place for herself, being totally confused, miserably unhappy and missing Steven. Then she decided to put it all out of her mind.

That night, Meggie and Peter brought in the New Year of 1970. The beginning of a new decade, closing the doors on the one left behind. The year North Vietnam invaded Laos. The year Charles DeGaulle died. The year of violence in the United States.

IX

Mid-January, Dottie returned to school with a great deal of enthusiasm about her upcoming wedding. She thanked Meggie for taking her to see Dr. Marcus, and asked her to be her maid of honor. The girls searched for dresses throughout Washington and Baltimore. Meggie was glad Dottie was back; she had really missed her.

A few days later, Meggie received a call from Ma, telling her Grandpa had died. On her way home for the funeral, Meggie couldn't help but think about this kind old man. She hoped he hadn't suffered. She thought about all of his stories and how chapped and scarred his hands were from working as a shoemaker. She recollected the time Grandpa took her for a walk near her parents' home and he pointed to a high stone wall.

"This is Seton Institute, a place for sick people," he smiled at a five year old Meggie, who thought the wall was huge.

"Mommy told me this was a bad girls' school and if I wasn't good she would send me here," Meggie remembered saying, with tears in her eyes. She recalled always finding wisdom from him.

"You bad? Never! My little love," Grandpa picked up this little package, swinging her around.

Meggie cried thinking of him and how lucky she was to have had his love all of these years. How she was going to miss him, how she loved him. He always used to say,

"East and west, home is the best!" Meggie cried harder.

By the end of January, Meggie's article on Bill Jones and Jay was published in the school paper. This time, Jay gave his consent for her to use names. Knowing he would appreciate it, she sent him a copy. Two days later she received a phone call.

"When would it be convenient for you to come to my office?" a voice on the other end asked.

"That depends on who this is," Meggie became aggravated.

"I am sorry: I should have identified myself. I'm Admiral Phillip Bennett from the Pentagon," he coolly stated.

"Oh!" Meggie said, surprised and at a loss for words, with a little fear coming over her.

"Friday would be good; I have no classes," she said, shaking.

"My office, Friday, eleven a.m.," he stated, before saying good-bye.

Friday morning Meggie rose quite early, showering and washing her hair; she began to dress conservatively.

"No way!" she said to herself.

She hung the pink shirtwaist dress back in the closet and removed a turquoise sweater mini-dress. Putting it on with no bra, watching it cling to her body, she smiled to herself in the mirror. The finishing touch was matching suede boots. Donning a white wool cape, Meggie set out for the Pentagon. Being frightened was an understatement. She felt this Admiral was definitely going to come down heavy on her, her instinct told her, for saying things this country didn't want to hear and the Pentagon didn't want said. She was prepared, however. Parking her car and carrying her portfolio, she made her way into the Pentagon. She was stopped at the front door.

"I have an appointment with Admiral Phillip Bennett," Meggie stated, starting to become aggravated with bureaucratic red tape. She didn't like being questioned, especially when she was nervous. The five-foot, brown-haired girl behind the desk seemed to be taking her time scanning a list.

"Security, you know. He's on the third floor," she said, finding the name, Meggie Hiken.

Meggie headed to the elevator, feeling tense and anxious, wishing she hadn't had any salt recently. Upon stepping from the elevator on the third floor, she saw another security person. She wondered what these Pentagonese were afraid of. She approached the man and stated her destination.

"Admiral Bennett's office is down this hall," he pointed in the direction.

Walking down the narrow corridor, Meggie noticed her hands were once again in fists. She approached a set of double doors marked 'Admiral Phillip D. Bennett' and wondered what the D stood for. She opened one to find a receptionist, or a secretary; it was irrelevant which, she thought.

"I'm Meggie Hiken. I have an appointment with Admiral Bennett," she said, to a short, slender, dark-haired lady.

"Miss Hiken, the Admiral's expecting you. Follow me, please," she led Meggie through another set of double doors. To find a man sitting behind a desk with his back to them, gazing through a large window.

"Admiral Bennett, Miss Hiken is here," she said. He swung his chair around, glancing at his secretary.

"Thank you, Miss Stone." She left, closing the door behind her.

"Sit down, Miss Hiken, please," he watched her remove her cape.

"You are Meggie Hiken?" Admiral Bennett questioned, hardly able to believe his eyes.

"Yes, why do you ask?" Meggie looked at this incredibly handsome man.

"I expected someone with large glasses, a little fat, maybe, even some curly hair. I never fathomed the author of those wonderful articles would be someone like you," he smiled.

"I anticipated an Admiral of at least sixty-five years of age, not one of thirty-five," Meggie smiled. They both laughed, still watching each other, both pleased with what they saw.

"Miss Hiken," Admiral Bennett said, trying to take control of the situation.

"It's Meggie," she stated.

"Meggie, I read your article of a week ago in the American University paper. I wanted to apprise you of the fact that not all of us here at the Pentagon are such bastards. I would like to present to you a different point of view. Afterward, if you feel it worthy of your editorializing, I promise there will be no ramifications," Admiral Bennett looked at her, waiting for a reaction.

"You seem surprised," he said, still with his eyes on her.

"I am. I honestly didn't expect this! Right here I carry a portfolio containing every article I have ever written about Vietnam, prepared to defend myself. You have totally mystified me," Meggie in shock.

"You need no defending. I read the college campus' papers to keep informed as to what is happening there. I have read many of your editorials. You are quite honest; that's why I desired to meet you. Everything is not exactly what it appears to be," he sat back.

"What does that mean?" she questioned.

"It simply means there were, and still are, other obstacles to conquer. We are in an untenable situation in Vietnam, and there are various other issues involved," Admiral Bennett stated.

"What other issues?" Meggie asked, alertly.

"I'm not at liberty to say," he said.

"I'm not surprised-typical bureaucratic close-out!" she was sarcastic.

"One moment! I didn't invite you here for a confrontation. I thought you'd be interested in a different point of view. I could be sticking my neck way out," he raised his voice.

"I will obviously listen; otherwise, I wouldn't be here," Meggie stated.

"I had a feeling you'd be interested. You seem so honest and open-minded in your articles," he smiled, pausing before he began.

"Unfortunately, we live in a society that is imperfect. We have Vietnam, there is nothing we can do to deny that! Whether we choose to accept it or not, the South Vietnamese need us. They have no choice, not desiring to fight their own war. However, we are working our way out. Be aware before we do, it will get worse. We are in desperate need of a change in policy. In reality, we are letting them down, basically because of the atmosphere in this country toward this war. There have been too many killed, too many injured. It is honestly unfair to continue any longer," Admiral Bennett leaned back in his chair again. Meggie, in shock, stared at him,

"How do you justify this duplicity?"

"I don't believe it's duplicity. Maybe your generation is too jaded to understand," he looked her in the eye.

"War, we understand: how senseless it is, an illegal diversion. It's the Detroit of bacteria," she stated, angrily. The Admiral smiled, liking her mind. It angered Meggie even more.

"You need not become angry," he saw it written all over her face.

"Feel fortunate. Anger is a tempered response," she glanced down, then to him again. "So why keep drafting people and why continue?"

"There are values in this world that have to be upheld," he firmly stated.

"Do you know what I was once told?" Meggie did not giving him a chance to answer. "I was told you guys here in the Pentagon don't care about the youth of this country, unless you can convince them to enlist and fight this war of yours. If you fail to succeed, their minds are undisciplined." She looked straight into his green eyes.

"Not true," he bluntly uttered.

"As you walk down these battle scarred-corridors of military- obligation every day, do you ever bother to embrace the day with open arms and hope all goes well?" she inquired, with furrowed eyebrows.

"You come through life one time. If it were up to me, I'd make everything right for everyone," Admiral Bennett, with a slight smile.

"Renaissance Man," she mumbled.

"What?" he uttered not understanding her.

"You have enlightened me. I'd like to hear more," she smiled.

"We call it the Americanization of the Vietnam War," Admiral Bennett said as he leaned back in his chair, looking more into space, then to her. He paused before continuing.

"Until 1960 the United States had supported the Saigon regime and its army only with military equipment, financial aid, and 700 advisers for the training of the army; as permitted by the Geneva Agreement. By the end of 1963, the number of advisers had increased by more than 20 times and they were joined by a rising number of U.S. helicopter pilots. All of this proved insufficient to halt the advance of the Viet Cong. In 1965 President Johnson ordered the bombing of North Vietnam, hoping to prevent further infiltration into the south. The bombing failed to stop Hanoi's support for the Viet Cong. On the contrary, according to our intelligence, the Hanoi government began to infiltrate its first regular army units. Four weeks later we sent our first combat troops to Vietnam - 3,500 United States Marines." Admiral Bennett paused again, glanced over at Meggie. Her eyes were fixed on him, taking all of this in. He broadly smiled before speaking again,

"With the Tet-Offensive of 1968; during which the Viet Cong and North Vietnamese attacked more than 100 cities and military bases, the situation became evident. There was a growing conviction here that a military victory was highly improbable. We restricted bombing of the north, which opened the doors for U.S. negotiations with Hanoi in May of 1968. By November of 68', bombing had been halted over all of North Vietnam. We have already begun a gradual withdrawal of troops. Though, they are still fighting in Laos and I fear soon the war will head into Cambodia. It has truly become an Indo-Chinese war. Be assured, we are on our way out." Admiral Bennett concluded, now moving forward in his chair a little.

"When will we finally be out?" Meggie questioned, not being able to take her eyes off this incredibly handsome man, and somewhat mesmerized by his speech.

"I couldn't venture to say. If it were up to me, it would be expedited," he stated.

"You're a democrat!" she said, surprised. He made no comment.

"Admiral Bennett," Meggie paused, then continued. "The horror of the Vietnam War is not just the misfortune it has brought to this country as a whole. It's a personal tragedy for those who have served there, and those who have died. In many cases there are men who are still living in a nightmarish hell."

"I'm quite aware of that unpleasant fact," he leaned towards her a little. "My dear, changes are not going to come about by you and I discussing this war. All changes take place in three worlds; the physical, the logical, and the emotional worlds."

"I believe if one is willing to stand by one's principals change may occur," Meggie said.

"That alone is not enough. In order to make a difference one has to be willing to put oneself on the line," he smiled.

"Like you," Meggie smiled, thinking, 'Renaissance Man' again. He glanced at his watch, then to her.

"We have a decent restaurant here. I would be honored if you would join me for lunch."

"Eating is one of my favorite hobbies," she smiled.

"You are cute," he rose from behind his desk.

"So I've been told, but I never paid much attention to it." She laughed a little, uncomfortable with the compliment.

Sitting at the table after they finished eating.

"What is your opinion of what I had to say?" the Admiral smiled.

"Why? Do you have political expectations?" Meggie inquired.

"You happen to be quite adept, but don't read into things. It's far from being healthy," he stated.

"Why did you call me instead of a real reporter, from the *POST*, for example?" Meggie pushed the food around on her plate.

Admiral Bennett was stunned. He had come across so few people who were this candid with him.

"I believe we all have the right to participate in the ebb and flow of current affairs. I think you agree with that," he said, seeing Meggie nod her head in agreement, liking what he had to say.

"I respect your convictions, your honesty and your ability to see through a facade. Besides, I didn't ask you here for notoriety; I desired to speak to the person who had written all of those intriguing articles," Admiral Bennett looked into her eyes. He thought, 'I never expected anyone quite like this.'

Rising from their seats they walked from the restaurant,

"Thank you for lunch and an extremely informative morning," Meggie extended her hand. He took it to shake, holding it.

"It was my pleasure," he smiled. "I would like to see you again," he still held onto her right hand.

Meggie glanced down, seeing a ring on the fourth finger of his left hand.

"I don't think so," she smiled.

Returning to her dorm, Meggie wrote the article. She found it easier when things were fresh in her mind.

> One Admiral's point of view: un homme sans peur, sans reproche - an honest man, without fear, without reproach.

Typing it, re-reading it, she smiled to herself before mailing a copy to Admiral Bennett.

The following Monday morning, the last day of January, Admiral Phillip Bennett sat behind his desk, staring at the many papers lying there. He was trying to decide which to tackle first when Miss Stone entered his office.

"This just arrived; I thought you'd like to see it," she handed him a large manila envelope.

Upon reading the return name and address, he opened it immediately. He smiled as he read, "un homme sans peur, sans reproche". After he finished reading, he sat back in his chair deep in thought before buzzing his secretary.

"Get me Miss Hiken."

In a few minutes his inter-office intercom buzzed.

"Admiral, she's not in; I left a message," Miss Stone said.

"Thank you," he swung his chair around, staring through the window, until his thoughts were interrupted.

"Admiral Bennett, you have a ten o'clock appointment with Senator Warfield," Miss Stone approached.

"Try to reach Miss Hiken again. Set up an appointment for seven this evening," he instructed, walking from his office.

Two-thirty that afternoon, Meggie arrived back to her dorm and received the message that Admiral Bennett had phoned. Curious, hoping he was pleased with the article, she returned the call.

"Hello, this is Meggie Hiken."

"Thank you, Miss Hiken, you saved me another phone call. Admiral Bennett is tied up in meetings all day. However, he asked me to arrange an appointment with you at seven this evening, for dinner," Miss Stone stated.

"I won't be able to make it. Please thank him for me," Meggie said before placing the receiver back in place. She thought, 'Who does he think he's dealing with?' She undressed and attacked a drawing, putting the episode out of her mind.

At six o'clock, Dottie came excitedly, rushing into their room,

"There's a gorgeous man in the lobby looking for you!"

"Oh shit!" Meggie rose from her bed, walking to the closet.

"Who is he?" Dottie curious.

"Admiral Phillip Bennett," Meggie stated, as she put on a hot pink clingy mini-dress.

"That's Admiral Bennett!" Dottie laughed.

"See you later," Meggie grabbed her cape on her way out. She walked into the lobby, finding the Admiral standing by the front desk. Upon seeing her, he approached,

"I would like to speak with you." Admiral Bennett took the cape and draped it over her shoulders.

"That's what I've been told," she smiled, as he led her from the dorm toward a chauffeur-driven limousine.

"Do all Admirals travel like this?" she watched him open the door.

"Hardly," he laughed, helping her into the limousine, then sliding in beside her.

"Since eating is your hobby, how about dinner?" Admiral Bennett asked.

"That would be fine," she nonchalantly stated.

He tapped the glass dividing the two sections of the limousine, signaling to his chauffeur. Then glanced at her,

"It occurred to me the reason you refused to see me again was because you had the notion I was married."

"Aren't you?" Meggie questioned.

"I won't be in one month; my divorce will be final then," he said.

"Why the ring?" she glanced at his hand. It was gone! He laughed,

"I should have taken it off long before this; I never really considered it. It was easier this way, not having to answer questions. My estranged wife and I have not lived together for five years now."

"The more I learn about people, the more amazed I am. Do you have any children?" she asked, curiously.

"Unfortunately, no. I used to believe it was because I traveled so much, but that was not the case. She didn't want any," Admiral Bennett became solemn. He gazed out of the window, not ready to share the rest. He turned toward her,

"Is that why you declined my invitation?"

"Partially; I don't date much. In fact, I think the last time I went on a date was sometime last summer. I have friends, though. I'm too busy," Meggie smiled.

"I find this difficult to believe," he looked questioningly at her.

"Why?" she inquired.

"You have too much to offer; I would think your phone would be ringing off the hook. It's obviously your choice,"

Admiral Bennett extended his arm around the back of her seat with his hand dangling on her shoulder.

The limo came to a stop, the Admiral helped her from the car.

"It's snowing!" she smiled.

"You obviously love the snow," he replied, taking her hand, leading her toward the door of his club.

"Admiral Bennett, do you know..." Meggie said, excitedly, not being able to finish her thought because she was interrupted. He stopped walking and gazed into those eyes of hers.

"I think it's time you called me Phillip." She laughed,

"Phillip! Do you know a typical snowflake falls at an average of two miles per hour?"

"No, I really was unaware of that piece of pertinent information," he smiled, placing his arm around her shoulder, leading her in.

Once inside, Meggie glanced around, extremely wide-eyed. It was aristocratic and formal. She had never seen anything like it before.

"Good evening, Admiral Bennett," the maitre'd took Meggie's cape and the admiral's coat. She looked curiously at Phillip. He simply smiled as the maitre'd led the way to a table. He pulled out a chair for Meggie first, then one for Phillip, before handing him the wine list. She sat, looking around for a few minutes, taking it all in. Then she stared at him.

"Don't we get menus?"

"After I order the wine, they'll bring me a dinner menu," Phillip smiled, finding her refreshing.

"Then will you please hurry up and order it," she said, with a tilt of her head.

"The selection of a fine wine can't be rushed; there's a part to selecting the perfect wine for the perfect evening," he stated very sincerely, with Meggie breaking into laughter.

Phillip finally ordered the wine and the waiter handed him a dinner menu. Meggie was in shock,

"Don't I get one?" He laughed,

"Sorry, no. This happens to be a men's club."

"And what is that supposed to mean?" Meggie asked, angrily.

"Women are allowed here for dinner; the men take the responsibility," Phillip said, finding it hard to control his laughter.

"What kind of chauvinistic place is this? Women have always been exploited by men!" Meggie stated irately, watching Phillip sitting back in his chair, laughing.

"I'm delighted you are finding this so amusing!" she said, before the waiter approached the table.

Phillip glanced at the menu again. Meggie eagerly watched, wondering what she was about to have for dinner.

"For the appetizer, we'll have two shrimp scampi," he glanced shortly at the waiter before returning to the menu.

"Two salads with the club dressing, two prime rib, medium rare, the oven potatoes and the asparagus," he closed the small menu and handed it to the waiter. The waiter walked away.

"You didn't even ask me what I wanted! What right do you have to choose for me?" Meggie irritated.

"You will like it," Phillip said with a smile.

"Whether I like it or not is irrelevant! I happen to have a mind of my own; I am an individual and I would like to be treated as such. I don't ever plan on being one of your little citizens in snug city!" Meggie stated her mind.

"You made your point," he took her hand. "From here on, you make your own choices."

She sat with a smile on her face, thinking him to be definitely different from anyone she had ever known. After the wine was placed on the table, Phillip lifted his glass to make a toast.

"To the libertine in my life." The appetizers were then served.

"This is fantastic," Meggie said to him.

"I knew you would enjoy it," he said, pleased with himself. "Why haven't you asked me?"

"I was waiting for you to say," she smiled.

"The article happened to be wonderful," Phillip said. Finishing his shrimp, he lay the fork down.

"You have a magnificent talent for finding the truth and elaborating on it, as well as a unique way with words," Phillip smiled as their dinner arrived. "Do you graduate this May?"

"Hopefully," she smiled.

"What are your plans?" He asked, finding it hard to take his eyes off of her, feeling drawn to her.

"I really haven't made any," Meggie stated, cutting her prime rib.

"If you would like a job with a paper, I would be happy to use my influence. I believe they would find you invaluable," he said.

"Thank you; I don't think that necessary," she laughed, laying her fork on the table, not giving him a chance to reply.

"I happen to be an art major. I love to paint. If you think I write well, you should see what I can do with a canvas and some oils."

"I would love to," Phillip said in shock.

"I'm really not a writer. I started writing for the school paper as an outlet for my frustrations. That was after I was arrested a few times for protesting against the war. Subsequently, I realized these sit-ins didn't do much good, only made a statement, so I started writing. I feel the articles I have written are somewhat more constructive. Being so against this war, I could not sit idly by; I had to participate in some way. Do you see?" Meggie looked at him.

"I do understand," Phillip took hold of her hand again.

"Admiral Bennett, which would you like?" the waiter approached with the dessert cart.

"Which one?" Phillip glanced at Meggie. She scanned the desserts,

"Thank you. I'll have the strawberry tart."

"Make that two," Phillip smiled. "Were you aware of the look on his face?"

"Honestly, he better get used to it. Women are starting to come out of the woodwork in this country," Meggie stated, then devoured her tart.

"Did you enjoy it?" Phillip laughed.

"I have to admit, the food here is good," she smiled.

"Eating really is your hobby!" Phillip still laughed, leaning back in his chair.

The snow was almost six inches deep when they left the club. The limo pulled up, Phillip opened the door, helping her in again and slid in beside her. He took her in his arms, kissing her as they drove away. Meggie was shocked, trying to keep her wits about her.

"Do you know how to keep milk from going sour?" she asked. He shook his head no.

"Keep it in a cow," she smiled. Phillip looked at her admiringly, never having known anyone quite like her. He put his arm around her again, leaning his head on top of hers,

"You are very surprising. You are also a well of obscure information." Phillip motioned for the driver to stop as they neared her dorm. He turned to Meggie.

"How about walking a few blocks?"

"In the sno-wonderful!" she smiled.

He opened the car door, got out, then extended his hand for her.

"Thank you, sir," Meggie took his hand on her way out of the limo.

Phillip put both of his arms around her,

"To you, I am never 'sir'." Then he kissed her.

She broke away yelling, "Sir Gallahad!" She picked up some snow, made it into a ball and threw it at him. He threw one at her as she ran. It took him nearly a block before he caught her, laying on top of her in the snow, kissing her. He gazed into her eyes,

"You have brought back a spark in me I thought was long gone."

"I can't remember the last time I was kissed like that," Meggie smiled. He kissed her again the same way, placing his tongue in her mouth, searching every space of it. He stood, helped her up, and walked toward her dorm with his arm around her shoulder.

"Will you have dinner with me again tomorrow night?" he smiled.

"Sorry, don't be offended. I have to finish a drawing I should have completed tonight, plus a painting that's due on Wednesday," she said.

"Wednesday then," Phillip said, before stopping, kissing her again.

"Not then, either. I have too much work to do. How about Thursday?" she said as they approached her dorm.

"I have no choice, Thursday," Phillip placed his arms around her, kissing her the same way as he did when they were on the ground.

"Goodnight Admiral" Meggie smiled, entering her dorm. He was still standing there in semi-shock, staring at the door, when his limo pulled up.

Meggie found Dottie already in bed when she walked in.

"Well?" Dottie looked up.

"I had a wonderful time!" Meggie threw her arms in the air, spinning herself around.

A few moments after undressing, Meggie lay in her bed with her head buried in her pillow.

"If that's the case, why are you crying?" Dottie rose from her bed to sit by her roommate.

"I honestly don't know," Meggie looked at her with tears on her cheeks.

"It's Steven," Dottie put her arms around her. "When are you seeing the Admiral again?"

"Thursday," Meggie sadly replied.

"Good! Maybe this will bring you to your senses," Dottie still held her.

Two days later, on Wednesday, Meggie had her painting class and afterward she worked in the S.D.S. office, as usual. At five-thirty, on her way to her dorm, she noticed a black limousine parked in front. She shook her head, aware of who it was. Seeing her approach, he got out and walked toward her.

"How about dinner?" Phillip took her portfolio from her.

"I told you-I have too much to do!" Meggie said, trying to get her portfolio back. He smiled, not allowing her to retrieve it.

"You have to eat."

"Look at me! I'm not dressed for one of your fancy places," Meggie aggravated.

"We'll go to a Hot Shoppes," he laughed, taking her hand.

After entering, Meggie removed her coat, revealing a pair of old paint-laden jeans and her lavender reefer tee-shirt. Phillip smiled at her as they slid into a booth.

"What did you expect? I was in painting class all day," she said, with her eyes open wide.

"You look adorable," he smiled, taking her hand, with his eyes focusing on her nipples extending through her tee-shirt.

Phillip looked at her after they ordered.

"Forgive me; I was impetuous. I needed to see you and I couldn't wait until tomorrow."

"So you are seeing me in my primary state," Meggie stated. "I've been meaning to ask you. What exactly do you do at the Pentagon?"

"One could say I analyze decisions," Phillip tried to avoid.

"A decision analyst, what does that mean?" Meggie asked, curiously.

"There are some things that cannot be discussed" He smiled.

"Top secret; I don't believe I like this!" she said, as their food came.

As they were leaving the Hot Shoppes, Meggie knew she would never forget this meal with a prim, proper, starch-collared admiral in a diner!

"Don't you ever drive yourself?" Meggie asked, sitting in the back of the limousine.

"No, I don't enjoy driving," Phillip responded.

"I feel bad for you," Meggie concerned. Phillip inquired, "Why?"

"Driving gives me a feeling of independence. Have you ever driven?" she questioned.

"Certainly; I think this nicer," he smiled.

"That's a matter of opinion, don't you think?" she smiled.

The limousine stopped in front of her dorm. Phillip kissed her before opening the door.

"You shouldn't do that to me," Meggie smiled to him.

He took her hands, helping her out of the limo, leading her toward the front door of the dorm. He placed both arms around her, kissing her again, placing his loose tongue in her mouth.

"Tomorrow, Meggie," Phillip looked into those beautiful aquamarine eyes before she walked away.

On Thursday evening, Phillip took her to another exclusive club for dinner. Friday evening, to a quiet restaurant overlooking the Potomac, and on Saturday night, to a fancy dinner club with dancing. He refused to elaborate on his job at the Pentagon, nor would he allow politics to be discussed. The entire subject of the war in Vietnam was off-limits. Initially, Meggie didn't like his attitude or control. Then, she thought, he might be right in wanting them to learn about each other without other issues clouding their vision.

Sunday morning, Phillip picked Meggie up at ten o'clock. The limousine stopped at an airstrip and Phillip rose from the car, extending his hand to help her again. 'He's always a perfect gentleman; it must be in the breeding,' she thought. He led her toward a small jet plane.

"Admiral Bennett, she's all gassed up and ready for you," a man in uniform said.

"Thank you, lieutenant," Phillip opened the door, helping Meggie in. She stood in shock, glancing around the inside of the plane. Finding the instruments and controls overwhelming, she was amazed.

"What's wrong?" Phillip placed an arm around her waist.

"I've never been in one of these before; it's a lot to digest," Meggie said, still taking it all in.

He laughed as he led her to one of the two pilot seats. After sitting and buckling up, Phillip started the engines and contacted the tower. The plane headed steadily down the runway and swiftly into the sky.

"You have been extremely quiet," Phillip said, once they were in the air.

"I'm simply taking it all in," Meggie very wide eyed, gazing into the clouds. Phillip smiled to himself.

"Where are we going?" she asked, not removing her eyes from the blue and white sky.

"I thought we'd fly to Norfolk for the day," he smiled. "It will take roughly half an hour to get there."

"Now I know why you don't like to drive! There's far more freedom in flying, and you love it!" Meggie smiled. Phillip leaned to kiss her,

"You're very perceptive."

"Look down there: it's one of our largest naval bases. Isn't it a marvelous sight?" Phillip motioned. Meggie looked through the window, seeing row upon row of large ships.

"Honestly, it's a relatively scary sight," she said, with her eyes not leaving the boats.

Phillip took her on a grand tour of Norfolk, then to an extremely elegant restaurant for lunch. After being seated, Meggie inquired,

"Were you stationed here once?"

"Yes, I also grew up here. I'm from a long line of naval officers. My father is an admiral and my grandfather before him," Phillip proudly.

Meggie sat back in awe. She had never known anyone like him, with roots such as his.

"Is that why you were made an admiral at such a young age?"

"My dear, the Navy does not believe in nepotism," he took her hand.

"Then how come?" she questioned. Philip laughed slightly. She possessed a way of doing that to him.

"I'd like you to be aware of the fact that I do not enjoy talking about this," he stated, with Meggie eagerly watching him. "I'm sure you are familiar with the saying, 'no guts, no glory'. In 1962, I was relatively instrumental with President Kennedy and the Cuban Missile Crisis."

"Go on," Meggie said, looking for more information.

"That's all I'm at liberty to say," he watched her perplexed face.

After lunch they toured the base, before boarding the plane for home. Once in the air,

"You never talk about your marriage," Meggie, curious.

"There's not much to say about it," Phillip watched the clouds.

"How long were you married?" she asked.

"Including the last five, a total of ten years. However, I look at it as five years; a mistake," he said.

"What's your wife like?" she asked. Phillip began to laugh,

"I feel like I'm answering a questionnaire."

"Sorry," Meggie leaned back in her seat. He leaned to kiss her,

"Don't be; you happen to have one of those incredible minds that never turns off."

"My very soon to be ex-wife is a spoiled Navy brat. Her father was always on one ship or another, never around too much. When he was around, she could do no wrong. He showered her with gifts, instead of love. Her mother died during World War II on Pearl Harbor. She was raised mostly by housekeepers," Phillip said, becoming solemn, reflecting on the past. He turned toward her,

"What is your father like?"

"He's wonderful; he's always been there for me. He's vice-president of a bank, his dad was a farmer and my other grandfather a shoemaker. You are looking at the all-American girl here!" Meggie laughed, throwing her arms in the air.

"I like what I see," Phillip smiled, setting the plane on the ground.

Under other circumstances, she would have accused him of being chauvinistic again, Meggie thought.

Once in the limousine, Phillip took her in his arms, kissed her, "What did you think?"

"You have given me the most extraordinary week of my life, filled with fascinating new experiences. I loved every moment of it!" she smiled, excitedly. "You have opened the doors to a whole new world for me!"

Phillip loved her vitality, her enthusiasm. Meggie saw him Tuesday evening for dinner, but explained she could not see him again until Friday because she had assignments to complete.

Wednesday morning, Admiral Phillip Bennett sat behind his desk again, finding a dossier. Opening it, he read: MEGGIE LOREN HIKEN. 'It finally arrived,' he thought. Then he read it in its entirety. Closing it, he sat back in his chair thinking, 'Some all-around American girl, who one day would be a millionairess!' He laughed, thinking, 'Whiz kid, nothing like an early education!' However, she was two years younger than he had anticipated. That should make a difference, somehow it didn't. She was young, but it was too late; he was already captivated with her. He hadn't laughed or enjoyed life so much in years.

His family would certainly find fault; her age, her religion, her mother. One saving grace, she would not be after his money.

Friday at noon, Meggie entered the reception area of Phillip's office.

"Hello, Miss Stone," she smiled, with Miss Stone glancing up.

"Miss Hiken, Admiral Bennett is expecting you. Please go in."

"Hello, handsome," Meggie smiled, entering his office. Phillip, flattered, rose from behind his desk, smiling. Walking toward each other, they embraced; he kissed her. She neared the large glass window behind his desk.

"Quite a view from here." He approached her again,

"I thought we'd have some lunch, then go to the National Gallery. I've cleared my calendar for the afternoon."

"Wonderful," she smiled.

Leaving the National Gallery, sitting back in the limo, Meggie checked her watch: six in the evening.

"Is it time for dinner?" Phillip smiled.

"Getting there," she laughed. "Do we have to eat out again?"

"Not if you're willing to risk my cooking," he laughed.

"Not on your life! I happen to be pretty good in the kitchen," she smiled.

The limo pulled into the parking lot of a grocery store. Meggie moved from the car, insisting she go in alone. Afterward, they were dropped off at a large apartment building overlooking the Potomac and took the elevator up to the penthouse. Somehow she was not surprised, until she entered the apartment, still carrying her bag of groceries. Very wide-eyed, she walked around the massive living room, seeing statues, paintings and ornaments, obviously collected from all around the world. Phillip stood, smiling, watching her. Meggie turned to him,

"You were in all of these places?"

"Yes," he replied, with a slight laugh.

"Jes, and I thought I traveled a lot," she walked into the kitchen.

This time, while she cooked, she cleaned up behind herself. She made veal Parmesan, Italian salad, spaghetti and garlic bread. At the same time, Phillip started a fire in the living room hearth. After the meal, Phillip sat back in his chair smiling at her.

"You are very surprising; this was an Epicurean adventure."

"Thank you," Meggie rose to clear the table.

"Allow me to do that," he took the dishes from her.

Later, Phillip returned to the living room, finding Meggie lying on her stomach, propped up on her elbows on the floor in front of the fire, reading the evening paper. Lying beside her, he placed an arm around her shoulder.

"You are one fantastic cook," he then kissed her. She rolled to her back placing her arms around him, kissing him back as his loose tongue explored her mouth again.

"You are one fantastic kisser," she gazed into his eyes, touching his hand on her hip. They kissed again and again. Meggie could feel the excitement brewing, until he moved his hand to her breast. She abruptly pushed him off her as she jumped up.

"What do you think you are doing?" Meggie angrily.

"I was under the impression you had this in mind when you wanted to eat in," Phillip replied in shock.

"And you have the audacity to tell me I read into things!" Meggie yelled, standing by the fireplace. "I'm not one for a casual dalliance! You sure like to make all of the decisions, don't you?" He approached her with her coat,

"I'll take you home now."

They rode the entire way back to her dorm without a word spoken. He walked her to the door, still without a word or a kiss. She went inside without even a passing glance. She was feeling extremely depressed again. She took a shower and climbed into bed and lay there, thankful Dottie wasn't back yet. She didn't feel like answering any of her questions. Then the phone rang. She answered it.

"Meggie, I'm sorry," Phillip said, sincerely.

"Me too; I really didn't mean the things I said to you," she said.

"I know. I was impetuous again; I was rushing you. Forgive me," Phillip asked.

"Of course; let's put it behind us," Meggie said.

"Don't forget tomorrow night," Phillip paused for a second.

"Do you know what the problem is?" She was silent. "I'm growing quite fond of you."

"Good night Phillip," Meggie said, placing the receiver back.

She lay in bed, deep in thought about what had happened that night and what he had just said to her. She decided to put it all out of her mind, then fell off to sleep.

On Saturday evening at precisely 6:30 p.m., Phillip watched in astonishment as Meggie walked into the lobby of her dorm. She wore a white, boat-necked, crocheted gown with long sleeves, which had slits from her ankle to about two inches above her knee; it clung to her shapely body. The only under-clothing she wore was a pair of panties. Part of her blonde hair was affixed on top of her head with the remainder flowing down her back. With her, she carried a silver fox jacket.

"You are a vision of loveliness," Phillip said, finding his eyes glued to her and helping her on with her jacket. He placed his arm around her shoulder, leading her from the dorm to the awaiting limousine.

Driving toward the Naval Academy in Annapolis, he inquired,

"Have you ever been there before?"

"No, never! I've never even known anyone in the Navy before," Meggie smiled, lifting her right leg a little to cross it over her left one. He couldn't help but notice.

"Don't you wear stockings or anything?"

"I wear nothing that I don't have to," she smiled. "Besides, pantyhose are the torture chamber of the twentieth century," she laughed, seeing him still staring at her legs. It brought a slight laugh to his face. He glanced up, into her eyes before kissing her.

Arriving at the Naval Academy, Meggie marveled at all of the uniforms. When Phillip removed his coat, Meggie realized how truly handsome he really was, especially in his Navy Dress. Leading her to dance, introducing her to his fellow naval officers and their wives, Phillip noticed how taken all of the men were with her. He couldn't blame them, he was!

"Miss Hiken, may I have this dance?" Rear Admiral Frost asked. Meggie looked at this fifty-year old man, then to Phillip who smiled.

"I'd be honored," she responded, giving him her hand.

Phillip stood watching, thinking how magnificently beautiful she looked-such class, such grace. 'A vision of sensual wonder,' he thought, with a smile on his face, until his thoughts were interrupted.

"Phillip, don't you think she's a bit young for you?" Mrs. Frost stated sarcastically. He smiled for a moment,

"I believe that's for me to decide." He glanced back to the dance floor, seeing Meggie dancing with Admiral Hopkins now. He smiled to himself again, thinking, 'The belle of the ball!' After a few minutes of daydreaming, he realized the music had stopped. He scanned the floor for her, not being able to locate her. He thought to himself, 'The food,' before walking toward it. There he found Meggie surrounded by a half a dozen young men who would graduate this June. Phillip approached,

"Meggie, I've been searching for you."

"Phillip, I'd like you to meet Mr. White, Mr. Burnett, Mr. Trens, Mr. Rogen, Mr. Paper and Mr. Thomas," she scanned the group as she spoke. Phillip extended his hand with the men taking it to shake.

"Admiral Bennett, you need no introduction. It's a pleasure to meet you," Mr. Burnett said, shaking his hand. Phillip glanced at Meggie,

"There are some people I would like you to meet," he placed his arm around her shoulder, leading her away.

"You sure have a way of getting around," he smiled, before kissing her. The undergraduates: they knew, hands off!

"What did he mean by-you don't need an introduction?" Meggie looked him in the eye. He stopped, taking her in his arms.

"I lecture here occasionally."

"Somehow, I think there's more to it than that," Meggie said, raising her eyebrows. Phillip laughed, leading her to the dance floor.

Later, sitting in the limousine with his arm around her shoulder again, Phillip smiled at her.

"Did you enjoy yourself?"

"That would be an understatement! I had an absolutely wonderful time!" she smiled, before kissing him. Another new experience!

"Have you ever heard of the 'rhododendron thermometer?'" she asked.

"No, I have to say I haven't," he smiled.

"A rhododendron is a plant. At sixty degrees, its leaves stick straight out, at forty degrees, the leaves drop. My leaves were drooping today. Prior to meeting you yesterday, I put it out for some sun, only planning to leave it there for five minutes. I ended up forgetting about it!" Meggie laughed.

"You ruthless killer of greenery!" Phillip laughed, taking her in his arms, kissing her passionately. Then glanced at her,

"Would you like to fly to New York tomorrow? I was given a couple of tickets to HAIR. I feel you will enjoy it."

"I love this!" Meggie excitedly threw her head back and laughed.

Phillip kissed her again. They sat, kissing, not noticing the limo had stopped in front of her dorm.

After walking her to the door of the dorm and sliding back into the limo, he sat deep in thought. He hadn't enjoyed himself so much in years, the past couple of weeks had been entrancing. That mind of hers-it was so refreshing! He truly believed he was falling in love with her, something he had felt would never happen again. He had lost all faith and trust in women. Was it her youth that was giving it back to him, or her vitality? He concluded it was everything about her!

The following Wednesday in the S.D.S. office Michael turned to Dottie.

"What's with your roommate? She's changed."

"Not really, she just has a lot on her mind," Dottie said, in Meggie's defense.

Meggie walked in, headed toward the closet where she retrieved her smock, and handed it to Michael.

"I quit!"

"You can't! We need you around here, your talent and your brains!" he grabbed her by the arm and looked her in the eye. "What is going on with you?"

"You mean on the level that man can never really grasp? I resign!" she sternly stated, before walking out.

Everyone was shocked. She had been too totally involved to turn her back like this. Dottie laughed to herself. It was obvious Meggie wanted to make a statement of some kind; what, she really wasn't aware of and she didn't think Meggie was, either. She felt pressure was getting to her roommate. Meggie was carrying an overload this year in school to insure graduation in the spring, she was having a relationship with the admiral and missing Steven. Dottie felt Meggie was cutting S.D.S. out to lessen the burden on herself.

That evening, Meggie had dinner with Phillip again. Sitting in another one of his fancy clubs, Phillip took her hand,

"You're very solemn tonight."

"I'm making some changes in my life," Meggie sullen.

"I don't understand," he said.

"I walked out on S.D.S. today. It's been a part of me for nearly three years now," she leaned back in her chair. "It hurts; I feel like I am closing the door on a piece of my life." A few tears ran from her eyes. He wiped her tears,

"We all make changes; it's part of maturing. Unfortunately, pain, now and then, is a part of growing up."

Now she really broke down and cried, knowing she had heard that before, from Steven. Phillip moved from his chair to embrace her.

"Look at it this way; you have made room in your life for new and rewarding experiences," he lifted her face to look at him.

Riding in the limousine on the way to her dorm, Meggie smiled.

"You remind me of Casanova."

"Why?" Phillip asked, in shock.

"You're so debonair, you always know just what to say and there's a degree of eloquence about you," she slightly smiled.

"Meggie, Casanova hated women; he used them to inflate his own ego," Phillip laughed.

"No!" she sat back, surprised.

"Yes!" he laughed harder, placing his arm around her shoulder. "Don't forget Saturday night at Admiral Hopkins'. The dress is formal."

"Oh! I did forget," Meggie said, surprised. "I made arrangements to go skiing over the weekend, I leave after my last class tomorrow. I'm sorry, I forgot to tell you."

"What?" Phillip surprised.

"I am sorry; I really am," she took his hand. "I wanted to get one last run in before the slopes closed." Phillip smiled, "I didn't know you skied."

"It's not something that arises in everyday conversation," she laughed.

"Where are you going?" he rubbed her shoulder.

"Osmond Springs. It's in Virginia, only a couple of hours away. The slopes aren't the greatest, but nothing that close is. And this beats nothing," she smiled. Phillip looked at her,

"You are beautiful." She stared down.

"Why do you find it so difficult to accept a compliment?" he placed his hand on her cheek to turn her face toward his.

"Flattery is a narcotic; too much, and you can OD.," Meggie smiled.

"Who's going with you?" Phillip said embracing her.

"No one. Dottie used to, but since she's getting married in May she refused to. She's afraid she'll break a leg or something. I can't fault her for not risking it," Meggie glanced through the window.

"You're going alone?" Phillip surprised again.

"Sure, why not? If I wait around for other people, I may never do what I want," she said. He smiled,

"I agree. Who and what you are, are the only things you'll have forever."

Helping Meggie out after the limo stopped,

"It's been an extremely informative evening," he kissed her. "When will you be back?"

"Sunday evening sometime," she replied as he kissed her again.

Sitting in his limo on his way home, Phillip thought how much Meggie was like him. She didn't wait around when she saw something she wanted; she went after it. She was not afraid of life! He felt he was really getting to know her. Now he knew for sure he was falling in love with her; it was easy to do.

Thursday afternoon, Meggie drove toward Osmond Springs, Virginia. She arrived at six in the evening, just in time for dinner.

On Friday morning she hit the slopes at nine-thirty, going there to ski and to think-that is exactly what she planned on doing. At eleven that same morning, a chauffeur-driven limousine dropped off an extremely handsome gentleman clothed in ski attire. He searched the slopes and laughed, seeing a spot of purple on its way down. He moved closer to where she would see him, watching her, finding she skied incredibly well. He was surprised. She was on her final run, picking up more speed. He loved it! 'Damn, she's good!' He thought, when the lady in purple made a direct stop in front of him.

"Phillip!" Meggie surprised. "Did you come to participate or spectate?"

He pointed to his skis. Meggie noticed they were not rentals; they were his.

"Let's get them on," she laughed, watching him through the goggles she wore over her eyes. No more teary-eyes was how she felt.

Phillip smiled, standing in front of her,

"I need a kiss first," he kissed her.

Meggie thought, he does kiss well! They sat in the lift on the way up the slope. He informed her,

"The last time I skied was in Switzerland, this past December."

"Lucky you!" she stood from the lift.

Meggie marveled, watching him; 'His ability is phenomenal,' she thought. He was the first man, other than her father, she'd been with, who could ski as well as she. In Phillip's case, he was better. They skied for the remainder of the day, until, reaching the bottom, they saw '4:00' on the outside clock. Phillip smiled at her,

"Have you had enough for one day?"

"I certainly have. How about a drink?" Meggie removed her skis.

"One hell of an idea," Phillip carried his skis and hers, locking them in the outside bin. He took her arm and led her into the lounge toward a small table. After they sat, she smiled,

"You're good."

"So are you," he said, with the waitress approaching the table. Phillip glanced at her,

"Your choice." .

"Scotch and water," she smiled. She had developed a taste for Scotch when she was with Jay. Phillip ordered the same,

"I never heard you order that before." Meggie leaned across the table and looked him in the eye.

"Maybe that's because you never allow me to order." She laughed with him joining her.

The drinks were served, Meggie asked, "Where are you staying?"

"A friend of mine has a chalet not too far from here," Phillip said.

"From the Pentagon?" she smiled. He nodded, yes, smiling.

After finishing their drinks, they walked to the parking lot. Meggie glanced around,

"Where's your limo?" Phillip laughed,

"After he dropped me off, he stocked the chalet with food. I told him to return home."

"Then how did you plan on getting to and from the slopes every day?" she very confidently asked.

"I thought I could hitch, or one beautiful lady we both know and love, would do me the honors," he smiled at her.

Meggie burst into laughter and took the two sets of skis that Phillip was carrying from him,

"Go hitch!" she said. Surprised, he looked at her still laughing, with tears rolling from her eyes.

"Simply walk out to the road and hitch. I have to see this!" she still laughed.

Phillip walked to the road, shaking his head, not knowing why he was doing this, with a smile on his face. Meggie walked with the skis to her car and clipped them on the back. Pulling from the parking lot, she stopped in front of him, knowing he wouldn't recognize her, never having seen her car before. Seeing this little car stop, he reluctantly opened the door, only to find Meggie laughing.

311

"This figures!" he uttered.

"Would you like a ride?" she smiled.

Phillip got into the car and felt his legs begin to cramp. Meggie started to laugh again, seeing this tall man in this little seat.

"How tall are you?" she still laughed.

"Six-feet-three and a half inches, to be exact," Phillip said, trying to make room for his long legs.

"There's a little lever under the seat on the right side. Push it back," she instructed. Upon releasing the button,

"Modern technology; what would we do without it?" he found somewhat more room for his legs.

Meggie put the car in gear, driving forward before inquiring, "Where are we going?"

Phillip pulled a map from his pocket.

"We are going in the wrong direction!"

Meggie slammed on the brakes, skidding the car around to go the other way. He looked at her. "Nice!" he said, sitting back in his seat and buckling his seat belt.

He gave Meggie directions. She stopped the car in front of the chalet. Getting out, she glanced around.

"Government over-indulgence," she said to Phillip. He took her in his arms and kissed her.

After leading her into this extremely modern and obviously costly chalet, Phillip headed toward the kitchen and the refrigerator.

"Let's see what Henry bought." From the refrigerator Phillip took out two Delmonico steaks, some potatoes and an already-made salad.

"Bless Henry's heart for making the salad! I'll make my oven potatoes; baked will take too long," Meggie said.

Phillip walked to the cozy living room and lit the wood in the fireplace. Meggie was busy in the kitchen, putting the potatoes in the oven and setting the table. Walking from the kitchen, she took a joint from her pocket. Lighting it and taking a few drags.

"It will be about half an hour," she smiled, taking another drag. He stood surprised, staring at her,

"What are you doing?"

"Try it," she extended her arm with the j.

"Do you do this often?" he asked. Meggie laughed,

"No, not anymore. After skiing, it tends to relax me. Before eating, it's good too. Come on, try it," she handed it to him. He took a hit and coughed. Meggie laughed,

"Not so much; it's pretty potent. I get it in Hawaii."

After finishing the j, Meggie lay back on the sofa for a few moments. Phillip was fooling with the fire, then he turned to look at her in the light from the glowing embers.

"You are even more beautiful," he walked toward her for a kiss.

"That's the pot talking," she laughed.

They lay on the floor in front of the fire after dinner. Phillip massaged her back,

"Either that was the best steak I have ever eaten or there really is something to this marijuana." She laughed. He continued to stroke her back, now with his hand under her ski sweater.

"You're not wearing a bra," he said, surprised. Meggie turned over, with his hand sliding to her right breast. She smiled,

"I never do. I told you, I never wear anything I don't have to."

Phillip kissed her again and again with his hand fondling her breast. He lifted his torso, looking into her eyes,

"I desire to make love to you."

She placed her hands on the back of his neck drawing him towards her, before kissing him. Then sat removing her sweater, revealing her firm breasts, as he watched. Passionately he attacked her torso, then sucking each round breast. She threw her head back in delight. He lifted the front of his sweater, pressing his bare chest against hers and kissing her ever so passionately. Then smiled as he stood to undress. She watched this sandy haired man with such magnificent green eyes and a truly beautiful face. When he removed his ski sweater, she had to keep herself from gasping. She never would have dreamed anyone could be built this well: so muscular and virile. What a body! As she stood, she removed her ski pants, then lie completely nude on the animal skin rug in front of the fire. She smiled seeing him move toward her; he savored every part of her body. She thought to herself, 'He's not only a good kisser, he's an incredible lover!'

Laying nude, still by the fire, holding each other afterwards. He whispered in her ear,

"I finally received my divorce papers this morning."

"Does that make this a time to rejoice or to mourn?" Meggie asked.

"You're a riot!" He squeezed her tight. "This day has been far better than any celebration I could have envisioned. It was you who made it that way: your beauty, your athletic ability, your wit, and best of all, your love-making. If you haven't figured it out by now, I'm in love with you," he kissed her. Meggie rolled over a little to see his face,

"What happened five years ago to have made you leave her?" Phillip rolled to his back, gazed at the ceiling and thought for a moment. Still holding her with one arm, he placed his other arm behind his head.

"It was beyond my comprehension as to why she couldn't conceive. I told you once I thought it was due to my being away so much. That was not so; a complete falsity, in fact. I accompanied her to see quite a few gynecologists; I even had myself checked out. I was informed everything was absolutely normal.

Five years ago, I was asked to fly a secret mission. So much of me is the navy and my country, I naturally said yes. She was aware of when I might return if everything went my way. I entered our home extremely excited because I had been successful, only to find her in bed, bleeding. She had an illegal abortion that same day. Here I was, risking my life, and she was destroying one, a part of me!" Phillip said, with a tear in his eye. Meggie noticed this, feeling for him. She embraced him, then lay her head on his chest. He continued,

"She had the nerve to ask me to help her. I told her she did this without me, therefore, she could take care of the rest the same way. She couldn't believe I could be so unfeeling. I reminded her, she was aware of how badly I wanted a child and she had no right to destroy what was part mine. I headed to the closet and packed. She had ended whatever we had. Before I got out the front door, she yelled, 'I've been using a diaphragm all of these years. This time it didn't work!' I knew she wanted to get to me. I left, slammed the door and haven't been back since."

"Are you still in love with her?" Meggie lifted her head up to look into his beautiful green eyes.

"She destroyed whatever feelings I may have had for her. Honestly, I don't even hate her. Sometimes I wonder if I ever loved her at all," Phillip held Meggie tight. "Besides, I'm in love with you." He kissed her.

"Is that mission too secret to tell me about?" She inquired. Phillip laughed, thinking, 'That mind, it never does turn off.'

"I'll tell you as much as I can." He hugged her first,

"Five years ago, Naval Intelligence turned up information that the KGB was planning on kidnapping a team of our nuclear scientists. They were in a meeting in Vienna at the time. I was sent solo to stop their plan. It's called, "low profile" instead of "show of force." Our government's been using it for years now. I did succeed." He smiled, "Two years later I was made admiral. That's about all that I can say."

"I knew there was more to it!" Meggie excitedly moved her body on top of his. "Who are you, my super hero? Renaissance Man!"

"Renaissance Man?" He chuckled.

"I thought that from the first time I met you. Chivalry, Lancelot, duty and selfless honor," she kissed him before they made love again.

They spent the remainder of the weekend talking, even a little about politics, skiing, eating and making love.

The following Tuesday night Meggie in the dorm, was busy with a painting when she was paged. There was a man waiting for her in the lobby. Her first reaction was anger because, she had explained to Phillip, she was carrying a very heavy schedule this semester and she needed her space to work. He said he understood as long as she made time for him. Meggie entered the lobby armed for bear, then stopped in her tracks.

"What are you doing here?" She stared at Peter.

"A hell of a way to greet a friend bearing food," Peter smiled, before kissing her. She hugged him.

"I wasn't expecting you. Why aren't you in school?"

"I have a major decision to make concerning my life and I need your input; I've always respected your opinion," Peter announced.

"Bullshit! You just have a difficult time making decisions on your own," Meggie stated. "What kind of food did you bring?"

"I brought you a culinary delight, straight from the French Quarter-Cajun," Peter smiled, leading her from the dorm.

Peter had checked into a small motel not far from the American University campus. He simply planned on staying the night and head back to New Orleans tomorrow. Thus, he chose not to inform his parents; they would have insisted he spend the night at home. The entire ordeal would have become too time-consuming.

They ate in Peter's motel room where Meggie happily told him about Phillip.

"The ultimate Professional!" She smiled describing him.

"What about Steven?" Peter glanced at her, hoping for a reaction.

"What about him?" She bit into her food. "Let's deal with this dilemma of yours. I don't have anymore problems."

"No!" he laughed.

"No," she said, giving him a dirty look.

"Okay, I've known you long enough to know when to give up. Mark my word, Meg, you're not finished with Steven," Peter smiled. "My professor, the one I'm going to Mexico with this summer, wants me to commit to working at Chichen Itza for an entire year."

"What about finishing school?" Meggie asked.

"I'll receive credit and graduate next May as I'm supposed to," Peter started to pace back and forth.

"So what's the problem?" She asked, with a slight laugh. Peter still paced, faster now,

"I don't know whether I can handle living in Mexico for an entire year, to be so isolated from everything I've grown accustomed to."

"You won't know unless you try. What's the worst that can happen? You come home and graduate a year later," Meggie looked at him.

"I never thought of it like that," Peter sat. "So I guess it wouldn't matter; nothing has to be that permanent, unless I want it to be."

"You'll go?" Meggie smiled.

"I'll give it a shot," he said.

"You've always had a difficult time making major decisions or any kind of commitment," Meggie sneered.

"I wish I could explain it. I freak out, like the world is going to fall apart. I'm quite aware I tend to overreact," he stated.

"That's an understatement," Meggie crawled into one of the two beds in his room.

"Settling in for the night," he laughed.

"I may as well. It's late and I'm tired. I know you'll remember about that wall between us," she smiled laying her head on the pillow.

Peter showered and walked back into the room to find Meggie still awake, engrossed in a Perry Mason re-run. He turned the lights out, then the television off.

"You'll become a couch potato," Peter laughed.

"Perry Mason is a unique show," she stated.

Peter climbed into the other bed. There was silence for a few moments. He turned toward her.

"Christine phoned me a couple of weeks ago."

"What did she want?" Meggie propped her head up on an elbow.

"Money," Peter stated.

"Did you give it to her?"

"Hell, no! She's really hurting," Peter said.

"I know; she's a coke junkie. You know, sometimes I feel sorry for her and other times I'm totally void of compassion as far as she goes," Meggie laid back down bringing the covers up higher.

"That's because you've never really gotten over Dennis," Peter attempted to see her face.

"How can you say that? My life's on an uphill swing," Meggie said angrily.

"Is it?" Peter questioned.

"Goodnight, Peter," Meggie moaned, turning over to go to sleep.

Over the course of the next few weeks, Meggie saw a great deal of Phillip. He flew her to the mountains for a weekend, where she painted a landscape. There were various dinner parties around Washington that he escorted her to. She thought this to be a whole new way of living, being quite intrigued by it and noting it would be easy to become accustomed to.

On a Sunday morning near the end of March, Dottie threw Meggie a copy of the *WASHINGTON POST,* "Look at this!"
Meggie picked the paper up, her heart throbbed.

March 20, 1970,
               Editorial: What It's Like To Be An
                 American Living in Israel
                   Byline: Steven Roth

Meggie read the entire article, digesting every word of it. 'He has a gift,' she thought, lying back on her bed with a smile on her face. 'But I always knew that!' Her thoughts were interrupted.
"I guess that's how he planned on lettin' ya know where to reach him," Dottie said with a smirk..
Meggie didn't answer, still lying on her back. When she first read his name she felt her stomach sink. She had goose bumps the entire time she read; they were just starting to disappear. All of this made her realize how much she missed him.

Phillip escorted Meggie to another one of his obligatory dinner parties that evening. He couldn't help but notice how quiet she was in the limo and now at dinner.
"We're finally going to have peace in the Middle East; two great men are going to see to it: Sadat and Begin," Admiral Phelps said, glancing around the table. "No one wants war anymore."
Meggie couldn't believe her ears.

"No! Iraq only wants Israel to be a test sight for its nuclear weapons!" she uttered.

Everyone was shocked, especially Phillip, but the conversation continued. About fifteen minutes later Admiral Phelps spoke again.

"I feel this world is going to be a better place to live in. We're making progress, don't you think?" He smiled. Meggie stared at him in shock.

"Why? Because nobody has been assassinated in the world today?" came out of her mouth. Phillip almost choked on his food; her prior comment was bad enough. The entire table went silent for a moment. After a few minutes everyone rose from the table and adjourned to the library for coffee.

Phillip pulled Meggie to the side and made her face him,

"What comes into that head, comes out of that mouth! What is with you today? You've never behaved like this and those comments were certainly uncalled for."

"He's a totally disenfranchised functionary!" Meggie stated.

"What unmitigated garbage!" Phillip said, still looking at her. "Something happened and I demand to know what it was."

"Maybe I've had my fill of your Washington bureaucrats or maybe I'm on the rag," she said, before turning to give him her back. He walked around so he faced her again.

"You are being argumentative," he barked. Meggie started to cry, then placed her arms around his shoulders..

"I know, Phillip; I'm sorry."

Later that night Phillip sat in his bed reading the Sunday paper. He was engrossed in an article on Israel, finding it extremely interesting and informative. He found it to be uniquely written. Then he checked the byline-Steven Roth, angrily he threw the paper on the floor.

"That's it!" he thought to himself. I wonder if she's still interested in him. He remembered the dossier; she had spent over a year and a half with Steven Roth!

X

On the evening of April 10th, 1970, Phillip arrived to pick Meggie up for dinner. He rushed toward her as she stepped off the elevator, seeing her red eyes and blotchy face. Placing his arms around her, she leaned her head on his strong chest, crying.

"What's wrong?"

"My grandmother passed away today; I just found out," she said, clinging to him. She was happy to have him hold her right now.

"The funeral is going to be tomorrow."

"May I accompany you?" He rubbed the back of her neck, trying to release tension and comfort her. Meggie stood back to look at him.

"Will you?"

"I'd be honored," Phillip said, before placing his arm around her shoulder to lead her from the dorm.

Meggie explained it was going to be a small graveside service. She felt it was planned that way because her grandfather had passed away just three months prior.

The following morning, Phillip waited in the lobby of the dorm for Meggie. Seeing her enter, he approached her,

"I should have gotten you a black rose; you look far too glamorous to be going to a funeral."

Meggie wore a black V-neck silk dress, fitting her shapely body, and a black hat. She smiled at him,

"Thank you; I appreciate your strength and your humor right now." He hugged her, she was thankful he was there for her. She didn't deal well with funerals.

A chauffeur-driven black limousine pulled into an old cemetery not far from Rosedale, Maryland. It grabbed the family's attention, and curiosity was piqued upon seeing Phillip step out in his admiral's uniform. He then extended his hand to help Meggie. Seeing his daughter, Morris Hiken immediately approached.

"Oh, Daddy," Meggie hugged him, then stepped back.

"Daddy, I would like you to meet Admiral Phillip Bennett." The two men shook hands, Morris gave Phillip an extremely curious look.

Phillip followed Meggie as she walked to where her mother was seated. There was little exchange between the two women, very little familiarity and no affection. He remembered her mom remarried a few weeks ago and Meggie refused to attend the wedding, even though he advised her it would be good politics. Her comment was, "I'm not a hypocrite-I don't do what I don't feel!"

"I'm sorry to hear about your mother," Phillip said, touching Lil Hiken Mossowitz's hand, after Meggie introduced him. Lil looked at this handsome man, in shock; he was nearly old enough to have dated her!

The rabbi motioned he was ready to begin. Meggie stood, crying, with Phillip holding her throughout the service. Morris watched them, wondering what his daughter was doing with a man so much older than herself. Rabbi Winston finished and motioned for the mourners to leave. Lil and Morris exchanged strange glances. Their only common interest now was Meggie, and their mutual thoughts were about her.

Meggie approached the Rabbi, and asked if she could shovel some dirt on her grandmother's grave-to say good-bye, she explained. Rabbi Winston extended his arm around Meggie's shoulder and led her toward the grave.

"That's a beautiful thing for a granddaughter to do," he gazed at this girl whom he'd known for nearly twenty years.

Phillip watched and Morris moved to stand beside him. They both looked on as the rabbi recited the three blessings in Hebrew.

"Your daughter is truly amazing," Phillip smiled.

"Determined, headstrong and young," Morris said. The admiral understood exactly what he was saying.

Afterward, Morris walked them to the limo,

"Are you going to your mother's now?"

"I think I have to," Meggie hugged him. "Daddy, I love you. It's been good to see you."

"I'll be in D.C. next week for business; how about dinner?" Morris asked.

"I'd like that," she smiled.

Morris watched Phillip help her into the car and it pull away.

"Do you always call him Daddy?" Phillip inquired.

"Of course! What do you call your father?" Meggie asked.

"Usually 'sir', occasionally 'Dad'," he replied.

About forty-five minutes later, they entered her mother's home. Meggie saw Ma sitting on the sofa. For some strange reason she felt like hugging her, so she did. Phillip went to the bar, making two Scotch and waters, thinking Meggie could use it right now. After receiving Meggie's affection, Ma looked at her.

"Meggie, he's too old for you!"

"Your credibility is suspect. You can't dictate to me any longer," Meggie snapped. Seeing Albert sitting next to Ma and completely ignoring him, she walked away.

Finding Phillip, she took the glass he handed her and they walked to the kitchen. She leaned against the counter, sipping her drink,

"She hasn't seen me for months now, and the first thing she does is give me shit!"

"Because of me, no doubt," Phillip placed an arm around her waist. He smiled a little. He'd never heard her use that word before; she was always the perfect lady.

"If it wasn't you, it would be something else. That's her favorite hobby!" Meggie finished her drink. "Let's take a walk." She took his hand to lead him through all the people and out the front door.

Seeing Meggie walk out, Lil moved toward the window, looking through it and not liking what she saw. Phillip took Meggie in his arms and kissed her, before starting their walk with his arm around her. As she moved from the window, Lil wondered about Steven.

"Did you grow up here?" Phillip asked, as they walked.

"That's right, born and bred in suburban America! I lived in that house my entire life, until about a year and a half ago. And now I feel like a stranger there," Meggie said, becoming solemn.

"Is that when your parents got divorced?" he asked.

"When they separated." She pointed to a one-story building,

"That's where I went to elementary school. It was in third grade when they found out what a brainiac I was." Phillip smiled a little, keeping step with her,

"Your parents don't talk anymore."

"Are you kidding! The entire experience was far from pleasant. You've heard of Murphy's Law. Anything that could go wrong, did," Meggie said, walking faster. He still kept step with her, knowing all of this, but wanting her to open up to him. Then she stopped abruptly.

"That's where I went to high school. I had wonderful times in those days," Meggie stared at the large building. She started to cry. Phillip held her,

"Why the tears?"

"Someone special to me died a couple of months after graduation," she said, despondently. Phillip knew that was Dennis Fine. Meggie pulled away from him, noting her fists were clenched.

"I hate death and funerals and all of the connotations that go along with them! I hate this period of sitting shivah, having all of those strange people constantly around. When I hurt badly, I need to be left alone," she cried.

"This is one fucked-up world we live in!" she yelled.

Phillip took a step back in shock, never having heard such speech from her previously. He was aware her vocabulary was diverse but he had no idea it went to this extreme. He excused her because she was upset. 'Another one of her many sides,' he thought. Arrogance in disappointment! He then glanced at her.

"Are you quite finished?"

"I don't know," Meggie said, looking at him glassy-eyed.

"I believe you are. Let's walk back. Remember, we promised Ben we'd take him for a ride in the limo," Phillip embraced her.

They spent some time with Ben. Meggie smiled, seeing how interested he was in Phillip. She had never heard him so inquisitive. She thanked God that he was feeling well. Sometimes she felt guilty because she refused to discuss Albert with him, knowing he must have some heavy feelings on the subject. She couldn't help it; she felt she couldn't handle it.

Meggie decided they weren't going to stay around there. She felt too uncomfortable, she didn't belong. She and Phillip said their good-byes to the family before going to the Pimlico Hotel for dinner.

Tuesday evening at six-thirty, Morris Hiken picked his daughter up for dinner.

"Hi, Daddy," Meggie slid into the car and hugged him.

"Phillip made reservations for seven o'clock at one of his fancy clubs; he'll meet us there," she gave him the address. Dad knew where it was; he'd been there before. He stopped at a red light,

"I want to talk to you first."

"I know that tone," Meggie laughed a little.

"Don't you think he's a bit old for you?" Dad asked.

"No! Age is relative. That's what Ma said," she stated.

"I know," he said. Meggie was shocked,

"You've talked to Ma!"

"She called the other day; she's worried about you," Dad uttered.

"That day will no doubt be marked in the annals of history!" she laughed.

"Be serious, Meggie!" Dad raised his voice. Meggie moved closer to him, placing her arm around his shoulder,

"I have had the most wonderful three months of my life. In my wildest dreams, I never thought life could be this exciting, and we both know what an incredible imagination I have! We fly around the country in his plane, I've grown accustomed to being driven in a chauffeured limousine, plus I find the Washington social life entrancing. Phillip has opened up a whole new world for me, one I could learn to live with very easily!"

Morris Hiken sat back, thinking to himself, 'Now the big one,'

"Are you in love with him?"

"You know I'm not capable of being in love with anyone!," she became hostile.

"Not even Steven?" Dad asked. He looked at her face for some expression; he saw it.

"Not even Steven," Meggie gazed down. Morris realized she was fighting it and she still didn't know her own mind.

"Have you seen his articles?" He asked.

"Yes, they're wonderful," Meggie became solemn, thinking she had saved every one of those masterpieces.

"Do you know who Phillip is?" Dad still inquiring.

"Uh huh; Superman! George Reeves in disguise!" She laughed. Morris gave her a demeaning look, becoming somewhat angered,

"This isn't funny; it's quite serious!"

"I'm aware he has quite a reputation. A man who loves his country and is committed to it. A man of high principles, selfless and honor bound. A man of impeccable standards who commands respect. All qualities that I absolutely adore," Meggie smiled.

"He's also a member of an exceptionally wealthy family; one could say aristocracy," Morris said, soberly. She laughed again,

"You live in the dark ages."

"He's not Jewish, Meggie," Dad stated.

"Now you're being prejudiced," she kissed his cheek.

When they pulled into the club lot, Meggie turned to her father,

"Please give him a chance, for me."

"I'll think about it," Dad said, then gave his car to the valet.

The maitre'd took their coats as they entered the club,

"Miss Hiken, Admiral Bennett is waiting for you. Follow me, please." He showed them to the table. Phillip rose,

"Good evening." He placed a kiss on her cheek, then extended his hand to Morris.

"I'm happy you could join us tonight."

After they all were seated, Phillip inquired of her dad.

"May I call you Morris?"

"I should hope so," Morris eyed this man who was probably no more than seven or eight years younger than himself.

During dinner, every time Phillip called her dad by name, 'Morris', Meggie looked up. Dad was aware of this, thinking her feelings for Steven were hidden deep inside somewhere. Finishing dinner, Meggie excused herself from the table. She wanted to give them time to talk, wanted her dad to realize what a fine person Phillip was.

"You should be commended; she's been wonderfully brought up," Phillip said.

"Thank you," he answered, rubbing the rim of the after-dinner drink. "Are you aware of how old she is?"

"Yes; when I initially became interested in her, I wasn't," Phillip glanced at him. Morris looked up, making eye contact,

"She's always been advanced beyond her years. Still, don't you think you're a bit old for her?"

"Chronologically, you may have a point. When you stop to think who we are talking about and the kind of mind she has, I would venture to say no," Phillip smiled. He leaned back in his chair,

"It's obvious, I am totally in love with your daughter."

"I thought so. Do you know how she feels?" Morris curious.

"I don't think anyone is aware of how Meggie feels; not even she," Phillip honestly stated.

"That happens to be quite perceptive of you," Morris said. "She wasn't always like this. Something happened a few years back, and she hasn't been the same since. Being a parent, I hurt for her."

"Being a man in love with her, I intend to do everything possible to help her come to terms with her feelings. I hope, eventually, to make her my wife," Phillip leaned forward a little, watching Morris. Witnessing the shock on his face. Phillip smiled again, seeing Meggie approach the table.

"Here comes the all-around creative genius now," he rose.

Meggie sat, smiling at her dad and then at Phillip,

"Did you have nice talk?"

"Very informative," Morris nodded.

"I thought so!" Meggie said, taking Phillip's hand.

"I have to drive back to Baltimore tonight. I would ask for the check, but I'm familiar with how these clubs work," Morris thanked Phillip for dinner. He leaned to kiss Meggie before rising from the table. Phillip rose and extended his hand. The two men shook hands, looking each other in the eye again, before Morris left.

Morris Hiken was very perplexed as he drove back to Baltimore. He was astonishingly surprised. He did like this man; his honesty, his integrity and his forthrightness made that possible. He even understood what Meggie saw in him. He was still extremely bothered by Phillip's age and religion, along with Meggie's own complexities. He then sat back and thought about Steven!

On the next to the last Saturday in April, Meggie and Phillip boarded his plane for Norfolk, Virginia. She smiled at him,

"Can I fly us? Please." He was finding it increasingly more difficult to refuse her anything.

"I think so," he said, before kissing her.

Whenever she flew, he was somewhat apprehensive. Nervously, he watched her start the plane. She checked the controls, which he double-checked. She contacted the tower and proceeded down the runway; then she lifted the plane off the ground. Once in the air, Phillip was more at ease, giving her coordinates for Norfolk. He thought, 'Almost a perfect takeoff. She does pick things up quickly. Brainiac,' he laughed to himself. Meggie turned to him,

"When can I take my pilot's test?"

"Keep your eyes on the clouds," he laughed. "You haven't logged enough hours."

"I only have a few more to go. I know I could pass it," she smiled.

"Let's wait and see how you land today," he said. 'Nothing like a positive attitude,' he thought.

"Phillip, how big and fancy is this party tonight?" She asked.

"It's my dad's sixtieth Birthday. I would venture to say they invited a few hundred people. They are going all out, an extravaganza. Why, are you nervous?" he laughed a little. Meggie gave him a look from the corner of her eye,

"You don't exactly come from the average American family."

"We 're getting close," He put the headset on and contacted the tower.

"Hello, Norfolk, this is Admiral Bennett."

"We're expecting you, Admiral," said a voice from the tower.

"I'm not flying today; Miss Meggie Hiken is. Give her accurate coordinates. This is only her third landing," Phillip instructed .

"Yes, sir, Admiral."

Meggie received her coordinates, approached the landing strip and set the plane down very gently. 'Perfect,' Phillip thought.

"Miss Hiken, a seasoned veteran couldn't do better," said a voice from the tower. Meggie laughed, glancing at Phillip. He smiled, giving her directions to the hangar. After turning the engines off, she smiled,

"What do you think?" He took her in his arms.

"Soon, maybe," he said, before kissing her.

He carried her garment bag and his, as Meggie led the way from the plane. She turned to him,

"Does everyone in your family ride around in one of these?" He smiled, leading her toward the open door of the limousine.

Driving up the long drive of his parent's estate, Meggie looked around, completely astounded, never having seen anything like this.

"In the throes of mediocrity!" she stared out the window of the limo. Phillip laughed, hugging her.

Entering, Phillip took Meggie's hand and led her toward the library. She was even more shocked as she glanced around this massive place. Seeing them, his father stood and his mother approached to embrace him. Phillip shook his fathers' hand and introduced Meggie. She smiled as his mother coolly eyed her.

"Miss Hiken, would you like to freshen up?" Mrs. Bennett said.

"I promised Meggie we'd go riding," Phillip smiled.

"You'll have to change. Mary, would you please show Miss Hiken to her room?" Christine Bennett noticing Meggie wearing a royal-blue, silk shirtwaist dress.

Mary motioned to Meggie. She followed, thinking she was going to die from the formality and coolness! Once in her room, she noticed her clothes had already been unpacked. 'How'd they do that so fast!'

In the library, Phillip neared his mother,

"She prefers to be called Meggie."

"Phillip, don't you think she's a bit young for you; she's even Jewish," his mother raised her eyebrows.

"No. I think she's perfect for me," Phillip bluntly stated.

"She's from a different class," Christine Bennett uttered.

"She has more class in her one little finger than all of the other women I have known, put together," Phillip walked closer to his parents, having his fill of this. He looked at both of them,

"You are both aware of my feelings, with full knowledge I never would have ventured to bring Meggie here if I wasn't serious. She's an extremely passionate, involved, romantic and vulnerable young woman. I am totally in love with her. I would appreciate it if you would put petty prejudices aside and try to see her with an open mind. I believe you will be pleasantly surprised."

"Now, I better go change," he said, leaving the room. He stopped at the foot of the stairs, seeing Meggie on her way down in her riding habit. 'A vision,' he thought.

"You haven't changed; I'm always waiting for you," she said, with a slight laugh. On the stairs he took her in his arms,

"You've got that a little backwards; I'll be down in a minute."

332

Meggie entered the library, finding Phillip's parents still there.

"Meggie, come sit down," his father directed.

"If you don't mind, I prefer to stand and walk a little when I'm somewhat nervous," she moved toward the large bay window and gazed outside.

"Those lavender flowers are lovely-a daffodil variety? I've never seen anything like them before," she turned to Phillip's mother.

"Our gardener cross-bred. You're right; they are from the daffodil family. Since you like them, I'll have Mary take some to your room," Mrs. Bennett said, still eyeing her.

"Thank you; that would be nice," Meggie turned to the window again. "A tonal spring day." Phillip's father smiled,

"Phillip tells us you graduate in May. What are your plans after that?" .

"I know I'm going to paint," Meggie said, now feeling a little calmer. She moved to sit on the sofa a few feet from his mother and across from his father. She looked at the elder Admiral Bennett.

"Does Phillip really call you 'sir?'"

"Sometimes," he smiled slightly.

"Anyway, I really haven't made any plans. There's a small gallery in D.C. that is willing to take some of my paintings and drawings on a consignment basis," she exchanged glances between the Bennett's.

"What do you think you'll get for them?" The elder admiral watched her.

"Honestly, it doesn't matter. It's the quality of the work that counts, not the credit or the money," she smiled.

Entering the library Phillip was pleased to find her conversing with his parents.

"Are you ready?" he asked.

"Waiting on you," she stood. He led her out, placing his arm around her waist.

"What do you think?" Christine Bennett asked her husband.

"I think this time Phillip is going to make his own choice; you're not going to make it for him. No pushing, no interference. Look what happened last time," he stated, emphatically.

"That is not what I meant," she said.

"She certainly is a beautiful young woman. I like her honesty, her straightforward attitude and her ability to speak what's on her mind," the elder Admiral Bennett stared through the window.

A couple of hours later, Meggie and Phillip walked back through the front door. Seeing them, Christine Bennett announced,

"It's time for luncheon."

"Luncheon?" Meggie questioned.

Phillip led her into the dining room. He pulled out a chair for her, then walked around the table to seat himself. His parents sat at opposite ends. Meggie scanned the table as Phillip started to make himself a sandwich.

"No, Phillip! Wait!" Meggie walked to the kitchen, where she spoke to the cook and made Russian dressing. Carrying it, she neared Phillip,

"If you're going to eat kosher deli, you have to eat it Jewish." She made him a corned beef, cole slaw and Russian dressing sandwich on rye bread.

He laughed, watching her. His mom was shocked and his dad, intrigued. After sitting in her seat, she made the same for herself. She glanced up and saw Phillip had already devoured half of his.

"Oh, you didn't like!" she laughed.

"You have a wonderful knack of making any food taste incredibly delicious," he smiled. "Where did you learn to ride like that?"

"I've been riding since I was four. My zadie-that's Hebrew for grandfather-bought me my first horse, Nozzle," Meggie said.

"Nozzle," Phillip laughed.

"What kind of name do you expect a four-year-old to come up with? Besides, I still like it," she said. "My zadie had a couple of farms in Pennsylvania, so he lived there. Nozzle died when I was twelve and my dad bought me Nozzle II."

"What kind of farms does your grandfather have?" The elder Admiral Bennett inquired.

"They are all dairy farms. My zadie passed away when I was eight. The farms belong to my dad and my uncle now. They hired someone to run them. Since they weren't interested, but they wanted to keep the land. It's his daughter Helen who takes care of Nozzle. I haven't been able to get up there much since I started at American," Meggie said, becoming solemn.

"You were close with your grandfather?" Christine Bennett asked.

"I was close with all four of my grandparents. They were all wonderful people," Meggie smiled.

"How large are the farms?" Phillip's Dad curious.

"I really don't know," Meggie stated.

"They're massive," Phillip stated. Meggie gave him a strange look. "Your dad told me! They supply most of the milk for three states and encompass thousands of acres of land." As he spoke, Meggie simply stared at him, wondering where he got his information. She also wanted this topic of conversation closed; she was uncomfortable with it. Mary approached from the kitchen,

"Miss Meggie, if you are finished lunch, Cook would like to see you."

"Excuse me," Meggie quickly rose from the table.

"Mother, she's an excellent cook," Phillip said, noticing the surprise on his mother's face. When Meggie returned, he smiled,

"Miss Meggie." She laughed,

"We discussed it. Since I was uncomfortable being called Miss Hiken, Mary and Maria decided this was best."

"Are you ready for some tennis?" Phillip rose from the table.

"Now that's one of my favorite sports," Meggie smiled.

Phillip led her from the table and up the stairs to change.

Returning from tennis, Phillip entered the library, finding his parents again.

"You look like you had quite a workout," his father eyed him.

"Are you kidding? she slaughtered me," Phillip sank into a chair, totally exhausted.

"Where's Meggie?" His mother asked.

"In the kitchen," he said, still out of breath.

"Cook hasn't allowed anyone in there since one o'clock," Christine Bennett stated.

"Mother, Meggie is not 'anyone'," Phillip said.

Meggie entered the room wearing a white knit tennis dress and a sweat band around her forehead. The elder Admiral Bennett sat up, taking notice. He couldn't find one fault-and those legs. 'She really is a truly beautiful creature,' he thought.

Seeing Phillip collapsed on a chair, Meggie started to laugh. She walked toward him and knelt on the floor beside him,

"Was it a bit too much for you?"

"You didn't tell me you were that good," Phillip looked into those eyes of hers.

"You didn't ask. I'm going to bathe now," Meggie smiled, before excusing herself and going upstairs.

"I think it's time we all started to dress," Christine Bennett rose from her seat and exited the room.

Phillip smiled at his father.

"Did you see those eyes; they're like the Caribbean," he paused. "I have never known any female to have so many of the same interests as I and at the same time to be so damn good at them. Everything she does, she does well! I would venture to say she's one of the brightest women I have ever known. Yet, she's so damn beautiful!"

"I heard what happened at Admiral Phelps'," his dad said. Phillip started to laugh,

"She does have a way with words! She did apologize; ignorant comments have a way of annoying her. I think I better shower."

At the same time, upstairs, Meggie ran the water for her bath. She found bubble bath, luxury soap, muscle relaxers for the bath, tremendous fluffy towels and after-bath moisturizer. 'All of the amenities' she thought, planning to make use of all of them, as she sank into the bubbles and water. After washing, she lay in thought; another day full of new experiences. She wanted to soak for a while; her tush hurt a little because it had been a while since she had ridden. She could feel her legs and her right arm becoming somewhat tight because she hadn't played tennis since last summer. She knew from experience if she was patient and soaked long enough, she would be fine. She rose from the tub, not realizing exactly how long she had been in there. She looked at her hands; they were a little wrinkly. She smiled, remembering what Ma used to tell her when she was little.

"Meggie, if you don't get out of that tub, you're going to turn into a raisin." Ma used to say that because she hated prunes.

She dried herself off, with tears coming to her eyes.

Looking at her watch: five-forty. Phillip's mother had asked her to be downstairs at six-thirty. She figured she had time to rest for twenty minutes, crawling into bed nude. She was still thinking about Ma and missing her, then decided to put her out of her mind. Then she thought about Steven's last article on the affairs of the Middle East and put that from her mind as well. Thinking about the fact, she really didn't know what she was going to do after graduation and found that easy to put from her mind. 'Jay is right,' she thought, 'Some people are better at putting things out of their minds than others.' She closed her eyes and lay there with no thoughts, until six o'clock.

As Meggie dressed, she reviewed in her mind what Phillip had told her about his brothers. He was the oldest of four boys. Gregory was next, at age thirty-three, a Lieutenant-Commander in the Navy; and his wife's name was Anne. Then came William, at age thirty, also a Lieutenant-Commander in the Navy and his wife's name was Dina. The baby was Lieutenant Anthony. They call him Tony; he was twenty-five and unmarried.

Meggie entered the library promptly at six-thirty, finding Phillip's entire family there. She wore a detailed, thin-crocheted, light turquoise gown that clung to her body. It had a high, scalloped neck, long sleeves with scalloped cuffs and slits up the sides extending from the floor to two inches above her knees. Around her neck, she wore a simple one and a half carat diamond drop. She wore half-carat diamond stud earrings and a simple antique gold watch which had belonged to her Bubbie. Seeing her enter, Phillip rose from his seat and walked to her.

"You are a vision of loveliness, as usual." He took both of her hands in his.

Meggie noticed all of the men in the room rose upon her entrance. She greeted Phillip's parents and he took her around to meet the rest of his family. Phillip handed her a glass of white wine.

He led her toward a chair, on which she sat, and he sat on one of the arms beside her. She was definitely a bit uncomfortable. Formal conversation took place between the members of Phillip's family. He held her left hand the entire time. They both noticed Tony staring at her. It seemed like an eternity to Meggie before the first guests arrived; it happened to be only a few minutes.

Phillip led her toward the drawing room with the rest of the family to greet the incoming guests.

"Good evening, Miss Hiken."

"It's nice to see you again, Rear Admiral Frost," Meggie smiled.

Phillip smiled, not knowing how she did it. She remembered all of their names, having met most of them only once. After the last guest arrived,

"Do you know what I am?" She asked Phillip.

"Let's find the buffet," he laughed, placing his arm around her.

The elder Admiral Bennett looked at his wife,

"Did you hear her, remembering their names?"

"It was amazing," Christine Bennett said, taking her husbands arm and walking to the main room. Entering, they saw Meggie dancing with Admiral Burns; after that came a line of different naval officers and youngest brother, Tony.

Phillip was able to have two dances with Meggie before his youngest brother, cut in. He had been doing that all night. Dancing with Tony, she remarked,

"It must be kind of difficult having a big brother like Phillip."

"What do you see in a man fifteen years older than yourself?" Tony inquired.

"Maybe I enjoy his company," she smiled.

"Are you in love with him?" he looked at her. Meggie laughed,

"Honestly, I don't think that's any of your concern, do you?" She paused, "I find Phillip totally fascinating. It must be hard for you, though, having to follow Phillip, your dad and your grandfather."

"I could never follow in Phillip's footsteps; he's one of a kind," Tony said.

"Precisely my point," Meggie smiled.

When the dance was over, Tony led her to Phillip, looked at him and walked away. Phillip's father saw the exchange of dialogue and the abruptness with which Tony left her. He approached his youngest son,

"What were you two talking about?"

"It's amazing how she got me to say what she wanted said, making it only more believable," Tony dismally.

"She's one bright lady," the elder Admiral Bennett smiled, admiring the way she handled the situation. He felt Phillip intended to marry this young woman, whether he approved or not. He had better learn to accept the situation.

Later, after most of the guests had left, the music still played with Phillip and Meggie dancing. Meggie stepped back to see him,

"You and Tony are the most liberal in your family."

"We are the most progressive; we admire change and are willing to compromise, if that's what you're trying to say. I feel a great society is made by people who work for progress. The rest of my family is staunchly conservative; right-wing die-hards all of the way." He drew her toward him to dance.

"Do you argue with 'Sir' about this?" She whispered in his ear. Phillip laughed a little,

"We make it a rule not to discuss politics unless absolutely necessary. I believe we should have the same rule."

The elder Admiral and Mrs. Bennett watched them before moving to the dance floor. Christine Bennett turned to her husband.

"I hate to admit it; they do make a handsome couple. Phillip was right; she does have a great deal of class."

"Tell me, Christine, could you deal with having a Jewish daughter-in-law?" he said. She smiled,

"I won't have to. Phillip will see to it she converts."

"I wouldn't count on that," he led his wife to dance.

A few moments later, Meggie and Phillip said their goodnights to his parents. Meggie noticed his mother was far warmer to her than she had been earlier. Phillip led her up the stairs and toward her room, gently pressed her against the wall and kissed her. He drew his head back a little to look into her eyes.

"I love you. You have made me a very proud and happy man tonight," he kissed her again.

"Let's go in my room," she smiled.

"Not here," he whispered.

"Morality outdated!" Meggie smiled as she turned to open the door to her room. He caught her by the arm, bringing her close. Their bodies leaned into each other's; he kissed her again.

"Good night," he said, before releasing her.

"Good night, Renaissance Man," she smiled, before closing the door. It brought another smile to his face.

The following morning, Meggie walked into the library to find Admiral and Mrs. Bennett, Tony, Gregory, William and Phillip. She had a feeling she was interrupting a family coup. When they saw her, all of the men rose from their seats again and Phillip came toward her.

"You're up early, Meggie," Christine Bennett said.

"I've always been a relatively early riser," she smiled at Phillip. "Good morning, Renaissance Man." He laughed a little, as he placed an arm around her waist and led her farther into the room.

"You really tempted me last night. I hardly slept, envisioning you in the next room," he whispered in her ear. Meggie laughed and placed a kiss on his cheek.

All eyes in the room were on them. Meggie was on display this weekend. She was fully aware and decided not to let it bother her.

"Help yourself to some coffee," his mom said.

"No thank you; I rarely drink it," she responded.

Phillip sat back down to finish his coffee, then glanced at Meggie again. "I don't know what went on between you and Cook yesterday but this morning she wanted to know what your favorite breakfast was. I told her, eggs Benedict."

"Please excuse me," Meggie walked from the room to the kitchen.

She returned five minutes later, carrying a pitcher of fresh-squeezed orange juice and some glasses. She poured a tall glass of it, neared Phillip to see him still drinking his coffee.

"First or second cup?"

"Third," he said.

"Try some vitamin C and let's put the caffeine on hold," she took the coffee from him and placed a glass of orange juice in his hand. Phillip smiled,

"She's relentless about the amount of coffee I drink."

His parents returned his smile. Christine Bennett felt she better learn to accept this young woman. She may not have been too happy about it, but Phillip had taken the control of his life away from her years ago. Mary came in, interrupting her thoughts.

"Breakfast is served."

Phillip took Meggie's hand and led her to the dining room. He pulled out a chair for her and sat himself beside her. They were served freshly-cut fruit, croissants with preserves and butter, coffee and orange juice.

"Phillip, what time are you flying back today?" his father asked.

"We'll leave sometime after breakfast. Meggie's doing the flying," Phillip smiled, proudly.

"What!" Tony yelled, dropping his fork. Then, staring at his oldest brother. "Since when have you ever allowed anyone to fly you?"

"Since two months ago when she convinced me to give her flying lessons," Phillip laughed a little.

"That's a perfect way to destroy a relationship!" his dad stated.

"That's exactly what I told her. She told me, not if it's worth having! You should see her fly, she's a natural. Yesterday when she flew us in, even Norfolk tower was impressed. We'll log a few more hours this week and I'll make arrangements for the pilots test on Friday," Phillip caressed Meggie's hand.

The eggs Benedict were then served.

"I wish you luck, Meggie," the elder Admiral said, surprised.

She thanked him with Mary handing her a note.

"Please tell Maria, 'de nada' for me."

"I told Cook that was the best scampi she ever made. Is that what you were doing in the kitchen yesterday?" Mrs. Bennett asked.

"That, and eating," Meggie smiled.

A few moments later, Anne and Dina finally awoke and came to breakfast. They sleepily said good morning before pouring themselves some orange juice.

Those who ate prior were finished, and Meggie excused herself from the table. She returned two minutes later with a large thin package, wrapped in brown paper. She neared Phillip's parents.

"Admiral and Mrs. Bennett, this is for you. Thank you for having me this weekend and Happy Birthday, Admiral." She kissed them both on the cheek.

Phillip's dad tore the paper from gift as the rest of the family eagerly watched. He revealed a brilliant, multi-colored landscape in Meggie's own distinctive style. On the bottom right hand corner it was signed, 'Meggie Hiken, 70'.

"It's beautiful; you are a very talented young lady. Phillip didn't exaggerate. It was dear of you to give us a piece of yourself; thank you," Christine Bennett gently kissed Meggie's cheek. The elder Admiral Bennett rose from his seat to embrace her. The entire family was somewhat stunned. Displays of affection were rarely seen from these people.

Phillip stood, staring at the painting. It was the landscape she had started when they were in the mountains, but it looked completely different from when he had last seen it.

"In the throes of creativity!" He smiled. Meggie laughed.

"I want to show you something," Phillip took Meggie's hand, leading her from the room.

"I've never seen Phillip look better," Anne said, buttering a croissant.

"Maybe youth breeds youth," Gregory laughed.

"I don't know, but he's definitely happier, more relaxed. She seems to bring out the best in him," Christine Bennett smiled.

"She seems to bring out the liberal in him," the elder Admiral stated. Tony thought, now I know I like her!

Hearing the piano, Christine Bennett looked up.

"Beethoven's Fifth, Phillip's playing!" She rose from the table and moved toward the music room with the rest of the family following. Upon entering, they saw Phillip playing and Meggie seated on the piano bench beside him. Phillip finished, she smiled,

"Not bad." Meggie then yelled,

"Move over Beethoven!" She pushed him down the bench; Phillip was in shock. She started to play

Tchaikovsky's Symphony No. Four in F Minor, brilliantly. After she finished that piece, she went into her high school repertoire. She moved back a little, giving him room,

"This is a medley from high school days. Play with me; I'll cue you." They played, with his family eagerly watching and enjoying. When they finished, Phillip placed both of his arms around her, right in front of his prim and proper family.

"You are incredible! You do everything well."

"I beg to differ; I happen to be the worlds worst cleaner," she said.

"I don't think we'll have to worry about that," Phillip laughed.

A little later, Meggie and Phillip were preparing to leave. They walked through the front door to the verandah with his parents.

"I forgot something. Excuse me; I'll be right back." She walked into the house and to the kitchen to say good-bye to Maria and Mary.

"Phillip, there is a lot more there than meets the eye. She seems to be a rare breed," his dad smiled.

"She's quite unusual; the type that can grow on you. I like her, Phillip," his mom hugged him.

"I knew you'd feel that way," Phillip said, as Meggie approached.

Meggie said good-bye and thanked his parents. They both told her it was their pleasure and they hoped to see her again, soon. Phillip put an arm around her shoulder to lead her away.

"'Bye," she waved with her free arm.

"Phillip, what religion are you?" Meggie curious.

"Protestant," he replied, helping her into the limo. Meggie thought, 'White Anglo-Saxon, no doubt.'

His parents stood watching the limo pull from the drive.

"Anne was right; Phillip hasn't looked this well in years," Christine Bennett said.

Ellene Pomerantz

"Phillip's been speaking of going into politics. This young woman could be a tremendous asset. With her beauty, charm and cleverness, she could prove to be a terrific ally," the elder Admiral stated.

"Don't overlook her spunk," Mrs. Bennett smiled. "But she still seems so young to me," she said, becoming solemn.

Once in the air, Meggie turned to Phillip.

"How'd I do?"

"You did great! You made one hell of an impression on my parents" he smiled.

"I know I'm likable, but that wasn't what I was referring to," she said with a slight laugh.

"Oh, your takeoff! Perfect," he smiled.

"I like your folks, too, even if they are a bit stuffy," she gazed out into the clouds. "I'm not one to put on airs; I was uncomfortable in the beginning."

"I know, but you became yourself quickly enough," he said. "I am really proud of you. I don't believe you realize what a difficult task you accomplished. I'm aware of how difficult it can be." He leaned to kiss her.

"You are special." He smiled, she blushed.

"Still finding it difficult to accept a compliment?" he laughed a little. "What do you think of this idea? When we get back, we'll go to the penthouse. I want to teach you more about reading flight maps and logging coordinates."

"Sounds wonderful!" Meggie smiled.

"Besides, I had a difficult time keeping my hands off of you this weekend. I plan on making passionate love to you," he stared at her.

"Phillip! You know better than to say things like that to me, especially when I'm flying," she yelled. He laughed.

Walking into the penthouse an hour later,

"How was my landing?" Meggie inquired. He picked her up.

"Perfect, just like everything else about you," he kissed her, carrying her toward the bedroom.

"You're very demonstrative today," she smiled. She had never seen this side of the illustrious Admiral Phillip Bennett before; he had always appeared so reserved. He placed her down on the bed, kissing her, exploring every space in her mouth again. She watched him as he undressed. He was, without a doubt, the best looking man she had ever known, and knowing him only made him more attractive, she thought. She smiled at him as she lifted her tush to remove her white wool slacks. He smiled, watching her, then he lay his muscular body beside hers and kissed her. He kissed her ears and her neck; he unbuttoned her blouse and gently caressed her breasts. Lovingly he sucked her erected nipples. He gazed into her eyes,

"I love you with all of my heart."

After complete perfection, they lay in bed holding each other. Phillip laughed a little.

"What is it?" Meggie raised her head to see him.

"Just thinking about the weekend," he hugged her tighter.

"It was a weekend of memories! Right out of a storybook," she smiled. "Can I stay tonight?"

"You can stay anytime," he raised his body over hers. "You usually don't want to." He kissed her.

"I don't want this marvelous weekend to end. Besides, a girl has the right to change her mind," she smiled at him.

"I think it's time we got to work," Phillip rose from the bed and put on a pair of his Navy shorts.

"Is your entire wardrobe uniform?" Meggie asked, lying there.

"Mostly," he smiled at her. She questioned,

"Don't you ever get tired of looking like everyone else—no individuality?" He leaned over her and looked right into her eyes.

"My dear, who and what I am, I am proud of. Clothes do not make the man," he kissed her .

He went into the study to gather the flight maps. Meggie put on the turquoise Indian-cloth robe Phillip had bought for her when she stayed. They worked on the flight maps for a couple of hours.   He taught her nearly everything there was to reading them and gave her some easy clues on how to plot the coordinates.

"I think you have it down. We'll review Thursday night," he said.

Meggie hugged him before going to the kitchen to set the table for the Chinese food Henry was bringing. A few minutes later the chauffeur entered.

"Thank you, Henry, that will be all for tonight. Tomorrow morning we will take Miss Hiken back to school. We'll see you at seven-thirty," Phillip said, dismissing his chauffeur.

Meggie was famished. She didn't know what to eat first as she scanned all of the food on the table. She decided to sample everything. Phillip laughed, watching her, then helped himself. "Are you aware you are the only girl I have ever taken home?" Phillip asked.

"What about your ex-wife?" Meggie surprised.

"My mother did that; she pushed it. That's why I don't know whether I ever really loved her. I feel as if I wasn't given a choice," he paused. "That was ten years ago but it seems far longer."

Meggie thought to herself, 'Ten years ago he was getting married and I was a ten year old kid playing hopscotch and jacks.' She decided to put it out of her mind. She was too caught up in the excitement of the weekend, and she didn't want to lose the happiness she now felt.

"You're being very distant," Phillip touched her hand.

"Just thinking about what parents do to their children without really trying. I wrote a piece for the American paper a couple of years ago on parental misguidance, misjudgment and deception. I don't know whether you saw it," Meggie inquired.

"No, I don't believe I did," he said. "That robe really is you, it matches your eyes."

After they cleaned off the table and put the leftover Chinese food in the refrigerator, Phillip placed his arms around her again.

"You have an appetite comparable to that of our entire Fifth Fleet," he laughed. Meggie tried to pull away. He wouldn't allow her to.

"This isn't fair! You have the strength of Samson before his hair cut!" She yelled.

He laughed again as he brought her body close to his. He gazed into her eyes and became extremely serious.

Across the gateway of my heart
I wrote, "No Thoroughfare,"
But love came laughing by, and cried:
"I enter everywhere."
"By Herbert Shipman."

Meggie had a few tears in her eyes. No one had ever recited poetry to her before. 'Renaissance Man,' she thought, 'Perfect.' Seeing this, he smiled, before kissing her and leading her toward the bedroom. He disrobed and made love to her again. Cuddling together afterwards, Phillip turned to her,

"I'd like us to discuss marriage." Meggie stayed, lying on her back staring at the ceiling; she wasn't surprised. Only a fool would be, after the weekend. There was a moment of silence then she answered.

"It's an extremely intricate relationship. I wasn't aware it had even crossed your mind until this weekend."

349

"I desired my family to meet you. This was a perfect opportunity," he hugged her. He lifted his torso up over hers and stared into her aqua-marine eyes, "I think we should seriously think about marriage. I know you are wonderful for me and I believe I am good for you."

"If we're going to consider it, there's a lot more we need to learn about each other. We should do that first; then we can begin to tackle the problems that will undoubtedly present themselves," Meggie smiled, looking into his beautiful green eyes. She did love those eyes.

"Damn! You have great sense," he smiled. She laughed a little,

"I have thirty-five years to catch up on."

"And I have twenty." He squeezed her.

"That twenty won't be able to compare to five of yours," Meggie emphatically stated.

"Ladies first," he said.

"Alright, but don't expect too much. You already know some things. I was born Meggie Loren Hiken, May 21, 1950, to the proud parents Lil Mintz Hiken; resentful, ex-concert pianist and Morris Hiken; Republican, banker." Meggie went through her entire life in less than an hour and a half. Most of it had been in the dossier but there were a few parts that weren't. Phillip's favorite was when she smiled at him and said,

"Now you know I won't be after your money, Little Lord Fauntleroy!"

"That's it. Enjoy the saga, superhero!" she smiled. Phillip thought to himself, 'She covered about everything, except Steven Roth. Why did she omit him; because he wasn't important or because he is?' He glanced at her,

"You've dealt with a couple of tragedies in your life."

"I made it through those and I don't plan on any more," Meggie stated with determination. "Your turn, but wait." She rose from the bed and left the room. A minute later she returned with a container of Chinese food. Climbing back on the bed she sat with her legs folded in front of her.

"Cold!" Phillip laughed.

"I love it like this. You want some?" She held the container out to him. He shook his head no.

"Then start," she said.

"You already know a lot because of how inquisitive you are," he said. "I was born Phillip Dean Bennett." Meggie interrupted,

"So that's what the 'D' stands for." He smiled, then continued.

"August 3rd, 1935, I was born to my parents, Christine Dean Bennett and Admiral Walter Bennett."

Meggie learned that his great-great-grandfather arrived here prior to the Civil War, and he fought in it for the South. It was he who had accumulated the beginnings of the family fortune; consequently, each generation after had made it grow. His family was worth millions; he wasn't even sure how many. He attended military school from the age of five till graduation. He broke his left arm twice, both times were in fights. She found it amazing that his three brothers were all born during World War II when his dad was in the Navy. She questioned him as to whether they were really his brothers.

He was twelve the first time he had a girl, he couldn't remember her name.

"Nothing like starting young," she observed, he laughed.

His girlfriend in high school was Cynthia; he couldn't get into her pants. On the whole, he basically never stayed with just one woman until he married. He traveled with the Navy quite frequently, he explained. He was a graduate of the Naval Academy, Class of 1957.

"What number in your class?" Meggie asked.

"Out of 97, number 151," he smiled at her.

"Seriously, Phillip," she laughed as he came to kiss her.

"Number three."

"Not bad," she said.

Phillip told her of his many Navy exploits, of the various countries he had visited, their cultures, lifestyles, people and food. He talked about some of the interesting people he was fortunate to come into contact with. There were times he had risked his life for his country. He told her briefly of a few of those experiences. At four a.m., Phillip glanced at her, finding her sound asleep.

He rose from the bed, walked to his dresser and opened the top drawer. He took out a small box and removed its lid. Inside was a large marquise shaped diamond, un-set. He smiled, thinking about when he purchased it. A week and a half ago he had flown to Holland for a couple of days on Navy business. Meggie had accepted that, not asking any questions. She was learning. He placed the box on the dresser and took a piece of string from the drawer. As he neared her, he looked for her left hand. He wrapped the string around the fourth finger. He was cautious not to awaken her. She stirred a little as he walked away. After placing everything back in the dresser, he climbed back into bed beside her. He covered her with the quilt and placed a gentle kiss on her cheek.

"Sleep well, lovely lady," he said, before turning the lights off.

Phillip found it difficult to sleep. The events of the past weekend kept creeping into his mind. He was truly in love with her, then there was tonight. He thought of Steven Roth and asked himself again why she had omitted him. Sleep finally came over him.

Monday evening, Dottie walked into their room to see Meggie, sitting on her bed sketching.

"You didn't tell me about your weekend with the aristocracy."

The first thing Meggie told her about was the food.

"I'm from Texas, remember, I've never heard of steak tartar. What is it?" her roommate asked.

"It's sort of like hamburger but hold the heat!" Meggie laughed.

"It was the most marvelous and exciting weekend of my whole life!" Meggie smiled, throwing her arms in the air. "A totally new experience. Phillip wants me to consider marrying him; I think I will. Isn't that great news?"

"It's right up there with the bubonic plague!" Dottie yelled.

Meggie looked at her in shock, not understanding. Why wasn't she happy for her? Dottie walked over and sat on her bed,

"Meg, this is not one of Grimm's fairytales; this is the real world." Meggie sat, still in shock, not being able to say anything.

"I know you love Steven; don't do this," Dottie pleaded.

"I'm not capable of love! If I marry Phillip, I can have everything that life has to offer, as well as meeting various interesting people and seeing worlds I may never see. Phillip has opened the doors to a whole new way of living for me-a whole new world," Meggie explained.

"What about Steven?" Dottie questioned.

"What about him? He left me. He knew I would be alone. He didn't care and he left," Meggie said, becoming upset. Dottie quickly uttered,

"He loves you and always will. I know you believe that."

"Dottie, you don't understand!" Meggie said, as she lay back on her bed. "This is safe! Because Phillip is fifteen years older than me, I can expect him to die before me. Because he's fifteen years older than me, he won't hurt me. He's totally in love with me, that I'm aware of. I absolutely refuse to deal with the pain I felt after Dennis died, ever again. This is perfect, a dream come true; this is safe."

Dottie was finding it difficult to believe her ears. She became angered,

"Don't you see? You just as much told me you don't love Phillip!"

"Wrong! I do love him! Anyone who's taught me so much will always have my love. As far as being in love with him, no. That's not possible, not with anyone," Meggie stated. Dottie stared at her,

"It won't work! You are far too liberal and he's too bureaucratic!"

"It's worked so far; he's not adverse to compromise," Meggie smiled.

"Oh, I'm aware of that fallacy! You love when he makes decisions for you, even when he orders for you. Right!" Dottie raised her voice.

"Dot, I don't want to argue with you; we're not going to get anywhere. Tomorrow I'm going to log my final hours. We're flying to Myrtle Beach for the day. I'll need to get the notes for Franc's class from you-Oriental Art History. On Friday I take the pilot's test. I could never have done this without Phillip," Meggie still a little upset.

Dottie decided this was futile and climbed into her own bed.

"Good night," she turned the light off.

"What happened to your belief in my positive aura and all of those great vibes you used to receive from me?" Meggie inquired.

"Lately, as far as you are concerned, my vibes have a limited frequency," Dottie stated quite bluntly.

The following morning, Meggie flew them to Myrtle Beach, South Carolina; another perfect takeoff and landing. Phillip was proud of her, and of himself for teaching her so well. This was when Meggie discovered he did have an ego after all. Arriving at his friend's condominium, Meggie dressed in her bikini, preparing for the beach. Phillip stared at her in shock,

"That's how you're planning on going out?"

Meggie gave him a questioning eye; she didn't understand. He approached and took her in his arms.

"It's one thing for me to see that beautiful body of yours, but it's something else for others to see it. An admiral's wife simply does not go walking around like this."

"I am not an admirals' wife yet, and even so, this is me," she stated.

"Meggie, we have reputations to uphold. Gossip can be quite dangerous," Phillip said, still with his arms around her.

"Honestly, I haven't been one to care what other people thought or said for some time now! Most admiral's are at least fifty years old and their wives are old and wrinkly. You happen to be thirty-five and I am twenty. Don't ask me to give up my youth. I am me, and I'm also proud of that. You were the one who told me: who and what I am are the only things I will have forever. Don't try to change me and I certainly won't try to change you!" She announced.

Phillip elected to drop the subject for now. Feeling that after they were married, he would have far more control. That afternoon, as they frolicked in the ocean, he found that he enjoyed the bikini. She appeared so natural with it and as he touched her bare skin beneath the water, he thought, 'I presume she'll be allowed to wear this.'

Phillip kept his promise. Friday morning he took Meggie for her pilot's license. Entering a small building on a naval base outside of Arlington, Virginia, he glanced toward the man sitting behind a desk.

"This is Lieutenant Barnes; he'll be monitoring your test."

Seeing them enter, Lieutenant Barnes rose from his chair and walked toward them, saluting Phillip.

"Hello, Lieutenant Barnes; Meggie Hiken," she extended her hand to shake his.

"Let's get started," he glanced at her and then at Phillip. "It will take about three hours."

"Good luck!" Phillip smiled and touched her hand, before he left.

"Sit down, Miss Hiken," Lieutenant Barnes motioned for her to sit behind a desk. 'Just like the ones in high school,' she thought.

"The first part is written. It should take you about an hour to complete," he handed her a booklet and a pencil.

"Thank you," she took it from him.

Phillip had prepared her for this. He also informed her it wouldn't take her anywhere near an hour. He was right; she finished in thirty-five minutes. When she raised her eyes, she observed Lieutenant Barnes staring at her.

"All finished," she smiled, rising from behind the desk and walking toward this blonde-haired, blue-eyed man. As she handed him the booklet, she thought, 'He's adorable-typical goyish (gentile) looks,' as her grandmother would say.

"That was quick!" He extended his arm for the booklet.

Meggie walked back to her seat while he checked it.

"Perfect!" Lieutenant Barnes announced.

"Now, step two," she stood. When he rose, Meggie figured he was about six feet two inches tall, had a nice body and he was about twenty-eight years old. She smiled for having these thoughts.

"This way, Miss Hiken," Lieutenant Barnes opened the door leading to the airfield, interrupting her thoughts.

"Are you a relative of Admiral Bennett's?" He inquired, as they crossed the asphalt.

"No, why do you ask?" Meggie questioned.

"The Navy is generally not in the habit of giving this sort of test to outsiders," he stated.

"He taught me to fly," she smiled.

Lieutenant Barnes opened the door to the small jet plane and Meggie led the way in. She took her seat in the left pilot's chair and he in the one on the right.

"Miss Hiken, there's no need to be nervous; just relax," he said, going over the controls quickly.

"Please call me Meggie," she smiled.

"You are an extremely attractive girl, Meggie," he smiled.

"You're not too bad, yourself," she said, with a slight laugh. "Can we get started now?" She was nervous.

"Take her up," he instructed.

Lieutenant Barnes watched very closely as she checked the controls, started the engines and scanned her flight map. She set her coordinates on it, contacted the tower and moved the plane cautiously down the runway. Then she made a gentle lift-off into the sky. She followed the instructions he gave her for turns: when, where and how large. He had her change altitudes at various times, with only a second's notice. She flew them for about an hour and a half.

"Are you from D.C.?" He asked.

"I go to American University; I'll graduate in a couple of weeks," Meggie smiled. "You're a graduate of the Naval Academy."

"How did you know?" he asked, curiously.

"I guess I can tell," she said.

"Let's see how you put her down," he directed.

Meggie contacted the tower, received coordinates and prepared for landing. When the plane touched down, one could barely feel it hit the ground.

"Beautiful!" Lieutenant Barnes said, giving directions to the hangar.

She brought the plane to a gentle stop, turned the engines off, undid her seat belt and stood directly in front of him.

"How'd I do?"

"Phenomenally!" He stood directly across from her, feeling himself magnetized to her.

"Does that mean I get my pilot's license?" She smiled excitedly.

"It certainly does," he said, before hugging her. This was not like him; there was something about her that made him want to. He took a step back,

"I'm sorry."

"Never be sorry where feelings are concerned," Meggie smiled. "Thank you for your trouble today."

"We'll return to my office and I'll complete the paperwork. Today I can give you a temporary license. You should receive the permanent papers in about two weeks," Lieutenant Barnes led her from the plane.

Meggie was all smiles. Another new experience, another conquest! Lieutenant Barnes glanced at her smiling, from ear to ear.

"A penny for your thoughts."

"I'm simply happy! After you accomplished this feat, what were your feelings?" she still had a broad smile.

"You're right; I have been there. I remember experiencing a great deal of gratification from it," he said, leading her toward his office.

Once in his office, he checked his watch.

"We finished early." He proceeded to fill out the papers, then gave them to her to sign.

"That's it! Congratulations, you are now a pilot. I'd like to take you to dinner tonight, to celebrate," Lieutenant Barnes noticed her start to blush; he thought it becoming.

"That would be nice, but I don't think Phillip would appreciate it," Meggie said.

He thought, then he said, in shock,

"Admiral Bennett!"

"None other than that 'legendary' man of steel that flies triumphantly into the dawn!" She laughed, slightly.

Phillip entered the room with a broad smile on his face and a little chuckle.

"You did it, right?"

"Right!" She yelled, throwing her arms around him.

Lieutenant Barnes stood in shock. He never would have thought-the age difference! Phillip extended his hand to shake the lieutenant's.

"Thank you; I will remember this."

Phillip placed an arm around Meggie's shoulder to lead her out.

"I know of a wonderful little restaurant; we can dine outside by a lake," he said before kissing her.

"I'm famished!"

Lying beside Phillip in bed that evening, Meggie turned to him.

"When can I fly again?" Phillip started to laugh,

"I was expecting that." He leaned to kiss her. Then he gazed into her eyes,

"When will you consent to marry me?" She smiled,

"I thought we were in the stage of consideration; that's why I'm spending the weekend."

"I have already done my considering," Phillip stated.

"But I haven't!" She laughed a little. "Besides, I haven't spoken to my dad yet. Let's wait a little bit longer."

The doorbell rang. Phillip rolled over to see the clock, Seven-fifteen. He rose from the bed and put on a pair of pants. Meggie watched him, thinking, 'Saved by the bell,' and laughed at the cliché'. Phillip walked from the room, thinking, 'This is why I need a maid around.' He recalled over a month ago, when Admiral Hopkins came at an inopportune time. Meggie told him not to answer. He explained he couldn't do that. That technique may work for some people, but not for people like him; he carried too much responsibility. He made her stay in the back; was she ever resentful. So you think I'm an embarrassment, she told him. Hardly, it's just not proper, he informed her. 'She's learning,' he thought. Still walking to the door, he hoped it was nothing pressing, he desired to continue their conversation.

"Tony!" Phillip was surprised as he opened the door.

"You're obviously not real happy to see me," Tony eyed his shirtless brother.

"Simply surprised," Phillip moved toward the study, Tony followed.

"Where's Lena? I expected her to answer," Tony asked.

"Meggie's here and she's a little uncomfortable having the maid around," Phillip stated. Meggie walked into the study wearing her turquoise robe.

"Tony!" She placed her arms around him and a kiss on his cheek.

"It's nice to see you two have a normal relationship," Tony smiled, with an arm around her waist.

"Why shouldn't we?" She asked.

"I didn't know what to expect," he laughed slightly.

"So you came to check up on us," Meggie raised her eyebrows.

"No, I needed to speak with Phillip," Tony said.

"In that case, I'll make dinner and you are expected to stay," she walked from the room as the two men watched her.

"Does she always do this?" Tony inquired.

"What?" Phillip said.

"Allow you your privacy," Tony smiled.

"Always; I wish I could do the same with her," Phillip said, as he made a pitcher of martinis.

"Why can't you? You had a dossier done. You know everything; nothing to fear. Dad wants to see it," Tony sat on the couch.

"He's not going to. I regret having it done. I brought it home from the office and I plan to shred it," Phillip stated, stirring.

"He'll have another one done," Tony said to his brother.

"I won't permit it! Anything he wishes to know, Meggie or I will be happy to tell him. She has nothing to hide. I know she would not accept the idea of a dossier. I'm not willing to risk it. She's into personal privacy, freedom and independence. She worked for S.D.S. It goes against everything she believes in," Phillip glanced at Tony.

"How are you going to handle her and our system?" Tony inquired.

"We'll break her in very gently," Phillip smiled, just prior to Meggie entering the room again.

"You guys can munch on this until dinner, about forty-five minutes," she placed cheese and crackers on the table.

Phillip neared her, handed her a martini and one to Tony. She left, returning to the bedroom to change into a pair of jeans and a thin lavender sweater.

In the study, Phillip sat near his youngest brother, "What brings you here?"

"Dad's talking about retiring. He's upset that we're slowly withdrawing from Vietnam. You know he agrees with Westmoreland, 'We should invade the land with 1,000's of more troops.' Now that your prediction has come to fruition, Cambodia's' involvement and the war being Indo-Chinese. Dad wants to fight more than ever, and his hands are tied." Tony sneered.

"Maybe Dad should get out. He's far too right for these times," Phillip stated.

"Mom doesn't think he'll be able to handle it. He's always led such an active life," Tony took a sip of his drink. "Mom would like you to fly down sometime soon and talk to him. You were the only one he respected enough to listen to. Though, I'm not so sure, now that you've turned more liberal. He's not going to like that."

"You do," Phillip smiled. His brother nodded in agreement. "Besides, I've already made him aware of my political deviations."

"I'm sure Dad had a difficult time digesting that news. I was even taken back a little by your present outlook," Tony smiled.

"When you keep your mind open, it's amazing what you're capable of learning," Phillip stirred his drink.

"To think a woman was responsible for altering the view of the eminent Admiral Phillip Bennett," Tony laughed a little.

"Not just any woman," Phillip smiled.

They spoke for a while longer, Meggie walked back into the study.

"Dinner is ready; how about you two?" Phillip approached her,

"You could have stayed." He took her in his arms.

"You know how I feel; you should have your space and me mine," she said. He kissed her a little; then, a kiss placing his loose tongue in her mouth. Tony watched, taking it all in.

"Phillip," Meggie out of breath. "I think you should put a shirt on. It's not that I don't enjoy looking at your gorgeous chest..." she smiled, not able to finish her thought with him kissing her again before he left the room.

Placing dinner on the table, she checked to make sure she left nothing out-veal Marsala, Italian salad, fettucini Alfredo, ratatouille, garlic bread and a bottle of red Italian wine. Phillip entered the dining room wearing a green Lacoste short-sleeve knit shirt.

"When did you become preppy?" Tony asked.

"Meggie felt my wardrobe needed some diversification. She bought me this to wear around the house," Phillip laughed a little.

"Your pilot's test today; how'd you do?" Tony glanced at Meggie.

"Not only did she pass the test with flying colors, but Lieutenant Barnes' own personal test as well," Phillip said, and saw the surprise on her face. "I was in the hallway; I couldn't help but overhear your conversation with him."

"Renaissance Man, you were spying on me," Meggie laughed.

Meggie lay on the floor by the fireplace after dinner, reading the evening paper. The two men entered from the study. Phillip smiled,

"That is her normal spot." Phillip sat beside her. He whispered something in her ear and she rose and headed toward the bedroom. When she returned, she lit a joint and handed it to Phillip.

"Since when do you do this?" Tony asked, in shock.

"Since recently; I know you have for some time now," Phillip smiled.

"True," Tony took the j from Phillip and wondered how she managed this.

"The folks think you two will be getting married," Tony smiled.

"It's under consideration," Phillip smiled at Meggie. "When you're finished considering, let me know. I believe in long engagements." There was a moment of silence.

"About three days long!" He said, then burst into laughter.

Meggie threw a throw pillow at him and yelled,

"You're being impetuous again!"

After all was calm, Tony inquired, "Meggie, are you also considering converting?"

Phillip sat up straight, Meggie turned white. He looked at her,

"I wouldn't ask you to do that. Your heritage is part of who and what you are. Without it, you wouldn't be the same."

The following Tuesday evening, Morris Hiken picked Meggie up from her dorm. Entering a steak restaurant, Meggie glanced around and thought it seemed familiar. She didn't realize until they were seated, it was the same restaurant where her dad first met Steven. She smiled at her father,

"I passed the pilot's test last Friday."

"Mazel tov," he replied.

"Daddy, I've been doing a great deal of thinking." She paused, trying to find the right words to say this. "You are aware I went home with Phillip to meet his family. I've decided to marry him. I wanted to tell you before Phillip approached you."

"Why have you chosen to marry Phillip?" He looked at her.

"Why do most people get married?" Meggie asked.

"For love, and because they want to grow old together," Morris stated.

"Is that why you and Ma got married? It worked, didn't it?" She said, sarcastically. Dad thought, 'touche'!'

"Without love, marriage doesn't have a chance to work at all," he placed her hands in his.

"I disagree. I believe you need mutual respect and honesty. Besides, I'm incapable of being in love. So your philosophy doesn't apply," Meggie stated.

"You are very capable of love. I know because I have seen it," he said, then paused. "With Steven! What are you afraid of?" He noticed tears in her eyes as she withdrew her hands from his. "What's wrong, I struck a nerve?"

"No, you don't understand," Meggie glanced down toward her clenched fists. Dad intently watched her,

"Then try explaining it to me."

"I want safety and security. Phillip can provide that for me," she explained.

"That is not what life is all about," Dad was upset.

"That's what I want from it," Meggie stated.

"I feel you should think about this more, before you jump into something you will regret," Morris took her hands in his again. "I love you more than anything else on this earth. My greatest desire is your happiness. I want the best life has to offer you. You, my little love, you are running away from it."

Later that night, after returning home with tears running from his eyes, Morris phoned his ex-wife. He was extremely concerned for his daughter and he knew he didn't get through to her. Maybe her mother could; it was certainly worth a try.

One week prior to the end of the semester, Dottie was in the shower and Meggie was finishing a drawing in their room. The phone rang, she answered it.

"Meg, is that you?" a voice asked.

"Yes," she said, not recognizing it.

"Meggie, it's Ma. I'm going to be in Washington today; I'd like to have lunch with you."

"I'm pretty busy today. You understand-finishing projects before the semester ends. Sorry, I can't make it," Meggie said, very nonchalantly. All of a sudden Ma wanted to see her!

"I have to talk to you. Whether you choose to believe it or not, you are my daughter and I love you," Ma stated.

There was silence for a few seconds. Meggie had never heard this tone from Ma before. She couldn't remember the last time she heard Ma tell her she loved her.

"Ma, what do you want from me?" Meggie said, tears ran from her eyes.

"I would like you to have lunch with me," Ma stated.

"Meet me at the Peppermill in Georgetown at twelve-thirty," Meggie coolly, controlling her tears, before placing the receiver back on the phone.

Lil Hiken Mossowitz arrived at the restaurant one half hour early and sat in the bar waiting for her daughter. She had no previous plans to be in D.C., but she needed an excuse for Meggie to meet her. Ma needed to be with her daughter, to try to help her because she loved and hurt for her. After her third martini, she cried for her.

"Ma, isn't the table ready?" Meggie walked into the bar.

"I was waiting for you. Do you want something?" Ma said, with a glass in her hand.

"A coke," Meggie stated.

Ma motioned for the maitre d', who led them to a table. Nothing was said until after they ordered lunch and another martini for Ma.

"What's so imperative?" Meggie inquired. Ma leaned across the table a little and looked at her daughter.

"You are my heart, just as much as Ben is, if not more. You were conceived from true and honest love. At the time, I loved your father so much and I believe he loved me. We were young and foolish. I didn't know what kind of resentments I was going to have by giving up my career for Morris. I was so afraid that I couldn't stick up for myself nor fight for what I wanted. As time went on, I started taking out my frustrations on your father. I know now, many of the things I did, I did to hurt him. It was at this point in my life Albert and I came into contact again. I was feeling miserable about myself; he made me feel whole and wonderful again."

"Ma, please! I don't want to hear this!" Meggie said, loudly.

"You have to hear me out. You owe it to yourself. Your grandmother, my mother, was a very frightened lady. We all loved her, but at times she instilled such fear in me that

I was afraid of my own shadow. She tried to do it with you," Ma said.

"Do you mean the stories she was always reading in the newspapers?" Meggie asked.

"A perfect example. You probably don't remember, but when you were very little and she would start, I would tell you the opposite and that she was too old to know what she was reading. I didn't want you to go through life afraid; it's too painful. I was afraid for so long, sometimes I didn't even know what of," Ma took a sip of her martini before continuing.

"Meg, I swore to myself I was not going to allow that to happen to you. Are you aware your father wanted to put your trust fund money into securities for you, redeemable when you turned thirty? He wanted the control, not allowing you your freedom or independence. I was against it because, not having it myself, I knew how important freedom and independence was to one's self esteem. I spoke with Uncle Bob and Aunt Helen and they agreed with me. They spoke with your father and two comparable funds were set up for you and Lori. Morris went along with the idea, even though, to this day, he protests it. It's because he loves you so much. I think being a man, he really didn't understand," Ma glanced at her daughter.

"Why are you telling me this?" Meggie questioned.

"Because I love you," Ma said.

Meggie started to cry. Lil took her daughter's hands in hers and cried with her.

"Meggie, I don't want you to make the same mistakes I have. I know they may seem different to you, but in the long run, they are quite similar. Mistakes made from fear are alike. In the past, even as a child, you were always one to go after what you wanted, to knock down walls if they existed and to exhaust all possibilities as a means to an end. Do it this time, too," Ma said, Meggie looked at her questioningly.

"Your relationship with Dennis was a teenage love; I'm not making light of that. What I am saying is, it was obvious you were out growing him months before he died. I saw this, and so did your father. I know you loved him as much as you could then. It was your first love; we all remember our first loves. The difference is, most of us don't have to carry the albatross of death with us," Ma held Meggie as she cried.

"Steven loves you so much and I know you love him. I have never seen you happier as when you were with Steven. You glowed with him. Find him, seek him out as he wants you to do; he's a wonderful man. Love like you two have is so rare, don't allow it to pass you by. Go after it, Meggie-go after your happiness," Ma cried, still holding her crying daughter. They never touched their lunch.

Meggie drove back to her dorm, crying the entire way. She found a space close by, turned off the engine and leaned back in her seat, crying. She was oblivious to everything around her, including the black limousine, until someone opened her car door. Meggie jumped from shock.

"Why are you sitting here?" Phillip asked, then noticed her tears and the look of fear on her face. He climbed in the passenger side and placed his arms around her.

"I had lunch with Ma today," she whimpered.

"My love, I refuse to allow her to hurt you anymore. An end will be brought to this," he said, sternly.

"It wasn't like that," Meggie sobbed. "Take me away from here."

Phillip helped her from the car and held her tightly as he led the way to the limousine, while she still cried.

In Phillip's penthouse that evening.

"I'd like to plot the course to Houston for Dottie's wedding," Meggie said.

"There are some flight maps in the bottom drawer of the desk in the study. Be my guest," Phillip smiled. He was by the bookshelves in the living room, filing some papers.

As she opened the bottom drawer of the desk, she noticed something fall from under it. After finding the flight maps, she picked up what had fallen on the floor, intending to put it back. Her eye caught the boldly typed letters: MEGGIE LOREN HIKEN. She turned red as she read it. Briskly walking into the living room, she yelled,

"You fucking asshole piece of shit! What the hell is this?"

"I love when you talk gutter," Phillip laughed a little, with his back to her. He turned and noticed what she had in her hand. 'Damn! I forgot to shred it!' he thought. Looking guiltily at her,

"It's called a dossier."

"Is this what the taxpayers spend their money on? You bureaucrats in the Pentagon don't even understand the words money, dollars, blue collar workers, Abbie Hoffman, now me! Anyone who would do something this vile, should have guilt eating away at him the rest of his life!" Meggie screamed, tearfully, trembling with rage.

"When did you have this done? I bared my soul to you and you knew everything there was to tell about me. But you couldn't trust me. Now I know how you knew about my grandfather's farms! I was a real idiot!" She shrieked.

"Meggie!" Phillip in a raised voice, walking toward her. He wanted her ranting to stop. "It came a couple of weeks after I first met you."

"Why!" She screamed, clenching her fists.

"It's the system, in the scheme of things. I am sorry. After getting to know you I was especially sorry, because I realized you wouldn't approve," Phillip hoped an apology might calm her down. It did not.

"This system of yours is as antiquated as a World War Two Sailor!" Meggie yelled.

"That really doesn't matter now, does it?" He sternly asked, walking closer to her, "Who is Steven Roth?"

"You read the dossier; you know who he is," she said, still aggravated.

"Wrong; because you didn't tell me," Phillip stated.

"I would have; it's just that...." she couldn't bring herself to finish.

"Just what?" he demanded, making her look at him. .

"Alright! Fuck you! You want to know about Steven! He is the most beautiful, most intelligent, most sensitive man I have ever known. He has the inner strength of Gandhi and the wisdom of Socrates. The deities would want him as one of their own, if they could have him. But he's not buyable! He is perfection with a capital P!" Meggie verbalized.

"If that's the case, why did he leave you?"

"Because I refused to marry him or to go with him. He told me he would find a way to let me know where he was, so I'd know where to reach him when I was ready to tell him I loved him and could commit myself to him," she cried.

"*THE POST* was the way," Phillip stared at her.

"Obviously!" Meggie screamed, throwing the dossier at him.

"Put that in your dossier to make it complete!" She yelled, running from the penthouse.

She saw Henry by the limo, but took a cab back to her dorm. Crying the entire way; there were so many things going on in her head. She tried to sort out the truth from fiction, fact from fantasy and reality from illusion. She thought she must have shed enough tears today to overflow the Potomac. Running through her dorm, into her room, she literally threw herself on her bed, still crying.

"What the hell happened?" Dottie asked, in shock.

"I'm a victim of macho male power!" Meggie cried. "We've talked about illusions-well, my bubble has just been popped."

Dottie approached and put an arm around her,

"Meg, you are no longer going to be looking at him through rose colored glasses. It's what you think of him that matters."

"I have treated you rather shabbily; you are one spectacular friend. I love you," Meggie cried, throwing her arms around Dottie.

The following morning, Meggie was paged from the lobby. She knew who it was. She hadn't slept all night; she had finished her projects and thought. Her mind would not turn off. As she walked from her room, she knew how terrible she looked and didn't care. Walking down the stairs, she put her thoughts in order. Entering the lobby and seeing him, she didn't even know what she felt anymore. He approached, and noted the bags under her eyes.

"Are you alright?" Phillip asked, trying to hug her. She pulled back, not allowing him to.

"No; let's take a walk," she led the way from the dorm to the outside. After walking for a few minutes in silence, she turned to him,

"Phillip, in a few days the semester will be over. I'm going to Houston for Dottie's wedding, and I'm going alone. From there, I plan on flying to Honolulu. I need some space; I need to think."

"I'm sorry; I wouldn't hurt you for anything in the world," he looked at her, pleadingly.

"But you did," she met his eyes. He pulled her toward him.

"I love you; I need to make this up to you."

"Not now; I can't handle it right now," she said.

"I'll be here waiting when you get back. I love you," he said, before he kissed her gently.

He watched as she walked away. She turned to give him a big smile with a wave. In her heart, she knew he was basically a good man, it would never work. They were simply too different.

XI

The semester was over, Meggie packed her things one last time. As she said her good-byes to her friends, her instructors and to American University, she did so with a heavy heart. Thank God she didn't have to say good-bye to Dottie; they'd be seeing each other again in a few days. She cried the entire time she drove from D.C. to Baltimore, partially for what she had lost, and some for what she had gained. Mostly, she cried because she was closing a door on another part of her life. Steven and Phillip were right; growing up did hurt.

While driving through downtown Baltimore, she was amazed to see how the city had changed, in the process of renewal. The old row houses were being knocked down, replaced by new high-rises. Old buildings were renovated; the city was taking on an entirely new dimension. The refurbishing of Baltimore's inner harbor was in progress, a process that would take quite a few years.

As she pulled into the Charles Center, newly built high-rise apartments in the heart of the city, she wondered what she would tell her father. He had already agreed to her staying with him for a few days. When he had asked her about her plans to marry Phillip, she told him she was taking his advice to think about it. She didn't want to tell him about the dossier-basically, because she didn't want to discuss it. She simply couldn't handle it. She put it all from her mind, including her mixed feelings for Phillip. She preferred to leave everything hanging in the air. She figured, why not? That's how her life seemed to be.

After spending a few days in Charm City, Baltimore's new nickname, Meggie decided it might be nice to live there. She enjoyed walking everywhere she needed to go: shops, food stores, theater and restaurants. It was at this point she thought it may be beneficial to go back to the

Maryland Institute of Art. She needed some direction to her life and going for her Master of Fine Arts might be the answer.

One morning in mid-May, Meggie drove uptown to Maryland Institute and dropped off her application and college transcript to the admissions office. After that she went over to the Beethoven, the apartment that Alex and Christine shared. She couldn't help but stare at Alex as she walked in.

"How did it happen?"

"I don't know how familiar you are with coke," Alex said.

Meggie's only knowledge was what happened to Dennis and Christine's addiction. "I'm naive on the subject."

"You know, Christine was doing a lot of it. Between snorting and free basing, her system was loaded. Coke gives people who use it a lot a feeling of grandeur; it gave it to her. Yesterday, when I came home, there was Christine, standing on the window ledge. She saw me and said, 'Alex, watch me fly.' Before I could get to her she was out the window. I looked down to see her lying on the pavement. I was never so scared in my life. I phoned for an ambulance before running down the stairs," Alex wiped her tears before continuing.

"She was dead before the ambulance ever got here. They think the impact of hitting the cement killed her instantly." Meggie was also crying. There was obviously no love lost between her and Chris, but the loss of such a young life brought back memories.

"What are you going to do now?" Meggie asked.

"Chris and I were going to hang around here for a while; now that has changed. We had talked about moving to Oregon to live on a peace commune. She wanted to wait, to try to kick the habit. Now there's no reason to wait.

I think I'll drop out for a while, maybe forever," Alex said, sadly.

The two girls embraced and said good-bye, feeling they might never see each other again. Meggie gave her Dad's number in case she should need her for anything. Walking to her car, upset, Meggie thought, nothing constructive came from dropping out. On her drive back to the Charles Center, she thought how she almost dropped out by marrying Phillip.

Later that day, she flew to Houston for Dottie's wedding. Her mood was strange; erratic, as Dottie put it. One moment antagonistic, another, lovable. The girls spent that night together in Dottie's room.

"Do you realize this will be the last time we will probably ever share a room?" Dottie smiled.

"I didn't think about it quite like that," Meggie said. "I need to apologize to you, for not being there for you, not helping with the wedding plans."

"I didn't have anythin' to do with this weddin'. My parents wouldn't allow me to have what I wanted. Since it's their show, I told them to take care of it. There's nothin' to apologize for," she smiled.

"Yes there is! If I hadn't been in fairytale land, I would have realized long before this the lack of birth control pills was not your only problem with Mark," Meggie glanced at her roommate.

"What are you talkin' about?" Dottie asked, not understanding. Meggie knew she had to choose her words carefully.

She walked over and sat beside Dottie. "You know I love you and it's because of that I want the best for you. I feel you are selling yourself short by marrying him."

"I love him, Meg," Dottie looked down, then at Meggie. "Do you know why we found each other?" Meggie bit her bottom lip, looking at Dottie, remembering the first time she ever laid eyes on her.

"Yes, because you're a pushy broad!" Meggie laughed.

"Maybe, but that's not why. We were two lone ships, in desperate need of each other. I shouldn't have said, 'ships'," Dottie noticed the tears in Meggie's eyes.

"It's okay," Meggie smiled at her.

The girls lay in their beds talking, Meggie started to cry. Dottie wanted to know why.

"Everyone thinks I can do everything well. The most important thing I'm terrible at-managing my own life," Meggie tried to stop the tears. She had to for Dottie. The next day would be Dottie's wedding. Another new experience. This one she wasn't looking forward to; she didn't like Mark.

On May 21st, Meggie turned twenty and boarded her flight to Honolulu from Houston. For the following month and a half she did nothing but play tennis, swim, worship the sun, eat and sleep: a complete cleansing of the soul. Lori and Victor were engaged; the wedding was to be the first week in October.

"Are you sure?" Meggie asked her cousin, as the girls sat on their beds polishing their toes. Lori smiled,

"Positive!"

"Why don't you try living together first?" Meggie suggested.

"My dad would have a fit. Besides, I don't intend to run away from life, like someone else in this room," Lori glanced over to her.

"That's not fair!" Meggie loudly, hurt was written all over her face.

"No! It's the truth! You're afraid to take chances, only run away and hide like a frightened child," Lori rose from her bed to approach her. "Oh, Meg, don't you see what you're doing to yourself, or to Steven? He is so in love with you and I know you love him. You haven't been the same since he left. Take a chance, what have you got to lose? You know the old saying, jump in the water and see how it feels."

"What if it's too deep?" Meggie mumbled, the tears flowed from her eyes. Lori hugged her,

"You won't drown." .

Meggie lay back on her bed recalling what Richard had said.

"You're not right. You're pretty as ever, but you're pale." She gave him an argument about it, telling him about all of the changes that had occurred in her life recently. He told her if she wanted to wallow in her self-pity, she could do it without him.

Later that day, Meggie was in the drug store. She glanced over to the newspaper rack and saw yesterday's *WASHINGTON POST*. Reaching for it, she noticed an item at the bottom of the front page in a small square:

> For the next four weeks, our man in Europe,
> Seven Roth, will be writing a series of articles,
> "The Decay of Venice."
> Look for them in the Wednesday evening
> WASHINGTON *POST*.

Immediately the paper fell from her hands to the floor, she abandoned her purchases on the counter and ran directly back to the beach house. Extremely excited she made a phone call. She packed haphazardly and left Lori a note:

> *Thanks a lot, cous. I don't know what I*
> *would have done without you. I decided*
> *to try the water!*
>
> *Love you, Meg*

A few hours later, Meggie closed a book and leaned back in her seat. Glancing at the title, *WAR AND PEACE*, and the author's name, Tolstoy, she laughed to herself. It only took her two and a half years to read it! She enclosed a note: "To good friends, colorful tomorrow's." She didn't have to sign it; Richard would certainly know who it was from. Her plan was to mail it when the plane landed. A voice interrupted her thought.

"On behalf of United Airlines and your flight crew, we welcome you to New York's John F. Kennedy International Airport. We hope you enjoy your stay in The Big Apple."

With the thought America would always remember him, she disembarked the plane. Heading straight to the TWA counter to confirm her reservation to Paris, then to Air France, to reserve a seat from Paris to Venice.

By the time she finally landed at Venice's Aeroporto Marco Polo, it was eight in the evening the following day. Being beyond exhaustion, she took a water taxi to St. Mark's Square. She marveled at the sights of this glorious city, but was far too tired to appreciate them. After finding lodging in a hotel on one of the little inner canals, she relaxed a little. The proprietor was kind enough to bring her a tray because she was famished. She ate, showered, collapsed in bed and fell into sleep, thinking, tomorrow.

The following morning, after eating breakfast, Meggie asked the hotel owner where an American, who would be spending well over a month in Venice, might stay. He wrote down the names of five small hotels or pensions and handed them to her. She thanked him and embarked on her search at 11:00 a.m. Clothed in a white, revealing sundress and a white, broad-rimmed straw hat, she headed in the direction of the Grand Canal. Glancing around as she walked she thought, 'What a fascinating city, but it will have to wait!' There was more pressing business at hand. After stopping at two of the hotels with no luck, the realization hit her, she was taking a shot in the dark. She thought it had to pay off, it simply had to! Walking up the Grand Canal at Riva Del Carbon, she checked her map to get her bearings, and crossed it. Two more pensions off the list, still no Steven. She figured, one left, then the real hunt will begin.

"I'll find him, even if I have to go to every pension and hotel in this city!" She thought out loud and smiled to herself; her perseverance even astonished her. Looking up, she saw the Hotel Paradiso, the last on the list. She thought, 'This has to be it.' Crossing her fingers, she walked inside and spoke to the man behind the reservation desk.

"Buon giorno" she said, hello. "Vorrer Signore Steven Roth?" She asked if a man by the name of Steven Roth was there.

"Si," he informed her he wasn't in and asked if she wanted to leave a message.

"No, grazie!" Meggie said, excitedly before leaving.

Walking outside, she jumped with tears rolling down her cheeks. She found him! What luck! What irony! 'The gods can certainly be kind to mortals,' she thought, as her stomach growled. Looking at her watch, seeing it was 1:30 p.m., she recalled passing a trattoria only a block away. She sat at an outdoor table, near a canal, and ordered an ensalada and pasticcio de lasagna. Taking out pen and paper, she started to write Lori a note. She sat engrossed in her food and her letter, not noticing the bearded man leave from the rear. He walked to his hotel, upon entering, the man behind the reservation desk excitedly informed him,

"Signore, there was a beautiful lady looking for you."

"What?" He was surprised.

"Very beautiful, bello long hair, about so high," the man motioned with his hand as to her height.

"Grazie!" he yelled, running from the hotel. He knew who it was. 'Damn,' he thought. Running back toward the trattoria, he recalled seeing someone out of the corner of his eye. He never dreamed it could be her; he had waited so long! As he approached the trattoria, he noticed she was gone! Just an empty table with a dirty plate. Where could she have gone? He stood back looking in both directions, nearly falling into the canal. Spotting her buying some flowers, he started to run again. He smiled, still watching her, remembering what she said two years ago in Greece,

"I always buy flowers from the women street vendors; they're so poor and they have children to feed."

Stopping and watching for a moment, to catch his breath, he couldn't take his eyes from her. God, she hasn't changed, she's so beautiful! Then, he laughed to himself at her indecision; she could never decide which ones to buy. He approached her from behind and spoke to the lady vendor.

"Per favore, give the lady the blanco ones."

Hearing his voice, she quickly turned around; her eyes swelled with tears. She had never seen anything so beautiful in her life. He was gorgeous! Their eyes met, but not a word was spoken. He paid the woman twenty lire for the flowers, never taking his eyes from Meggie's. They walked away together.

"Grazie," the old woman said, but no one heard.

They stopped at an outdoor cafe close by and sat at a small table by the canal, still looking at one another. He ordered a cup of coffee and she a coke. Finally, Meggie broke the silence.

"It's good to see you."

"How have you been, Morris?" Steven stared at her as he leaned back in his chair.

"Lonely," she smiled.

"One wouldn't know to look at you; you're just as beautiful as ever," he smiled. She laughed a little,

"Love is blind, you know."

"Is it?" Steven said, seriously.

"It was pretty clever of you," she smiled, with a trace of mischief in her eye.

"What?" He asked, still serious and not taking his eyes from her.

"How you let me know where to find you," she still smiled.

"I knew you'd pick up on it; a bright lady, such as yourself," Steven smiled, pleased with himself. "So why did you come?"

"I decided to try the water!" She smiled with a slight toss of her head. Her hair flowed over her shoulders.

He loved when she did that! Gazing at her curiously, he was somewhat nervous, accidentally spilling his coffee. Meggie rose to get some napkins; turning around, she looked into his eyes and smiled,

"Steven Roth I love you!"

His eyes met hers. He sat in shock for a few seconds, then swiftly rose from the table and threw his arms around her, tightly embracing her. He stepped back to look in her eyes; he had tears in his.

"Do you have any idea how long I have waited to hear those words?" He didn't wait for an answer, before kissing her. Once wasn't enough; they stood holding one another and kissing.

The waitress cleaned the table before they sat down again. As they sat across from each other, they tightly held hands.

"Morris I have missed you so much. I love you; I always have and I know I always will. This was the hardest thing I have ever had to do."

"I love you; I'm sorry," Meggie said, with tears running from her eyes. Steven brought his chair close to hers and took her in his arms.

"You understand why I couldn't stay in D.C.?"

"Uh huh, you wanted me to suffer," she smiled. He laughed, before becoming serious again.

"I had to give you your space. I couldn't do that if I were around."

"It feels so good to have you hold me again," Meggie leaned her head on his shoulder.

"It feels even better to have you in my arms again," he kissed her. Meggie drew back, glanced into his eyes and took his free hand in hers.

"Do you remember, you once told me, truth is the child of time?" He nodded yes.

"I have to tell you something, but before I do, I need you to know how much I love you, how much I have always loved you. I ran away from it because I was scared," tears ran from her eyes again.

Before Steven could say anything she began her story. She had collected her thoughts as to how to say this while she traveled on the planes and on her walk through the streets of Venice. She told him all about Phillip, because their relationship was based on being up front and honest.

Steven took it all in and when she finished, he asked,

"Let's see if I've got this right. The legend in his own time, the 'Low Profile' Admiral Phillip Bennett? The James Bond twin?"

'How did he know that!' She thought. Then, 'History!'

"He's far better looking than James Bond," she said. He started to laugh; he couldn't stop. Meggie watched in shock,

"I was hoping you wouldn't be upset. I certainly didn't expect you to react like this."

"Oh Morris. I haven't exactly been celibate; it's been fourteen months. Of course none of my liaisons ever lasted

382

long because they weren't you. I was simply passing time waiting for you. I certainly never neared marrying anyone else," Steven said.

"Why, Mr. Roth, I thought you loved me so much," Meggie said, with raised eyebrows. He embraced her and whispered in her ear.

"I do, but you know me!"

"I deceived us," the tears still flowed from her eyes.

"You did it the way you had to. I understand. You're here now and I'm never going to let you go," he kissed her again.

Steven paid the check and they walked from the cafe. He led her in the direction of his hotel. As they walked through the lobby, Steven noticed Signore and Signora Jeni, the proprietors, watching them. He introduced Meggie and told them, "This is the beautiful woman I have been waiting for all of these months." After entering his room, Steven took her in his arms.

"I can't believe you have finally come."

"I never want to lose you again," she hugged him.

"No way! I promise; I always keep my promises," Steven laughed a little. Then he kissed her more passionately than ever. She became limp again-he could still do that to her! He slipped her dress off, placing her on the bed, still kissing her as he undressed himself. Lying there, just holding one another felt wonderful; both needed this closeness. It had been far too long. He rubbed her back, never knowing anyone who could become so turned on by a back rub as she. Then he thought, 'Every part of her is sensual.'

"Oh Steven," Meggie sighed. "You have always had the most incredible hands." He made love to her, remembering her most sensual parts and she his. They both felt it was better than the first time. Holding each other for a while afterwards, Meggie lifted her head,

383

"It's as if your body talks to me." He squeezed her, because it happened to be true.

It was now dark outside. Meggie excitedly jumped from the bed and opened the doors to the balcony. Steven lay watching her, knowing he would always love her energy. Completely nude, she walked out to see this glorious city. She knew this would be her favorite place in the whole world! Turning around, seeing Steven watching her, she threw her arms in the air, yelling.

"I feel whole, I feel free and I love you!" She ran and jumped on top of him.

"Morris, I love you!" Steven kissed her and gently, sliding his hands down the front of her body. He still found that he could never get enough of her. She was such a part of him, a tremendous part of him. They fell to sleep holding one another. At eleven that night he woke her with a kiss,

"Aren't you hungry?" She sat up, stretching,

"I'm still a little jet-lagged, but I am starving."

Meggie rose from the bed and walked to the bathroom. Steven didn't move, he smiled, recalling the events of the day. She was finally with him. There were times he was on the verge of giving up hope, but he never did. He saw her walk toward him; she had something in her hand. He began to rise from the bed.

"Let's go eat," he said.

"Not yet!" Meggie approached him with a razor. He held her arm,

"Hey! What do you think you're doing?"

"It's time to shave your beard!" She smiled.

"Okay, okay!" He laughed, taking the razor and placing her in his arms again. "I hope you never change. You are still you, and I love it," he kissed her.

He walked to the bathroom with Meggie following. As he shaved, she stood watching and gave instructions. He glanced toward her,

"I've been shaving for quite a few years now."

"But none too recently!" She said.

He turned the razor over to her with a slight reservation, but he did trust her. When she finished, he inspected himself in the mirror.

"You did a good job Morris. You didn't cut me once."

"I wouldn't do a thing like that. I was too anxious to see that gorgeous face of yours; I missed it," she said, as Steven extended his arm and drew her toward him. Their nude bodies touched again, this time on the bathroom floor. He ran his fingers through her hair,

"Some say nothing can ever be as it was before. In our case, it's going to be better"

"I wonder if any place is open where we can eat?" Meggie rubbed her stomach.

"Always thinking about your stomach. I know the perfect place for beautiful, hungry people in love," he laughed slightly. She turned her body toward him, placing her arms around him.

"I remember when you first laid that expression on me. God, how I love you."

"Morris, have you any idea how good it feels to hear you finally say that, how good it felt the first time you told me today? We're good for each other; you know that too." He rubbed her shoulder starting to excite her again. She stood to put her dress on,

"Marathon Man, we have to feed me."

Steven stared at her and thought, 'Thank you, Lord; she's my life, my joy!'

Meggie rolled on top of him the following morning.

"Happy Birthday!"

"I can't believe you remembered!" Steven placed her in his arms.

"It's not every day a person becomes a quarter of a century old," she kissed him, then rose from the bed.

"Where are you going?" He asked, wanting her back.

She returned with a small package.

"Oh Morris," Steven sighed.

"Open it," Meggie sat beside him with her legs bent under her.

Steven tore the paper off, opened the box to discover a beautiful, antique gold pocket watch, which had etched engravings over the front.

"It's beautiful," he wasn't able to take his eyes from it.

"It belonged to my Zadie," she smiled, thinking she would have an inscription engraved when they returned home.

Steven smiled with a tear in his eye; he turned and took her in his arms. He kissed her more passionately than ever, fondling her breast. Than the rest of her.

Afterward they lay completely content, holding each other. Meggie raised her head a little,

"What would you like to do on your birthday? The day is yours."

"Wrong! The day is ours; what's mine is yours," Steven propped himself up on an elbow to look at her. "I feel we should get married. With all of my heart I know we are right for each other."

"That wasn't quite my plan," Meggie gazed into his eyes. Now he knew for certain she wasn't running anymore: "I thought we should live together first, just to make sure."

"I am sure. I couldn't bear living without you again. Call me selfish, I want to make sure I have you for the rest of our lives," Steven quite seriously. Meggie thought for a minute, then smiled,

"You have brought out a side of me I didn't know existed. I feel fulfilled; I feel loved. I'm sure, too!"

"You will!" Steven yelled. She laughed,

"Why not? I have nothing else planned today."

He kissed her, then lay back on the bed, bringing her to lie on his chest.

"We have to discuss some things first," he squeezed her. He was happy; his dream was finally coming true. "Not that I don't think one major decision isn't enough for one day. I have one more article left to do on Venice. Then maybe we should take a few weeks to ourselves before going home. I'm sure the POST will give me a job in D.C., or I'll find another paper that will."

"What about your book?" Meggie curious.

"It's coming along," he said, nonchalantly.

"If you want to know what I think..." she raised her head to see him. He laughed again,

"You have a great mind; I always want to know what you think."

"I think we should travel for as long as we want. You can write and I'll paint. See the world and experience life together. There's nothing pressing at home," she stated.

"Life is a school and experience our teacher! That would be nice, but we have to eat! What they're paying me for these articles, the two of us could never live on," Steven eyed her. She gazed into his beautiful light blue eyes.

"Steven, if you give up your dream, a piece of you dies! I don't want that for you or for us. I love you and because I do, I want you to be the most you can be. I feel you should concentrate on finishing your book."

"Morris, that is beautiful, but we are still back at square one. What are we going to live on, the sale of your paintings?" He laughed, before kissing her.

"You're not far off," she smiled. He glanced at her curiously.

"I did leave some paintings and drawings on consignment at a small gallery in D.C. However, that's uncertain. Didn't I ever tell you about my trust fund?" she loved to surprise him. "That's how I've been able to travel and be me. My zadie passed away about twelve years ago, and left me a sizable amount. The conditions were set, at the age of eighteen, I have control of the yearly interest and at twenty-one, I can have the principal."

"You never told me! How much interest?" Steven hugged her.

"It varies; Daddy takes care of placing it where it will earn the most each year. I've never spent it all; he reinvests it. The initial trust was for half a million," she smiled.

"You are always doing that to me-dropping bombshells," Steven said, in shock. Meggie hugged him.

"I have to be the luckiest man on earth. To finally have the woman I love, who's not only beautiful, but bright and talented. Now I learn that she's almost an heiress!" He kissed her. "How I love you!" he kissed her again, caressing her breasts.

"Steven, if you want to get married today, you better stop that!" Meggie laughed, with a twinkle in her eye.

"I still can't get enough of you," Steven smiled.

"Tell me that twenty years from now," she rose from the bed.

"I will; I promise," he still smiled. "I wonder how easy it's going to be to find a synagogue in Venice?"

It turned out not to be that easy. Through determination and perseverance, they finally located one. Initially, the rabbi refused to marry them without blood tests. He informed them it was illegal without the results. They convinced him to perform the ceremony with the provision they would get the tests first, then they would return, at three in the afternoon, for the ceremony. Steven thought the only reason the rabbi agreed was because Meggie spoke to him in a combination of Yiddish, Hebrew and Italian. He embraced her,

"You are amazing! I have never heard those three languages spoken in the same sentence before."

"I needed to be understood," Meggie laughed.

They left the synagogue and headed in the direction of the hospital for the blood tests. Afterward, Meggie told him she would meet him at the synagogue at three. Steven was surprised, but he agreed to it. He knew she had her reasons, she always did. He smiled, he still knew her so well.

Meggie walked away and out of sight before entering a little store on the Calle Dei Fabbri. She smiled to herself as she looked in the mirror, wearing a white, eyelet, vee-neck dress with short puffed sleeves, a fitted waist and a short, straight skirt to just above her knee. Deciding she would purchase it, she walked around the shop trying on hats. Finding a white cotton one with a short rim in the back and a stiff, broad rim in the front, she tried it on. Meggie decided it was her and told the salesgirl it was perfect for her afternoon wedding. The salesgirl excused herself and returned with a piece of white netting and a needle. Meggie smiled at her, saying, grazie! A few minutes later, she left the store and headed in the direction of the synagogue. Not noticing anything or anyone as she walked, she thought about Steven. She never thought it possible to love someone as she loved him, to trust someone so explicitly, to respect so fully and to want so much for someone else. She couldn't recall ever being happier, so fulfilled, so loved. Seeing him waiting on the steps of the synagogue, she smiled; a few tears ran from her eyes. 'God certainly does give us what we need,' she thought. Steven smiled, nearing her.

"I see now why you wanted your space."

"In my scheme of life, I plan on being totally in love with one man and marrying only once," Meggie smiled. He took her in his arms,

"I enjoyed hearing that. You look breathtakingly beautiful."

He led her through the large doors of the synagogue. Seeing them, the rabbi motioned they should approach the altar. Meggie stood still. It frightened Steven, afraid she was about to back out.

"We didn't check me out of my hotel," she said. He laughed,

"Is that what you're worried about thirty seconds before we take our vows?" He clenched her hand, leading her down the aisle and up the steps to the bema. The rabbi began his service in Hebrew. Midway through, Steven motioned for him to stop. He held Meggie's hands in his. Looking into her eyes,

> "You are my love, my life, my spirit,
> You are my best friend, my confidant, my lover,
> You are my world, my soul, my heart,
> The love I have for you, is yours forever."

Meggie's eyes never left his as tears rolled from them.

"Oh, Steven," she whispered.

The rabbi proceeded with the ceremony. He appeared to be touched. He placed the glass on the floor. Steven, in keeping with tradition, broke it. In Italian the rabbi said, "You are now man and wife." Meggie glanced at the rabbi,

"Man and woman."

"Oh, Morris," Steven smiled.

"You can now kiss the bride," the rabbi instructed.

Steven took her in his arms and kissed her passionately. They turned to the rabbi and thanked him. Giving him lire that he wouldn't take. He told them it was an unusual pleasure and wished them much happiness. Meggie kissed his cheek, telling him to give the lire to the synagogue or the poor. Steven led her back down the aisle, through the large doors of the synagogue to the front steps. They took pictures, in between kissing, laughing and talking to the passersby. Then they headed in the direction of her hotel with plans to check her out.

"Nice accommodations," Steven said, entering the room and glancing around. He took her in his arms. She looked up at him,

"What you said back there was beautiful. I had no idea you were a budding poetic genius."

"Only for you, Morris," he kissed her.

"If you want to stay here, we can," she said.

"Maybe for an hour or so," Steven said, before kissing her again. "I feel we should consummate our marriage."

"No! I want to do that," he stopped her as she started to undress. "I love taking your clothes off. In fact, I love everything about you," he kissed her, feeling her body go limp again.

Over the next five days, Steven showed Meggie Venice.

"It's a fantastic dream," he said, holding her.

She couldn't get over how romantic and sensitive he was. She loved him more each day; she couldn't believe it possible to love anyone so much. The wall she had built around herself, Steven had torn completely down. She had never felt so free.

Steven took her to St. Mark's Basilica, the Doge's Palace and a late dinner at one of Venice's finer restaurants. A vaporetta ride back to the hotel on this moonlit Venetian night. Modesty was not one of his virtues either as he caressed her breast and whispered in her ear,

"I love you."

"I love you so much. I fought it for a long time. I'm glad it won!" she smiled, holding his face in her hands, then kissing him.

The next day he took her to the Campanile, a red brick bell tower, where she could look over all of Venice. They saw the Correr Museum. He knew she would love it: the costumes, the paintings and the replicas of boats, plus work by Bellini, Carpoccio, Canova and Lotto.

"This is definitely a city for lovers," Meggie sighed.

"That's what we are, what we will always be," he kissed her.

Awakening on the tenth day of their marriage, Steven held her,

"I have to write my last piece on Venice. Then I'm all yours."

"Okay," Meggie she rose from the bed. "You gave me my space, I'll give you yours!"

"Do you have any idea how I love you?" Steven watched her dress. She leaned over to kiss him,

"I have a pretty good idea."

Meggie spent the entire day going through this marvelous city again, enjoying her freedom and her piece of mind. She spun herself around, and threw her arms in the air,

"Of all the feelings in the world, is there a better feeling than feeling free?" She stood in the middle of St. Mark's Square with people watching. "I'm happy!" she smiled at them.

Eating lunch at a nearby trattoria, Meggie wrote Ma a letter first, then her dad and one to Lori. After finishing, she smiled at the sequence; a year ago it never would have been like that. She picked up the photographs from the farmacia and ran back to the hotel. Seeing her enter the room,

"I've been waiting for you."

"You're finished already! You do work fast!" Meggie laughed.

"With everything and everybody but you!" Steven smiled.

"Look at these," she excitedly lay the photos out for him. "Which one would you like to send to your folks?"

"This one," Steven picked the one taken immediately after they were married, standing on the steps of the synagogue. "I think they'll appreciate it." He placed it in the envelope with the letter he had written that day.

"Did you tell them I can't wait to meet the people who brought up such a gorgeous person?" she said, before kissing him.

"Of course! They basically know you already; they'll understand," Steven drew her toward him for another kiss.

That evening, they mailed their letters and Steven's last article on Venice. Now time was theirs.

They spent four wonderful weeks in Europe, driving around in a rented car. Steven would not permit her to drive; he told her she had far better value as a navigator. She took him to Interlaken, Switzerland, where they could ski in the summer. This was going to be a real trick, Steven had never skied before. Meggie found the entire experience quite amusing. She laughed,

"I'm afraid you're not going to make it as a skier."

"If God had intended for man to do this, we would have been born with long sticks for feet," Steven said, removing his skis.

"How do you plan on getting down from here?" she still laughed.

Steven took her hand, carried his skis in his other and led her toward a cave he had discovered earlier.

"Most people would be content simply to play in the snow in the summer," she smiled.

"We're not most people," he said, unzipping her ski jacket.

Afterward, Meggie put his skis back on him and held his hand the entire way down the slope.

The following day they went into a little shop in the heart of Interlaken. After a brief financial discussion, Meggie ordered one of those one-foot-thick down comforters she had wanted for over two years. The salesgirl informed her it would take at least three months.

"I don't care; I want it," Meggie said, then glanced questioningly at Steven as he wrote.

"I take copious notes on you," he laughed. Meggie gave him a look as if she could read his mind before she burst into laughter.

Arriving in Paris a few weeks later, Meggie placed a call to Air France.

"I would like two first class seats on your next flight from Paris to New York, to Washington D.C., or to Dulles." Steven took the phone from her.

"Can you book us to New York, two for coach?" he looked at Meggie, finding her quite surprised. He laid the receiver back on the phone. "You're being wasteful. What's the big deal about flying coach?"

"My legs get cramped. Being a tall person, you should understand that! Besides, I've never flown coach in my life!" she smiled.

"We have to start economizing sometime, Morris," Steven extended his arm to draw her toward him.

"Why now? What's money when love is in bloom?" She laughed.

"To my despair, I'm going to have a rough time teaching you about economics," Steven laughed, sliding his hands up and down the sides of her body, seeing her quiver.

Their flight landed at J.F.K. International Airport in New York. Steven made arrangements for a flight to Friendship. Disembarking from the plane in Baltimore, Meggie ran and yelled, "Daddy!"

Morris Hiken hugged his daughter, as he released her, "Have you any idea how happy I am to see you?" He extended his hand to Steven before embracing him.

"Thank you," Steven smiled.

They went with Dad to his condominium with plans to spend a couple of days. Before dinner, he handed Meggie and Steven the deed to piece of property in Howard County.

"I was under the impression this would not be mine until I turned twenty-one," Meggie said, with raised eyebrows.

"Your zadie made a codicil to his will. If you married before then, and as long as your mom and I approved, it would be yours. When do you plan to move in?" Morris smiled.

"Isn't someone living there now?" Meggie asked. Dad smiled,

"Certainly; that's why I asked. I have to give him notice."

"Don't," she bluntly stated.

"Mr. Hiken," Steven said, and was interrupted.

"Don't you think now you should call me 'Dad', 'Morris'-something else?" Morris Hiken stated. Steven would now realize her effrontery didn't only come from her grandmother. Steven smiled,

"Dad, Meggie and I are planning to travel for a while."

"In that case, our lessee can stay. However, when the two of you decide you are ready to settle down, please give me enough notice," Morris said. Meggie placed her arms around her father.

"I love you, Daddy! Sometimes you can be so understanding."

"I told you once; all I want is your happiness. I believe you have found it," Dad said looking into her eyes. She smiled to him,

"I certainly have."

The following morning, Steven drove her to Washington. Stopping the car, he leaned to kiss her,

"If, when I return from *THE POST*, you're not waiting on these bureaucratic steps, I will consent to come in and meet your admiral." She swung her arms around him.

"I do love you!" she said, before opening the car door. Steven watched as she walked up the steps, snickering to himself.

"God, how I love her, her convictions, her righteousness!" He sat in thought about what Meggie had told him earlier, "One can never have too many people to love. However, one can only be in-love with one person. That's you, Marathon Man!"

Meggie entered this large building, found she still had clearance and proceeded in the direction of Phillip's office.

"Good morning, Miss Stone. Is Admiral Bennett busy?"

"He's alone; go right in, Miss Hiken."

Meggie simply nodded and walked toward the double doors. Seeing him engrossed in work as she entered,

"I don't believe I have ever seen your desk so cluttered." Hearing her voice he rose from his seat and walked toward her.

"I do work at times," he smiled. He couldn't help notice her white, off-the-shoulder sundress and the white, broad-rimmed straw hat, before placing both of his arms around her.

"You are still a vision of loveliness." Meggie returned the smile. Phillip led her farther into the room to the brown leather sofa in the corner. They sat; Phillip placed both of her hands in his.

"How was your summer?" he gazed into her eyes; he needed honesty. Meggie smiled, looking at him, still adoring those green eyes.

"That's why I've come," she took a deep breath before continuing. "You are aware I went to Dottie's wedding and then on to Hawaii. I had a great deal of time to think. I thought a great deal about us, about the times we shared, the things we shared and the many things we learned. I think it wonderful when two people know each other this well." Meggie paused; this was harder to do than she had anticipated.   Seeing confusion on Phillip's face she immediately spoke again.

"After nearly two months in Honolulu, I flew to Venice."

"To Steven?" Phillip questioned, dropping his eyelids somewhat.

"To Steven. We were married two days later," Meggie said, softly.   He immediately released her hands. She placed his face between her hands, forcing him to look at her.

"You are one incredible human being, I will always love you in a special way. It was simply not meant to be. You came to me at a time in my life when I felt restless and undirected. I will never forget what you did for me. I needed to be the one to tell you. I couldn't let you hear this via a transatlantic phone call or some idle gossip. We returned yesterday evening; I had to come here. You and what we had mean too much to me," tears rolled from her eyes.

"Are you truly happy?" Phillip inquired.

"Don't you see? You were the one who set my heart free. I have honestly never been happier. I need for you to know how special you are, how much you have taught me, how I will never forget you." She placed her arms around him. After a few moments, she sat back; he could only watch her.

"How are your parents? Did your dad decide to retire for political reasons?" she asked. Phillip smiled a little,

"The folks are amazing. Dad's retirement was two-fold. He also desired to share with my mother all of the marvelous things this world has to offer. Being in the Navy, he had seen most of them," Phillip said. "I conveyed to them your message to visit Hawaii in October or November, not in the winter, that is the rainy season."

She smiled at him, he didn't know how to react; still loving her.

They sat talking for a short while. Phillip found it increasingly difficult to take his eyes off her. Miss Stone's voice was heard through the office intercom, startling both of them.

"Admiral Bennett, there's a Mr. Roth here to see you. I have informed him you are busy, but he's quite persistent."

"Please ask him to come in," Phillip glanced at Meggie. He rose from the seat next to her on the sofa and walked toward his office doors. As they opened, Phillip extended his right hand with Steven shaking it.

"Mr. Roth, I've enjoyed your articles in *THE POST* immensely. I hope I can look forward to more of them."

"Thank you, Admiral Bennett; it's a privilege to meet you," Steven eyed this man. He saw certain characteristics, he could understand why Meggie may have been attracted to him.

"You are quite fortunate," Phillip said. Steven smiled,

"That I am. I've learned patience in my two-and-a-half-year wait."

"Give it a rest, you two," Meggie stated, with raised eyebrows. Steven neared her,

"What's the matter Morris, are you afraid we're going to start on you?" He sat beside her and kissed her cheek. Phillip sat in a black leather chair adjacent to the sofa. He noticed they wore identical antique gold wedding bands on the third finger of their left hands. He felt this was Meggie's bright idea. She always had to be different, a non-conformist, having to make some sort of statement. Phillip smiled about that to himself before glancing at Steven.

"Meggie tells me your plans are to travel for a while. I happen to carry a little clout in certain areas. If there should ever be a problem, feel free to call on me. One never knows what to expect when traveling outside of the States."

"That's very generous of you. I hope we won't have to take you up on it," Steven said rising,

"What stage is this from? Either good depression or undirected?" He was referring to a painting hanging on Phillip's wall. She laughed,

"I'm honored to hear you've learned enough, after all of the art lessons I've given you, to pick out my style. But-wrong periods! This is called, 'Flight'." At that moment the door to Phillip's office opened.

"Miss Stone said Meggie's here," Tony said on entering. He walked toward her,

"It's nice to have you back. You sure put the light back into this office." Meggie glanced Steven,

"This is Tony, Phillip's brother. And this is my husband, Steven Roth." Tony extended his hand as Steven stood to shake it.

"Nothing like putting my foot in it? Congratulations," Tony surprised.

"Morris, we have to see Michael. He's been drafted." Steven said.

"Knowing Michael, he's definitely not taking this well," she glanced at Phillip, deciding to keep her mouth shut. Politics were not to be involved today.

"He told me you gave him a real tough way to go last year. One minute delightful, the next minute a cobra," Steven smiled.

"He's referring to when I walked out on the S.D.S.," she smiled at Phillip. "You remember that."

"I have to agree with him," Phillip laughed, recalling her moods.

"I don't think that you guys..." Meggie stated angrily, with Steven kissing her before she could finish her sentence. Phillip then learned how to control her arrogance and temper.

"Morris, I believe it's time to go," Steven rose from the sofa. "I'll be waiting in the outer office." He shook Phillip's hand,

"Admiral Bennett, it has been an honor meeting you."

"Thank you. Good luck on your book," Phillip now eyed him. Tony followed Steven to the outer office, Phillip walked over to the window. Meggie neared him, forcing him to look at her before taking both of his hands in hers.

"What we had was very special. I will always remember it, and you. There will always be a place in my heart that belongs to you. I do love you; it's just different from the way I love Steven. I will always love you." She hugged him and whispered in his ear,

"Be happy, Phillip; I really want that for you." He tightly embraced her,

"Remember, I once told you, if you need me to call. That still applies. I will always be here for you. You see, I know I will always love you." Phillip drew back to gaze into her eyes one last time.

"Thank you; I will remember that," Meggie smiled as she walked away.

"Meggie," he called and she turned. "May your life be beautiful and rewarding. That's what I desire for you."

"That's my prime objective," she smiled again, before leaving.

Tony returned to find his brother standing and staring through the office window. Tony still surprised,

"That was a shock; a capricious turn of events, I would venture to say."

"Not at all. I've known about Steven. I simply wish I didn't like and respect him," Phillip turned to his brother.

"There is a lady sweet and kind,
Was never face so pleased my mind;
I did but see her passing by,
And yet I love her till I die."

"I can't take the credit for that, it's by Barnabe Googe. It's quite fitting, don't you think?" Phillip turned back to the window. He couldn't help but see Steven and Meggie walk down the steps from the building but was unable to hear the interchange of dialogue.

"What did *THE POST* have to say?" Meggie interested.

"I must be on a run of good luck-first you, and now *THE POST* is willing to print almost every article I write, with an increase in salary. They informed me Mt. Kilauea is due to erupt again by the end of October. Wouldn't that be fantastic! That's when we'll be there and I'll be able to write about it!" Steven excitedly picked her up and spun around. They were totally unaware two men were watching from a third floor window.

"Let's have lunch," Tony suggested, trying to pull his brother from the window.

Meggie rose from the mattress on the floor, from the three day sit-in she had been staging by herself. She walked to the bathroom and looked in the mirror. Such a sight: swollen red eyes, a very drawn face and the palest she had ever been. She entered the shower to rid her body of the grime that had accumulated without her knowledge, washed her hair and allowed the fresh water to run down her face. She heard a knock on her bedroom door as she turned the water off.

"Miss Meggie, I made you a breakfast tray; you have to eat something," Anna stated. She opened the door to her room for the first time in three days.

"Thank you, Anna. You're right, as usual," she took the tray from her, not noticing the surprise on Anna's face.

"I'll be going out in a little while," Meggie informed her, before closing the door.

She sat to eat; first the fresh-squeezed orange juice, then the soft boiled egg with a little bit of sea salt. She decided to fore-go the coffee, she was hyper enough. She stared into space and recalled a conversation she had with Steven a few years back.

"Morris, you use too much salt," he bluntly stated.

"A little hypertension never hurt anyone," she smiled. "You drink far too much coffee. You even see mirages from all of the caffeine!" Meggie laughed. From that day on she cut down on the salt and he the caffeine.

'God, I miss him!' she thought, and began to cry again.

She pushed the breakfast tray aside and stood, with the thought of pulling herself together. She proceeded to dress in a light turquoise sundress and hat. There was even a trace of a smile on her face as she eyed herself in the mirror. Her body hadn't changed much. She may even look better after having had two children. Her hair was the same; long, wavy and many different shades of blonde. Her face showed some sign of maturity, but no lines yet. She briskly left the house and drove her car from the driveway onto Route 29, south-destination, Washington D.C. Before she was aware of what was happening her mind wandered again.

Steven and Meggie entered Michael's apartment, finding it in disarray. There were boxes and suitcases everywhere.

"Did a tornado happen to come through here?" She smiled, glancing the place over.

"I'm not in the mood for your mouth!" Michael sternly stated.

"Sorry," Meggie stood back. Steven placed his arm around her shoulder. Few people realized how sensitive she was, but he knew.

"I thought you were drafted, not extradited," Steven said.

"I'm going to Canada. I refuse to fight in a war I don't believe in," Michael sealing a box. "I call it the philosophy of living. If you don't have the right philosophy, you won't stay alive. You've got to stand up for what you believe in. If you're not a part of the solution, you're part of the problem."

"Michael, it's not the explanation that's important, but knowing your own mind and heart," Meggie uttered.

"Look who's talking here, our altruistic friend!" he blurted out.

"It's true I had a lapse there for a while. However, I am starting to form a resentment at how you are treating me!" she announced. Steven stood back: he knew they had to work this out for themselves.

"Adult choices are somewhat different. They're not, should I wear the red dress or blue one!" Michael sarcastically.

"Oh! The virtues of independent thought and deed!" She cut in.

"I don't have the strength for this. How long can we keep up this subterfuge? I've always adored you. You really hurt me last year. I think a part of me enjoyed hanging onto that anger. I believe it's time to forgive you; we've shared too much. We fought for causes we loved together." Michael approached to embrace her.

"Apology accepted," Meggie kissed his cheek.

"Since all is at peace now, let us help you," Steven took a box.

"A few weeks ago my parents bought me a van and gave me some bread to live on. They don't want to see me killed. I know when I get there it won't be easy, especially to find work. There are some guys from the States there now; I've learned how to contact them," Michael very solemnly.

"Have you thought about the fact that you won't be able to come home?" Meggie asked, as she closed a box.

"Of course! I honestly feel that when this whole affair is put to sleep, when this idiotic war and the climate in this country has somewhat turned; a way will be found for those of us who managed to escape virtual assassination to return. When that time comes, it comes. Presently my main concern is saving my own skin." Michael sealed another box.

After a while, all of the packing was complete. They all rested on Michael's bed. Michael slightly smiled,

"I'm glad you two finally made it together. I knew you were meant for each other ever since your first meeting in the trailer. Remember?"

"I'll never forget it," Steven with his arm around Meggie.

"Me either," she stated. Steven glanced toward her,

"Do you suppose your admiral could help Michael?"

"He's Navy, not Army; he'd want me to enlist!" Michael yelled, with Meggie nodding in agreement. "I'm one of the draft losers with nothing going for me. That way if I'm killed, there's no loss. They can't draft us while we are in school. Only after I receive my degree am I touchable. They must like their dead educated! Federal law requires us to register within thirty days before or after our eighteenth birthday. Failure to do so is a five thousand dollar fine or five years in prison. I should have failed to do so. I'd take prison over Vietnam anytime. Or better yet, maybe they would never have found me."

"Put the army out of your mind and try to get some sleep. You have a long drive ahead of you," Steven stood.

"Sure; I'll try counting jeeps," Michael responded.

"Good luck; I'd like to know where you are and how you are doing. Please write. We can be reached through my dad or Steven's folks," Meggie kissed his forehead, placing the addresses in his hand.

"Be well, my friend." Steven embraced him.

They left with heavy hearts, thinking, 1967 revisited.

A few days later, Steven and Meggie relaxed on a plane headed toward Phoenix, Arizona. She sat thinking about the time they spent with Ma and Ben. Ma had been genuinely happy for her and Ben was extremely distant. She smiled recalling a conversation with Steven,

"Ben's gotten weird."

"Maybe puberty is rearing it's ugly head," Steven smiled.

"Doubtful," Meggie felt Ben would have rather seen her marry Phillip. He had appeared so impressed with him. She decided to write Ben a letter, to explain how much she loved Steven.

Her thoughts were interrupted as the plane landed. They disembarked with Steven's arm around her waist. He was aware of how nervous she was. It brought a smile to his face. He felt that no one knew her like he did.

"Steven!" his mother yelled as she ran toward him. His dad did the same. They embraced.

"Come here," Steven pulled her into the family group. "This is Meggie," he smiled proudly.

"I feel I've known you for years now," Ian Roth stated, before hugging his new daughter-in-law. Meggie smiled with a few tears in her eyes as his mom kissed her cheek.

Ian Roth proceeded to drive through quite a few acres of orange trees before reaching a large frame home. After entering the house Meggie turned at Steven,

"You know me by now; I need a shower. Besides, you should have your space with your parents." She walked up the stairs as his mom led the way to the kitchen.

"I'm waiting, Steven," his dad announced, as the two men seated themselves at the kitchen table.

"I wrote telling you everything," he said.

"True, you did that. What I'm curious about is why you did it the way you did?" Ian Roth looked at his son.

"I love her more than anything else on this earth. You are quite aware of that," Steven said, before telling them the story. "Every age is the same; it's love that makes them parable."

"You deprived me of the joy of seeing my only child marry. That hurt," Mom said, slicing a coffee cake. Steven took her hands in his,

"I never meant to hurt you. You and Dad raised me to think for myself and to have the judgment to do what was best for me. You have always given me my independence, even when we lived in the neighborhood where the state flower was asphalt," Steven smiled. His parents laughed a little.

"Freedom means making my own decisions. This was one Meggie and I made for ourselves. We did what we felt right for us. I'm confident you're going to love her, once you get to know her. That's why we're here for a few days before going to Hawaii. It seems I've waited so long to bring her home," Steven looked up to see Meggie walk in wearing a purple silk blouse and a pair of jeans.

"How about a piece of cake and a cup of coffee?" Mom asked.

"Thank you, but no coffee," Meggie eyed the home baked cake.

"She's not big on coffee, but she loves fresh orange juice from oranges grown out of love," Steven removed a pitcher from the refrigerator and poured a tall glass for her.

"Thank you," she took the glass from him and tasted the cake.

"This is delicious! Can I have the recipe?"

"You bake?" Mom was flattered and surprised.

"This is a bobka; my mom makes something similar, but not quite as good," Meggie said, still eating.

"Mom, she's a regular Betty Crocker," Steven laughed.

"Are you ready to see the orange grove I've been talking about?"

"That's what I've been waiting for," she smiled. "Thank you," she said as Steven led her through the back door of the kitchen.

As they walked toward the grove, Steven took her in his arms,

"Living with the confidence of youth."

"What is that supposed to mean?" Meggie laughed.

"Us!" he kissed her. She broke away and started to run through the orange trees. They were both laughing. Steven's parents stood by the kitchen window watching. His mom glanced at his dad.

"She's a beautiful young woman, and down to earth. I like that."

"Steven's been in love with her for a long time," Ian Roth said, still with his eyes fixed out of the window.

"She gave him such a hard time. I don't know if I can ever forgive her for the heartache she put him through," Mom said, watching them.

"Meggie's only twenty, Steven knew that he had to give her time to grow up. That's what real love is about," he smiled.

"What are they doing now?" Mom still stared through the glass.

"They're so in love; the same kind of love we have," Ian smiled.

"I wonder what our grandchildren will look like," she mused, as Ian took her in his arms and kissed her.

Steven tackled Meggie. They landed on the ground as he began to undress her.

"What are you doing?" She squirmed, trying to get away.

"You, me and nature," he unbuttoned her blouse.

"You are incorrigible!" She yelled. Steven kissed her,

"Life is what you make it."

They said good-bye to Steven's parents a few days later,

"Your mom told me your room was in terrific shape. I was surprised, after what you had told me in the past," Dad said to Steven.

"She truly has grown up. They're calling our plane, Morris," Steven took her by the hand to lead her away. Meggie waved good-bye with her free arm. It had been an extremely pleasant visit.

Their plane landed at the Honolulu airport. Finding Uncle Bob had placed one of his rental cars, a Ford Mustang convertible, on reserve for them, Meggie walked to the driver's side.

"Oh no, Morris," Steven eyed her.

"You have no idea where you are going," she sat herself in the seat.

"I have a feeling I'm going to regret this," Steven placed the bags in the car, then sat in the passenger seat. Meggie peeled the car from the airport, to Steven's dismay. She headed up the coast to the Kahala Hilton. Her family had rented a block of rooms for Lori's up-coming wedding. Morris Hiken was due to arrive in a couple of days with his sisters and their husbands. Meggie laughed, thinking what she had told Lori a few months ago after seeing the guest list.

"In deference to limited space, your mom invited the entire population of the Hawaiian Islands!"

"What's so funny?" Steven asked, feeling left out.

"Thinking about the number of people they invited-three hundred and fifty," Meggie drove through downtown Honolulu and up the coast.

"Look! That's Diamond Head, the infamous," she smiled, Steven gazed out over the cliff, seeing surfers for the late afternoon tide.

"It looks the same as in the movies."

A few minutes later they pulled into the parking lot of the Kahala Hilton. They checked in and went directly to their room.

"Have you ever seen anything like this?" She asked. Steven glanced around this massive room, first noticing the king-size bed, then two bathrooms, one with a tub and one with a shower. It had it's own private bar with a refrigerator and a balcony that overlooked the Pacific Ocean. 'All of the amenities,' he thought. Steven placed her in his arms,

"I always said you liked the better things in life."

"My creature comforts, remember," she smiled.

"I'll never forget." He kissed her and picked her up, placing her on the bed. He started undressing her,

"I think we should consummate our room."

"Tomorrow we'll consummate the beach!" Meggie smiled, before hearing a knock at the door.

"I have this feeling we won't have any privacy while we're here," Steven rolled to his back as Meggie went to answer.

"Lor!" Meggie happy to see her cousin. The girls embraced before Lori entered the room.

"Something tells me I came at a bad time."

"No time is bad for you," Meggie smiled.

"It's been a long time, Steven," Lori smiled.

"I believe I'm indebted to you," he rose, embracing her.

"You two seem happy," Lori sat on the foot of the bed.

"Never happier!" Meggie said, joyfully.

"I knew it! Only came for a minute; we'll talk tomorrow. Dad made reservations for tonight at the club, seven o'clock," she stood to leave. Meggie walked her to the door and the two girls stood in the hallway talking for almost half of an hour.

"You two are like a Roman orgy; don't you ever quit?" Lori smiled.

"Never!" Meggie laughed. She went back into the room to find Steven going through his suitcase. She was curious,

"Have you lost something?"

"Morris, I want you on the bed."

"That's where you always want me, but you've never been so blatant about it before," she laughed, as she sat on the bed. Very wide-eyed she watched him. "What now?"

Steven sat down beside her handing her a bank passbook,

"Before we left Phoenix, dad gave this to me. They were saving it for when I married." Meggie opened it to see a balance of $35,000.

"Marathon Man, I thought you seemed more relaxed when we left," she kissed him.

"You didn't ask," he said.

"I knew when you were ready you'd tell me," Meggie placed her arms around him. Steven smiled at her,

"Meggie, will you marry me?"

"I thought I already did," she laughed.

"Just answer the question."

"Steven, my love, I would marry you one hundred times if it would make you happy." Steven held her right hand and placed a two carat marquise-shaped diamond on her fourth finger. She sat in shock. He smiled, 'Gotcha,' for once.

"I'm positive this ring has a history," she gazed into his eyes.

"This ring belonged to my third great-grandfather, he gave it to his wife. It has been passed down through the generations in my family. Now, it's your turn," he kissed her. "When we have a son and he marries, it will pass to his wife. This is my legacy and now yours."

"And you told me I was full of surprises." She smiled gently sliding her finger nails around his chest.

"Oh Morris," he sighed with a slight laugh. He tightly embraced her and laid her back on the bed. He straddled himself on top of her, rubbing his hands up and down her torso, feeling her body move.

Sunday evening, Meggie was matron of honor for Lori. She had managed to clear up most of her differences with Victor and to place the past just where it belonged, behind her. Afterward, Steven took her in his arms.

"I think we really wracked tonight!"

"Certainly! My dad's entire family is here. I suspected they would be generous," she smiled. "Daddy told them we planned on traveling for a while, not settling down as yet. He asked them to give us money."

"That's exactly what we got," Steven smiled. She laughed,

"We're wealthy. What can I say. And you were fearful."

After a week stay in Honolulu, Meggie and Steven left for some privacy on the island of Kuai. They stayed in a small Hawaiian hotel on the south coast. After seeing the modern, larger hotels on the east coast, Steven questioned why. She explained it rained daily there, not as often in the south.

As they walked the gardens Steven told her, "This is heaven."

"No, tomorrow will be heaven," Meggie said, with a slight laugh. She had lined up a helicopter to place them in one of the islands alcoves for the day. They frolicked in the ocean, made love on the beach and had this piece of time and earth completely to themselves until the helicopter returned to pick them up at dusk.

The following day they took a river boat ride into the fern grotto, being married Hawaiian style in a fern-covered cathedral.

After that, on to the big island, Hawaii.

"A magical kingdom!" Meggie told Steven.

They checked into the Mauna Kea Hotel on the Kona Coast. Meggie explained, Rockefeller built and owned it for a few years before selling it to the Westin chain. First she showed him the think tank temple. She was always amazed by these totally unconventional people. She felt

Steven would love it, and he did! Then on to Kilauea. Ironically it erupted the following day. Steven's article began:

> A great mountain explodes, lava overflows in glasslike crystals. The natives say that it's hair from Pele'...............

Next stop, Maui. Meggie told Steven, "This is my favorite." After a few days of sightseeing they found a small two bedroom house for rent on the Ka'anapali Coast. It wasn't far from the old whaling village of Lahaina. Signing a two-month lease they immediately moved in, setting the second bedroom up as Steven's office.

"Morris, come here," Steven stood on the porch overlooking the Pacific. He placed his arm around her waist to bring her closer as she approached. She smiled,

"Sailboats on the horizon."

"It's like a wonderland," Steven said, before kissing her.

"I knew you would love it here. It's conducive to writing, don't you think?" Meggie inquired.

"I think," he smiled.

During their stay in Hawaii they ate a great deal of fresh fish, fresh vegetables and fruit.

"A very healthy diet," Meggie told Steven.

"The pineapples are the best," Steven ate a slice. Meggie laughed,

"Contrary to popular opinion, the pineapple is not native to Hawaii. In fact, very little is, even the flowers. Everything came here by boat or by the birds. When the pineapple first came here, it was round. It was Dole who changed its shape so it could fit into a can."

"You're joking, right?" Steven surprised. Meggie laughed again,

"No! Captain Cook had a great influence on these islands. That's why there are monuments to him on each one. On each landing he brought something new."

"This is interesting; this would make a wonderful article. Would you mind my picking your brain?" Steven inquired.

"It's a great idea. There's an archives museum in downtown Lahaina. I believe your facts would be better from there," she smiled.

Steven watched Meggie a few weeks later, sitting on the beach and deep in thought.

"You're very quiet today."

"I've got Dottie on my mind," she played with a stick in the sand.

"I'm sure she's happy," he replied.

"I don't think so," Meggie responded, explaining to Steven how Dottie lost her virginity. "When I finally met him at Dottie's wedding, he bugged me a little. I couldn't put my finger on it right away. Then I realized he never touched her. I never saw him kiss her and he never complimented or flattered her. I asked him about it."

"Morris, you have a lot of balls," he interrupted her.

"I'm the one with balls? Dottie is one of my closest friends. I know her and love her; she deserves better. This non-person she married told me: 'I'm not sensitive, I'm not emotional and I'm not affectionate. She has to accept me for me.' I asked him if he loved her. He replied he wouldn't be marrying her if he didn't. Then he looked at me and asked me what love is. I was in shock." Meggie had a few tears rolling down her cheeks. Steven embraced her,

"Dottie's pretty strong; she'll deal with it."

"Standing up for her the day she married this low-life was a difficult thing to do. I wish you had been there with me," Meggie laid back on the beach.

"I would have, had you come to me sooner," Steven kissed her.

Nearly two months after they rented this little house, Meggie awoke at five o'clock one morning. Finding Steven had not come to bed yet, she put her robe on and walked to his office,

"You need some rest," she said, spotting a half-empty bottle of Scotch.

"Edison survived on two hours of sleep a night. He took catnaps in his lab," Steven arrogantly stated. Hostilely Meggie yelled,

"Your attitude is less than constructive and you're drunk!"

"It's your doing! If you hadn't insisted we stay in these wondrous islands of yours, I wouldn't be at a lull in my book! The well has run dry. I can't seem to work and it's all your fault!" Steven yelled the slurred words. She ran from the room, through the front door of the house and down to the beach as tears flowed from her eyes. Steven picked up his glass of Scotch, took a swig, then threw it across the room.

"Oh, shit!" he yelled, as he saw the glass splatter. He ran from the house yelling,

"Morris!"

She heard him, but wouldn't stop. He finally caught her by her left arm, brought her against his chest and tightly squeezed her.

"I'm sorry."

"We promised that wouldn't be necessary," she leaned her head on his strong shoulder. "Peter wrote saying how quiet Cancun, Mexico, is. Maybe we should try there for a while? The Caribbean would be a refreshing change."

"I love you, Morris," he still hugged her tightly.

"I know," she smiled, as they walked back to the little house and sat, holding each other, on the front porch for a while. Their first disagreement since they married.

XII

Cancun, Mexico, one month later,

"Morris," Steven whispered in her ear.

"Why are you waking me? I finished the last painting for Christmas gifts yesterday," Meggie stretched. Steven lay the manuscript of his book on her chest. She briskly sat up,

"You finished!"

"I'll take your paintings to the post office and you read. I value your opinion. Remember, you have a great mind," Steven laughed.

"I can't wait! Is there any coffee?" Meggie rose from the bed.

"On the stove, but, you want coffee?" Steven stared at her.

"We all deviate at times." Meggie walked toward the kitchen.

"Morris, you have enough paintings here to cover the wall of Grand Central Station! Did you leave anyone out?" Steven yelled from the living room.

"I certainly hope not!" She yelled back to him.

"What is all of the noise about?" Peter sleepily entered the kitchen.

"Steven finished his book," Meggie announced.

"Obviously, you plan to read it today," Peter yawned.

"That's the plan." Meggie poured herself and Peter a cup of coffee.

"Steven, come to Chichen Itza with me today, you haven't seen it yet. This is a perfect opportunity because I know I'll never get Meggie back there again," Peter said, walking into the living room. Steven was busy organizing the paintings.

"That's a good idea."

Watching Peter and Steven leave the house they had rented on the Caribbean in Cancun, Meggie thought about how they came to live there. A friend of Peter's was renting it before them. He left for Egypt and Peter made arrangements for Meggie and Steven to take over the lease. After first walking into this small, three-bedroom house that sat virtually one hundred feet from the Caribbean, Meggie glanced at Peter,

"One high tide and we're done for."

"It's not that bad. He's only had water a few times in the past year." Very matter-of-factly Peter replied.

"Wonderful! I'm glad it's not hurricane season," Meggie gazed at the Caribbean only a few steps away.

Since then, Peter had become an almost permanent guest. She welcomed his company since Steven was so engrossed in his writing.

"Don't come back for dinner," Meggie yelled, through the front screen door, as they sat in a small rental car.

"We won't!" Steven smiled.

She took her coffee and a couple of slices of toast and climbed back on the bed preparing for a day of reading. She thought to herself, 'No matter how much I want this to work, it is imperative I be objective!' She stared at the cover:

ONE MAN'S LEGACY
by
STEVEN ROTH

The death of a president, November 22, 1963, 12:23 p.m. Central Time, Dallas, Texas. Ten bells flash on the wire service - urgent catastrophe! The violent death of John Fitzgerald Kennedy, which ended his young political career, brought about a loss of optimism in this country. The murder of the

35th President of the United States of America and how his death changed history twenty years ago. A hero of our time, he created a hope!

"Ask not what your country can do for you. Ask what you can do for your country!"

This statement, made by J.F.K. at his inauguration, Will live on in the annals of history. He had magic; it really wasn't charisma. He was a man of grace who reached out to others. He was a man who went to war, World War II...............

Closing the manuscript, she glanced at the clock: eleven p.m. 'Where are they,' she thought. She had been so engrossed in what she had been reading she had neglected to eat. Meggie headed to the kitchen to make herself a sandwich when Steven walked in with a hobbling Peter. Seeing them she couldn't help but laugh.

"It's really not funny; it hurts like hell!" Peter said angrily, looking at his bandaged broken ankle.

"How did you do this to yourself?" she said, helping Steven guide Peter toward his room. Steven shook his head,

"Those crazy little steps at Chichen Itza! Those Aztecs must have had the smallest feet. The steps are no wider than five inches. People who wear a size ten shoe like Peter and I have a difficult time making it up sixty of them."

"I know," she agreed. "Let's get you into bed," Meggie pulled the top sheet down, then assisted Peter as he slid in.

"I fell; can you believe it? As long as I've been working there-I'm even used to the steps by now," Peter complained.

Seeing to it Peter was comfortable, Meggie entered their bedroom to find Steven lying on his back on the bed with his arms folded behind his head. She lay on her stomach on top of him and smiled, looking into his eyes.

"You are a man with a great gift."

"You liked it!" he yelled, before hugging her. She kissed him,

"I loved it!"

"Now tell me what you changed." Steven pulled back to see her.

"Not much, a few words here and there, a slight revision on just one section," she stood to pick the manuscript up to show him. Steven was pleased. His expression showed it as he checked it over.

The following day, Meggie typed the revisions as Steven watched every word. When it was finished, he smiled,

"It's almost Christmas. Let's get a tree."

"I've never had a Christmas tree," she smiled.

"I grew up with the privilege of having two religions," Steven took her hand to lead her out.

"It seems strange to celebrate Christmas when it's so warm. No snow, no chestnuts roasting over an open fire," she gazed up at the hot tropical sun.

That afternoon they returned with a six-foot-tall pine tree.

"I find it difficult to believe we actually found this in Mexico," Steven said, as he carried it into the living room. Peter stumbled from his room.

"This part of the country receives a great deal of rain. Vegetation grows well here. The people are somewhat wealthier here than they are midland, such as Acapulco, where it only rains five days a year. Here they grow most of their own food. They don't need to beg on the streets as they do in Acapulco and other parts of the country. Don't forget the majority of Mexicans are Catholic and Christmas is very important to them. The trees grown in this area are shipped throughout the country. I have to admit it, you did get a beauty! Felice Navidad!" Peter smiled. He never had a Christmas tree, either.

One month later Steven was relatively down. All of his manuscripts had come back from the publishers with no acceptances. Meggie felt not one of them had read it. Being furious, she booked them on a flight to New York.

"Why bother?" Steven stated. Meggie looked up from the suitcase.

"Why not? What have we got to lose? Besides, I know it's wonderful and you're not getting a fair shake because it's your first book. Daddy got us corporate rates at the Americana. Notice, I thought of economics!"

Arriving in New York, Steven proceeded with his manuscript to various publishers. They refused to even take a quick glance at it. The next day, after Steven had left with his manuscript to see other publishing houses, Meggie left the hotel with a copy of his book. She walked a couple of blocks before taking a cab to the east side. Entering the office of a very reputable publisher, one who only handled quality work, not any of the junk novels seen on the market today, she stood by the receptionist.

"I'd like to see Mr. Strayer, please."

"Do you have an appointment?" the woman asked.

"Is he alone?" Meggie smiled.

"He is, but without an appointment, you cannot see him," the woman sternly stated.

"Then if I were you, I'd make one for now. The name is Meggie Roth," she walked to the door to Melvin Strayer's office and opened it. The receptionist quickly jumped up, followed her, yelling,

"You can't go in there!"

"What type of societal functionary are you?" Meggie stated, staring at a forty year-old man seated behind a large desk.

"Mr. Strayer, I'm sorry; she wouldn't listen," the receptionist nervously uttered.

"It's alright, Margaret. I think I'll hear her out," he smiled, sitting back in his chair gazing at this beautiful blonde standing in front of him.

"You were saying..." Mr. Strayer looked at Meggie for an answer and wondered what it might take to get her into bed.

"This!" Meggie looked straight into his brown eyes and threw Steven's manuscript onto his desk. Melvin Strayer wasn't surprised.

"So, a book. We read two hundred a month around here."

"But you haven't read this one," she said, with anger in her voice.

"It's impossible to read them all," he stated.

"You mean futile! Therefore, the unknown, promising and talented authors are thrown aside!" She was aggravated.

"It's difficult to differentiate sometimes," he said, wondering about this beautiful woman.

"If you had read this book when we sent it to you, or better yet, if you were to read it now, I guarantee you would publish it. It is obviously above your grain to take a chance in life, to venture in discovering new talent. It's far safer to stay with the old!" Meggie still stood in front of his desk, now with her hands placed on her hips.

"Please sit down, Miss....." he glanced at the manuscript, seeing Steven Roth as the author. Noting that he was somewhat interested, Meggie smiled as she sat on the chair.

"Mrs. Steven Roth, but you can call me Meggie."

"You obviously have a great deal of faith in your husband's work," Mr. Strayer leaned forward a little.

"It's worthy of it. In my opinion, feeling you won't take it too seriously, it happens to be the work of a gifted man. I think when you read it, you will be pleasantly surprised," she said.

"What makes you think I'll read it?" he asked.

"Human nature and curiosity," Meggie smiled. He smiled at her,

"I must admit, I am curious. It's a rare occasion when someone bursts into my office the way you did."

"Then you'll read it?" Meggie was excited.

"Right now I don't believe I have a choice. As you said, human nature and curiosity." He laughed a little. Meggie stood and handed him a piece of paper.

"I promise you won't be sorry. This is where we can be reached."

She proceeded toward the door, she heard him call, "Meggie." She turned to see what he wanted.

"What possessed you to come in here like that today?" He watched her for an honest answer.

"Number one, I stand by my convictions. Number two, if I had been a timid, shy little mouse, you never would have listened. I got your attention, didn't I?" She smiled, then exited his office.

Melvin Strayer sat back in his chair, thinking, if Steven Roth has a mind like his wife, this is going to be good. He started to skim through the manuscript. Before realizing it, he was engrossed and read it cover to cover.

Meggie returned to the hotel to find a disheartened Steven waiting for her. 'He obviously had no luck,' she thought. She had made a decision not to tell him what she had done until it became necessary, not because she wished to deceive him but simply because she didn't want him let down any more. This whole experience had been hard on him and devastating to his male ego. She loved him too much to see him hurt anymore. Even though in her heart, she felt any publisher who would read his book would publish it immediately, she was not willing to risk hurting him again.

Nine o'clock the following morning the phone rang, waking them. Groggily Steven answered.

"Is Mr. Roth in?" a voice said on the other end. Steven sat up as Meggie stretched.

"Speaking."

"This is Melvin Strayer's secretary. He would like to meet with you in his office at eleven this morning."

"I'll be there!" Steven excitedly.

"By the way, he loved your book," the secretary conveyed before hanging the receiver up. Steven smiled at Meggie,

"That was Melvin Strayer's office. He wants to see me!"

"I knew he would!" Meggie hugged him. Steven was surprised,

"You went there?"

"Yesterday; the only one I went to. Somehow, he agreed to read your manuscript. Don't be upset with me," Meggie said as Steven squeezed her.

"Upset with you? Never! You should have told me, though I do understand your reasons for not. I haven't exactly been a pleasure to have around lately." Steven kissed her and rubbed her back. Feeling her aroused he smiled before making love to her.

Later, he rose from the bed and threw her robe to her,

"You're coming with me today."

"Why? This is your thing," she said.

"No, this is our thing! I don't know what you did yesterday to interest him in reading my manuscript, but I do know it was something out of the ordinary," Steven pulled her from the bed, hugging her again.

Precisely at 11 a.m., Meggie and Steven walked into the Strayer publishing house. Meggie glanced at the receptionist,

"I believe we have an appointment today to see Mr. Strayer."

"Mrs. Roth, today you do. He's waiting for you; go right in."

"Thank you," Meggie said, as Steven followed her. She opened the door to Mr. Strayer's office. He looked up from the work on his desk,

"Hello, Meggie. You happened to have been right. You must be Steven Roth." Mr. Strayer rose from his chair to shake Steven's hand. "Your book is not only enjoyable, witty and informative; I believe it has the makings of a best-seller."

"I value your opinion. Thank you," Steven smiled, as Melvin Strayer sat and motioned for them to do the same. He handed Steven a few sheets of paper stapled together.

"Your wife told me yesterday she felt you were gifted as a writer, I'm inclined to agree with her. This is a contract which I am sure you will want to check over. Take your time. I would like very much to publish this book and I want first rights to all of your future work. You will see I am willing to pay you very handsomely for the first rights, along with a percentage of the royalties. Finances for your future books we'll negotiate at a later date."

He rose from behind his desk and left the office to Steven and Meggie. They read the contract over thoroughly.

"It seems to be quite fair. I'm surprised; I believe I'm going to enjoy working with this man. I think I should sign. What do you think?" Steven asked, still with his eyes on the document, taking in where his name was typed as author. Meggie smiled,

"Certainly!"

Mr. Strayer walked back into his office. Steven handed him the contract and the two men shook hands-a gentlemen's agreement.

"I had a feeling you would sign. Meeting Meggie yesterday, then reading your book, I was well aware the honest approach would be best. This agreement happens to be just that-honest and fair." Melvin Strayer glanced at the signed contract in front of him, then to Steven.

"It's uncanny; this is your first book and it needs very little editing."

"Meggie already did that," Steven smiled.

"Very little!" She stated, "When do you think it will be on the market?"

"In about two months. I'd like you to stay in New York for a few days. We will need an autobiography and some photographs," he said.

"It can be arranged," Steven smiled, as they stood to leave.

"Mr. Roth, you have a very determined wife there," Melvin Strayer smiled. Steven placed an arm around her,

"I am quite aware of that fact!"

Once outside of the building Steven took her in his arms, picked her up and spun her around.

"I knew I did something right when I fell in love with you!"

Late March, approximately two months later, Meggie and Steven were still residing in Cancun. She wouldn't leave until Peter had fully recovered. Late one afternoon, Steven and Peter entered the house to find Meggie knee deep in the middle of quite a few cases of books and rolls of brown wrapping paper. Steven picked up a book. Reading his name on the front cover, his stomach did a roll. He approached her and placed his arms around her.

"Morris, I didn't expect you to single-handedly make my book into a best-seller."

"It's not that many." She stated. Steven laughed,

"No! Just enough paper to diaper King Kong!"

"I'm proud of you! I want everyone I know to see it. Here, sign this one for your folks," she smiled. Steven took the book, kissing her.

A few weeks later Meggie and Steven sat on the floor of the living room with an atlas in front of them, trying to decide which part of this wondrous world to visit next. They were having a wonderful time joking and teasing, being high on life since Steven's book had been published. The art gallery in D.C. had even sold all of her paintings and had requested more. Things were going their way.

"We work hard, we do great; so much for the American green!" Meggie smiled before kissing Steven. There was a knock at the door and she rose to answer it.

"Lor!" She was surprised, opening the door wider for her cousin.

"Can I stay for a while?" Lori, upset. entered with a suitcase. Meggie looked at her questioningly.

"Of course."

"Steven, I received your book, but I haven't exactly been in the frame of mind to read it yet. Please forgive me," Lori burst into tears.

Steven rose from the floor and placed a kiss on Meggie's cheek.

"Don't worry about it. I need to go to town for a bit."

"You're terrific." Meggie hugged him, knowing what he was doing-giving her space with Lori. Steven left, Meggie led her cousin to the spare bedroom, and as she sat on the bed she stared at her,

"Okay, brown eyes, out with it."

Lori started to cry harder, sat beside Meggie, and rested her head on her shoulder.

"Lor, you've always been there for me. Let me help you for once."

"You are," Lori said, with tears still running from her eyes.

"Then talk to me. It helps to get it out. You always made me do it," Meggie said. Lori took a deep breath,

"You're the only one I could turn to; I couldn't go to my parents with this. Damn it, Meg, it's so hard!" Lori cried. "A few weeks ago I walked into Victor's office to find him and his secretary on the sofa. He made up some cock and bull excuse. For some strange reason, I chose to buy it. I didn't want to face the truth." She stopped and looked around.

"You didn't exaggerate in your letters; the Caribbean is beautiful. Getting back to it, from that time on, he started coming home late. I guess he thought I was a real idiot! Then he took to staying out all night. Last night he did it again. I have had it! I packed my bags without seeing or telling him where I was going. I needed to get away." Lori still cried with Meggie holding her. 'She didn't deserve this shit, he's so much like his father,' Meggie thought.

"From what I've read, many new husbands stray from home the first year of marriage. It has something to do with the male ego and having a difficult time adjusting to being tied to one person. They feel their masculinity is threatened. Some doctors have even called it immature self images." Meggie said, trying to comfort her.

"Sometimes you read too much!" Lori stated sarcastically. Meggie still held her,

"You'll stay for a while and play with us. Time has a way of healing all wounds. You told me that a few years ago, remember?"

Three days later, Lori, Meggie and Steven were relaxing on the beach, soaking in the warm rays from the sun. Meggie smiled at Lori,

"Our skin is going to be like leather when we get older."

"We'll worry about it then," Lori rose and headed to the water.

"This is far calmer than the Pacific," she yelled back to them. Not receiving an answer, she glanced up to see them kissing, and felt somewhat of an intruder. She knew it was unintentional; then she had a shock! Seeing a dark-haired man walking toward the water.

"Oh shit! What is he doing here?" Lori swam farther into the sea.

"Lori!" he yelled, running toward the water's edge. Thirty feet out into the sea, she stopped and turned around,

"What the hell do you want?"

"You!" He yelled.

"Too late!" she yelled, swimming farther away.

He undressed and headed into the water with only his jockey shorts on. Meggie and Steven sat by, taking all of this in with smiles on their faces. It was fun to watch Victor try to catch Lori, who swam every day of her life. Victor was no match for her. However, somehow he caught her. Out of breath,

"I love you! You fool!"

"You call me the fool!" Lori angrily struggled to get away but he wouldn't let her.

"I am the fool; I know that. I love you so much, I can't bear the thought of losing you," he embraced her.

"Then why?" Lori asked, with tears running from her eyes.

"I wish I knew the answer. I don't know what happens. Some say men are expected to stray to prove their masculinity," he said.

"To prove their immaturity!" Lori glanced into his eyes.

"It was only sex; no feelings involved at all," he pleaded.

"Except for mine! I can't comprehend how you could risk losing what we have!" She yelled.

"I love you and only you. I only care about you and what you think of me. I promise, it will never happen again," Victor kissed her and led her toward the house.

"I imagine all is forgiven," Steven smiled.

"He's a shit." Meggie said, watching them.

"Morris, such language from that beautiful mouth," Steven smiled as he pulled her to lie back, kissed her placing his tongue in her mouth and untied the top of her bikini. As it fell, he gazed at her breasts. He pulled her to lie on his bare chest, sliding his hands all over her body.

Stopping the car at a red light on Route 29, Meggie began to cry again. She missed him so much-everything about him, even his tongue! Life with Steven was such a joy. He knew how to make her laugh, when to let her have space. When she needed him, he knew how to love her. He was perfect! There has to be a way! I need him. I love him so much and I don't know whether I can face life without him. He's most of my world. 'There has to be a way,' she thought, as she watched the light change to green. She drove on again with her mind drifting.

January 23rd, 1973. Vietnam War cease-fire. A day to rejoice, a day to mourn and a day to remember.

One month later, Steven and Meggie were living in the small town of Negril, on Jamaica's west coast. They rented a small house on the cliffs. It overlooked the Atlantic Ocean and there happened to be water access down a ladder. Steven returned from town one day; he had mailed his publisher the remaining few chapters to his second book. He spotted Meggie swimming and smiled as he stood on the cliff watching her, loving her so. He never thought after two and a half years he could possibly love her more than the day they married, but he did. Steven ran; terror was written all over his face,

"Morris!" he yelled. Meggie looked up to see him motion toward the metal ladder that had been built into the cliff. Then she saw something near it as Steven yelled.

"Head for the boat; there's a barracuda!" Meggie swam to the inflated rubber boat as fast as she could. She climbed into it, totally out of breath.

"Catch this," Steven called to her, he threw her a rope. She caught it. Seeing the fish head out to deeper water, Steven pulled her to the ladder. Meggie climbed it, trembling. Once she reached the top, Steven helped her up. They held each other tightly.

"Sir Lancelot! My knight in shining latex," she kissed him.

After the encounter with the barracuda, Meggie was ready to leave for a different part of the world. Steven brought the atlas out again and they went through it. Meggie pointed her finger to a page.

"Stop right there! The Himalayas, the highest mountains in the world! One side, China; the other side India and Nepal."

"My, you're adventurous," Steven somewhat surprised.

"You're the one who said, 'Life is a school and experience our best teacher'. We may never have another chance to go there again." She stood and walked toward the small kitchen for some of that great Jamaican orange juice. Steven laughed as he watched her.

"We'll check into it tomorrow. Let's abandon the orange juice for once." He walked to the ice chest and pulled out a bottle. He approached Meggie, and placed an arm around her shoulder to lead her to the bedroom,

"Tasty Jamaican champagne under the covers."

"An erotic adventure," she smiled.

Lying in bed the following morning, Steven smiled,

"I have to check the post office again. While I'm in town I'll see what I can learn about the Himalayas and Nepal."

"You were just at the post office yesterday," she questioned.

"Melvin Strayer is supposed to send a new biographical sketch for my approval. If we intend to depart for parts unknown, it is imperative this be taken care of first. For demographic purposes, it will be a bit difficult to do from the other side of the world." Steven said, Meggie jumped on him, yelling,

"Charging the unknown!" She kissed him, sweetly touching his penis and seeing his face light up.

Later that morning, Steven walked to town, a mile away. He reminisced about how he was able to persuade Meggie they didn't need to rent a car.

"Fine; but the mail becomes your responsibility," she stated.

Steven laughed to himself as he walked into one of the town's few hotels. He was seeking out a travel agent and was finding it difficult to obtain much information on the Himalayas and Nepal. It wasn't one of the popular tourist stops for people from Jamaica, or for anyone from this side of the world, for that matter. He smiled, thinking he and Meggie had areas of mutual interest. The woman agent handed him two phone numbers: one in Montego Bay and the other in Kingston. Thanking her, he headed for the post office a block away. He didn't mind these walks, they gave him time to think. He thought about how primitive this place was. The houses on the cliffs had no electricity. They sat by candlelight at night, which was romantic for people in love. They had an ice chest in place of a refrigerator, propane gas was used for cooking, and Alexander Graham Bell hadn't been introduced yet, either. Their only contact with the outside world had been through the mail and a phone at the local post office. It was time to depart for other parts. They had been total recluses. He thought entering the small post office, the only one for miles around.

Back on the cliffs, Meggie sat baking in the sun with thoughts of Steven's last book. She was immensely proud of him. She smiled, recalling one segment:

> Any government that dictates what a person can or cannot do in his own home, is too much government! Circulating money-that's how our economy works!

She loved his mind. In reality, she loved everything about him. She stared into space after reading the second book for the first time, trying to digest it all. She finally saw Steven as he walked into the room and sat beside her.

"I think this one is better than the first. I feel it will sell better. More people will relate to it."

"A prognostication, Morris." Steven hugged her. She smiled,

"Call it a fearless prediction. I believe in you."

Entering the small post office, Steven smiled at its only employee,

"Good morning, Mr. Raymond. Has my letter arrived?"

"Early this morning," he responded in his English accent, just before he heard the click of the telegraph.

"Excuse me," he left to take the message. Returning, he handed Steven his letter, "This just came for you," he gave Steven the telegram. "I'm sorry," Mr. Raymond said. Steven panicked and couldn't speak; his eyes fixed to the telegram:

Mrs. Lillian Mossowitz
3642 Brenton Drive
Ashville, Maryland

Mr. and Mrs. Steven Roth
10 Cliff Road
Negril, Jamaica

Meggie and Steven return home immediately.......
Morris had heart attack...
Funeral Sunday...

Sorry, Ma.

"Oh, Shit!" Steven screamed, running from the building. He ran back the entire mile to the house. His mind was working overtime, trying to think of the right words to use to tell Meggie. There were no right words! Psychic scars! He was well aware of how difficult this was going to be for her and hoped they would hold everything together. He had cause for consternation, being totally knowledgeable of how incredibly hard it was on her the last time she lost someone she loved. Her grandparents were all more acceptable. They had lived full lives and were much older. This was different; Morris Hiken was only forty-five years old-too young to die. She would never be prepared for this. It sucks that death has to be a part of living. He was still deep in thought as he approached the house. Still running, his brain wave was interrupted.

"Steven, it's too hot to run. Look how sweaty you are," Meggie yelled, waving to him. Noticing he kept running, she yelled again.

"I know you can't wait to get back to me, but remember, the heat doesn't agree with your caffeine."

Meggie lay back down on the chaise lounge. A few minutes later, Steven walked over and sat on a small space beside her. He kissed her, held his head about three inches from hers and gazed into her eyes.

"What is it, Steven?" Meggie was nervous, always knowing when something was bothering him. Steven had tears in his eyes,

"This isn't going to be easy." Meggie lay there waiting, part of her wanting him to say what was on his mind and part of her wanting him to forget about it.

"We received a telegram from your ma today. Dad died. We're going home," Steven held her close.

"This is a joke, right, Steven?" Tears swelled in her eyes.

"You know better, I would never joke about something like this," he held her tightly.

Meggie cried hysterically, then she let out a scream that could be heard for blocks around. He held her for a long time as she wept, trying desperately to comfort her.

"We have to pack. I booked us on a flight home this afternoon. We're paid through the end of the month here; however, I don't think we'll be coming back. You wanted to visit the Himalayas, remember?" Steven took her hand to stand. He held her tightly against his chest before leading her into the house.

"I placed a call to your ma, letting her know when we'd be in, and a taxi is due here in one hour. So we have to hustle," Steven said as Meggie climbed into bed and pulled the covers up over herself. She watched his movements as he packed without a sound or a stir. When he was almost finished, Steven walked over to the bed and gently pulled the covers off her.

"Go take a shower and get dressed," he said softly.

Meggie rose from the bed in robot-like motions and did exactly as he instructed. Fifteen minutes later, Steven carried their luggage outside and saw Meggie standing by the edge of the cliff. He approached, placed both arms around her,

"You okay?"

"I'll be alright because I have you. I need you with me, that inner strength of yours, your love and warmth." Meggie said, still with tears in her eyes. He kissed her,

"Thank you for always caring enough to let me in, for always sharing your inner thoughts with me."

"It's still beautiful," Meggie glanced out at the water.

"We had some good times here," Steven still held her, hearing the horn from the cab.

As they walked toward the taxi Meggie turned to sneak one final look of the ocean. They got in and Meggie started to cry as they pulled onto the road. Steven took her in his arms, trying to comfort her.

"How long will it take to reach the airport in Montego Bay?" Steven asked the Jamaican taxi driver.

"About an hour and a half. It's a little over sixty kilometers," he replied in his English accent.

There was silence in the cab for quite a while except for the sound of Meggie's tears. Steven held her the entire time. Later she looked at him,

"A few years back, I imagine it was when I was in junior high, I asked Daddy why we lived the way we did, since we had so much money. He answered me with a very self confident smile and said 'To be simple,' said Emerson, 'is to be great.' I believe he lived like that."

"He was a terrific man. You were fortunate to have a father like him. I honestly liked and respected him. My only regret is that I didn't spend more time with him, to learn to know him better, though I do feel I know him through you," Steven glanced into her watery eyes. Meggie wiped the tears from her face,

"He loved you. I was happy for that. He was aware of what we had long before I was. Maybe that's because the two of you are somewhat alike. It's strange, I never thought that until now."

"His favorite author was Zachary. He told me it was because he's one who made you work a little," Meggie stared out of the window.

"Herman Wouk," she murmured.

"What?" Steven asked.

"Just thinking about Daddy's favorite books: the *CAINE MUTINY*........ World War II. *FROM HERE TO ETERNITY* by James Hershey. I'm certain you've read both of those," she said.

"I have. My taste is impeccable and so was your dad's." Steven hugged her as they pulled into the airport parking lot.

Steven led Meggie from the car and carried the suitcases to the American Airlines counter,

"We are now boarding, Mr. Roth. The plane is due to leave in a few minutes," a short Jamaican woman stated from behind the counter, before giving directions to the gate. After boarding the plane, Meggie said in shock,.

"First class! What happened to economics?"

"Now that I have one best-seller and with your infinite wisdom you feel this next book will do even better, the time has come for you to be treated to your creature comforts," Steven smiled.

The plane took off and she embraced Steven as it leveled off. "Some people have to wear diamonds, others have a certain specialness about them. Do you have any idea what a good man you are?"

"I must be wonderful to have you," he smiled, gazing into her eyes, watching the tears flow.

"Oh, Morris," he drew her to lie on his chest.

Later, as the plane made its decent,

"On behalf of American Airlines and the flight crew, we welcome you to Baltimore's Friendship Airport. The present temperature is twenty-five degrees with a wind chill of zero. Enjoy your stay in Charm City," the stewardess announced, following a three hour flight.

"Better get out your woollies, Morris," Steven placed a tender kiss on her cheek.

"You have a fantastic sense of humor. You've always been able to put a smile on my face. I guess that's one of the many reasons I love you so much," Meggie said, tearfully. They kissed before disembarking. Still holding each other on the way up the ramp, Steven spotted Lil. Meeting her in the waiting area, Lil actually embraced her daughter. After retrieving the luggage they all sat in the front seat of Ma's 1973 Buick LaSabre. Meggie questioned her mother,

"Where's Albert?"

"I thought the three of us should be alone for a while," Lil said, handing Meggie and Steven a letter. Meggie, with tears still flowing from her eyes, stared at the envelope,

"Ma, how did this happen?"

"Meggie, read the letter. He must have written it at least a dozen times, trying to find the right words. This one he wrote yesterday morning, shortly before he died. We decided this was the best one. It's for both of you," Lil said, driving the car from the parking lot. Meggie tore the envelope open,

"We, as in you and Daddy?"

"Yes," Lil said, with a tear rolling down her cheek.

> *My dear kinder,*
> *I know you've never heard much Yiddish from me in the past. I imagine when one's time comes we revert back to our heritage. Don't ever forget yours, Meggie. It's important to know who and what you are.*

Knowing you as I do, you're waiting for an explanation. Two and a half years ago, the doctors diagnosed me as having a degenerative heart murmur, it had been getting progressively worse. I was informed I could have quite a few years left, if I took it extremely easy. The advice was to quit my job, to get plenty of bed rest, and watch my diet. You know that is not me. I informed them of that fact. It would have been as if I had died then. They told me I might live two years at most if I refused to follow their instructions. I fooled them—I had two and a half. I could never have been happy being a shell of a person. I had to do it the best way for me; it was my choice. I think you would want to know that.

I do have a few last requests. The house in Howard County has been refurbished. I would be pleased if you, my brother and sisters would sit shivah there. A few months ago, I hired a couple to take care of the place and the two of you, when the time came. They're good people—Anna and Joel Wilkes and their twelve-year old son, Tommy. I think you'll like them. They're living there now. The house has been completely furnished. If you dislike something, the store will take it back without a problem. I brought a few pieces from my apartment there a few weeks ago and I smiled, thinking how pleased I was with everything. It was important to me to have the house comfortable for you. I think you'll approve. When Ma pulls into the driveway you will see a white MG parked there. Later, do what you want with the car and the house. Be happy, that's all I have ever wanted for you, Meggie. I'm confident you know it so.

Always keep in mind my philosophy of life. I conveyed it to you many years ago - to be happy, to learn and work for what you want. I still think it a good one. There are quite a few things I have learned over the years, I would like to pass on to the two of you.

Meggie, about five years ago we discussed the difference between dreams and fantasies. At that time I thought I knew, but it was Lil who taught me the difference a few weeks ago. Fantasies are when you sit back, put your feet up and wait. Dreams might come true with a lot of hard work. The two of you have never been the type to wait, to let life pass by. I would like you to think about this. Caution is a valuable trait. Try it some time; it may work for you.

Everyone we love is bound to fail us when we insist they be perfect. I learned that the *hard way. I feel you understand what I am saying.*

Always remember how much I love you and desire nothing other than your happiness.

Who knows, I could be a Phoenix, risen from the ashes! If not, I will still be watching.

One last request. Tell my future grandchildren that I love them. I love both of you.

Daddy

Meggie folded the letter, placed it back in the envelope then glanced at Ma as she drove down Route 29.

"It was a beautiful letter. I'm glad he wrote to say good-bye. I know it was a difficult thing for him to do. However, he should have told me. I can't bear the thought of him being by himself at the end; it's far too lonely," Meggie cried. Ma stopped the car at a red light and looked at her daughter.

"He wasn't alone; I was with him."

"I am puzzled. What about Albert?" Meggie in shock.

"He wasn't real happy about it, but I did what I wanted to do, what I was comfortable doing. There were too many things in my life that were out of my control. It was about time I started taking it back. When I learned how sick Morris was, I went to see him. At first it was uneasy for both of us. After a few weeks of talking, more than I think we had ever communicated, we discovered there was still so much feeling there. We had shared a life together. I searched my soul, I didn't want it to be pity. He wouldn't have wanted that. A man of principle!" Ma smiled, only one mile from the house, then continued.

"Some people when they're married, get into an emotional straight jacket. They have difficulty admitting to their feelings. That's how it was with your dad and me. There were also other factors involved. Morris didn't want to die in a hospital. I certainly couldn't blame him. It was far too cold of an environment, we are both aware of how he likes things to be homey and warm. His housekeeper was very willing to care for him, but that wasn't good enough for me. He needed love and no matter what had happened in the past, I have always loved him. He knew that and accepted it, because he had always loved me. I moved in there six weeks ago, took care of him and supported him until the end," Lil pulled into the driveway.

"Did you sleep with Daddy?" Meggie asked, still with tears.

"Yes," Lil replied.

"Did you do more than that; was he up to it? Did you make love?" Meggie raised her eyebrows. Steven smiled, thinking about her effrontery. Lil placed the car in park, turned the motor off.

"Your father was a part of me and always will be. Yes, I made love to him many times. It's what we both wanted; we needed each other. I will always love him. He was a very special man." She started to cry. Meggie embraced her mother.

"Thank you for being there for him. He should have let me know how sick he was. I would have liked to have been with him."

"You are his heart. He loved you more than anything else in this world. All he has ever wanted was your happiness," Lil paused.

"He didn't want you to see him like he was. Their male egos, sometimes make it difficult for men to admit to their human weaknesses, especially to their daughters. In the

440

past generations they were raised to present an example: the strong virile facade. He preferred for you to remember him as he was-a handsome, intelligent and energetic man. He loved you so much, Meggie," tears still flowed from her eyes.

"I know. I think he knew how much I loved him. I wish I could have told him one last time," Meggie cried with Steven holding her.

"He knew how much you loved him; there's no doubt about that. That's why he wanted to make things as easy as possible for you. He was aware of how hard his death was going to be on you. It hurt him to think of you being in pain. Since he knew it would be impossible for you to deal with this without pain, he chose the next best thing-trying to make you comfortable," Ma said.

Steven opened the door to the car, stepped out and glanced around.

"It's not the way I had envisioned it."

"It grew!" Meggie said, surprised, getting out of the car behind him.

"Your dad's refurbishing," Lil said, staring at this large, old, stone, two story home. She continued,

"He made an addition. He thought you may approve. Remember when you used to complain about how prudent he was? This was a definite extravagance for Morris. I think he was hoping you would stay."

They followed Ma up three steps leading to the house. A woman about the age of thirty opened the door. Lil motioned toward her, a man and a boy.

"This is Anna, her husband Joel and their son Tommy."

"Mr. and Mrs. Roth, I wish our meeting were under better circumstances. Mr. Hiken spoke of you frequently. We are sorry," Anna said, looking at Meggie. She smiled slightly, at Anna,

"My name is Meggie and this is Steven." He extended his hand to shake that of Joel Wilkes's.

"Please follow me. I'll show you around, Miss Meggie and Mr. Steven," Anna said, as she led the way from the foyer. Meggie remembered her experience with Phillip's family's housekeepers.

"Your father told me it's been quite a few years since you have been here. As you can see, there have been a few changes made." Anna led them through a large living room, where there was a baby grand piano, then to a family room.

"This was part of the addition and this, too." She opened a door, revealing a nice cozy library. The shelves extended from wall to wall and were filled with books. Many of them were her father's. Anna smiled at Steven,

"Mr. Hiken planned this room for you."

They followed Anna through a remodeled kitchen with a separate breakfast nook and playroom. Meggie smiled to herself, thinking how she had sensed Daddy was ready for grandchildren. Over the past two and a half years he had mentioned it nonchalantly on several occasions, but he never pushed. He truly wanted her to be happy. There was a mud room with a small laundry area and powder room. Anna opened a set of double doors,

"Mr. Hiken said you're an artist-this is your studio."

Meggie walked in and glanced around. It seemed huge. I t had a solid wall of glass and skylights ran across the ceiling for proper lighting. She was speechless. It was so unlike Daddy. Anna led the way out and up a flight of stairs. There were three bedrooms and two full baths along with the master bedroom suite. In it were a large tub, a separate shower and a dressing area. Before leaving Anna explained,

"This is the end of the tour. The house is vintage late nineteenth Century. They didn't dig for basements then; there's only space for a furnace and hot water heater. I've spent the past three months getting to know this old house. If there's anything you want to know, please ask."

Both Meggie and Steven stood in shock. She looked at him with tears flowing from her eyes.

"Daddy was never like this-not this extravagant and certainly not this controlling!"

"I have a feeling he was trying to tell us something. He felt it was time we settled down. He was trying to make the idea more alluring to us. It is a fantastic house; it has character. Each room has been faultlessly decorated." Steven took her in his arms.

"The furnishings.....I really didn't notice. My head is not there right now." Meggie broke from his embrace and headed down the stairs. He followed her to the kitchen, where Ma was busy organizing and cooking with Anna's help. Ma looked up,

"Your aunts and uncles will be here for dinner."

Tommy walked in, placed two grocery bags on the kitchen counter,

"Would you like to see the stables? Dad's down there grooming the horses."

"That would be nice," Meggie eyed this thin, blond-haired, blue-eyed, five-foot-tall twelve-year-old.

Entering the stable, Tommy walked to a horse.

"This is Nozzle III. Your Dad told us the story of I and II." He then walked to another horse, pet his nose and smiled at Steven.

"This one hasn't been named yet. He wanted you to do that."

"What do you think?" Steven said to Tommy.

"It's your choice. He's your horse," Tommy replied.

"I could use some help. What do you think of Lester?" Steven smiled at the child. Tommy nodded approval. "I like that," Meggie grinned. "Even though I have never heard of a horse called Lester."

"Nor a beautiful lady like yourself called Morris," Steven smiled.

"If it weren't so cold I'd take her for a ride," Meggie rubbed Nozzle III's nose.

"Dad and I exercise the horses every morning. It's warmer now, unless it's too cold for you," Tommy said.

"Me, I happen to be numb, but I'll ride," she said.

Joel and Tommy saddled up Nozzle and Lester. Joel told them of a trail he had shoveled out of the snow. Before he finished Meggie had taken off.

"Morris, wait! I haven't been on a horse in years," Steven yelled to her. She didn't wait, but he did catch up to her. She glanced at him,

"That felt good."

He understood. Taking out frustration by riding into the wind and having the cold air embrace her face somehow produced a cleansing sensation. Meggie pointed for Steven to look.

"That's the pond, totally ice-covered."

They rode for a bit when she suddenly stopped.

"Steven, I have always loved it here. My father was born in that very house, the one he wants us to live in. Can you imagine that? From the time I was a little girl he would bring me here to pick strawberries," Meggie pointed to the strawberry patch.

"That's the garden. Wait until you taste home-grown fresh vegetables, from dirt to stove. They're wonderful!" She motioned toward a low fenced in area.

"It sounds like you're ready to settle in here," Steven glanced around.

"Maybe until the spring thaw," she smiled, with some tears still flowing from her eyes. "Would it be that terrible?"

"No, it may even be interesting." He saw her tears, dismounted his horse and walked toward her,

"I think you have shed enough tears today to overflow the Danube."

"The largest river in Europe, the one that flows through three countries," her face was red and she gazed down at

Steven standing beside her. He took her hand, helped her off her horse and held her for a while, a long while, before returning to the stable. Tommy approached to take the saddles off the horses.

"Did you have a nice ride?"

"Under the circumstances, I guess we did," she said. Steven placed an arm around her shoulder to lead her away.

"Mrs. Roth," Tommy called.

"Call me Meggie," she smiled.

"Are you sure it's alright?" Tommy watched her to see her nod.

"I feel bad about your dad. We met a few times. He was really a nice man. I don't know what I would do if anything ever happened to my dad." Tommy now stared at the ground. Meggie moved closer to him and lifted his face up to look at her.

"I don't think you have to worry about that. It's the love from the people we love that help us through times such as these. I have Steven, so I know I'll be fine." She embraced the child.

"I have a feeling we're all going to be family here. Your parents, you, Steven and I-we're all living here. Mutual respect and understanding breed love. I feel we have the makings for that. Never worry about what could happen, otherwise fear would dominate your life. A few years ago Steven told me to live for today, tomorrow we'll worry about then," Meggie said, before placing a kiss on his cheek.

"We'll see you later, or tomorrow," Steven glanced at Tommy as he placed an arm around Meggie to lead her from the stables. He noticed Joel Wilkes look up and nodded to him.

Joel neared the door of the stable to stand by his son as they watched them walk up the hill. Tommy turned to his father,

"She's so pretty."

Joel placed his arm around his son's shoulder,

"She's a pretty extraordinary lady. She's going through a real bad time right now. Most people wouldn't have been as compassionate as she was toward you. She felt for you, that's a rare trait at a time like this. I liked her dad; he was good man. I believe I'm going to like her and Steven. I think we're going to be happy here," he embraced his son.

On the walk back to the house Meggie let out a little laugh. Steven looked at her curiously.

"I was thinking of what Tommy told us before our ride. Nozzle is a one-and-a-half year old female. Lester is a two-year-old male, perfect stud material. I think Daddy was determined to have a grandchild one way or the other, even if it were to be a horse." Meggie walked, holding on to Steven.

"He also let us know his father has had a great deal of experience with breeding, even raising a couple of geldings," Steven smiled, before kissing her. Meggie stopped walking and gazed into his eyes,

"I need you to make love to me."

He held her tightly, led her toward the house and whispered,

"I always want to, now more than ever. First we'll initiate our shower, then the bed. I may never let you out of it." Steven kissed her, placing his tongue in her mouth and feeling her go limp in his arms again. He smiled as he led her inside, thinking sex was a wonderful release for built-up anxieties and frustrations. He felt happy Meggie realized this, the need to let go. They definitely possessed symbiotic instincts! He couldn't wait to make love to her as they walked through the kitchen, passing Ma and Anna, then the foyer and up the stairs. He unbuttoned her blouse on the way to the bedroom, placed one hand inside and gently caressed her bare breast. As he turned the shower on, he was not releasing her. He held her, fondled her and undressed her. Meggie looked at him as tears rolled down her cheeks.

"Steven, you are the best thing that ever happened to me."

"That's because we love each other. When you love another you share everything. Your pain is mine, your grief is mine. You are the most important thing in my life," he led her into the shower, then kissed her again. He rubbed his wet hands up and down the front of her body.

"Oh Steven," Meggie sighed as he kissed her. The tepid water beat over them as they passionately clung to each other before falling to the shower floor.

"Release it; we need this," Steven whispered, as he placed himself in her. As he felt her body go into orgasm, his did the same.

"Good, but not enough," he lifted her and carried her into the bedroom. Both still sopping wet from the shower. He lay her on the bed and rubbed his hands over her entire body again.

That evening, sitting at the dining room table with her dad's family, Meggie glanced around and thought this to be a very peculiar situation. She looked at Steven engrossed in conversation at the far end of the table. She headed the other end. 'Reversed roles,' she thought, as she watched her aunts and uncles, not knowing whether she was ready for this part of adulthood. She recalled the time when she couldn't wait to become an adult, feeling it would give her more space and freedom. It did that, but it brought along a great deal of responsibility with it. Her thoughts were interrupted by Aunt Gertrude, Daddy's oldest sister,

"I haven't been this upset since the price of gold went down."

Steven gave Meggie a very strange look as Ma walked in with a platter of chicken and placed it on the table.

"What gives you the right to be here after what you did to Morris?" Aunt Gertrude arrogantly stated. Ma didn't answer. Her face turned red and she briskly walked back to the kitchen. Meggie stood and gave Aunt Gertrude a piercing look..

"My mother has more of a right to be here than you! While you were in sunny Miami for the past six weeks playing bridge, Ma was busy taking care of Daddy." Meggie left the table and went to the kitchen. Ma was standing by the stove, crying. Meggie placed an arm around her shoulder,

"You know a chimp has a higher IQ than she does."

"Gertrude doesn't bother me. It's the culmination of everything that has happened over the past two days. She simply triggered it." Ma took Meggie's hand and led her to sit at the kitchen table. She held both of her daughter's hands in hers.

"Yesterday morning after Morris had finished the letter to you, we watched the movies from when you and Ben were little. He enjoyed doing that and listening to the recording from your first piano recital. Remember that?" Ma glanced at Meggie, she smiled.

"At eleven o'clock he was getting quite tired. I told him to take a nap. I had noticed over the past week he was growing weaker. He asked what I would do while he was asleep. He had been asking questions like that over the past few weeks. It's strange, years ago I wanted him to care. I've learned that he did, he just didn't show it. Now when it's too late..." Ma started to cry. After a minute she pulled herself together.

"I kissed him and said I would be in the kitchen making him a gourmet lunch. Over the past six weeks I made him all of his favorite dishes. It's amazing what the mind is capable of remembering. During this time we had together, we only talked and thought about the good times. We reminisced frequently. We laughed a lot, loved a lot and gave each other strength. We completely forgot about all of the hurt and heartache," Lil said, with tears running from her eyes.

"Thank you for being there for him." Meggie hugged her.

Lil held Meggie's hands tighter.

"As I left the room he said, 'You're a good woman Lil; I don't think I ever told you that before but I always thought it'. I told him that he was a wonderful man and to get some rest. I prepared a crab meat soufflé' and a spinach salad waiting for Morris to wake up. At one o'clock I went to check on him. It didn't seem like he was breathing. I shook him trying to wake him and I screamed his name. I know I was hysterical when I phoned Dr. Marcus. He came over immediately, checked Morris, then confirmed my worst fears. He was dead, I went completely to pieces. He helped get me back together and to put things in their proper perspective. There was a lot that had to get done. I was the only one to do it. I owed that to Morris, to myself and to you." Lil cried, embracing her daughter. Meggie also was crying,

"I'm sorry you had to deal with this alone. You've always been such a strong lady. I only wish I could be."

"You two alright?" Steven walked in, not accustomed to seeing Meggie and Lil like this.

"We'll be fine." Lil sat back a little and smiled at Meggie. "Morris would be happy to see us now. He always wanted us to be closer."

"Steven, you were great in there," Lori laughed, entering the kitchen. Meggie and Ma stared at him curiously. He smiled,

"I told dear Aunt Gertrude, her comments this evening were far from constructive, not to mention the fact I didn't approve. If she couldn't learn to control her mouth, she could leave. I would not permit this behavior in our home."

449

"Do you think it possible she could be a relative of the witch of Endor?" Meggie rose to hug him. "You're a wonderful man, Mr. Roth."

"Let's go for a walk," Steven said, leading Meggie from the room.

Lil smiled, watching them, feeling in her heart they had a good marriage. She knew Morris felt that, too.

They walked outside in front of the house,

"Ma said Ben will be here in a little while. He's at the airport picking up Peter, Dottie and Jay. It's nice of them to come? Good friends."

Steven awoke the following morning to find Meggie standing by the window, staring into space. He rose from the bed, neared her and placed both of his arms around her.

"Deep in thought?"

"It's a beautiful day. I think Daddy would have liked that," Meggie still stared into the bright sunlight. Steven looked in her eyes,

"I think so, too. We're going to make it through this."

"You know me and funerals. Thank God, now I have you," she kissed him, thinking how lucky she is. She was well aware of how much she relied on his enormous strength, understanding and wisdom and felt if it weren't for Steven, she didn't know where she would be.

Sitting in the limousine on the way to the cemetery, shortly after Steven delivered the eulogy, Meggie smiled.

"That was a beautiful soliloquy."

"It was all true," he smiled.

"I think I fell in love with that mind of yours first. You are the brightest, most eloquent person I have ever known," Meggie put her arms around him, squeezing him tightly. Steven kissed her as the limousine pulled from the drive.

They arrived at the cemetery and walked to the grave site, noticing a bouquet of white roses, the only flowers

450

there. It was a Jewish cemetery. Rabbi Winston said the prayers and the mourners the Kaddish. Steven held Meggie the entire time as she cried. When it came time for the three blessings, the Rabbi handed Meggie the shovel. She placed three shovels full of dirt over her father's coffin. Steven took the shovel and did the same. Rabbi Winston motioned for the mourners to return to the limousines. Steven started to lead her away.

"One moment," Meggie walked toward the flowers and removed the card attached. She smiled as she read it, then handed it to Steven as they stepped into the limousine.

"Your admiral, you had a feeling they were from him," Steven said, as the car pulled from the cemetery. Meggie replied, still with the tears running from her eyes.

"It wouldn't take Einstein to figure out. Only someone not familiar with our religion would send flowers to a Jewish funeral. Besides, Phillip always sent me white roses."

"It's a strange feeling, knowing another man is in love with my wife," Steven glanced at her. She smiled a little,

"Why, Mr. Roth, one might think you are jealous."

"No. Well, maybe a little," he embraced her.

The following morning, after most of the people had cleared the house from the morning minyan service, Meggie entered the kitchen.

"You deserve the asshole of the year award!" Lori yelled at Victor. He approached her,

"Lor, you're overreacting."

"Then where were you last night? Just because I chose to stay here, you took the night off to go fucking around! You were even late for services this morning!" Lori screamed. Victor became aggravated,

"You know I spent the night at my mom's. You're so suspicious."

"Bullshit! Two and a half years of living with you would make the Pope suspicious! I spoke to your mother last night and this morning!" Lori stared him in the eye. Victor now yelled,

"Why can't you ever take what I say at face value?" Lori turned red,

"Because I am not as adept at manipulating the truth as you are."

Steven entered the room, then sternly stated,

"Enough! What is going on in here?"

"The chameleon has turned lying into an Olympic event," Lori glanced at her cousins. Steven was puzzled,

"Chameleon?"

"Lori started calling him that two years ago in Cancun, because he finally showed his true colors. Remember?" Meggie smiled. Lori looked at Meggie,

"He's still in a state of flux!"

"I must know what a state of flux is," Steven laughed. Even Victor was curious. The two girls laughed. Meggie calmed herself,

"A state of flux is our definition of what comes in between adolescence and law school, so to speak."

Meggie took a smiling Steven to one side.

"Will you talk to him? If anyone can understand what is going on in his head, it's you."

"Morris, a little personal animosity exists here. On my part," Steven stated.

"Please. For Lori, for me." She kissed him, then turned to Lori.

"Want to go for a ride? You can have Lester." Meggie led her through the rear door of the house.

"I'm the one who's supposed to be consoling you," Lori cried.

"We've always had confused roles," Meggie smiled, hugging her cousin. It even brought a smile to Lori's face. Meggie held her,

"Are things as bad as they appear?"

"Lately it's been like trying to put toothpaste back in the tube," Lori said, with tears in her eyes as they entered the stables.

In the house; "Let's take a walk," Steven put his jacket on and threw Victor his. They walked along a narrow path which led to the pond. Steven bluntly stated, "Don't you think it's about time you came to grips with your feelings? It's obvious Lori can't go on like this much longer."

Steven felt the element of surprise would give him a better chance of getting to the truth. By the look of shock on Victor's face, he achieved his goal.

"I'm quite aware of my feelings," Victor uttered.

"You're probably the only one who is. I know Lori isn't," Steven picked up some snow and formed it into a ball. Victor looked at him,

"She knows I'm mad about her. I love her more than anything."

"Then, why? Why all of this garbage, the fooling around, the lying, the heartache?" Steven questioned.

"You think you have the humanity market cornered? I'm not as insensitive as you all may believe me to be." Victor paused, kicking a pebble.

"How do you deal with it? But it's different for you. You came into your marriage with some money and you don't happen to be working for your father-in-law. Do you have any idea how it feels to sense nothing is really yours, you owe someone for everything, you have no self worth?" Victor stared at the ground. He finally said it, finally got it out.

"I'm having a difficult time following you. You're being a bit ambiguous," Steven responded.

"Let me ask you this. How did it feel when your first book was published? Now I hear your second will be out in another month. How did it feel, Steven?" Victor glanced at him. Steven smiled,

"It felt good, no, it felt great! A wonderful sense of accomplishment."

"My point is I haven't had any of those feelings since Lori and I were married. My self-esteem level has hit rock bottom. I feel as if my manhood is being stolen from me, and I don't know how to deal with it. It's obvious that what I'm doing is not lessening the problem, only making it worse," Victor kicked more stones.

"Have you ever discussed any of this with Lori?" Steven asked.

"No; I don't think she would understand," Victor upset.

"I think you should talk to her. Communication is essential in all relationships. Without it, there's no relationship. You're well-educated. Why don't you try a different job, not working for her dad," Steven stated.

"That has crossed my mind, but the money is too good. Besides, I don't think they would understand," Victor said, seeing Meggie and Lori ride by a block away. "They're both marvelous."

"I know, and you're willing to throw it all away without an honest fight, simply because you think they wouldn't understand. I'm sure Lori would understand it better than what is happening right now. Money is really far from the issue here. It's honesty, and doing what is going to make you happy; in the long run, what will make you both happy," Steven met Victor's eye. Victor smiled,

"I have to admit you make a great deal of sense. How do you think Lori would feel about me working for someone else?"

"Ask her," Steven smiled, as he saw Meggie and Lori approaching.

"Thanks, I plan to do that," Victor neared Lori, leading her away.

Meggie approached Steven and put her arms around him.

"Well, Marathon Man, did you get through?"

"I may have," Steven said, before kissing her.

"I knew you would," she smiled, as Steven unzipped the front of her jacket. He placed both of his hands under her sweater and caressed her breasts. He looked into her eyes and saw how excited she was. He felt the same way,

"Anyone in the stables now?"

"They're all gone," Meggie smiled, biting her bottom lip.

XIII

"You are the most important thing in my life!" Meggie screamed as she stopped the car at another red light on Northwest K street in D.C. The woman in the car next to her heard, and stared at her curiously. She had all of the windows down and the sun roof wide open, even though the temperature was well above ninety degrees. Being shut in a room for three days made her look pale. She needed air, a lot of it, and she welcomed the warmth of the morning sun. The light turned green, she drove on with her mind drifting back again....

One evening in mid-August, almost six months after Morris Hiken died, Meggie and Steven strolled a trail near their home. Joel Wilkes had shown it to Steven earlier that day. He seriously inquired,

"Morris, what pen name did Samuel Clemens write under?"

"Another game!" Meggie laughed. "Mark Twain. Who made the "V" for victory the famous symbol of freedom?"

"The hippies! Before them, Winston Churchill," Steven pulled a leaf from a tree. "Who found an immunization against rabies?"

"Louis Pasteur. That and pasteurized milk," she answered. "Who fathered a baby to be born in mid-March?" At first it didn't penetrate. Then Steven stood still for a few seconds. He held her tightly,

"Morris! That was quick, but you've always been. When did you find out?"

"Today," she smiled.

"The fates can indeed be kind to mortals," Steven said, before kissing her.

"I think they've been kind to us for quite a while now," Meggie said. Steven led her back toward the house. She stopped, "I imagine Daddy's getting his wish. It's strange. I feel more control from him now then when he was alive."

"That's only because we have more responsibility now," Steven still with his arm around her and walking.

"Are you referring to the money?" Meggie asked.

"No, that's minor. We have more responsibility for ourselves, to take control of our own lives-and we're going to have a baby!" Steven yelled, picked her up and spun her around. She loved when he did that!

Entering the house, Steven carried her up the stairs.

"What are you doing?" Meggie laughed.

"A woman in your condition should not be doing anything too strenuous," Steven said, a little out of breath. Meggie laughed again as he placed her on the bed,

"Stairs are far from strenuous. That's an old wives' tale."

"Let me pamper you. I want to," as he undressed her. He gazed inquisitively at her nude body.

"You don't look pregnant."

"It's early yet," she smiled. Steven looked at her stomach,

"Show me where."

"Right here," Meggie pointed to the area below her belly button.

Steven kissed the entire area, then rubbed those hands over it. Noticing he had already aroused her. Passionately he attacked her mouth with a kiss and her breasts with his hands.

Afterward, Meggie lay watching him sleep and she allowed her mind to think. She was scared, but found some relief in knowing she had Anna to help her. They got along really well with the Wilkes's. She and Steven liked them a lot; they had become family. Steven told her they would share the responsibility of the baby equally. He wanted to know and love his child. All of this helped, but she was still frightened. So much of it was her responsibility, especially the pregnancy part. She cried herself to sleep feeling guilty. She loved Steven so much and she really did want this baby, but it meant more responsibility. Days of youth are gone! Come to the realization you are an adult already, lady!.

Before rising from bed the following morning, Meggie placed a call to Houston. Steven glanced at her curiously,

"What are you doing?"

"I want to tell Dottie," she smiled.

It wasn't only that. She had a dream about Dottie during the night and awoke with an uneasy feeling concerning her.

"Hello," a voice on the other end answered. It seemed familiar but Meggie couldn't place it. She felt her heart skip a couple of beats.

"Hello, this is Meggie. Is Dottie there?"

"Meggie, it's Dottie's mom," the voice could barely utter. Meggie started to shake.

"Is Dottie alright?"

"We lost Johnny last night. The doctors don't know why. Crib death, or as they call it, sudden infant death syndrome," Dottie's mom in tears.

"Oh my God!" Meggie cried in shock. "How's Dottie?"

"Not good, none of us are. We decided the best thing for her is to have the funeral as soon as possible-tomorrow."

"Tell Dottie I'm on my way, and give her a hug and a kiss for me. 'Bye," Meggie placed the receiver back on the phone.

"What is it?" Steven asked.

Meggie explained and Steven immediately made plane reservations to Houston that afternoon for both of them. All morning Meggie lay in bed with thoughts of Dottie. She recalled how happy Dottie was the last time she saw her. It was at Daddy's funeral. Dottie was pregnant then. How happy Dottie sounded on the phone after she gave birth to Johnny. Damn! He was only three months old. Dottie didn't deserve this. Meggie knew in her heart that no one did, but not Dottie! She cried, now wanting the seed planted inside of her more than anything else on earth. She was still frightened, but she had faith everything would work out.

Arriving in Houston, Meggie and Steven went directly to Dottie's before checking into a hotel. Meggie was sitting on Dottie's bed with her when she checked her watch.

"It's getting late; we better go now."

"You're staying here," Dottie pleaded. Meggie looked at her,

"You don't need the burden of guests at a time like this."

"Damn you! I need you around!" Dottie cried. Meggie hugged her, allowing her to cry on her shoulder.

"Shhh, we'll stay."

In the guest room, as they lay in bed, Steven turned to her.

"I understand what you were saying about Mark."

"Tell me what you understand," Meggie placed an arm behind her head to see him. Steven had a sallow look on his face,

"I have never come across anyone so cold and unfeeling."

"Did you notice? He didn't touch her once tonight. He knows how miserable she is and how much she needs his love and support right now. He was absurd, putting her down about minuscule things," Meggie said, with tears rolling from her eyes.

"I saw it, too. If it were anyone else, I would not have butted in, but it was Dottie. I'm indebted to her." Steven paused,

"I tried talking to Mark. He was rudely evasive. I asked him why he felt he had to be so evasive and why he couldn't say what he meant? His reply was, 'You can't insult me. I'm a lawyer.' I laughed in his face! I then informed him of what his role as a husband should be right now and what Dottie needed desperately." Steven stared into space. Meggie still had tears rolling from her eyes. Her heart went out to Dottie, who deserved so much better. Steven continued,

"'Short circuit the advice, buddy', he said to me. My mouth fell open. He informed me in a blunt manner he is what he is and Dottie has no choice but to accept him for that. If not, it's her problem. I tried real hard to keep my cool and I asked him if he ever once considered Dottie's needs. He firmly told me no, she'll take care of them, they're not his problem. I told him when you love someone, especially in a marriage, you help each other through things. 'That's not me', he said. I asked him what was him but he couldn't answer. I don't believe he knows. He's extremely shallow," Steven glanced to her,

"'You don't know!', I raised my voice at this point. 'Have you ever thought maybe you should be single and it may not be possible for you to love anyone, not even Dottie?' I asked. His reply was, 'If I didn't love her I wouldn't be married to her'. At this point, I was becoming totally frustrated and I began to yell, 'Even at a time like this, you won't stand by her.' 'What is love?' He asked me. Before I could reply, he jumped all over me. I just stood there, watching him, not being able to comprehend and feeling my blood pressure rise. I thought about your description of him-a-non-person, and totally agreed. That's when I came upstairs to be with you and Dottie," Steven put his arms around Meggie. She looked at him,

"He's really put her in a different space. She seems to have lost all confidence in herself. She cried about Johnny and on top of that pain she cried about Mark. She told me that behind the walls she has built around herself, there's a warm, caring and loving human being! I told her that I have always known. Her husband couldn't see that, so she built these walls to lock the world out, not wanting to deal with further pain of rejection."

"I consider myself extremely fortunate to have you, you gorgeous person," Meggie slid her hand all over his chest. Then, with her nails to his stomach, she encircled his belly button. She abruptly stopped and lay back on the bed,

"I've got to find a way to get Dottie out of this marriage."

"Morris!"

"I have to. She would for me," Meggie said, looking at him.

"I know, but you really had me going there. It's time for us now," Steven kissed her and fondled her breast.

Nearly seven months later and almost two weeks before their baby was due, Meggie walked through the family room,

"What time is it?"

"What do I look like, Big Ben?" Steven bluntly stated. Under normal circumstances she may have laughed, but not now. Steven had been extremely irritable as of late, ever since Dr. Marcus told them not to make love the last month of her pregnancy. So Meggie didn't respond and walked past him to the kitchen to fix herself something to eat again. Steven followed, sat himself at the kitchen table.

"I want you to hear this," he said, not waiting for an answer, and read her the last piece he had written under assignment for *THE POST*. Meggie didn't respond immediately and he gave her a very strange look. She looked him in the eye,

"It's terrible."

Steven stared at her in shock. She always loved everything he had written. She was his most loyal fan. Meggie walked toward him,

"You are missing the point here. This senator has been on the take for years. You have evaded that. Plus, he has screwed around with half the women on Capitol Hill, his secretaries included. There's nothing on that. Why don't you go see one of his former mistresses?"

"I'm doing an unbiased article, not a Harlequin romance," he said angrily. Her eyes became very wide,

"Sorry! You asked for my opinion. I gave it."

"I think you're not being honest with yourself or with me!" He said loudly. She started to get a little hot under the collar,

"I've always been honest with you. Think about it, would I lie to you?"

"You're clever enough to have told a lie here or there and me never to have known it!" He yelled. She screamed back at him,

"Bullshit! I can understand Swahili better than this!"

"I'm going out!" Steven bellowed as he threw the article on the table and stormed from the house.

Meggie watched him leave, with tears in her eyes. She couldn't blame him for not wanting to be with her. She was a walking blimp and waddled like a duck. However, she went back to her food and when she finished she crawled into bed with a book. Before she started to read, she looked at the clock: six-thirty in the evening. Lately, all she seemed able to do was eat, lie in bed and read. She was too uncomfortable for anything else. She even had difficulty sleeping. She knew what celibacy meant to Steven, but it wasn't her fault. He wanted this baby more than she did in the beginning, and she was starting to resent the way he was treating her.   .

After midnight she lay the book down and turned off the bedroom lights. As she lay in bed she thought, 'He's not home yet.' She cried because she was too uncomfortable to sleep. It was 2:00 a.m. when Meggie checked the clock, hearing the front door close. She pretended to be asleep when he entered the bedroom. He undressed, crawled into bed and kissed her cheek.

"Sleep well my love," Steven said, before he passed out.

Meggie lay there deep in thought. She decided not to say anything about his whereabouts, even though she felt she knew what he was up to. To love someone is to forgive him, no matter what his shortcomings are. She thought about what Daddy had written to her.

Over the course of the next few days, Meggie was semi-cool to Steven. She was never really good at hiding her feelings. He was as pleasant as he could be. She noticed he wasn't as tense and felt no guilt! He never spoke a word about that night. She really thought he would since there had always been honesty between them. Things started to get back to normal. Steven rarely left her alone and he even took interest in what she was reading. He re-wrote that piece on the senator, taking her advice. It was three in the morning on the 18th of March when she woke Steven with a smile.

"We're having a baby!"

"I'll call Dr. Marcus!" Steven excitedly jumped from the bed. Meggie stood,

"I already have. He's going to meet us there."

"How far apart are they?" He glanced at her as he was putting on his pants. She felt another contraction and checked her watch.

"About three minutes."

"You waited too long!" Steven yelled, hurriedly buttoned his shirt.

"No, from what I have read, first labors take much longer. Uh!" Another contraction came, taking her off balance as Steven came to catch her. She gazed up at him,

"I guess I'm an exception to this rule."

"Morris, you're an exception to every rule. Let's get out of here," he picked up her overnight case, then carefully led her down the stairs.

As they drove up Route 29 toward the Baltimore Beltway, her contractions seemed to be coming closer together. Steven glanced at her,

"You okay?"

"I'll make it," then, "Oh shit!" She yelled.

"What?" Steven was frightened. Meggie laughed a little,

"My water just broke all over your beautiful new car!"

"Fuck the car! Will we make it?" Steven asked, very serious. Meggie gritted her teeth as another contraction came, then laughed,

"Put the pedal to the metal and go!"

"Where did you pick that up from?" Steven ran a red light and nearly hit 90 miles per hour on the speedometer.

"Who knows, T.V., books, I don't remember now," she said, before screaming, "Oh!" Steven quickly glanced at her,

"Another one! How close?"

"Two minutes," she said, panting. He was aggravated; now he neared 100 on the speedometer.

"You cut it too close!"

"Steven, if you don't want to deliver a baby, you better burn some rubber," Meggie said, just as another contraction started. He yelled,

"Oh shit! I'm glad one of us has his wits about him."

Steven pulled the car in front of the hospital and stopped. He leaned across to open her door.

"Out with you, Morris."

"Wrong! I need some help. I feel like Hoover Dam burst between my legs," she laughed a little. He stared at her in shock,

"I can't believe you're laughing at a time like this."

"What should I do? Cry because I'm scared and it feels so wonderful? Aren't you aware laughter is a nervous reaction? Now help me in," she instructed. He quickly turned the motor off and helped her out of the car. As he led her into the hospital, she smiled,

"I feel like a walrus."

They entered through the large doors with Steven placing Meggie in a chair in the lobby as he checked her in. The elevator doors opened, Dr. Marcus quickly neared Meggie and signaled a nurse to bring a wheelchair. She sat in it, with Steven's help. Dr. Marcus asked,

"Where are we?"

"Her water broke and the contractions are less than two minutes apart," Steven said, before Meggie could open her mouth. Dr. Marcus began wheeling Meggie toward the elevator. He turned to Steven,

"We're going up. We'll see you there."

Entering the labor room, Meggie heard women moaning and one, in particular, was screaming from the pain. She looked at Dr. Marcus,

"Is this necessary? Let's go somewhere else!" He ignored her. He was busy with the task before him.

"Are you sure you want to go natural? It's too late for an epidural but I can give you a saddle block or twilight sleep."

"There's no question, it's natural. I despise needles and I want to see my baby as soon as he is brought into this world." She gritted her teeth as another contraction approached. He motioned for Meggie to spread her legs,

"I have to see how we're doing. I don't think we'll be in here for long."

"Morris, how do you feel?" Steven entered. She gave him a peculiar look,

"I feel just great."

"Steven, look here. The more she dilates the farther down the baby's head will be," Dr. Marcus showed him. Steven saw the top of his baby's head. There was blood, but he thought it wondrous! He went to hold Meggie and each time a contraction came, he helped her to breathe, just as they were taught in the natural childbirth classes.

Ten minutes later, Dr. Marcus checked again, Steven was right beside him.

"It's time," he smiled.

They wheeled her down the corridor to the delivery room, with Steven holding her hand.

"It hurts like hell!" She screamed. He placed his arms around her.

"I know it does. When Dr. Marcus tells us to, we'll push, you and I together, as always."

Another contraction came. Dr. Marcus looked at her,

"Push with everything you've got! Push!"

"Good," Dr. Marcus said, inspecting the baby.

"We're almost there," the good doctor said, not taking his eye from the baby's head.

Meggie gritted her teeth and screamed at the same time with the onset of another contraction. In unison, Dr. Marcus and Steven commanded her to push.

"With the next contraction push as hard as you can and we'll have a baby," Dr. Marcus instructed.

"Ahhh!" She screamed again. Steven hugged her tightly.

"Push! Push! Push!" Steven said before placing his mouth on hers, then his tongue in her mouth. Dr. Marcus was amazed, not having seen anything like this before in a birthing room. It worked-out came the baby! He placed the baby on Meggie's stomach before the umbilical cord was cut and he sewed her up.

"It's a boy!" Meggie screamed in delight.

She and Steven smiled at each other before he kissed her.

"I love you," Steven smiled, before kissing her again.

"I know. This is a symbol of our love." Meggie stared at her baby as Dr. Marcus snipped the umbilical cord, then at Steven as she bit her bottom lip and tears of joy flowed from her eyes.

They informed her the baby had to go downstairs to the nursery to be checked over and she, to recovery. When she was admitted to her room, they would bring her baby to her. Steven walked with her to the recovery room.

"Ma and Albert are waiting downstairs. I think I should inform them you are doing great and we have a beautiful baby boy." He had tears in his eyes before he kissed her again.

"It's a miracle!" He put both arms around her and squeezed her tightly, before leaving the room. She yelled at him,

"I'm starving!"

"I'm not surprised. I'll see what I can do," he laughed.

Meggie lay back in the bed in thought about this beautiful baby she had just brought into this world. She hoped the world would be free and at peace for him to grow in. She thought about how lucky she was to have Steven. She didn't know if she could have made it through this without him. Then she thought that Ma went through this with her and Ben. How wrong she had been all of the years she thought Ma didn't love her. She wondered if Ma really loved Albert. She knew she still didn't like him, only tolerated him for Ma's sake, and because he gave Ma her space when Daddy needed her. Her thoughts were interrupted.

"They told me breakfast wouldn't be up until seven-thirty. So for you, my love, I went to the machines and purchased an unbelievable feast!" Steven sat on the edge of the bed and lay the food before her. Meggie reached for the orange juice.

Later that morning, Ben came to visit. Meggie smiled at the sight of him. He stood six feet tall, shoulder-length wavy brown hair adorned his head, and he had rings on his fingers and beads around his neck. He placed a kiss on her cheek and sat in the chair beside her bed.

"I have to admit, I didn't think you had it in you."

"I'm not sure how to accept this wonderful compliment from my brother" Meggie stated. He smiled,

"The baby is gorgeous!"

"Thank you," she smiled, before becoming serious.

"Ben, what was the outcome the other day when you left Ma's after Albert yelled, calling you a Bohemian, hippie parasite-type?"

"Later that night when I got home, he was still in the same space. He said to me, "What are you? Poet, artist or communist?" Ben laughed. Meggie glanced at him,

"He's worried about you. You dropped out of school. What are you planning to do?"

"You know I've been in a band for a while now. I'm going to play music. It's just not the right kind of music as far as Albert's concerned. He even feels it's non-music. We have a creative difference," Ben stood and neared the window,

"It's really strange. For the longest time I didn't know who I was. Now that I'm finally learning, he's standing in my way. Life seems to be made up of obstacles that take a great deal of effort to tear down to get what you want."

Meggie thought, 'He's learning. We all have to grow up in our own way and it is a hard thing to do.' Ben interrupted her thought,

"He and I have been at peace for a record forty-eight hour period. A good friend of his told him to let me go my own way and I'll find it back to him!"

"That guy did you a favor. I can't believe Albert bought that bull!" Meggie laughed. Ben glanced at his watch,

"We all believe what we want to. I've got to go-rehearsal." He kissed her cheek again. She grabbed him and gave him a big hug, whispering,

"Be happy Ben."

Steven walked back into the room. Meggie smiled,

"You just missed Ben."

"I saw him in the hallway," he sat beside her on the bed.

"Where were you?" She was curious.

"With our beautiful baby," he smiled.

"I thought he was having his bath?" she smiled at him.

"He was. I helped. I've also made arrangements to stay here with you. I'll feed him at two and six in the morning so you may get your beauty sleep," he said, before kissing her. "Our son needs a name."

"I like the name Matthew, after my dad," Meggie said.

"Perfect; I had the same thought. I told you great minds work alike," he kissed her again. Meggie moved to one side of the bed making room for him. She pulled the covers up so he could slide under. He placed his arms around her.

"I never had a middle name. I want Matthew to, what do you think of Jay?" he asked.

"Matthew Jay Roth-I like it," she kissed him and massaged his strong chest. He leaned back a little,

"How much longer?'

"Since yesterday, thirteen days," she bit her bottom lip.

"Shit!" He yelled.

"Shh," Meggie said, kissing him and touching him all over. She lay her body on top of his and looked into his eyes. "You belong to me. I know a few years back we said neither one of us would ever belong to anyone. Somehow, growing up has changed that. I belong to you," she kissed him again.

"I love you so much," he hugged her tightly as his body moved rhythmically with hers.

"I know, because I love you and that's why we are blessed with a beautiful baby boy," she said, with tears in her eyes.

Matthew's Bris took place one week later, another Jewish ritual that appalled Meggie. She decided to stay in her bedroom because she couldn't bear the thought of her baby being cut and the surface skin around his penis removed. She thought, 'Today they call it circumcision.' Meggie lay back on her bed, allowing her mind to wander, not wanting to think about what was happening downstairs. She remembered her conversation with Dottie, how Dottie wanted so badly to come and how that controlling bastard she was married to wouldn't allow her to spend the money on plane fare. Dottie's father had lost a great deal of money in the stock market recently, thus he wasn't able to help them out anymore. Mark was an attorney and always had the money for what was important to him. 'That shit!' She thought, still trying to find a way to get Dottie out of that marriage.

Her thoughts turned to Peter, who wanted to come and to bring his new lady friend, Adina. She wished they had, wanting to see Peter happy and to meet Adina. He couldn't get away from Chichen Itza.

Smiling, she thought of Steven's parents. They were so happy to come and to meet their first grandchild. In fact, it was the first time they had come to visit. Ma made them feel totally welcome and a complete part of the family. She'd never seen Ma quite like this, like a child with a new toy. She wondered if Matthew was going to fill the void in her life. Meggie decided not to think about it, only wanting happy thoughts today. She laughed, because in her wildest dreams, she never would have envisioned her baby would ever be spoiled by Ma.

Her thoughts were interrupted as Lori entered the room carrying a Bloody Mary and handed it to her.

"Mazel tov, it's over."

"How is he?" Meggie took the glass. Lori smiled,

"A real trooper. He hardly whimpered."

"After all of the wine they gave him, I was hoping he would sleep through it," Meggie replied. Lori sat beside her and smiled,

"Victor and I will be having a baby in September."

"I knew everything would work out for you. Good things come to those who wait!" Meggie embraced her cousin.

As the girls walked downstairs, so Meggie could greet her guests, she felt happy for Lori. Following the scene they had after Daddy died, Lori and Victor had a heart-to-heart talk. They laid all of their cards on the table. Lori wanted to lend him money for his own business but he wouldn't accept it. Instead, he went to the bank, received a business loan and another loan from Honda to set up a dealership on Oahu. He sold motorcycles, repairing them and was his own man. Meggie had found new respect for him.

Later that night, Meggie and Steven opened all of Matthew's gifts. She smiled at Steven as he held Matthew on his lap,

"Our son may have enough money here to make it through his first year of college."

"I told you that you have a lot to learn about economics! By the time he gets there, it will probably cost twenty thousand a year." Steven laughed, watching her unwrap a small box and take out a small silver fork and spoon with the initials MJR engraved on them. Meggie read the card and smiled at Matthew as she held the silver in front of him,

"This is from Uncle Phillip."

"Your admiral!" Steven yelled. Matthew started to cry. Meggie laughed as she took both father and son in her arms.

Approximately one week later, at three in the afternoon, Steven walked into the kitchen with Matthew and an empty bottle.

"He took the whole thing," he handed Anna the bottle. He smiled gazing at his baby in his arms. "We finally have things back to normal around here, since we got rid of your naughty nurse."

"Steven, can I see him?" Meggie asked. He handed her the baby,

"Where have you been?"

"He's sleeping," Meggie said, as she watched Matthew at rest.

"That's about all that babies do-eat and sleep," Anna smiled.

"That's not the only thing that's back to normal around here. I went to see Dr. Marcus," Meggie smiled at Steven.

"You mean I can stop eating now!" He looked at her, excitedly.

Meggie bit her bottom lip and shook her head, yes. Anna took the baby from her. She laughed because she had grown to know them.

"I'll stay to give Matthew his ten o'clock feeding. After that you're on your own," Anna smiled.

Steven went to the refrigerator and took out a bottle of champagne. He announced,

"Watch how I open this. You won't even here the cork." There was a big "pop." Meggie laughed,

"So much for that!"

Steven placed an arm around her and led her from the kitchen and up the stairs. Anna phoned Joel, telling him to come to the house for dinner with Tommy. Joel laughed, recalling the time he found them in the stables and another, by the pond.

After they entered the bedroom, Meggie turned to Steven,

"Okay, lock the door and we'll turn this visit into an x-rated movie! But I hope it won't hurt."

Steven poured the champagne before coming to undress her. They spent the following ten hours in bed making love, exploring each other's bodies again and totally loving one another. The first time it did hurt a little, but not after that!

Mid-September, six months later, Meggie was in a great mood. She had just received news that Lori had a little girl and Dottie was pregnant. The phone rang and she happily went to answer it, feeling things travel in threes and this, too, had to be good. As she placed the receiver back on the phone in the kitchen she turned to look at Steven and Matthew with tears in her eyes.

"That was Peter," she paused. "Remember Peter talking about the woman he's been living with, Adina?" He nodded, yes.

"She's dead," Meggie said, with tears flowing from her eyes. Steven rose from the kitchen table to hold her.

"Oh, Morris, I know you hurt for Peter. Did he tell you how it happened?"

"The best I could make out with his crying was that she had been having a difficult time sleeping. She took to taking long walks on the beach when she would awake in the middle of the night. She didn't want to disturb Peter. When Peter awoke this morning, Adina was nowhere in sight. He started running along the beach in search of her, yelling her name. You should remember about a mile and a half up from the house, the beach is divided by a group of large rocks." Meggie saw him nod, yes.

"One of the reasons Peter awoke so early was because he heard the waves. They were real rough. He found her on those rocks with her head split open. All he could conclude was that a wave came and had so much force she lost her balance and fell. The funeral's tomorrow. He wants us to come. I told him we'd be there," Meggie wiped the tears from her eyes. Steven still held her and glanced at their son in his high chair.

"Morris, you go. I don't believe it's a good idea to take Matthew to Mexico-the water."

"Anna and Joel can take care of him." Meggie nodded to Anna who smiled, shaking her head in agreement. Steven still held her,

"I have a responsibility to *THE POST* -the editorial on the fuel crunch."

"That can wait! We won't be gone for more than a couple of days," she pleadingly gazed into those light-blue eyes of his.

"It really can't wait. You're the one that Peter really needs now. You're his best friend," Steven hugged her.

"I hate being separated from you," tears flowed from her eyes. Steven hugged her tighter,

"The last time was for fourteen months because you wouldn't admit you loved me and you almost married your admiral."

"We weren't going to bring that up!" She yelled, breaking away from him. Steven laughed, grabbing her to bring her close again,

"It's kind of hard to forget when he sends gifts."

Steven looked at Anna and she smiled at him. It was their signal. He led Meggie from the kitchen and up the stairs. The following morning, Meggie flew alone to Cancun to a waiting, distraught Peter.

Following the funeral that afternoon, Meggie and Peter entered his small house on the beach, the same one she and Steven had rented a few years ago. She glanced around, noting not much had changed, and Peter went to the kitchen. He came back into the living room with two glasses of tequila and handed her one. After fifteen minutes of Peter being non-communicative, Meggie neared him,

"How about a swim?" He nodded in agreement.

A few minutes later she walked from the bedroom wearing a pink knit bikini. It brought a slight smile to Peter's face. He was sitting in the same chair; he hadn't moved. Meggie gave him a peculiar look. He stood, removing his shirt and lowering his pants. Under his clothes he wore a red nylon man's bikini. She smiled at him, denoting flattery. He was built exceptionally well. She always wanted the best of everything for Peter. After taking his hand and leading him toward the water, Peter sat on the beach and watched her walk to the waves. Watching Meggie play with the waves, loving when they hit her body, he thought Adina was the same way with the water. Adina was a truly beautiful creature inside and out. She tried to make him happy in so many ways. Peter had tears running from his eyes when his thoughts were interrupted.

"Peter! Come on in; it's fantastic!" Meggie yelled to him. She felt the ocean seemed to have a cleansing feeling, just like riding a horse in thirty degree weather.

Watching her, Peter neither moved nor made a sound. He simply sat and stared. All of their past experiences together traveled through his head: from the time she was a caterpillar, to now! To look at her, no one would ever think she gave birth just six months ago. She hadn't changed. He knew from the beginning Steven was good for her, and as time went on, he became more certain of it. These thoughts warmed him on the inside because, when two people are as close as they have been, it's only natural to want the very best for your best friend. Meggie came out of the water and a flash went through his mind like the first time he saw her in a bathing suit, with Dennis. He wasn't aware of what was happening to him until Meggie knelt in front of him, looked into his eyes and took his hands in hers.

"Peter, will you please talk to me?" She felt for him, his loss. He stared into her eyes for a moment before aggressively pulling her to lie on top of him, kissing her passionately. He pulled his head back a little to whisper in her ear,

"I want to fuck the shit out of you."

Stunned, Meggie stood very wide-eyed, staring at him.

"Peter, you don't exactly induce excitement!"

"You are my best friend and I love you," Peter stood.

"I know that. I love you too," she responded.

"I need you now, I want you now!" Peter tried to look in her eyes. She gazed at the sand.

"Meg, I don't feel it's possible there could be a wall of any kind between us," Peter placed his hand under her chin to lift her head so that she would look at him. Meggie thought for a while, about when her father died and making love was a wonderful release for frustration and anxiety. Without saying a word she took Peter by the hand and led him toward the house. Once inside, Peter kissed her like he did on the beach and untied the top of her bikini.

"Peter!" Meggie was surprised. She placed a hand on his cheek,

"I guess I will finally find out what half of the girls in our senior year were talking about." He led her toward the bedroom. They lay on the bed.

"I know I'm asking a lot of you," Peter said, holding her.

"You have always been there for me. Remember when Dennis died, you held me for days and you hurt, too. You even put up with all of that shit from me afterward," Meggie hugged him.

"This is different. I want all of you," tears ran from his eyes.

"I know you want to bury all of you into me. I know what this kind of pain feels like," Meggie said, before kissing him.

"I'm asking far more of you than you have ever asked of me," he sighed.

"You're asking something different of me and if you don't shut your mouth, you're going to find yourself alone in this bed," she smiled. Peter kissed her even more passionately than before and passed the palm of his hand alternately over her breasts.

"Unadulterated fun!" She laughed.

"Quiet," he said, as he nibbled on her ear, then the rest of her.

Afterward, he collapsed on her for a few minutes, not wanting to ever let go.

"That felt so good," Peter whispered in her ear.

"It was nice," Meggie smiled.

"It was great!" he picked his torso up to look at her. As he rolled off, he placed his arm under her so their bodies still touched.

"Now I know why Steven loves you so much and was willing to wait for you," he laughed.

"Steven loved me before I ever went to bed with him!" Meggie said, emphatically.

"I know; just teasing my best friend," Peter laughed.

"Has anyone told you, you have fantastic breasts, the kind I would never want to let go of, that you are totally captivating in bed," he was teasing a bit but also being serious.

"Of course," she laughed a little, not knowing quite how to take this.

"Meg, if there should ever be a strange turn of events in your life, if you should ever find yourself destitute and poor, I'm certain you could earn a handsome income as a prostitute," Peter laughed. Meggie pulled the pillow out from under his head and proceeded to hit him with it.

"Gee thanks! Meggie, the sperm depository!" She laughed. Peter pinned her back on the bed.

"What did you learn about me?"

"You like to bite," she still giggled.

"It's not biting; it's using teeth. I'll show you what a bite is," Peter opened his mouth wide, moving near her shoulder. Meggie struggled and yelled,

"No, Peter. No!"

"I thought you liked it," he lay beside her again.

"I loved it. I can't wait to do it to Steven. You are good, you know. I imagine I found out, didn't I? You are also quite large." Meggie smiled as he hugged her. "I guess what they say is true. When you share your bed, you share your secrets. I learned a few about you today."

"And I about you," he said, as he brought her to lie on him. "Are you sorry?"

"No. I have a feeling this may have brought us even closer as friends," she said, before kissing him.

"I feel the same way. I have never felt closer to you," he smiled.

"I'm starving," she said.

"Up and out!" he pushed her off him before he stood. "There's a place not too far from here that has the world's best barbecued shrimp. Notice, I remembered how you love shrimp."

Walking back after dinner, Peter smiled,

"Being aware of how important food is to you, did you enjoy it?"

"It was a culinary delight," she laughed a little.

"What's so funny?" Peter curious.

"I was thinking about our ski weekend when this girl-I can't remember her name-asked you to make love to her. Afterward, you found out she was a virgin," Meggie grinned, as they walked.

"Carol. She's a real nice person. She came to visit last winter. Adina went to stay with a friend to give me space with her. She lives in L.A. and is in broadcasting. I think half of the girls in our senior class lost their virginity that weekend," Peter gazed at the beach.

"I was one of them," Meggie laughed. "Though, I disagree with you. Many had lost it before. Remember, Dennis took it from quite a few."

"Those who didn't are probably married in boredom and still have no conception of what an orgasm is, let alone multiple orgasms," he laughed. "Remember our music? We had some fun with it back then," Peter reflected.

"It's a gift I hope to pass on to my children. It's pure joy! Being able to play the piano is an invaluable lesson, one you keep for life. I remember hiding behind the music," Meggie said sullenly.

"You hid there and in your paintings," Peter laughed.

"True," she smiled. "I always believed you had a real talent and would eventually have a career in music. I never would have thought, archeology!"

"Maybe that's what college teaches us. It broadens our horizons, opens new doors and enlightens us on matters we never would have explored," he walked with an arm around her. They strolled for a few blocks. Shortly after, Peter became solemn again,

"I think I'm going back to Egypt for a while to lose myself. It's a healthy environment."

"Sure, just as healthy as me saying that I'm going to the Manhattan library to lose myself in all of the Jane Austin books because she's a dependable author," Meggie replied arrogantly.

"It's not the same!" Peter snapped.

"No! You're running away! Something you have always gotten on my case for doing!" She sternly stated.

"Did you know that Egyptians get stuffed before they get wrapped?" he asked. Meggie started to laugh,

"Of course not! Egyptology was not a course I even wanted to take!"

"It will be an educational experience as well as a change of scenery. I need that now," Peter had a few tears flowing from his eyes .

"Oh, Peter, Egypt is one great national resource of death," she embraced him. "Tell me about Adina. I'd like to know her; I'd like to listen."

Peter put an arm around her shoulder and led her toward the beach. "It's nice and even a little calming here." Meggie nodded in agreement.

It seemed as if Peter talked for hours. Adina appeared to be a very warm, compassionate and understanding person. She definitely did love Peter and tried to make him happy. She was aware Peter didn't know whether he loved her or not. Meggie felt a great deal of warmth for this woman and was sorry she never had the pleasure of meeting her. Afterward, they sat in silence for a while, listening to the waves.

"Who have you ever loved?" She asked seriously.

"You," he smiled.

"Bullshit!" Meggie stated.

"Maybe I'm one of those guys who doesn't know how to love," he saddened.

"What kind of crap do you think you're feeding me. Maybe you're afraid of making that decision, of a commitment," Meggie said. He placed his arms around her,

"You are the only person I have been able to admit any kind of love for. Maybe no one else could compete with you."

"More garbage, you're a veritable cesspool today. You're able to admit your feelings for me because I'm safe.

You never had to commit yourself. What the hell are you afraid of?" she stared at him.

"I don't know. I never thought about it like that before," he stood.

"Maybe you should. There's a wonderful life for you out there. All you have to do is want it," Meggie followed him into the house.

"You're right. I'll definitely think about it," he crawled into bed. He was tired and he wanted this conversation over with.

A couple of days later, Peter and Meggie waited in the airport for her boarding call, he smiled,

"You are super. I certainly did something right when I chose you as my best friend." She laughed a little.

"I do love you, my best friend. Thank you. I would never have made it through the past few days without you and your wit, my little sperm depository," Peter laughed, hugging her. She embraced him,

"I love you, too. I only wanted to take some of your pain." Just before hearing the final boarding call for her plane. "Take care of yourself and please reconsider going to Egypt again," she said, before heading toward the plane.

"I'll take it under advisement," he waved to her. She threw him a kiss, then a final wave before walking on board her flight home.

When Meggie returned home that night, she went straight for Matthew's room. She wished he wasn't asleep. She had really missed him. Both she and Steven stood watching their baby for a short while.

"He's so beautiful, Steven," Meggie said, not taking her eyes from her six-month-old baby.

"Morris, we're going to wake him," Steven placed an arm around her shoulder to lead her from the room.

Meggie showered, her normal routine after flying, because her skin felt clammy. Afterwards, she sat at her vanity to brush her wet hair. In the mirror's reflection she could see Steven lying nude on the bed. Knowing he could see her reflection as well, she smiled,

"How were things while I was gone?"

"Anna and I managed. How's Peter?" Steven watched her reflection in the mirror.

"I think he'll be alright. They're making plans to develop Cancun into a resort city," she gazed at his image.

"They'll ruin it!" Steven stared at her. Seeing her eyes in the mirror on him,

"Come here, you wonderful creature," Steven extended his arms. Meggie walked toward him and removed her white silk robe, revealing her nude body. She smiled as she lay her body on top of his,

"I think you missed me." He hugged her,

"Maybe. Damn it, Meggie! You have no idea!" They kissed.

"Did you finish the article?" she said.

"Yes; we'll talk about that later," Steven kissed her again. His hands on her breasts made her quiver. She ran her fingernails gently over his chest, then softly with her teeth she nibbled his breasts.

"Morris," he sighed. She smiled, laying her body on top of his, then forcefully kissing him. Feeling those hands rub her back, she placed him inside her.

"God, how I love you and I missed you so much," Meggie hugged him tightly afterward.

"That's nice to hear," Steven said, lying on his back and drawing her to lie on his chest, placing his arms around her. Meggie loved laying her head on his hairy, masculine chest, feeling his shoulder muscles flex under her ear.

"Morris," he said softly.

"Uh huh," Meggie quietly.

"Did you go to bed with Peter?" Steven said, still softly.

"What makes you ask?" She said, with surprise in her voice.

"I just sensed it," he said, nonchalantly.

"From what we just did?" she questioned.

"No," he started to laugh, hugging her tighter. "Though the biting was a bit uncharacteristic."

"It wasn't biting, it's using teeth. You loved it!" she smiled. He nodded in agreement. "Is that why you sent me away by myself?"

"No! I didn't sense this until a day after you left," Steven gently massaged her arms.

"Peter asked me. He needed me. I knew how he felt so I did. It wasn't just that; I wanted to, knowing that it would ease his pain. Are you angry?" She glanced at him.

"No, not really. I understand, somewhat," Steven solemnly.

"I told Peter this would be your reaction!" She kissed him. "Mr. Roth, you see, I know you," Meggie smiled, before placing her head back on his chest, feeling so fortunate to have a man like him.

"Meg, do you remember the night we had an argument about five days before Matthew was born?" He said.

"Of course," she buried her face deeper into the hair on his chest.

"That night I went to a bar. I know it's not my style; maybe that's why I did it. I picked up a girl there and had sex with her. When I returned home you were feigning sleep. I knew you were because your cheeks were wet from tears," Steven made her look in his eyes.

"I know," she stated.

"Then you understand why I did it?" Steven said.

"Honestly no! Even being aware I was fat and ugly, I was carrying our child! What is making you tell me now?" Meggie emphatically.

"Morris, you could never be ugly and the only fat you have ever had has been all baby. I love you. I didn't want you to feel any guilt about Peter," he hugged her. She broke away,

"You shit! That's not what I want to hear." She hit him over the head with a pillow.

"Stop! We'll wake Matthew," Steven said, in a controlled scream as he grabbed both of her arms.

"I love you. I saw her only that one night, I have never even had a desire to see her since. You are my love, you are my life, you are all I have ever wanted. It was only sex, like with you and Peter," he lay on top of her, pinning her down.

"That's where you're wrong! I love Peter as a friend. I've known him for well over ten years. He's far from being a total stranger!" Meggie yelled. "Plus the fact you weren't sitting home feeling fat, neglected and despondent about yourself. What you did was completely selfish." He lay back in thought,

"You are right."

"Damn right I am. But I love you anyway!" She laughed, as she hit him over the head again with a pillow. Steven was able to throw her back on the bed and tickled her. He loved when she laughed like that and couldn't conceive how anyone could be so damn ticklish. They were both laughing hard when they heard Matthew cry.

"I'll go," Meggie rose from the bed.

"No way! Whenever you do, he never goes back to sleep," Steven stated, before leaving the room. Meggie thought, 'I'm glad one of us knows how to be a mother.' A few minutes later Steven returned and Meggie feigned sleep. He gently crawled in bed beside her.

"I know you're up," he placed his arms around her.

"How?" She laughed.

"I told you over four years ago-you are me and I am you. In reality we are one," he said. Meggie turned to face him,

"I love you. I want to share everything with you. I wish you would have come with me," she said. He laughed,

"Why? So we could have indulged in a menage a' trois?"

"You're starting again!" Meggie rolled off of him. He placed his body on top of hers.

"Don't you understand how much I love you, how difficult it is for me to share you and how this entire incident is a bit hard for me to digest!" He gazed into her eyes.

"You! Mr. live and let live," she said, shocked.

"Except when it's mine!" Steven frankly stated. "You really liked that!"

"Maybe I needed to hear it," she smiled.

Steven walked into the kitchen the following morning to find Anna by the sink and Meggie with Matthew.

"Did you miss Mommy?" Meggie hugged her son, unaware Steven was awake. He approached from behind and placed her in his arms,

"We all missed Mommy."

"Good morning," she turned to kiss him.

"I missed seeing that smile in the morning," he kissed her again.

"And I missed that morning kiss," she took his hand and led him to the terrace on that beautiful warm autumn morning. "We won't be able to have breakfast out here much longer. Jack Frost is due to arrive soon." Meggie poured the orange juice and placed honey melon filled with strawberries in front of Steven.

"Are you ready to tell me about your article?" She asked, then quickly rose from the table. She returned with a basket of Steven's favorite buns, which she baked earlier.

"What time did you get up today?" Steven curious.

"Matthew and I were early risers. He must have sensed I was home," she smiled.

"I didn't even hear him," Steven said, as he ate his melon.

"I know. We got to sleep pretty late and you were really out of it this morning. You were even snoring," she smiled, clearing the table, returning with eggs Benedict.

"You really outdid yourself this morning," he eyed the food.

"I wanted our reunion to be special," she smiled.

Steven finished and leaned across the table to kiss her, "It was absolutely delicious."

"I'm still waiting to hear about the article," Meggie leaned back in her chair.

"It's grown," he smiled.

"I suggest you explain that to me," she said.

"The article is finished. It will be in the editorial section of this Sunday's *POST*. I have a copy in the study for you." He paused, "It's developed into the makings of a good book. I'll let you read my notes."

"That's wonderful! I want to read everything!" She hugged him.

"There's one drawback. I have to visit Saudi Arabia and Iran for a couple of weeks," Steven said.

"I'm going with you," she frankly stated. He shook his head NO,

"It's too dangerous."

"It's dangerous for you," she said.

"Having only myself to worry about is one thing. It would be far more difficult having to worry about your well-being too. I'm going to make it as quick as possible. I'll get in, get the information, then I'll get out," Steven took her hands in his.

"I don't want to be separated from you again. When are you leaving?" Meggie asked, with tears in her eyes.

"Sometime within the next couple of weeks. Arrangements haven't been confirmed yet. I wanted to talk to you first," Steven stood and helped her up so she could face him.

"It's going to be hard for me too. I don't enjoy being apart from you either," he kissed her. Steven saw Anna as she came to clear the table. He gave her their signal, and Anna shook her head in agreement. He led Meggie into the house.

"Time for dessert," he smiled.

"Not yet; I have reading to do first," she said. He went to the study to retrieve the article and his notes on the fuel crunch. He handed them to her, "In bed you can read."

Steven lay beside her as she read. When she finished, she stared into space for a few moments in thought. He became a little concerned. Then Meggie abruptly threw her arms around him,

"I always said you were a man with a great gift."

"You agree? It's worth following through," he said.

"The approbation of honest critics!" she laughed. He became serious,

"What are you going to do while I'm gone for two weeks?"

"It's nearing Christmas. I'll paint and spend more time at the gallery. You know he's asked for more paintings," she replied. Steven glanced at her,

"Great, with Ronald Lowstein, the oil and canvas Casanova!"

"What are you talking about?" She laughed.

"He's had the hots for you from the beginning," Steven stated.

"You're nuts!" Meggie kissed him and placed her tongue in his mouth.

"I know what I'm talking about, Morris," Steven said, becoming excited. Meggie held her face over his.

"In that case, the next time I go there I'll wear something from Frederick's of Hollywood, the passion fashion," she laughed, and rolled off of him.

"That's not funny," he held her arms down.

"Why? You're the one with the dangerous libido in this family." She was still laughing.

"Not any longer," he smiled, seeing the surprise on her face. "Men have their sexual peak in their late teens, women usually at around age thirty."

"I'm not even twenty-five yet," she said.

"You're building up to it" he laughed, before kissing her.

"Will you be there for me?" She smiled.

"Always," he said, before kissing her again, touching her erect nipples. Abruptly Meggie came to a sitting position,

"You have to promise me a couple of things."

"Anything!" Steven said in surprise.

"First, when you go to the Mideast, you won't get hurt and you'll come back alive," she said, very seriously.

"I promise. Now come back here," he said, touching her arm.

"Not so fast! You'll be away for two weeks. Promise you won't be with any other women," Meggie looked him in the eye.

"I'm not sure I can promise that," he laughed, then pulled her back to lie with him. "A little jealously on your part."

"Not really. Selfishness yes. I, too, don't like sharing what is mine," she said, before kissing him. "Now promise!"

"I promise my love. I promise, I'll save it all for you," he kissed her.

"Oh, shit! Damn you, Steven! Where the hell are you?" Meggie screamed as she slammed her foot on the car brakes, coming back to the present. Hearing screeching tires and a horn from behind her, she placed the car into park and got out to make sure no one had been hurt. She had full knowledge she was out of control and had no business driving but she didn't know what else to do. She had to do this!

"Are you alright?" She approached a man of about thirty-seven sitting behind the steering wheel and seeing no one else in the car.

"Terrific! I love this kind of excitement in my day!" He gave her an evil look.

"I'm sorry," she said sincerely, with tears running from her eyes.

"Where was your head, lady?" He yelled at her.

"I don't know, but I assure you it was unintentional," Meggie said, with tears flowing down her cheeks.

"Women drivers!" He grunted as Meggie removed her sunglasses. He stared at her, thinking, 'She's a beauty. Damn, she looks familiar.'

"I said I was sorry. There doesn't seem to be anything else I can do right now," Meggie walked back to her car. After she closed her car door he approached.

"I don't think you're this upset because you nearly caused a major accident. Would you like to tell me what's bothering you?"

"Honestly, no," Meggie said. He handed her his card.

"If you should change your mind, feel free to call me," he had an uneasy feeling in his gut about this meeting.

"Thank you, Mr. Thompkins," she glanced at the card. "I think you should go in front of me to ensure this doesn't happen again."

"I believe I will do that. You be careful," he said, as she nodded her head in agreement.

Seeing the car behind her pass by, Meggie disengaged her car from park and continued on her way. Before she was aware of what was happening, her mind drifted again, going back in time to 1978, the year Vietnam draft evaders were pardoned. The year of record unemployment and inflation. The year after the peanut king, Jimmy Carter, became President. The year she and Steven were blessed with their second son, Seth Michael Roth. They named him after Steven's grandfather, Samuel Mervis, his mother's father. Seth was a truly beautiful child, looking like his father. Meggie noticed even his facial expressions were exactly like Steven's.

Stopping at another red light and seeing twin girls walk in front of her car with their mother, she thought of Dottie.

A year after Seth was born, Meggie and Steven went to a writer's convention in Houston. Dottie was insistent they stay with her. Meggie reluctantly agreed, not because she didn't want to spend time with Dottie but because she didn't want to subject Steven to Mark. Over the past few years they had visited one another for a few days at a time. Mark had not changed. In fact, he was worse. On this visit, Dottie opened the door to her home, Meggie and Steven stood in shock.

"What the hell happened to you?" Meggie stared at her friend's bruised face.

"I was in a car accident," Dottie led them toward the den.

That night, Meggie and Steven were lying on their backs in bed in the guest room and staring at the ceiling. Steven broke the silence,

"Dottie's twin girls are adorable. They're almost four now, if I remember correctly."

"Uh huh. I honestly feel Dottie would leave that jerk if it weren't for the children," Meggie uttered.

"Jerk-when did you start calling him that?' Steven smiled.

"Tonight. It fits," she stated.

"I agree. He did lend me a tie for tomorrow, since I left mine home. When I walked into his closet and saw more suits than Saks has, I became hysterical. I couldn't stop laughing. His priorities are ass backwards," Steven propped himself up on an elbow to look at her.

"I know. Dottie showed me tonight. And yet, he allows her to buy very little for herself, for the girls or for the house. I have never had the displeasure of knowing anyone so controlling. That's not the half of it," Meggie said, tears began to fill her eyes. "I'm not going to go with you tomorrow. I have to talk to Dottie. She's in deep trouble here. Those bruises weren't caused by any accident. Dottie finally admitted he beat her. Can you believe it, he beat her!" Steven hugged her,

"Oh shit!"

"She admitted she doesn't love him and hasn't for quite some time. How can you love someone who only wants to manipulate you, who doesn't give a damn about your welfare and cares only for himself? When he saw the verbal abuse he was dishing out wasn't working any longer, that's when the physical abuse started-to get her to do what he wanted her to do." Meggie cried and held Steven tightly. They fell to sleep holding each other.

The following day, Meggie encouraged Dottie to hire a baby sitter so they could go out for the afternoon, like old times. The idea excited Dottie. She put the thought of what ramifications might lie ahead out of her mind.

Sitting in a restaurant in one of Houston's new malls, Meggie looked at her friend,

"How much longer do you plan to take this?"

"We worked thins out last night. He loves me and has promised to change," Dottie stared across the room.

"Come back to the living! He'll never change! That jerk only cares about one person-himself!" Meggie said, loudly.

"Dottie, you're the one who's changed. You specialize in vulnerability lately."

"Meg, don't! We go back too far. Remember the time I was paintin' a still life and my bowl of fruit kept shrinkin in size?" Dottie laughed a little. "I didn't know what was happenin and you were sittin there very innocently. Then I caught you eatin it!"

"Only the nectarines. You're not changing this subject!" Meggie said, with a piercing look. Dottie didn't respond, Meggie continued,

"How much more can you take? How much longer are you going to allow him to bring you down, put you down and make you feel bad about yourself?" Dottie started to cry, Meggie placed an arm around her.

"I'm trying to stress to you the futility of this situation," Meggie had tears in her eyes.

"I'm so scared," Dottie cried. "If I try to get out of this marriage, he'll do everythin he can to destroy me."

"And if you stay, he may kill you. Accept it, he's lower than a turtle's butt. He's a low-life who belongs in the gutter," Meggie stated.

"I have nowhere to turn. If I force a separation, he'll take all of our money. He already has it hidden. He'll see to it I get nothin, not even my girls. Remember, he's an attorney. What he lacks in common sense, he makes up by knowin every sneaky passage of the law," Dottie said.

"Steven describes him as snake rational," Meggie responded.

"So you know what I'm talkin about," Dottie looked at her with some relief that another person saw him as she did.

"Let's put this in proper perspective. Correct me if I'm wrong. Over the past year he has broken your nose twice, given you a fractured rib and multiple bruises over your body on various occasions," Meggie stated bluntly. Dottie nodded in agreement. "You have definite grounds for divorce and no court is going to award custody of your children to that jerk!"

"I know, but our system is ass-backwards. He could drag this out for years and durin those years, I would be subjected to his harassment. I don't think I could take it. He would cut off all money and my children have to eat. Since my dad died, my mother has had to work. She can't help me. I'm alone. I feel like I'm sinkin and I'm alone," Dottie cried on her shoulder.

"You're not alone. You have me, you have Steven and you have your daughters," Meggie cried with her. "We're not going to allow this greenback junkie to wipe you out. I have plenty of money and if it can't be used to help those I love, what the hell good is it?"

"I can't take your money." Dottie cried.

"Why not? In fact, you have no choice," Meggie paid the waitress and led Dottie out. "Our first step is to find a good attorney. Then find where the House of Ruth is here. Houston must have one. Let's find Steven at his convention. Through his contacts, he may be able to help."

Dottie stopped the car in front of the Hilton. Meggie went in alone to find Steven. Instead of looking herself, which could prove futile, she went to the front desk to have him paged. A few moments later he entered the lobby. After a brief discussion with Meggie, Steven placed a phone call and Meggie returned to the car to be with Dottie. Shortly thereafter, Steven slid into the back seat of the car and gave Dottie the address of the attorney she was to see.

"How did you find him?" Meggie inquired.

"You must remember Paul?" Steven said.

"Your old roommate," Meggie smiled. Steven nodded,

"He's a lawyer living here. I ran into him today. He doesn't handle divorces but one of his partners does."

"How's his little boy?" Dottie asked.

"He says he thinks he's okay. He doesn't get to see him much. His son lives with Marrianne in Arlington, Virginia. They couldn't manage to work things out. They were divorced," Steven said. Meggie laughed,

"It seems he was thrown out of the Catholic Church after all."

Dottie pulled the car into the underground parking facility of a large office building in downtown Houston. They walked toward the elevators, Steven put both of his arms around Dottie,

"I know this is hard. I want you to know you are not alone. We love you and we will always stand by you." She started to cry.

"I'm so lucky to have friends like you," she whimpered.

"You deserve some luck after everything you've been through and yours is about to start changing right now," Meggie moved in on this embracing.

A couple of days later, Dottie's husband, Mark, disembarked his flight home from New York. He was an attorney for the Ottis Oil Corporation and traveled a great deal with his job. Nearing his car in the airport parking lot, a man approached and handed him some papers. He took a good look at them and broke out into a cold sweat. That bitch is suing me for divorce! He was not about to allow her to get away with this. Driving straight home in record time, he was becoming more and more angry. Tearing rubber from his car tires as he stopped in the driveway, he tried to unlock the front door. No luck; she had the locks changed!

In fact, Dottie had followed her attorney's instructions implicitly, from locks to doctor records, to an injunction to keep him from the house and her. It was called survival!

"Dottie, I want to talk to you!" Mark yelled.

"Go away. You can talk to my attorney," Dottie yelled back, shaking with fear.

Mark became angrier, breaking the glass of the front door and trying to reach in to grab the door handle. Steven caught his hand,

"It's not going to work. I should let you know the police are on their way." Thus, Mark withdrew his hand. Meggie had phoned the police as soon as she heard the car in the driveway.

"Dot, we can work this out," Mark pleaded.

"The only thin you want to work out on is me! Then to walk out with everythin in this house. You're nothin but a greenback junkie who switched all of our assets to your name solely!" Dottie yelled, still trembling.

"You bitch!" Mark screamed in a fit of rage, just before ramming into the door and shattering the remainder of the glass. Steven opened what was left of the door, forcing Mark to step back. He walked out to face him,

"I think you better go."

"I'm going to make her life miserable. I'm going to break her and maybe even bury her," Mark said, angrily, as he saw the police arrive. He then hastily left.

The next day they had the door fixed. Steven returned home, but Meggie was to stay for a little while longer. That evening, Meggie dropped Dottie off at The House of Ruth for a group discussion with women in the same situation as she. A couple of hours later, Dottie slid back into the car.

"Ya know, it's good to have friends like you and Steven to talk to, but it's not the same as sharin with people who have been where I am," she said, sullenly.

"I imagine it isn't," Meggie pulled from the parking space.

"I learned I'm sufferin a double whammy. The pain I feel is more emotional than physical. I feel as if I've been violated, as if my insides have been torn out of me and thrown about and I'm tryin to find a way to put them back, to be whole again. Plus I'm also in mournin over the death of a marriage. And at the same time I feel totally humiliated and ashamed. These feelins transcend all language barriers," Dottie cried.

"I wish I could help," Meggie glanced at her friend.

"You have, but there are some thins in life one must do for oneself. This is one of them. What did you buy?" Dottie said, glancing at the packages in the back seat. Meggie smiled,

"I think it's time you started painting again. There was an art store down the street."

"It may not be a bad idea-to take out my hurt, anger and frustration on canvas," Dottie replied.

"I don't understand why you ever stopped. You have a real talent, far better than mine. I've always thought of myself as one of those people who could do well at some things, a jack of all trades so to speak. You have a gift. Why did you stop?" Meggie said, driving.

"Meg, you're gifted at so many thins," Dottie said.

"The only reason people think that is because I pour everything I've got into what I do," Meggie stated.

"You don't call that a gift, I certainly do. But, the most special gift you have is the way you love. The way you love Steven, your children. The way you love your friends, I'm thankful to be one of them," Dottie leaned to place a kiss on her cheek. Meggie smiled,

"You didn't answer my question."

"It was Mark. I allowed myself to believe what he said. He told me I wasn't any good and to stop wastin my time. When I think how I believed everythin he said to me, how stupid I was," Dottie still had tears running from her eyes.

"He sure got his way, didn't he? He deserves the asshole of the year award! Have you any idea how long I have wanted you out of this farce of a marriage?" Meggie asked.

"Since the beginnin," Dottie smiled a little. "Meg, I had to be the one to want out. Besides, I didn't want to leave prematurely."

"The only way to have left prematurely was to never have started it," Meggie with raised eyebrows.

"How did you hear about the House of Ruth?" Dottie inquired.

"From DEAR ABBY," Meggie smiled.

"I thought I was the only one who still read her column," laughed Dottie, slightly.

"There are millions of us," Meggie laughed with her.

A few days later, Meggie entered Dottie's kitchen to find her crying as she was hanging the receiver of the phone back on the wall.

"What, that the jerk again?" Meggie walked closer to her.

"No, his rejection I can deal with now," Dottie cried, placing her head on Meggie's shoulder, needing warmth and compassion because she felt so empty inside. Dottie stepped back and started to pace the kitchen, Meggie waited patiently. Dottie had opened up so much; she knew she'd get it out.

"That was-I thought-a friend of mine, Carla. She called to see what she could find out, I believe to tell Mark. I told her to stay out of it. We didn't need her to make an already volatile situation far more explosive," Dottie said, in disbelief.

"Good for you!" Meggie said excitedly

"You've met our little group of friends; at least I thought they were friends," Dottie cried, Meggie nodded yes. "They're all goin to testify for Mark. Can you believe this? They're goin to say what a wonderful person he is and I must be crazy because he says I am. He would never hit me, never lay a hand on me, but I scratched him. He showed them his scratches. True, he had them. When somebody sits on you and pounds on your back, your legs and your arms, you fight back!"

497

"Dottie, these people are ignorant fools. Let's put this in perspective. All of us who are brighter than Mark, know the truth; those of lesser intelligence are blinded by his snake rationality," Meggie hugged her.

"Thank you. I guess the worst of all was when she told me not to count on any of them for support because their husbands had been friends with Mark longer," Dottie cried.

"I know the past year I haven't been the best of a friend to anyone, but I was goin through hell. I thought they would understand." Dottie glanced at Meggie, who also had tears running from her eyes.

"It was Emerson who said, 'One measure of success is to endure the betrayal of false friends,'" Meggie smiled.

"Why does it have to hurt so much?" Tears still flowed from Dottie's eyes. Meggie cried with her. It seemed like Dottie's whole world was caving in. She wanted to take some of the pain from her friend, but this kind of pain she didn't know how to take. All she was able to do was be there for her.

XIV

After nearly running a red light, Meggie brought the car to a screeching halt. She glanced around and noticed she was nearing her destination and returned to the present again. She spotted children playing in a playground, and her mind drifted again as she drove on; April, 1980.

"Morris, you have to see this," Steven called from Matthew's room.

"What!" she rushed in, curious.

"These, Mom!" Matthew excitedly said, pointing to his new guinea pigs running around his room.

"AHHHHHH!" Meggie screamed, quickly jumping on a chair, then on top of her son's desk.

"Get them out of my house!" She shrieked, with tears in her eyes.

"Morris, they're not mice," Steven said, in disbelief.

"Bullshit they're not! I want those little rats out of here!" She yelled in a very distraught state.

Steven helped Matthew and two-year-old Seth put the guinea pigs in their cage. Meggie left the room immediately. Steven carried the cage with the little animals and set it outside the house. He spotted Meggie walking toward the woods.

"Morris!" He yelled. She turned around to see him running. "I didn't know they would frighten you so badly."

"I know," she replied, he embraced her.

"Boys are boys. He wanted them. I didn't think you would object,"

"Next time, think first. I may be the only woman living in this house, but I have rights, too," she stated.

The guinea pigs went back to the store and they returned with a parakeet. Right away, Meggie didn't like it; it shed everywhere. She refused to say anything, feeling badly enough about her fear of guinea pigs. In a few days, Matthew was bored with the bird and it, too, was gone. Four days later Steven found Meggie in the kitchen.

"Morris," he placed his arms around her.

"I'm a little dubious about this technique," she smiled.

"We have a new member to our family," Steven chuckled.

"I'm almost afraid to ask. Tell me they're not mice!" Meggie said.

"No mice; I promise. Andrew gave him his monkey," he laughed.

"You're joking, right!" Meggie said in shock.

"No, I'm not." Steven still laughed.

"Get him out of here! No monkeys! What are we running here, the National Zoo?" Meggie screamed, breaking away from his embrace.

"Morris, didn't you ever want a pet as a kid?" Steven smiled.

"A dog maybe. I may have been peculiar, but never little rats or a monkey," she walked back to the sink. Steven started out of the kitchen, then turned,

"By the way, the monkey's name is Horace!" Meggie threw a wet sponge at him.

Over the course of the next few days, Horace was nothing but destructive. The entire household, except for Meggie and Anna, cleaned up after him. Meggie explained to the guys she and Anna were on strike until all critters were removed from the premises. Steven finally decided Horace had to go-it was only after every book in his study had been torn from the shelves. He found a place for him in the Baltimore Zoo. Matthew was unhappy about the situation. Steven explained they could visit Horace at any time. It helped ease the pain.

The following Saturday morning, there was a special delivery package for Meggie. Signing for it, she removed the letter attached and noted the return address.

"It's from Dottie," she tore open the envelope.

Hi Meg,

I've found out that we women are made of strong stuff. Wish me a mazel tov, as you would say. The non-person finally signed separation papers. It only took him 14 months. It doesn't matter. It was 14 months I had to work on me. I honestly believe I'm back to normal. Thanks to you, Steven, the House of Ruth and my psychologist. He dismissed me two months ago. There will be an exhibit of my paintings next week. I know you're proud. Enclosed you'll find a clipping of part of a Dear Abby column from the paper. It made me think of you, of a conversation we had.

"To laugh often and love much; to win the respect of intelligent persons and the affection of children; to earn the approbation of honest critics and to endure the betrayal of false friends; to appreciate beauty; to find the best in others; to give of one's self; to leave the world a bit better, whether by a healthy child, a garden patch, or a redeemed social condition; to know that even one life has breathed easier because you have lived——this is to have succeeded."

Ralph Waldo Emerson
(1803-1882)

P.S. My dog had puppies. The crate is for the boys.

I love you guys,
Dottie

Matthew and Seth opened the crate to find a little puppy.

Excitedly, Matthew looked at his parents, "Can we keep him?"

"Certainly," Meggie smiled.

"I think I'll name him Oscar," Matthew said, placing the puppy in his little brother's arms.

Meggie came back to reality again as she stopped the car at another traffic light. She thought, 'D.C. has more red lights than the North Pole on Christmas.' When the light turned green, she thought of her recent phone conversation with Dottie.

Dottie had married again a year ago. He was a wonderful man who wished her to be happy, to be the best that she could be. Putting her needs and those of her children in front of his own, he was a selfless man. She and Steven had met him and liked him immediately. They wanted only happiness for Dottie and felt this man could provide it.

The reason for Dottie's phone call was to deliver good news: she was pregnant. Meggie had never heard her sound so happy.

"I know you're always up for a good laugh. My ex-husband phoned the other day. He said he finally recovered from our divorce and he's learned from it: it's always darkest before the dawn, there are plenty of other fish in the sea and never put a three piece suit in the washing machine," Dottie laughed hysterically. Hearing silence from Meggie on the other end.

"Remember, he's a lawyer. He makes his living conning people!"

"You are unbelievable! It is beyond my comprehension how you can talk to that jerk!" Meggie bluntly stated.

"I'll admit it took some doing, but I learned if I didn't learn to forgive him, I couldn't get on with my life. I had to let go of all of the old resentments and that unbelievable hatred. Remember how intensely I hated him? That was unhealthy for me. I don't hate him anymore, nor do I resent him. That doesn't mean I like him. I don't at all. In fact, it's dislike and disrespect, and that's why I call him a non-person. A human being would never have violated my personal trust the way he did. Believe me, I can't wait for the day when the twins are grown and I don't ever have to talk to him again. He's not worth my breath or my ear," Dottie uttered.

Meggie drove on, with a slight smile on her face and tears still flowing from her eyes. So many things had happened over the past thirteen years. They had lost complete track of Michael, having kept in touch for almost a year before their letters started returning. When amnesty had been granted, they thought they would hear from him. Steven had seen to it they were listed in both the Baltimore and D.C. phone directories. If Michael had wanted to find them, he could. To this day there had been no word from him.

Richard spent a few more years in relative solitude in Hawaii before returning to the mainland to teach at Berkeley. He finally published his poems and was currently in the process of writing a textbook on poetry. A few years ago, he married a woman a couple of years older than himself. Richard told her that his wife was highly intelligent, well read and had a wonderful head on her shoulders. Meggie still thought of him as her free spirited friend.

Ben was traveling the country with his rock band. He and Albert were still at opposition. He hadn't settled down; however, he had lived with quite a few women along the way. Meggie wondered when he would finally grow up, then thought maybe he never would. Maybe Ben would remain a kid forever. If it makes him happy, so what!

The last time Meggie saw Jay was not that long ago. He, his wife and three children came to D.C. On November 11,1982, for the dedication of the Vietnam Veteran's Memorial in West Potomac Park. She recalled the look on Jay's face as he read aloud the names of those he served with. She would never forget that day, nor the more than 58,000 names on the Memorial. She would never forget the monetary cost of that war: 200 trillion dollars! She would never forget that war!

Ma and Albert were such a mismatch, Meggie thought. Albert could never even hold a candle to Daddy. He was one of those people who thought he did everything right and no one else could do it as well as he. It definitely got on her nerves, along with his closed mind and tunnel vision. Since he was a musician, Meggie had anticipated he would to be freer in thought. Was she ever let down. She decided she would never like him, only tolerate him, for Ma's sake, and she let her opinion be known. At times she felt guilty about this, because he was very good to her sons.

After Adina died, Peter spent two years in Egypt before returning home. Then he went back to Cancun and Chichen Itza. Having a few other liaisons before he finally contacted his old high school girlfriend and invited her to come visit. Carol eventually quit her job in broadcasting and moved in with Peter in Cancun. Two months ago, Meggie received a phone call from them. They had finally gotten married. She was happy for Peter. It took him long enough to make a commitment, but he ultimately did. Then she wondered what would have happened if he hadn't wasted all of those years. She decided to put it out of her mind because it wasn't important anymore. They had each other now. One can never go back in time.

Meggie smiled a little as she thought of Lori. Victor had made a success out of his Honda motorcycle business and now that Honda manufactured cars, he had a car dealership as well. She wished Lori was with her right now. It would not have been fair to ask her to come and forgo her own responsibilities. She had a wonderful marriage with Victor and two beautiful children; a little girl six months younger than Matthew, and a little boy the same age as Seth. Uncle Bob had become ill, heart problems. This is when Ma finally told Meggie that she had been born with a slight heart murmur. But had outgrown it when she was quite young. Growing up certainly carried a great deal of responsibility with it.

Parking her car, Meggie sat crying for a short while. "Steven where are you!" She screamed inside the car. She stood and locked the car door, the tears still flowed from her eyes. She walked toward the building which appeared even more massive than she had recollected. This time she counted the marble and concrete steps on her way up. "Thirty-five!" Her mind started to slip again as she made her way into the large building.

So many things had transpired over the past thirteen years. We had been through four Presidents: Nixon, Ford, Carter and now Ronald Reagan. Ex-movie star turned president, Reaganomics, the Reagan Revolution! The Vietnam War had ended and there had been Watergate and a recession. The American hostage situation in Iran, and the U.S. and Russian talks on disengaging nuclear weapons. Margaret Thatcher is the first woman Prime Minister of Great Britain.

This was the year 1983. The year Datsun engineered their cars to talk. The year pinball machines dating back to the 1950's were replaced by arcade video games. The year of "NIGHT RIDER", a television show starring a computerized car named Kit. The year of the Space Shuttles.

Opening the door to the office, she hesitated before walking in. She smiled slightly at the slender woman behind the receptionist's desk,

"Is he free?"

"Go right in," the woman responded, taken by surprise. She recognized her. 'It's been a long time,' she thought.

Meggie walked toward the double doors, opened them and stepped in. She smiled again, as she glanced around his office.

"If one didn't know better, one would think you to be a collector of fine art," she said to the man rising from behind a desk. She again glanced around the room at all of her paintings.

"A very special woman sends me a painting, along with a picture of her wonderful family every year for Christmas," he smiled, nearing her.

"It's good to see you. How have you been?" He asked, just before Meggie removed her sunglasses, revealing swollen red eyes. He placed his arm around her shoulder and led her toward the brown leather couch. Sitting down, he placed her hands in his and gazed into those eyes of hers that he vividly remembered. "Try telling me what's wrong."

"Phillip, you told me once if I ever needed you, you would be there," Meggie burst into tears.

"I meant it then and now," he said, curious.

"This is so hard. I've never been very good at facing reality, especially without Steven. I didn't know who else to turn to," she cried and drew her clenched fists up to her face.

"Tell me what happened," Phillip concerned. Meggie dropped her hands to her lap; they were still in fists.

"Steven's been in El Salvador for a couple of weeks doing research. A few days ago, I received a phone call from the State Department, informing me the helicopter he was traveling in was shot down! This took place approximately twenty miles northwest of the capital, San Salvador, and they said they knew no other details. They couldn't tell me whether he was dead or alive," Meggie still cried. Phillip placed his arms around her to comfort her.

"I know in my heart he's alive and he's been hurt," she whimpered, burying her face into his strong shoulder. "I can't explain it. I've never been psychic before. All I know is I feel it and I can't stop the pain." She sat back to look at him as the tears still ran down her cheeks.

Phillip moved from the sofa to his desk and buzzed his secretary,

"Miss Stone, I would like you to get me Franklin Harris with the State Department, Admiral George Frost and my brother, Tony." Releasing the intercom button, he glanced at Meggie.

"Tony's with Naval Intelligence," as his intercom buzzed. Meggie thought, 'A contradiction in terms,' but put it from her mind.

Phillip remained on the phone for quite a while, juggling various calls. She sat there like a stoic, trying to gather bits of information, but not really discovering anything. He then turned to her,

"Tony's will handle it now. Mr. Harris and Admiral Frost will get back to him. What do you say we have some lunch?" He glanced at his watch. Sitting quite still, she made no comment. Her mind was busy digesting everything.

"I remember, eating is your hobby," Phillip helped her up and led her from his office. Even Meggie had a slight smile on her face, thinking, 'History!'

After being seated in the restaurant downstairs in the Pentagon, Phillip ordered.

"I know your mind is always at work. What's going on now?" He took her hand in his. Meggie composed herself,

"If memory serves me correctly, twenty miles northwest of San Salvador is around the Santa Ana volcano in the Metapan Mountains."

"Santa Ana is inactive," he said, wondering where she was heading.

"There are many active volcanoes in El Salvador. What I was referring to is, Santa Ana is the country's highest peak, at 7,812 feet. Is it possible to land a plane there?" She said, very wide-eyed. Phillip smiled,

"It's near impossible!" He squeezed her hand. "Just because the helicopter went down in the highlands doesn't make him trapped or solitary. El Salvador is one of the most densely populated countries of the world, nearing five million people. That's over six hundred people per square mile," Phillip stated, seeing a man approach the table.

"Admiral Bennett, would it be possible for me to have a few minutes of your time?" The man inquired, just before noticing Meggie.

"Hello. These are far better circumstances in which to see you."

"Phillip, this is Mr. Thompkins with WBYE News," she said, as the two men shook hands and Phillip motioned for him to sit. He found it curious, but recalled how Meggie had always managed to get around.

"In my profession, it's rare when someone knows my name before I am acquainted with theirs," Mr. Thompkins said. She smiled a little,

"It's Meggie Roth." Mr. Thompkins turn red,

"Are you related to Steven Roth?"

"He's my husband. Why do you ask?" She stared at him.

"There were four people on the helicopter that went down: the pilot, your husband and two newsmen. One of the newsmen was a close friend of mine-Danny Shotz. Through the wire service, we've learned Steven Roth was the only survivor," Mr. Thompkins expected to see relief on

Meggie's face, but there was no sign of it. He turned to Phillip,

"Admiral Bennett, would it be possible for you to give me some assistance in bringing Danny's body home for burial?" Phillip rose, Mr. Thompkins followed him to the corridor.

"My brother, Tony, is in a far better position to deal with this. Inform him I told you to call," Phillip handed him a piece of paper with Tony's number. "Is there anything else you can tell me that you've learned through the wire service?"

"The helicopter went down exactly twenty-two miles northwest of San Salvador. They're not sure of the cause of the crash. They need Steven Roth for that and right now no one has been able to locate him," Mr. Thompkins said, then recalled where he had seen Meggie before. It was in the file in the newsroom pictures. He glanced at Admiral Bennett,

"Rumor has it quite a few years back you almost married. Was Meggie Roth the one?"

"Mr. Thompkins, it's been nice meeting you," Phillip smiled, shaking his hand before walking back to join Meggie.

"Thank you, Admiral," Mr. Thompkins watched Phillip walk away, and felt he received his answer.

They returned to Phillip's office after lunch to find Tony on the phone, sitting behind his brother's desk. Seeing them enter he placed the receiver down,

"Meggie, you're just as beautiful as ever." He neared to embrace her.

"Thank you," she said, lowering her head.

Phillip smiled, thinking, 'She still has difficulty accepting a compliment.' He led her to sit on the couch and he sat beside her. Tony sat on the edge of the desk. Meggie couldn't help but notice how handsome he was. At the age of 38 his features had matured. He now resembled his oldest brother a great deal.

"I was able to learn a few facts. Steven is definitely alive," Tony said.

"We discovered that ourselves," Phillip stated.

"It's still rather vague. The helicopter went down, thanks to the guerrilla opposition. Steven Roth was seen running from it before it exploded. To our knowledge no one else made it out. It is believed they were already dead. There was a great deal of gunfire when Steven escaped. My source tells me he may have been wounded. He made his way into the brush before dropping out of sight. It is believed a pro-American Salvadoran may have given him shelter. Intelligence is still working on this and will continue until we have some answers," Tony said, as tears flowed from Meggie's eyes.

"Thank you," her voice cracked from her crying. Phillip placed his arm around her shoulder and helped her up.

"I'm going to drive Meggie home now," he glanced at his brother, as he led her from the office.

"Phillip, can I see you for a minute?" Tony said. Meggie waited in the outer office as Phillip conferred with Tony.

"What is it?" Phillip said.

"Do you think your involvement now is wise?" Tony said.

"I thought you learned a long time ago people make their own choices," Phillip smiled, before leaving.

Walking outside and toward her car, Meggie took his arm.

"Why are you doing this? You hate to drive?"

"In your present frame of mind, I have no intention of allowing you to. Besides, Robert Thompkins informed me of what almost happened on your way here," Phillip helped her into the car. He sat in the driver's seat and placed the key in the ignition, then put it in gear.

"Parking brake is on," a woman's voice uttered. Meggie laughed, seeing the shock on his face.

"Only you would have a car that speaks to you!" He laughed slightly.

"It says lots of other things, too," Meggie turned the radio to Q107.

"You're the same; you still like small cars and rock music," Phillip pulled the car from the space.

"Age is what you make it. Determination as a kid, growing up means making adult choices. Like the one I've made: an economical, mid-size car with the radio having eight speakers," she smiled a little, then gave him directions to her house. He smiled at her.

"I'm familiar with where you live." Seeing the surprise on her face. "I've known since your dad passed away. You don't think I'd allow you to get too far away, do you? All of your paintings had return addresses. I still think of you in terms of, "in the throes of creativity," Phillip laughed. "Have you done much painting lately?"

"One has to want to paint to need to paint," she replied.

"Would you like to explain that?" Phillip stopped at a red light.

"Simply, as a child I thought I could hide anywhere, especially in my paintings. Now I cannot," Meggie said, sullenly.

'Damn,' he thought, 'She can still get to me.'

"Growing up means coping with what life deals us, taking the reins of our own destiny," Phillip quickly glanced at her.

"Should I frame that quote?" She smiled as he laughed,

"Only if it will help you remember it." He parked the car in front of her home. As they stood, Meggie noticed him looking it over.

"Superficial perusal."

"Irish you are a jewel!" He laughed slightly.

"Irish, they are always in the right, believing they will do almost anything to win. Especially when it comes to fighting for freedom. Sounds like the Jews!" She said, as they walked toward the front door.

"Sometimes I think you are an illusion I chose to create," Phillip grabbed her by the arm, forcing her to look in his eyes.

"Highly doubtful, Phillip, you would have chosen someone far kinder than myself," a few tears ran down her cheeks. He didn't know how to answer that.

Meggie opened the front door, led him into the house and toward the large den. Hearing voices, Anna entered the room.

"Anna, I'd like you to meet Admiral Bennett," Meggie said. Anna stood in shock for a moment, staring at him. Over the years she had heard talk of him, but never expected any gentleman as handsome as he.

"It's nice to meet you, Admiral Bennett," Anna finally said, before turning to her employer. "I made veal for dinner tonight."

"That's wonderful! Admiral Bennett will be joining us," Meggie smiled at Phillip. They heard the front screen door slam shut. Two young boys ran through the house toward the den, yelling,

"Mommy, Mommy." Matthew and Seth arrived home from camp and were anxious to see their mother, not having seen her for a few days.

"Are you feeling better?" Seth embraced her. Matthew approached giving her a big hug as well. Meggie stood with her sons beside her,

"Guys, I would like you to meet Admiral Bennett."

"Your admiral!" Matthew yelled, with surprise in his voice as he went to shake Phillip's hand. His younger brother followed.

"We're starving," Matthew turned to his mother. Meggie smiled,

"I doubt that. Anna's in the kitchen. She'll give you something. Dinner will be in a short while."

The boys left the room, Phillip glanced at her,

"Your sons are beautiful." Then giving her a very questioning look,

"'Your admiral?"

"That's how Steven refers to you. We've followed your exploits-from saving the Vietnam orphans to your dilemma in Iran. When someone means a lot to a person, they find a way of keeping track," Meggie smiled. "No politics. Was that a dream or a fantasy?"

"You flatter me, then interrogate me," he was a bit indignant. "Politics has a way of draining a person. I'm committed to what I do. Besides, I didn't have anyone to stand beside me."

"I'm sure there are lots of women who would love to go out with you," Meggie said, noticing his graying temples and feeling it only made him more attractive. Phillip laughed a little.

"There are plenty of them, but I tire of one-way conversations," he closed his eyes in thought for a minute. He opened them and looked at her. "When you're smart, ambitious and independent, it's far easier to maintain a career than a relationship."

"Oh, you put the no thoroughfare sign back up!" Meggie said, watching him. Phillips' face turned white, 'She remembered the poem!'

Anna entered the room to announce dinner was ready.

Phillip smiled at the boys when they had finished dinner,

"Would you like to go outside and learn to pitch like Fernando Valenzuela?"

"Yes!" they screamed in unison. Meggie sat in shock,

"Who or what is that?"

513

"He's a great pitcher for the L.A. Dodgers. I call it Navy know-how!" he walked to the door. He turned to her, "What one works so hard to build, others take great pleasure in tearing down. You must never give them the chance. I will not allow that to happen to your children. They are our future." He possessed a strange look in his eye, before he walked through the doorway to join the boys.

Meggie sat at the table, not being able to move for a while, trying to digest his statement. Then she ran out to join them.

"Baseball peddler," she yelled. Phillip laughed,

"Don't worry, I may just experiment a little! That's what Dr. Frankenstein once said."

Later that evening, after tucking her sons into bed, Meggie walked into the den to find Phillip on the telephone. She sat on the sofa just as he was putting the receiver in place.

"That was Tony," he said. She sensed it was with her infallible instincts. She smiled a little,

"Anything?"

"Nothing different," Phillip stated, solemnly. She sat back farther into the couch and relaxed a little.

"We were apprised that El Salvador was politically volatile. However, I never dreamed the situation there was this extreme and I don't believe Steven did either."

"Steven was fully aware of what he was getting himself into. He's too thorough a writer to have left anything to chance. He simply didn't desire you to live in fear," he sternly stated.

"I feel like an idiot. I could have stopped him," Meggie's tears ran from her eyes.

"You really don't believe that," Phillip said. She looked at him,

"I don't know what to believe. I read all of Steven's notes. The situation didn't seem that tenuous to me.

Especially since a new constitution is now being drafted which would allow the people to elect their president."

"That's true, but it's hard to picture what may be in parts of the world that have been in turmoil for years. For years the government has been plagued by opposition from both the left and the right wings. In the 1970's, violence by both groups increased and the government was accused of atrocities and was ousted in a coup. The resulting junta promised reform, order and free elections. It never happened. In 1982 the elections set up a government, the power of which centered on the popularly elected sixty member Constituent Assembly. They were given the authority to legislate and draft a new constitution. That assembly assumed the power to appoint the president, vice-presidents and judges and to veto presidential appointments," Phillip stood to stretch his legs.

"What you are saying is that the people have been lied to and disappointed for so long now, they have no faith in what this new constitution may say," Meggie said. 'He was always so knowledgeable.' He smiled a little,

"That's a very astute observation, but only part of it. There are numerous political parties and organizations active in El Salvador. There are three main parties and then there are the guerrillas. The most significant guerrilla opposition to the government comes from the left-wing Farabundo Marti de Liberacion Nacional. It is a coalition of several groups. Some are communist. We believe this guerrilla group is responsible for Steven's helicopter going down. The government forces and the guerrillas are still fighting and thousands of lives have been taken."

"War! I never understood it!" The tears still flowed from her eyes. Meggie stood, glanced at Phillip.

"Would you like a tour of our home?" She walked toward the doors to the rear of the den, not waiting for an answer. Phillip rushed to catch up with her, she was already outside. "I needed some air."

515

Phillip placed his right arm around her waist and smiled,

"I desire the same in-depth tour that Virgil gave Dante'."

"Hell; you were there," she threw her head back to toss the hair from her face. He noticed the tears were still rolling from her eyes. He placed both of his arms around her, just trying to give her comfort and whispered in her ear,

"There are many different kinds of hell. We all have our own." She leaned her head on his strong shoulder for a minute, welcoming his strength.

"I want to hear about yours," she pulled back to look into his eyes. He couldn't help but smile at her before they walked toward the stables in the light from the full moon that evening. He kept his arm around her and proceeded to speak very seriously.

"I believe my worst was in Brazil in 1965. It was shortly after Kennedy died and L.B.J. was in the White House. Knowing my allegiance to the Kennedy administration, I was invited to accompany Bobby as part of his diplomatic team," Phillip was deep in thought as they entered the stables.

"Brazil; a country that outlawed political parties and denied basic freedom," he placed a hand on Nozzle's nose.

"Is that when Bobby turned liberal?" Meggie inquired, never seeing him quite like this before. It was as if he went back in time; a whole new side to the illustrious Admiral Phillip D. Bennett.

"I would venture to say so. The people hated him-not really him, but the fact that he represented a government that supplied aid to their dictatorship. J.F.K. once said he would see to it communism would stay out of the western hemisphere. Brazil's youth were turning Marxist. It wasn't because of us. It was the poverty, the disease, the illiteracy and the mass murders. We weren't helping, though. It was a very rude awakening," Phillip stared into space.

"You really are something out of the dark ages," Meggie took his hand to lead him back to the house.

"It's similar to what is now happening in El Salvador. The government depends on foreign aid for survival due to falling production and escalated military expenditures. More than one half of that aid comes from the U.S.," he glanced toward her.

As they entered the house the phone was ringing. She answered it, then handed it to Phillip. He placed the receiver back,

"That was Henry. He's waiting in the drive."

"He's still with you?" She slightly smile.

"We'll grow old together," he placed his hat on his head.

"I can't picture you old," she said.

"My dear, I'm forty-eight years old," he stated.

"You know, you don't look it," she walked him to the front door.

"I'll phone you as soon as I know something," Phillip placed a kiss on her forehead. She watched him walk toward the limo.

"Phillip!" she yelled. He turned.

"Thank you!" Tears ran from her eyes. There was simply too much history tonight, coupled with a missing Steven.

That night, when Meggie lay in bed, her thoughts were of Phillip, Renaissance Man. Steven would be in good hands with him. She then thought, 'Chivalry, Lancelot, duty and selfless honor.' She fell into sleep for the first time in days.

On his way home, Phillip sat in the rear of the limousine recalling their relationship. He wondered whether Tony was right-his involvement at the present time may not be in his best interest. He couldn't help himself, he smiled, recalling the first time she walked into his office. His smile broadened as he thought of the first time he made love to her.

A few nights later, Meggie was dressing and thought about her conversation earlier with Phillip. He had phoned to invite her to dinner and didn't wait for her to question him, informing her he had more information on Steven. Meggie thought before responding, Steven would want her to go. He would tell her she needed to be with people, because being alone was a catalyst for depression. She felt she had already had the solitude to locate herself, but she still felt so lost inside. She said yes, knowing deep in her heart her marriage to Steven was based on heartfelt trust and honest loyalty.

That evening, she sat across from Phillip at one of his fancy clubs. He ordered for them and smiled at her,

"I'm disappointed. No sharp wit as to how this club is managed."

"It doesn't seem important anymore. There's only one thing on my mind," Meggie said. He smiled,

"Steven is safe, though he was shot as he fled from the helicopter, taking a bullet in the shoulder. He's being well cared for and hidden by a pro-American Salvadoran family."

"Thank God! Which shoulder?" She stared at him. He laughed slightly,

"I really don't know."

"Have you been informed of his exact location?" She was curious.

"Not yet. In this business, one must learn to be patient," Phillip slightly smiled.

"I know patience is a virtue and I'm not very virtuous! If he's not too far into the highlands do you suppose we could fly in and get him?" Meggie said, with her eyes opened wide. Phillip leaned into the table,

"We are not flying anywhere."

"Are you?" She gazed into his eyes and knowing him so well. He laughed a little as he sat back in his chair,

"Do you still have your pilot's license?"

She hesitated for a moment. He had avoided her question, but with her past knowledge of Phillip, she had received her answer.

"Certainly. Do you recall the day I earned it?" She smiled. He laughed,

"That I do. You didn't need a plane to reach the clouds that day."

"Anything I worked so hard for I would never allow to go to waste. One never knows when it may come in handy," she said.

"Have you purchased a plane?" He said, as the salad arrived.

"My economics professor pointed out how wasteful it would be. I would fly to Hawaii and Houston, then home," Meggie smiled a little.

"Your economics professor?" Phillip glanced at her.

"Steven! He's been trying to teach me economics for years. We rent a plane so I can keep in practice. He says he feels far safer with me in the cockpit than he does with me behind the steering wheel of a car," she laughed slightly. He laughed, recalling the way she drove.

"Personally I feel it says a great deal about the skills of my flying instructor," Meggie gazed at him. Noticing a broad smile on his face.

The main course arrived. Phillip had ordered Chateaubriand for two. Meggie's eyes were still on him as he began to eat,

"It baffles me why you never went into politics. You're a natural. It would be refreshing to have a man of honest mind helping to run our country." He continued to smile,

"That already is part of my job."

"Think about it. You're well educated, well read and have a reputation beyond compare. Your charisma alone could get you elected. Plus, you are the most handsome man I have had the pleasure of knowing," she said with a smile. He blushed uncontrollably.

"Well, look who else has a difficult time accepting a compliment," she laughed. He smiled at her,

"You've never told me that before."

"Phillip, you are perfectly well aware you are quite handsome," she smiled.

"I haven't heard it in a very long time," he said, flattered.

"Then I guess you're traveling in the wrong circles," she said, just before finishing her dinner.

Meggie watched the dessert cart as the waiter wheeled it to the table. She scanned the cart,

"We have some military favorites here. Napoleon War, Pie Alamo, and Colonel Custard." Phillip smiled, shaking his head in disbelief.

In the limousine on the way to Meggie's house, "I'm aware that you and Steven are still involved in the protests against nuclear weapons," he said. Meggie was in shock,

"Are they still making lists of whom they feel dissidents to be? What no comment concerning our pro-choice involvement's?"

"My dear, we all deserve the right of freedom of choice."

"Renaissance Man," she mumbled.

"What?" He said.

"Nothing," she replied, with a slight laugh. Realizing what her comment was, Phillip smiled,

"I recall the first time you said that to me."

There was a lull, silence for a short while, before Meggie spoke,

"Faulkner, have you read him?"

"Some," Phillip replied nonchalantly.

"Steven told me if you read him in chronological order, you see the depth of his humor. I've been trying to for the past twelve years," she grinned.

"It's a thought," Phillip stared into space. He found Steven and himself to be somewhat symbiotic.

Walking Meggie to the front door of her home, he placed a kiss on her forehead again,

"Sleep well and thank you for a very convivial evening."

"I've given up on sleep. Nuclear paranoia took over," she smirked.

"Meggie, it's enough!" He walked away from her.

"To World War None!" She yelled. Phillip turned to look at her,

"Do you know what happens when your life seems to go wrong? You have a feeling you are being punished. I will personally see to it that it doesn't happen to you," he opened the door to the limousine. She watched with tears in her eyes as he drove away.

On his way home, Phillip could not get Meggie out of his mind. He felt her pain. She didn't have to talk about it, it was ever-present. A tear came to his eye as he thought about what she was dealing with and how she was hurting. He made a vow to himself: he would find Steven.

On the nineteenth day of July, Phillip was busy at work behind his desk, when he heard three raps on his door. Tony entered before being invited. He walked to the wall on the far side of the office, reached high and pulled on a small tab.

"The average person would never know these exist," Tony said, as he exposed a large map of Central America. "There's one more detail to tie up, then you're off. It should be sometime within the next thirty-six hours. If I were you, I'd cancel the appointment with the Diat today."

"I'll consider it. Will your contact be ready?" Phillip said.

"He's one of my own men. He's prepared," Tony turned toward the map. "You're going to have to humor me. I'm merely refreshing your memory. El Salvador is bordered on the south by the Pacific Ocean, on the northwest by Guatemala and northeast and east by Honduras. It is the smallest of the seven Central American countries and is divided into two highland mountain ranges and three lowland areas." He pointed to what he was referring to.

"Our man will move Steven Roth here, the northeast base of the Metapan Mountains. It's a flat, lowland area, north of the village of La Palma, with just enough open space to land a small plane. This is guerrilla country," Tony said, still pointing on the map. Phillip sat, taking everything in, knowing there was no room for error.

"Here's the weather report," Tony neared his brother and handed him a sheet of paper. Phillip glanced at it,

"Rain; I expected it. I would have been surprised if it were different. The rainy season in El Salvador is from May to September."

"Which plane have you readied?" Tony inquired.

"The Hornet, there was never a question," Phillip said.

"The F-18 Hornet does not have the vertical climbing ability that the F-16 Eagle is capable of. Nor can it rotate on take off. Don't you think you should reconsider?" Tony stated.

"No, I'm perfectly comfortable with the Hornet. The Eagle has far too much fire power, I'm not venturing there to start a war," Phillip looked at Tony, seeing he accepted his decision.

"Are you certain you want to do this?" Tony asked knowingly.

"Positive! When I saw her, it was as if someone opened the shades and let the sun in, then I felt her pain." Phillip retorted.

"Do you plan on telling her?" Tony said.

"Certainly not!" Phillip replied, witnessing Tony glance around the office.

"Archaeological relics from the tombs of love," Tony sneered.

"Don't be so cynical," Phillip said with a slight grin. Tony shook his head in bewilderment,

"Woman-Jupiter made the first one to punish his brothers for stealing fire from heaven." Phillip laughed a little. They were interrupted by Miss Stone's voice over the intercom,

"Admiral Bennett, Mrs. Roth is on the line." Phillip reached for the phone. Tony stopped him,

"I want you reachable today," Tony then walked from the office. Phillip sat in thought for a moment before picking up the phone,

"Good morning, my dear."

"Hi! There's a new exhibit at the Baltimore Museum of Art on the Muses, the goddesses that artists communicate with," Meggie said, with a slight laugh. "I'd like to go, but I don't feel like going alone. I was hoping, per chance, you were free." Phillip thought carefully for a minute, not wanting to tip his hand to enlighten her of the upcoming event. The best way he could imagine, was to be with her. Plus, she always educated him in museums.

"I'll check with the Diat and see if they can spare me today," he replied.

"What does Japan's legislature have to do with this art exhibit?" She questioned.

"I have a luncheon engagement with two of them. Would you care to join us?" Phillip said with a smile.

"Hardly! You get me there and I'll turn into a banana Republican," she said quite seriously.

"Highly doubtful. You're not capable of shooting anyone. I'll change my appointment for later this week," he said, then continued. "I'll pick you up at one."

"I have an appointment in Baltimore this morning. How about if I meet you in front of the museum?" She said.

"See you at one," Phillip placed the receiver down.

A few minutes prior to one o'clock, Meggie sat on the front steps of the Baltimore Museum of Art, waiting for Phillip. She was in a trance, digesting what Dr. Marcus had just told her.

"Meggie, I'd love to know what's going on in that head of yours right now?" Phillip stood in front of her, interrupting her thoughts. She smiled, stood and placed a kiss on his cheek,

"Thank you for meeting me. I really appreciate it."

"I could use a diversion right now," he said. She took his arm, they walked a few steps, then she stopped.

"Phillip, I need to fly to El Salvador and bring Steven home." Tears ran from her eyes. He placed both of his arms around her,

"You're like a shark. When you get hold of an idea you refuse to let go of it! However, we have received more information confirming he's still in the highlands. There's no way to fly in there right now." She pulled back to look at him,

"When?"

"He's safe, Meggie. That should ease your mind," he tried to reassure her.

"The truth is irrelevant when the mind has the power to take you places you don't want to be. When?" She adamantly stated.

"As soon as I know something, my first priority will be to let you know," Phillip noticed she bought it. He took her by the arm.

"*THE THINKER*," he looked at the statue on the museum's front steps.

"There are seven of them. The first time I ever saw him was on *DOBIE GILLIS*, " she said, as Phillip led her into the large building.

"First, I want to show you my favorite room. The Cone sisters lived in Baltimore in the old Beethoven Apartments, not far from the Maryland Institute of Art. Neither one ever married, one was a doctor. I don't recall much about the other sister, except they were both collectors of fine art. When they died, they left this wonderful collection to the museum," Meggie explained, entering the Cone sister's room.

"They were even friendly with many greats, including Picasso, my favorite square," she smiled, motioning to his cubist paintings.

"Whenever I accompany you to a museum, I feel as if I am receiving an intelligence surge," Phillip amazed at this collection.

"Short sightedness, tunnel vision," she laughed, as they walked from the room. He placed an arm around her shoulder,

"Only when it comes to fine art, my dear." They neared the muses.

Entering the large exhibit, Meggie recalled the first time she ever saw it, in Honolulu in 1966.

"The first time I saw these deities was with Lori around the time of my 'coming-out,'" she said, as they neared the painting of the sun god.

"I never knew you had a coming-out," Phillip interested, gazing at Apollo.

"Because the dossier didn't say so," she snapped.

"You will never forgive me for that. If it's any consolation, I will never forgive myself either," he looked at her. She smiled and squeezed his hand tightly,

"Phillip I forgave you years ago. We all do things how we do them. I couldn't expect to change you, just as it would have been impossible for you to change me. My coming-out was far from in the society sense. It was more like a coming out of hibernation."

"'Of this great world both eye and soul' - Milton," he glanced back to Apollo.

"'That orbed continent, the fire that severs day from night' - Shakespeare," she led him toward Diana. "'Diana, the moon, also known as Phoebe, Cynthia, Artemis, Hecate, Luna or Astarte. The maker of sweet poets' - Keats." Meggie was engrossed in the painting.

"'The sovereign mistress of true melancholy.' I know Shakespeare too," he smiled, as they walked toward Hades. Then on to the fates.

"The sisters three. The weird sisters - remember Macbeth? In Greek, they are Clotho, Decuma and Atropos. In Rome, they are known as Nona, Decuma and Norta. I wonder how much control they actually do possess over our lives?" Meggie stared at them.

"I doubt if any. You see, my dear, we make our own good luck. It's the bad that seems to creep up on one," Phillip placed his arm around her waist as they walked to the war gods.

"Ares, Mars and Odin. Now you're in your element, Phillip," Meggie smiled.

"Whether you choose to realize it or not, our ninety-six percent of the world is only good as long as we can hold everyone else at arm's length," Phillip eyed her.

"Therefore, we need nuclear weapons!" she replied.

"Abolition of nuclear weapons-don't ever hope for it," he said, as they walked from the museum.

"Sometimes, Phillip, I think you live in a zinc plated, vacuum tubed culture," she shook her head.

"Hardly, my dear. I live in the real world," he replied with a smile.

"Where's your limo?" Meggie glanced around, not seeing Henry anywhere in sight.

"I saw no reason we should have two cars," he said, with the knowledge that Henry was nearby and would remain so for the next thirty hours, if necessary.

Meggie persuaded Phillip to join her and the boys for dinner that evening. She had been acquainted with many of the sides of Admiral Phillip D. Bennett, but never this one. Never had she recalled him so serious, and at the same time there was a gleam in his eye. She didn't understand, but she needed to stay close to him, to be around if there should be information on Steven.

Dinner was interrupted by a phone call for Phillip. Returning to the dining room, he was in the process of putting on his jacket.

"That was Henry. He's waiting in the drive; I have to go." Meggie stared at him in shock,

"You haven't finished dinner!"

"I'll get something later," he said, walking toward the front door.

"Phillip, where are you going?" Meggie rose from her chair to follow him. He turned toward her,

"You should be familiar with my behavior. My country calls, I respond."

"Where are you going?" She sternly eyed him. He looked away and proceeded through the front door,

"You know I'm not at liberty to discuss this."

"Phillip!" Meggie yelled, standing outside on the front porch, seeing him open the rear door of the limousine.

"I'll be in touch," he said loudly, as he slid into the back seat and closed the door. He had far too many things going on in his mind right now, and had to get her totally out of it.

Arriving at a small navy air base in the Virginia suburbs of Washington D.C., Phillip proceeded immediately to check on his plane. There were a few minor details he desired worked out before take-off and directed the staff to do so. Then he proceeded into the building and entered a small briefing room where Tony was awaiting him. They had been over this many times before, once more could not hurt. Tony pulled down the map on the wall and pointed to the area north of the village of La Palma, El Salvador. He checked his watch and motioned for Phillip to do the same.

"Steven Roth will be there at exactly O one-thirty hours, Central time. That has to be your exact time of arrival. We cannot afford to have him waiting, nor you. The guerrillas have learned he's alive and have been actively searching for him. In all probability this will be far more difficult than either one of us had envisioned," Tony stated.

"I have always thrived on challenges," Phillip said with a smile, noticing a disconcerted look from his brother. "I've handled myself under fire before. However, I will be guarded and keep my time on the ground to the bare minimum. I figure forty-five seconds should do it." Tony was shaking his head,

"I'm not happy about this. Your risk is now far greater"

"Let's get on with this. I have a mission to fly," Phillip stated, not wanting Tony to dwell on the fact he would be risking his life. Tony walked to sit beside him,

"We're not going to notify the White House until you're out of U.S. .air space. As you fly over our bases you will not be contacted on your way to El Salvador. Our people will see to it. As you requested, this is being treated as a Priority One, Top-Secret Assignment. There are only a handful of us who are aware of it, all of whom you personally chose. If anything should go wrong, it will be in El Salvador. We couldn't notify the government there; not that they wouldn't cooperate, but we couldn't risk a leak and I'm certain they're full of them. You're on your own. Phillip, for Christ's sake, guard your ass!"

"I have full intentions of doing so. See you tomorrow, O five-thirty hours," Phillip glanced at his watch, stood and proceeded to the door.

"Phillip!" Tony called, Phillip turned to see him.

"Vulnerabilities are exploitable weaknesses," Tony stated, woefully.

"True," Phillip smiled. "This is a world of rewards and punishments."

"And you'll see to it that you receive your share of both!" Tony said, noticing a peculiar smile on Phillip's face.

"Nothing is like it was. The three worlds that create change have been altered. You were married and now you're not, there's now peace between Israel and Egypt, and next year they predict a woman will run for Vice-President. We've been through Watergate, the ending of the Vietnam War, hostages in Iran thanks to Ayatollah Khomeini and a recession," Phillip said, then checked his watch again.

"What are you saying? You're not in love with her any longer?" Tony asked. Phillip laughed a little.

"Hardly; there's no room in my life for her. Since I do love her, I desire her happiness. She had taught me things I never envisioned possible to learn. In all of my relationships past and present I was always the teacher. With Meggie I am also the student. Besides, my integrity is a pearl beyond price," he looked directly into Tony's eye.

Phillip walked briskly from the briefing room toward his waiting F-18 Hornet aircraft. He smiled to himself, because he had such great confidence in his powers of persuasion. He desired to tell Tony that love was not something you planned; it simply happened. If you keep your heart open you make room for someone to come in. When he had first met Meggie, he hadn't loved for a very long time, just as Tony was now experiencing. He couldn't tell him because he wouldn't understand. It was something he had to learn on his own. Maybe someone stubborn, willful, trying to grow up and not knowing exactly how to go about it, would walk into his life, turn it inside out and make him a far better person for it. Phillip smiled again as he climbed into the cockpit. She had grown into an extraordinary woman.

He lifted the plane from the ground and wiped all prior thoughts from his mind. After further discussion with Tony, he was to set his course for Arizona, then backtrack and enter El Salvador from the west. They would not be expecting anything from there.

Meggie was home alone pacing the floors. After Phillip left, she called Ma and asked if Matthew and Seth could spend the night. When she returned from Ma's house, she tried phoning Phillip's penthouse, only to find his answering service. She tried his office. There, too, the service answered. The same was true of the limo. Not knowing what to do, she took out the Washington phone directory and looked up Tony's number.   His ex-wife answered. Meggie explained why she was calling and she was thankful she was given Tony's number. No luck there either-the answering service again! She left a frantic message for him to phone her as soon as possible, regardless of the time. She told the service to inform Tony she would be on her way out soon, to every air base in the area if necessary. It was twelve-fifteen in the morning when her phone rang.

"Where's Phillip?" Meggie said, knowing that it had to be Tony. No one else would be calling at this time.

"On government business," Tony responded coolly.

"Don't give me that bull!" She yelled.

"Calm down!" Tony ordered.

"Not until you tell me the truth," she said, still hostile.

"I already have," he responded, as Meggie then realized he had-an American citizen trapped in a foreign country was government business. She burst into tears.

"Meggie, are you alright?" Tony somewhat concerned.

"Depression, circa 1930. October 24,1929, to be exact. Economic upheaval; in this case, emotional upheaval," her voice cracked.

"You weren't serious with the message you left with my service?" Tony questioned.

"Want to bet? My car keys are in my hand," she stated firmly.

"Don't go anywhere, I'll be right over," Tony aggravated. He had no plans to leave the base that night. His brother was risking his life for this woman, and she was now threatening to cause problems. Damn her!

Meggie now paced the front drive of her home, crying. Then she saw lights entering her driveway. Totally unaware of how long she had been out there, she ran toward the approaching vehicle. As he stopped the car, she walked to the driver's side and watched him get out.

"Where's Phillip?" The tears ran from her eyes. She needed to be told. Her mind was busy conjuring up all sorts of things.

"I've already told you! I am not the type of guy you want to even try to handle" he said sternly.

"I'm a connoisseur of fine bouncery when I don't get what I want," she smiled, still with the tears running down her cheeks.

"I make my own decisions, Meggie. You can't push me," he said to her. She glanced at the ground, then back at Tony.

"Would you like to come in?" Knowing she wasn't about to get her way just now; maybe another tactic would work better.

"Did you know that certain primitive tribes feel pictures steal your soul?" She asked, opening the front door and he followed her in.

"Honestly, no," he smiled slightly. She led him toward the kitchen, to the already brewed coffee.

531

"Do you know that in Scotland they call lakes 'lochs'?" Tony said, seating himself at the kitchen table. She shook her head, no, as she placed the coffee on the table. Meggie smiled at him,

"You have an inimitable style all your own."

"I had no choice with three older brothers who would beat me any way they could," Tony smiled, flattered.

"You and Phillip are the closest in the group?" She sipped the coffee.

"The oldest and the youngest, we're the most alike. Yes, I would venture to say we are the closest, but it wasn't always like that," Tony said, before going off in thought. We weren't this much alike or this close, until thirteen years ago. He then stared at Meggie, not hearing what she was saying, but recalling what Phillip had said to him earlier. Tony now felt indebted to this woman he had resented. His thoughts were interrupted.

"Where were you? I become offended when people ignore what I have to say," she said.

"I'm sorry; please go on," he lifted his cup.

"As I was saying, you and Phillip happen to be a great deal alike," she said, hoping he would love the compliment even though she was being quite honest. She felt a degree of comfort with Tony there. It brought her confidence that her instincts were right.

"In which way?" He said with a smile.

"Attitude and spirit," she glanced over at him.

It was nearly one-twenty-five in the morning, Central time, as a jet fighter aircraft crossed the Metapan Mountains from the west, flying at the lowest possible altitude with no lights on. He spotted the village of La Palma, then the small landing area to the north. Not wanting to take any unnecessary risks, he found it possible to set the plane down without circling. The oncoming passenger would hear the sound of the plane's engines.

There would be no need to blink the lights. As he lifted the hood of the cockpit he heard gunfire. "Shit!" He said, glancing around, trying to find someone running. There, to his right, was Steven, running from the brush. Phillip turned every strong light of the plane on, hoping to blind those that were shooting and to divert the gunfire. If at all possible he desired to avoid using weaponry, the ramifications would be astounding. He didn't desire to risk it. Then he witnessed Steven stop. He thought, 'He's been shot;' no, he stooped to pick something up from the ground.

"Steven, a bit more ventre a' yerre!" Phillip yelled over the sound of the roaring engines. As Steven approached the plane, Phillip noticed his left arm was in a sling. Phillip extended his arm to help him climb into the back cockpit. As briskly as he could, Phillip sealed the plane and lifted it steadily from the ground, they were still experiencing heavy artillery fire.

"I should have known it would be you. How did she persuade you to do this?" Steven extremely out of breath.

"She didn't have to ask. Besides, it's no big deal," Phillip flew steadily into the clouds. He desired out of this part of the world as soon as possible. He plotted his course for the Caribbean.

"Flying a mercy mission into a war-torn country is not exactly a trip to a treetop," Steven stated. Phillip smiled as the plane rose above the clouds.

"Alright, you owe me. But first, look up there at the five stars in the shape of a W. That's Cassiopeia, the Queen," he said. Steven gazed in bewilderment.

"What was so important you had to stop and risk your life for," Phillip questioned. Steven took it from his pocket.

"My pocket watch fell. It's become my good luck piece," he opened it staring at the inscription. Tears filled his eyes,

Ellene Pomerantz

Aurora My Love!
your Meggie

"Relaxed now?" Phillip asked.

"I will be as soon as you tell me how she is," Steven's eyes were fixed to the back of Phillip's head.

"Stubborn, determined and still sharkish. She took this very badly," Phillip responded.

"She's my best friend, my soulmate, my partner for life," Steven's voice cracked and a few tears flowed from his eyes. "My sons?" Tears still ran down his cheeks.

"Incredible, like their parents," Phillip said earnestly. A warm feeling ran through his body as Steven thought of his family. There was silence for a few moments. Phillip broke it,

"Why do you jeopardize yourself ? Steven, with your experience in foreign affairs, you could attain a cushy job with the State Department. With your writing credentials you are in a position to do almost anything you desire. Why these risks?" Phillip turned the plane a little.

"You're one to talk. It's irrelevant, anyway. Meggie wouldn't settle for that," he paused, then continued.

"When you love someone as we love each other, you want that person to be the best he can be. She told me once, if I gave up what I love doing, I would only be half a person. She fell in love with the whole me and refuses to settle for less. We discussed it in depth after Matthew was born and she made me realize you can't make much of a difference in the world if you're not willing to put yourself on the line," he stared into space, longing for his wife. Phillip smiled, 'He had taught her that!'

"She is incredible. My father once told me: great men have two loves-what he does and who he's with," Phillip responded.

"El Salvador, a place where people aren't," Steven said, changing the subject, uncomfortable discussing

534

Meggie with him. He paused in thought, "We're in quite a nefarious position there. It's not illegal; however, it is underhanded."

"I'm aware this country is relatively afraid to become involved in any war since Vietnam. Skepticism, if you wish," Phillip said, still flying over the clouds.

"This has absolutely nothing to do with Nam. Vietnam wanted us. They never wanted us to leave. Here we are not wanted. We're pushed on them because of our aid. We certainly do not belong, even if it means withdrawing the money. They're hoping to be able to have free elections next year. Even if it's so, I don't trust it. The military runs the system. They could fake anything," Steven said, eyeing Phillip from the back. He was certainly humble and noble. He understood why she called him 'Renaissance Man'. Steven cleared his head.

"We heard about your Silver Star for bravery. You certainly proved it tonight as the bullets flew from everywhere," he said.

"All that star means is that I was brave five minutes longer than the next person. Emerson said that first," Phillip with a smile.

Steven sat back in thought. He liked this man and wondered why he never went into politics. He decided he was far too honest. His thoughts were interrupted by a voice over the radio.

"This is United States Navy, McAllen, Texas. You have just entered our air space. Identify yourself!"

"This is Steel Hornet, United States Navy," Phillip spoke proudly into the speaker.

"Steel Hornet, what is the present status of your mission?"

"Affirmative," Phillip coolly responded.

"Alright!" The voice yelled excitedly. "Welcome home, Admiral. You too, Mr. Roth."

"Steel Hornet, may I quote you?" Steven asked with a smile.

"I'll have to think about that," Philip laughed a little.

"Now I understand!" Steven said. Phillip waited for him to explain. "The rush you receive from this. As I overheard that conversation, chills ran up and down my spine. This is why you never went into politics-this uncanny feeling!" Phillip merely smiled.

Meggie and Tony were still sitting in her kitchen talking when the phone rang at three-forty-five in the morning. Answering it, she handed the phone to Tony. Glancing at him as he placed the receiver back,

"Vice-Admiral!" He placed his hat on his head,

"I have to go now."

"Where?" She asked.

"Don't start," he said, he followed her to the front door and watched her remove a white sweater cape from the hall closet.

"All right; you may accompany me if you promise to keep that mouth shut," he said, opening the door.

Meggie didn't care where she was going. All she knew was, she was going, and at the end of that line somewhere, there would be Steven. She agreed without hesitation to be quiet.

Tony drove to a small Navy air field, it looked familiar. She recalled being here before with Phillip, but she really couldn't place it. Her mind was not working properly-lack of sleep coupled with too much caffeine. Taking deep breaths to clear her head, she quietly followed Tony into a building, then up a large flight of stairs. At the top, she glanced around. All four walls were glass. It was an airport control tower! An elderly man approached Tony and shook his hand.

"Job well done, Vice-Admiral," he said, before he looked at her.

"Nice to see you again, Mrs. Roth." Meggie flashed,

"Rear Admiral Frost! Thank you."

"It's Admiral now," he said.

"Congratulations," she smiled, he nodded and walked to the front of the tower. She then saw someone else congratulating Tony, noting he also looked familiar. He neared her,

"Hello, Mrs. Roth. Do you remember me? Captain..."

"Barnes," she interrupted him

Being led to the rear of the tower by Tony, Meggie carefully scanned around the room. Only a handful of people, a selectively chosen few. 'Undoubtedly Phillip's doing,' she thought. She watched Tony standing calmly next to her, not being able to understand how he could remain so placid. Witnessing Tony check his watch frequently, she looked at the time: 5:20 a.m. Then there was a voice over the radio,

"This is Steel Hornet. Do you read?" Meggie whispered to Tony,

"That's Phillip's voice!"

"Shhhh!" He commanded.

"We read you, Steel Hornet! You're twenty-five miles southwest. The air is clear and so is the ground. Bring her on home!" The man at the radio said excitedly. Everyone in the tower seemed excited, but they were containing themselves. A mission isn't over until the plane has landed safely on the ground.

"He certainly is that legendary man of steel who flies triumphantly into the dawn!" Meggie said to Tony, with tears in her eyes.

"Be quiet," he ordered, though he liked her description of Phillip.

Meggie watched the clouds, waiting, with tears uncontrollably flowing from her eyes. Then she saw it! Never in her wildest dreams would she have imagined a jet fighter plane to be one of the most beautiful sights her eyes would ever behold. Intently she watched as it slowly descended from the morning sky, then gently land on the ground and travel down the runway. Not being able to control herself any longer, she ran from the tower, down the stairs and forcefully pushed her way through the guards by the outside doors. Tony ran after her, yelling,

"Meggie! Meggie!" She wouldn't listen! He yelled to the guards,

"Stop her!" Then decided against it and hollered,

"Let her go!"

Running out to where the plane had come to an abrupt stop, she saw Phillip climbing from the cockpit.

"I Thank God you're all right," she threw her arms around him, squeezing him tightly. She stood back to look at him.

"You should have taken me with you."

"My dear, where would we have put you?" Phillip smiled and motioned toward the two-seater aircraft Steven had just climbed from.

Meggie stood watching him for a moment as tears ran from her eyes. She thought, 'He's still the most beautiful thing I've ever seen, even with a beard.' Then she noticed his arm in a sling. He walked toward her and she put both of her arms around him.

"Oh Steven!" She whimpered.

"Oh, Morris," he laughed slightly.

"How could you do this to the four of us?" She said. He stood back a little to look into her eyes.

"Are you trying to tell me..." he smiled. She slightly nodded her head,

"Do you think you can handle the two a.m. wake up call again?"

He lifted her off the ground, spinning her around.

"Steven, your arm!" Meggie yelled.

"Aurora my love!" He screamed blissfully, just prior to kissing her.

THE END

Ellene Pomerantz

ABOUT THE AUTHOR

Ellene G. Pomerantz resides in Maryland with her husband and their youngest of three sons. She always loved to paint and to write, to put her imagination on paper. As she grew she transferred this creativity to design and received a B.F.A. degree from the Maryland Institute College of Art. She is currently working in her trade, as a designer of unique custom invitations. After discovering that this artistic thinking process knows no boundaries, she has channeled this creative energy into writing.

With the awakening of numerous emotions through life experiences along with many hours of research, Ellene has written her first novel, *AURORA*. *AURORA* is the first of two novels completed by this author. Her second book *PURPLE*, now ready for release, is a spin-off of *AURORA*, but with a surprisingly different twist. She describes design and writing as her passions, cooking and crossword puzzles as her hobbies.

Printed in the United States
6378

9 780759 633278